CLEMMONS

A NOVEL

Hilary Masters

DGR

DAVID R. GODINE · *Publisher* · BOSTON

All the characters of this novel are wholly fictitious; however, there is a hamlet of Boston Corners, N.Y., where a prize fight as described did take place. Moreover, the New York State Historical Society did place a marker on the supposed site of the Morrisey-Sullivan fight and it did bear the wrong date. The sign mysteriously disappeared several years ago.

First edition published in 1985 by
David R. Godine, Publisher, Inc.
306 Dartmouth Street, Boston, Massachusetts 02116

Library of Congress Cataloging in Publication Data

Masters, Hilary.
Clemmons.

I. Title
PS3563.A82C5 1984 813'.54 84-47639
ISBN 0-87923-542-X

Set in Sabon by Dix Typesetting, Syracuse, New York
Printed and bound by Haddon Craftsmen, Scranton, Pennsylvania
Designed by Anne Chalmers

First edition

Printed in the United States of America

. . . especially Polly

❦

My thanks to Yaddo and to Ohio University for the support, encouragement, and fellowship given as this book was written.

Books by Hilary Masters

NOVELS

Clemmons

Palace of Strangers

An American Marriage

The Common Pasture

BIOGRAPHY

Last Stands:
Notes from Memory

PART ONE

Chapter One

Would he accept a collect call from Daisy?

Outside his bedroom window the mountains loomed. The Berkshires have been barely sculpted from the dark by the early sun and look like a continent cut loose and set afloat unaccountably, nudging the meadows of Boston Corners. Or sometimes to Clemmons, the hills take on the sensuous line of a woman lying beside him, sharp fall at waist and rise of hip, about to turn and enfold him; while at other times he thinks of the ridge to the east as a dam holding back Massachusetts—all of Great Barrington, Springfield, Worcester, and even part of Boston. Or, he might also think, it was a natural barrier that kept up the property values on this side of the border.

"I'm in Grand Coulee, Pop," the young woman's voice said. So it wasn't a dream. "Washington," she tried to be more specific.

"Grand Coulee. Isn't there a dam in Grand Coulee?"

"Boy, is there ever! I'm standing right on top of it now." Her voice became childlike. He remembered her screaming, almost in pain, when she'd found the hidden prize at a birthday party. "I'm in a phone booth right on top of it. It's fan-tas-tic."

"Daisy, what time is it out there?"

"Well, it's early, or late—depending how you look at it, you know? But it's all lit up." She had picked up the real question in his query. "They've got all these lights all on it. It's just like day. How's Boxer? Are you feeding him right?"

"Yes. He's just fine."

"I bet you give him a lot of that canned shit to eat." Her accusation contained no anger.

"No, only what you told me to give him. The only meat that passes his lips is the occasional rabbit or groundhog he kills himself. I'm afraid there's nothing I can do about that." She said nothing and he pressed the receiver close to his ear. Was that a rush of water in the background, the sound of traffic, the milling of a bar scene? Daisy did not always report her locations truthfully, but he could see her standing in the phone booth, if she was standing in a phone booth, sulking, because he had made a joke about her dog. "Daisy? Daisy?"

"Hey, I'm back. I was just getting a cigarette from Jason. Jason's the friend I'm traveling with. Oh, you know what happened?"

"What happened?" The new day had arrived outside his windows.

"Well, he was taking this blacksmithing course in Salem and they stopped giving it."

"That's too bad."

"Yeah. So that's why he left Salem, and he's got a job in Spokane and the university there has a whole program for blacksmiths."

"That's wonderful." It would be a warm day, very warm for this time of spring. The mud season was not yet over.

"That's where we're headed for now, but I'll leave him there and get home from there."

"You're coming to Boston Corners?" Clemmons was now sitting on the edge of his bed and he scratched one knee. He looked at the window beside his bed. About a hundred years ago, a carpenter had installed it here at a 45° angle under the roof line. Clemmons cranked his head to one side to be agreeable.

". . . not to stay," her voice said firmly. He had not suggested that, he thought. "But I got to be in the wedding, I've never been in a wedding before."

"What wedding?" Strange that he had never noticed this drop of paint on his window before, all the times he had turned on his side in the morning to watch the mountains reappear. It was not a teardrop, but a scraggly dribble the shape of a shepherd's crook. "Wait a minute. Milly's getting married?" He returned to the voice in his ear, the endless flow of water.

"Jesus, Pop. You mean she hasn't written you?" Then she stopped, spoke to someone out of range. He imagined a long line of people stretched across the Grand Coulee dam waiting to use the phone. "Just a minute. I'll be there in a minute." Then it sounded as if the connection had gone dead, as if she had been forcibly removed from the booth by someone eager to use the phone, perhaps to report a fire, an accident in the water. Then she was back.

"That sonuvabitch. I'll be glad to dump this creep when we get to Spokane. Jason's nice but he's a real drag."

"I think you're right," he said, still trying to make out the nature of the paint spot. It could be a question mark, something drawn by a child. "It must be difficult traveling with all of those heavy tools."

"What tools?" she asked. He could hear the suspicion in her voice, see the dark clouds forming on the horizon of her brow. "He doesn't have any tools."

"Not even his own anvil?" But before she could reply, "Now Daisy—fill me in on Milly."

"Well"—she sounded as if she had flounced down in the phone booth—"she's coming home to get married to this guy she met in Key West. He's the leader of Stanley Livingston, the rock band! You know? And she wants to get married at home, in the field where the old fight was. I'm to be in the wedding, sister of honor."

"Maid of honor," he said.

"Something like that, but she wants you to give her away. Will you, Pop?"

"When did all this happen?" He was standing up. The morning had formed too suddenly. "You people can't just arrange everyone's life to suit your whims. I can't do that. I have an option on that piece of property."

"You're selling it? You're selling the old fight place?"

The hurt in her voice surprised him, that she had even cared about it surprised him. She was now talking to someone outside the booth. He could hear some of the words: ". . . sit in the cab and . . . be there . . . in a minute . . ." Then back to him, the voice of a schoolgirl. "Listen, Pop, I have to go, this guy is getting anxious to move."

"Wait a minute, wait a minute. Daisy? I want to know about this. When is this wedding supposed to take place?"

"She said she wrote—just like that bitch. You should have a letter from her. I think it's May 8th. Mama's birthday. Isn't that Mama's birthday? Oh, yes, that's why she asked me to call you—would you talk to Mama, see if she'd come up for it?"

"Wait a minute, wait a minute." He paced the floor of the bedroom, his range limited by the length of the telephone cord, the two-thousand-mile-long connection between their voices. "Your mother and I . . ."

"Listen, Pop. I gotta run. Don't fail us now. It'll be real nice. Just think, it's the only wedding I've ever been in. Hey, I'll probably be the only straight girl in the wedding, including the bride."

"None of that. Don't say that," he replied, confusion sidetracked momentarily, but before he could return to the main point, she had hung up, had somehow waved goodbye more than spoken, and the line went dead. Even if he knew the phone number and called back, it would be no use. He imagined the aluminum cage of the booth like a counter on a board game, isolated on its utility square, waiting for some player to move it. That call must have cost him twelve, fifteen dollars; he checked the time—the high rates were in effect.

With his thumbnail, he removed the small fleck of paint from the windowpane, but the shadow of the mark remained, a scraggly, hesitant questioning. He would have to have the place painted. He would have to get Benny Smith up here to paint the place, though he was not sure that he had not been reminded of Benny by Boxer, who sat under one of the old, very large maple trees that grew in front of the house. The dog, a boxer by breed as well as by name, sat like a lovesick Romeo, body tense and face lifted to the balcony of the tree's boughs where squirrels frolicked in the eastern sun. So much for the animal's dedication to vegetarianism, he thought, and pulled on the heavy shirt he used for a robe.

Now, one might suppose that living alone like this, furnishing his solitude with moments of aloneness collected with the same care as those Sunday antiquers expend on the back roads around Boston Corners, Clemmons would have been outraged by this sudden threat to his solitude, the handling and breakage that was bound to happen. But anyone who knew him from the old days, in urban haunts, can easily recognize his peculiar ambivalence. He could never decide where he wanted to be, alone or together with someone, not so much because he couldn't make up his mind, since he always had a clear idea of what he wanted—it was as though a special kind of clock told him when to walk out of the noisy scene of the old Ruban Bleu and climb a peak in Boston Corners. Nor was it because he got bored with one scene or another, but more like one of those pioneers, he had to move out of one settlement only to start up another one someplace else.

But now he moved through the hallway that connected the two front rooms of his house—a living room–library and a dining room—with the kitchen. A wall of glass was on his right, on the north side of the house, and the inside wall of this passageway was decorated with reproductions of various sizes, some framed, others merely taped to the surface or stapled (as was the case with a large poster that had been distributed by an airline company), and all of them madonnas, serenely squinting against the morning light. They were all from Siena, so their eyes would be half-shielded even if the north light was dull, even if they peered into darkness; a crafty expression put there by Martini and Giovanni di Paolo or others from that mountain town where the brilliant light in those studios had given the models a confidential look, the look of a secret shared. It was the same look Daisy had, the same look her mother had, though Daisy's hooded eyes were rinsed of Old World guile, the Machiavellian glint, by guarded wonder. He carried this look with him into the kitchen, imagining her looking this way as she talked to him on the phone. He missed her. He opened the back door and Boxer raced through followed by three cats, who dashed across the floor of the back room, together and with tails up, like the members of a carnival high-wire act entering center ring.

He did not like cats, yet he was feeding three cats; one of them belonged to Daisy, he could not remember which one, and the other two had been left by Milly. "You need them," his older daughter had told him with that no-nonsense tone of voice, a temper that entertained no disagreement; she must have been about nineteen then, but that made no difference, for she had been that way as a little girl.

"But I don't want to be the evil stepmother anymore," he could remember Daisy saying outside his window. "Why can't I be the girl going to the ball?"

"Because that's my part," Milly had replied. "You will play the evil stepmother or we won't play." That was her tone of voice.

For a moment, he missed them both, then turned to the stove, set out a frying pan, and opened the refrigerator to get out a package of bacon. He pulled one, two, three strips of bacon from the pack as Boxer watched from under the table. The dog's eyes glazed over as each piece of bacon passed through the air from package to pan. He seemed to vibrate with anticipation, his square jaw closed tensely, a silly scrap of pink tongue fixed on one side.

"You poor sonuvabitch," Clemmons said, holding a strip of bacon above the dog's head. Boxer rolled over on his back to expose his smooth underbelly, as if the look of his sheathed penis and neat knob of testicles would win the prize. "Ah, you hypocrite. You backslider. Look at you, aren't you ashamed?" The coral tip of the dog's penis had emerged from its furry scabbard. "Where are your ideals? You forget it all, give it up for a slice of pork. No, I won't let you do that, my friend." Clemmons went back to the stove and threw the bacon into the pan. "I'll keep you honest. You'll eat your bean sprouts and like 'em." The dog rolled back over and began to pant open-mouthed, disinterested. If Boxer had had a tail, it would have thumped the floor.

As Clemmons ate breakfast, sitting in the bay window of the kitchen that faced south and overlooked the field where the old prize fight had taken place, he let the flavors of the food arouse his palate, tasting an egg, bacon, and bread for the first time. He sorted through his reactions to his daughter's phone call, the information it had brought him. Milly to be married. They had, more or less, lost contact and now she wished to return, to be married with his blessing, his bestowal of affection. He still had affection for her, even love for her; but sometimes a terrible rage seized him—an anger not unlike Milly's—a fury that made him swipe a clear radius around himself, as if he had been pressed too hard, and his survival demanded space; point of fact, some put the tag of "Regency" on him for this characteristic, and though he was not what one might call a fop, there was the feeling that if he carried a cane, a sword would be hidden within it.

The morning sun flooded through the bay window to

spill upon the breakfast table and collect in his empty plate, to make a dazzling pool like a mirror, or a screen—for he did not see his own reflection, but the faces of others: of Daisy and her sister, of their mother and others; each one appearing and disappearing like the cameos that used to introduce the cast in early films. It was a cast of women.

He needed to talk to someone about all this and he thought of Claire, not that he would be able to say anything beyond the original problem. Claire would carry off the first query to spin an answer around it for hours, for hours talking extemporaneously as if she were taking a final at Mount Holyoke, filling one blue book after another, as she constructed a thesis around the original statement, so it resembled one of those models meant to demonstrate the molecular makeup of the universe. He would listen, though he understood only half of what she said, but listening always helped; his confusion purified as it passed through the intricate net of her intellect.

Then he saw her turn and lift her arms, her hands going to her hair to pull out the large pins that held it up—large Old Testament hairpins, for he thought she looked like one of those Biblical seductresses, an amused look in the large eyes, the delicate lips slyly turned up, as if he had solved, unwittingly come upon the solution to, the problem she had held secret for centuries, and now he would be rewarded for his lucky guess.

But he never knew what he had said, what the magic word had been or the secret gesture; perhaps to hold up to the light one of the colored glass bottles she had all over her apartment, a red one, or the amber one, the green, the purple—it wasn't just any bottle, but had to be a particular one she had been waiting for him to touch and lift to the light so that, then, she could raise her arms, undo her hair, and turn to him.

The morning light had also warmed his legs and his lap

as he sat at the table, a gratuitous supplement to the heat his thoughts of Claire had aroused.

"We are two horny bastards," he told the dog. "Here we both sit in Boston Corners with hard-ons. Except you, you dumb bastard, get it up for all the wrong reasons." The dog looked wild-eyed and affectionate, stood up and put his head out to be stroked. "Maybe I'll call her," he said and leaned over to the wall phone just as a large station wagon pulled off the road below the house and parked. A well-dressed couple got out. They looked to be in their late sixties; the woman had beautiful snow-white hair.

He ran through the back room and out into the garage, which had been made into a home office. He looked at the large appointment calendar that hung on the wall above his desk. A. W. CLEMMONS—COUNTRY REAL ESTATE. In the printed square for the day, he made out his own scrawl, "Walker . . . 9 A.M. . . . Desmond place . . ." He grabbed a set of keys off a board by the door. The Walkers were solemnly reading the historical marker at the edge of the field. Upstairs, Clemmons quickly dressed in jeans and a pullover, and slipped into a pair of boots. He wrestled an old jacket off its hanger. He got downstairs to the front door just as the couple approached the other side, a quizzical look on the man's face as if afraid they may have walked up to the wrong house.

"Good morning."

"Mr. Clemmons? Well, good morning. Horace Walker and . . . Mrs. Walker."

"Good morning," Clemmons said again, shaking hands. "Should we go in my car . . . or . . ."

"I'd like to take my car," Mr. Walker said. "Just to see how it does on the road up to the place."

"We were just reading that marker down there," the woman said. They walked down the lawn toward the station wagon. "I don't know anything about prize fighting but this seems like an odd place to have a championship fight—it's so quiet, remote." Her eyes were a bright blue and were the striking features of a face that was still smooth and very pretty. "It must have been even more remote in 1853."

"Prize fighting was illegal in those days," he told them, "but neither New York nor Massachusetts claimed Boston Corners. So the law could not be enforced here." He unfolded the cloth of narrative along the usual lines; he had told the story of the Yankee Sullivan-John Morrisey fight so many times, to so many prospective buyers, that he could relate the details while saying to the driver "Turn here" or "Take the next right" without interrupting the story, as if the directions were part of the story, like instructions given by the referee in the course of the fight itself.

Clemmons could tell Mrs. Walker was charmed by his speech but Mr. Walker listened to him suspiciously, probably thinking no one who spoke so easily could be trusted. It was this same gift of language, putting assorted lots of fact into pleasing relationships, that accounted for those successes he enjoyed in the old days. But—here's the ambiguity—at the core of those successes, with women or as a press agent, there was a deafness that would not hear the full range of his words, nor credit him a full range of meaning. It is at this core, perhaps, that everyone wants to be heard.

". . . About twenty years," he is answering Mr. Walker's question. "Though actually I've lived here longer if you count the summers, since my Dad used to have a summer place south of here. No, it hasn't changed much. Here we are."

The Desmond house sat handsomely on a hillside, with terraces, patio, and a screened porch on one side. It was not too old a house, but had a quality in the use of stone and dormers that suggested an earlier time. Two bedrooms, bath and a half, full basement, two fireplaces, workshop, and garage. Mr. Walker was particularly interested in the basement. Mrs. Walker looked as if she wanted to respond immediately to the charm of the setting but glanced quickly at her husband, who sat stiffly behind the wheel. She said nothing and got out of the car.

"Now what are they asking?" Mr. Walker looked as if the price might have changed during the course of the trip, the course of Clemmons's talk.

"Sixty-five," he replied. It was thirty thousand dollars more than what the Desmonds had paid him originally. "There's a small mortgage you can take over, or it can be refinanced. The local banks are pretty liberal. The estate is not interested in a second mortgage."

Mrs. Walker skipped up the brick steps stiffly, a last fling at girlishness. Her husband mounted the steps soberly.

"You know"—he turned to Clemmons at the flagstone terrace—"it's getting so bad in the city these days—you have to speak Spanish just to get along. And you have to speak some kind of gook talk just to buy apples. Think of that." His voice was light and its tone was more one of amazement than anger. "It's unbelievable what's happening down there. All those people." His face had flushed as he spoke. Clemmons had not responded, only nodded and passed by to unlock the door.

It was his habit to let clients be on their own, to be handy to answer questions, and to let the property sell itself, but this sometimes confused people, threw their resistance off balance if they had expected to wrestle with a sales pitch. Also, he enjoyed being alone in the empty rooms of these houses, not to pry into their pasts but to commune with them. In fact, there were some rooms of certain houses where he and Olive had enjoyed good times, dined and talked with the previous owners, and this was the case here. There were still some clothes in the closet and a tweed cap on a hook. Magazines and newspapers several months old had been neatly stacked on the coffee table. The refrigerator door stood open, the interior clean and empty, but a half-full jar of instant coffee sat on the drainboard of the sink and a bag of birdseed rested against the window sill. He passed Mrs. Walker in the doorway to the study and she nodded at him as if to say *yes,* or *hello,* or *not so bad.* Mr. Walker had gone immediately down to the basement.

Records were stacked on a cabinet top still marked with the dust outline of the turntable that had once been there. They were mostly of musicals. The Desmonds had gone to all the Broadway openings, bought the recordings of the shows they had liked, and played and replayed the music as they sat outside on the patio on long summer evenings. He shuffled through the albums. Walker moved directly beneath him in the basement, paused, then moved again, apparently taking measurements, because Clemmons heard a whir and snap of what sounded like a metal tape-rule. So there was no one present to see Clemmons start as if the sunlight had suddenly lost its heat. It wasn't fair, he thought, and looked down at the face printed on the old record jacket; another face in an album he did not want to open. JENNY SEVEN SINGS RODGERS AND HART. The record cover was worn rough on the edges. He must have loaned it to the Desmonds; in fact, he now remembered that he had misplaced it, had forgotten the loss of the record though not the sound of the voice carried in its grooves. She stared out from the cover in the vacuous fashion of those times; her hair permanently pagodaed, and the same curves repeated in the mouth, open and song-shaped, in the turned-up nose and the deep parabolae of the eyes; the arched, plucked eyebrows—a pasteboard, dimensionless, printed, put-together image.

He turned it over to read the brief biography, which he knew, because he had written it: a clever collection of almost-truths and not-quite-lies that were part of the press agent's style.

> After featured roles in the leading musical tents, Miss Seven left her native Providence, Rhode Island—folks there still remember her as the *Sunny Singer* on WPRO—and challenged fame and fortune in New York City.

"It's a little steep. How about fifty-five?" Walker's voice came over his shoulder.

Clemmons said nothing, made no movement for he had been tuning out a hash of sounds, an anonymous mixture that choked him like smoke in a dark room; and by the time he returned to the clear silence of the empty house, Walker had already upped his proposal.

"I could maybe do better if the local banks are as liberal as you say." The man had taken his silence as a bargaining chip. "The basement will take a lot of work."

"The sills were all replaced just recently," Clemmons countered.

"Oh, the basement is structurally sound," Walker agreed. He came to a window, studied the condition of its sash. He held the metal tape measure in one hand, a notepad and pencil in the other. "But I figure I'll have to put eight, maybe ten thousand into the basement." Clemmons's look amused him sufficiently so he added "For the shelter."

"The shelter?"

"Mrs. Walker and I will have to be self-sufficient down there for at least ten days—two weeks more likely—and that means a self-contained water system, storage, and supplies. Auxiliary power unit, of course . . ."

"Oh." Clemmons nodded and looked back at the record album. It had been used as a coaster for cocktail glasses many times, circular water marks forged a loose chain across the printed copy like a magician's set of metal rings.

"For sure, the foundation is pretty good," Walker continued. "But there has to be a complete subfloor erected; steel beams, enforced concrete. Plus ventilation. I think I can put that through the west wall." As he spoke he began to play with the measuring tape. "It will be tricky, but I think it can be done. The airshaft, vent, and exhaust can be worked through what looks like it may have been a cistern of some sort."

"These old houses often had cisterns to collect rain

water." Clemmons tucked the record album under one arm. "I thought bomb shelters came cheaper."

"You're probably thinking of those prefab jobs back in the sixties." Walker's manner was casual. "What was it—four hundred dollars' worth of sandbags? Rockefeller's idea of survival? Wouldn't last a minute in the fire storm these babies can start today. Brother, when that megaton cleans up Times Square, it's going to do a number for hundreds of miles around too. Mrs. Walker and I intend to have our eggs and coffee the morning after—powdered eggs and coffee, to be sure, but probably the best breakfast to be had in the lower Hudson Valley." Walker laughed and punched Clemmons lightly in one arm.

"Oh, there you are." His wife had stepped into the room. "Take your ruler and measure these windows. I think the drapes in our bedroom will fit here." Good-naturedly, Walker followed his wife's directions and measured the different casements, calling out their dimensions in a businesslike manner.

"Seventy-three . . . forty-six . . . seventy-three . . . forty-six . . ."

Clemmons had walked out of the house. The planting around the patio still suggested the former owner's meticulous gardening: crocus and snowdrops with wild flowers—trillium, rue anemone, Jacob's ladder, too. Clemmons admired their fresh variety in this crisp sunlight of early spring, but he had been thinking of night, and of one night in particular.

The record album had spun his memory, though the man's talk of bomb shelters had sounded a peculiar harmony. Lexington Avenue at four in the morning. Empty, no one on the street. Not a machine or person moved, save for the automatic click-clocking of red and green traffic lights strung out like beads of a necklace. Jenny had just finished the last show at the Ruban. It was June, already warm, and a cloudburst had wet down the streets so the air was redolent with the lush, worn aromas of the city. New York was turning in an embrace, waiting for something to happen, as the two of them waited for a taxi, kissing. The humid breath of the city had enveloped them.

"Here's the village of Stout Falls." Clemmons leaned forward and spoke over the front seat. They had just left the bank. It is a crossroads similar to Irondale, the same loosely lapstraked cluster of buildings, but without a general store. A flagpole with flag set before a trailer marked the post office. "In the summer it's quite busy here," he continued. "Also an interesting ethnic shift takes place. A lot of Jewish summer camps in the area." He could feel Walker's eyes bounce off the rear-view mirror.

"Look," Mrs. Walker said. "There's one of those roadside vegetable stands. Can we stop? Let's stop."

"He won't have much," Clemmons told them. "It's too early in the season for anything to be in."

"Oh, let's stop anyway," Mrs. Walker begged, anxious to join her new community, and her husband pulled off the road and parked before an open shed that contained tables and bins.

"Mr. and Mrs. Walker"—Clemmons made the introductions. "This is Earle Hicks. The Walkers have just bought the Desmond place," he told the tall, red-faced man behind the counter.

There had been only a slight shift of eyes toward the newcomers, an obligatory glance, for the man behind the counter continued to stare at the realtor, and his eyes seemed pressed out by the same force that puffed the muscles of his neck.

"How have you been, Earle? I haven't seen you for a while."

"I've been in the hospital," the man said cheerfully.

"You don't say. I'm sorry to hear it. I hope everything's all right."

"Well, I guess so. They took out a couple of tumors." He was almost chortling, but there was little humor in the tone. "So I guess it's all right, A. W. I guess it is."

The Walkers had selected a can of local maple syrup, about all the stand had to offer, as Clemmons had warned; though his attempt to discourage their stopping at Earle Hicks's stand was not so much to benefit them, to save them a waste of time, as it had been for him to avoid seeing Earle Hicks. The man's eyes scored him like the jets from acetylene torches, probably made more intense by the news of his condemnation. Clemmons had known of the man's hospital stay, and the verdict was common gossip.

"Well, you're right," Mrs. Walker said amiably as they got back on the highway. "He doesn't have much. But I guess in a month there'll be peas and lettuce."

"Maybe." Clemmons nodded and sat back; maybe in two or three months the bins would be empty and the shed would have lost its square lines to slant like a trapezoid, because there'd be no one around to give a twist to the large turnbuckle fixed on the cable stretched diagonally across the rear wall that kept the structure upright. Then, one day, driving by, he'd see the whole thing flat like a deck of used cards, and then, a day later, it would be all gone. Earle Hicks's outpost gone; the last of the Hicks family, the first white people to talk to the Iroquois—so Earle always said—all bulldozed and covered with gravel so that coming down Route 22, no one would be able to tell that Hicks, his vegetable stand, or the Iroquois had ever existed. All of that had been in Earle's expression, for the sentimental range on which such thoughts were prepared had also cooked the hate in his eyes so hard they resembled boiled eggs. Clemmons had looked away. He had not exiled Hicks to this pitiful spot on Route 22; the man's own father had done it when he had sold the village of Irondale to Clemmons. Even in summer, the produce was limited, and Clemmons often suspected the man had set up the stand on this stretch of highway so he could wave to him as he went by, to remind him that the deal with old man Hicks had somehow expelled the son from his own house, his own community;

maybe had even ignited the cancer that slowly blackened his life.

"Thank you, thank you." They were back at his house and he was standing beside the Walkers' car. Boxer was on the lawn, gnawing on a freshly killed groundhog. It was about lunchtime, Clemmons thought. They would meet again at the closing, the lawyers would now take over, so good-bye until then; they had to get back to the city.

"*Adios,*" Clemmons said and turned to his mailbox. He spotted among the circulars and bills a square envelope of a salmon pink, the sort of paper Milly would use, and indeed he recognized her large, oval hand in the address—an expensive kind of handwriting, and formed to ornament the creamy stationery and double envelopes of fancy invitations. The postmark was somewhere in Florida, the town's name blurred, and the stamp was upside down. He knew that if he carefully removed it, a secret code would lie underneath.

But he would have to finish with business first, before he opened her letter, before he could call Claire, before he could even forage the refrigerator for something to eat.

He called his main office, in Irondale, and told Rita Pickens about the sale, asking his manager to complete the paperwork. He made a few notes to himself and then leaned back in his chair, boots on the desk. He felt let down, as he usually did after completing a deal, as he used to feel in the old days when he had managed to put someone with Garroway on the *Today* show, or had booked a client, say someone like Jenny Seven, into the Green Room—the Green Room in the old Forrester Hotel that had offered a menu of spareribs and black-eyed peas. The menu had been ahead of its time, and the hotel was torn down a few years back.

There had been the excitement before the deal, the tension of the artless talk and careful silences, but even the thought of the Thirty-Six Hundred Dollars earned that morning—put together with a few other similar commissions; put together with the option money from that filmmaker for the field; put together with the record he had found—even all that could not stir up his desultory mood. Maybe he would take a walk in the woods with Boxer. Or maybe he'd go to New York. Maybe he'd open the letter from Milly.

Dear Pops,

Now, don't be mad, but Paul and I want to get married. He's good for me, A.W., he truly is. You'll like him. He's a musician—I mean serious. He writes music and plays all kinds of instruments. He has his own band. It's called Stanley Livingston.

Now don't be mad (I said that, didn't I), but I want to be married at home, in the field below the house. Will you please? It means something to me. A big wedding. Everybody—Mama, Grandma, Daisy (I already wrote her)—everybody. We can all be together. Will you do this, Pops . . . Let's start over. Can't we? You know that—

He laughed ruefully, reached for the phone, and looked at the wall clock. He could drive down to Dover Plains and take the 3:30, which would get him into the city just in time for drinks somewhere—maybe Claire could meet him at the Carlton bar. Or he could pick up some wine and they could make a picnic in her living room. No one was answering. She was looking at Persian rugs. Maybe at an auction. Maybe down in the Village at that building she was redoing. Maybe she was out of the country.

"Claire Wolferman's."

"She's just stepped out?"

"Can ay have yo nom-bur?"

"Where is she? Is she around?"

"Yo num-bur, pliss?"

"Wait a minute." He paused. *"Señorita, habla Andy Clemmons."*

"¡Ah! Hola, Señor Clemmons. ¿Cómo le va?"

"Bien. ¿La Señorita Wolferman, está en la ciudad o qué?" Just speaking Spanish to Claire's answering service made him feel not so removed from the city, from the old days.

One more call. He dialed the long number in the back of his address book; there was no name next to it. A flat voice with no accent surprised him.

"Hello? Six-seven-two-four-one-four-one."

"May I speak with Olive Clemmons, please?"

"Who is this?" It was a cool inquiry, unhurried and calm. "You've just dialed a private line into the residence of Governor Chase. Who is this?" He could hear a signal being made, another assistant starting the process that would trace the call, make the voice print.

Clemmons took a breath and recited the terms of his relationship, almost a curriculum vitae, that seemed required of him whenever he called his wife.

"Just a minute." The voice sounded automatic, and he wondered if he had been speaking to a human being at all; recorded music tinkled in the earpiece. Some old hymn, he first thought. Then he identified the melody: "The Sweetheart of Sigma Chi." He took several deep breaths and tried to shake the stiffness out of his left shoulder.

"Mr. Clemmons?" It may have been the same voice, but it sounded more human. "Awfully sorry to keep you waiting. Mrs. Clemmons is attending the Southern Governors' Conference at White Sulphur Springs. She and the Governor will be there through the weekend. Is this an emergency?" The tone had flattened.

"Something like it."

"Well, I could give you a number for them down there, but perhaps it might be quicker if I got a message to Mrs. Clemmons and had her return your call. I suppose she has your number?"

He was no longer hungry, but the dog might be, so he got

out a can of chickpeas and mixed them with leftover green beans and some vegetable oil. Boxer was nowhere around and did not respond to his call. Perhaps, in his desperation, the animal had cornered a bear up on the mountain. It was not fair, he thought, the events of this whole day so far. And he had been good, he reminded himself. This morning, right after Daisy's call, he had gone into the bathroom and there had been a spider in the sink. He could have turned on the tap, or could have flicked it away, but he had waited patiently as it placed each of its eight feet one after the other up the sides of the porcelain bowl, over the counter, and down behind the molding. The Greeks probably had a god who turned himself into a spider, he thought, and perhaps this was that god. Maybe it had been Zeus, hotfooting it toward a rendezvous in Boston Corners, say, with that blond girl at the Irondale store. In any event, he had let the spider go and, according to the rules, he was supposed to be rewarded. Such benevolence should bring luck, make things fair.

Chapter Two

The old Café Nicholson used to be not on 57th Street or the later place, but tucked under the Queensboro Bridge; diners had to bring their own wine and there was only one waitress, a pale girl with long blond hair, and this is the period Clemmons turns in his mind as he puts the record of Jenny Seven on the turntable. Boxer is inside, the cats are out, and the night is strummed aggressively by peepers.

He met her first in Moriarity's, on 51st Sreet across from Radio City Music Hall—it's not there anymore either—or rather, heard her first, but not as a singer. As he told the story, he had been sitting at a rear booth having a late lunch with his boss and a client, and this commotion took place in the front, at the bar.

Some of the Rockettes had come in from the Music Hall for a snack between shows and they were noisier than usual; something peculiar had happened, for they laughed and talked excitedly. But her voice rose above the clamor like a fire bell.

"Jesus, Mary, can you imagine me trying to do 'Blue Skies' up to my ass in water? And it kept coming down. I looked down at Oscar and I wanted to say, what time does the ark leave? You know? Is this the Easter number or the Old Testament number?" Her voice projected like Stan Kenton's brass; her laughter was hard-edged and unmuted.

Clemmons excused himself and came to the front of the restaurant, thinking there might be an item in the event—he sometimes picked up a little extra money by giving different columnists reports of incidents he came across. He was more than surprised to trace this strong voice to the long, elegant throat of a young woman who looked like she might be the younger sibling of one of the dancers, in from the country on a visit. She was almost plain beside their theatrical manners, all still wearing stage makeup, and they surrounded her like protective aunts. That is, until she opened her mouth and spoke. "I looked up in the flies and saw those bastards trying to shut it off and I nearly choked in the middle of 'Never saw the sun shining so bright.' "

But it was the smooth vulnerability of her neck that struck him, how it seemed to bend slightly under the weight of a long, ovaled head made heavier by a dense mop of short curly hair; even the back of the neck was exposed. He said he was reminded of Lena in *Victory,* the same curve of throat, and for perhaps the same reasons.

"So what happened?" she answered his question. "I'll tell you what happened, Charlie. There we were, doing our little Easter number and they couldn't shut off the fucking rain machine. That's what happened." He was blasted by her laugh, though she stood some distance away. Up close, even under her makeup, she still looked like a girl on the way home from her first communion. "These poor broads were falling on their asses all over the place and I'm standing there trying to sing through the downpour like the poor little match girl. Then comes 'Tiptoe Through the Tulips,' and one of 'em slips and knocks over one of these three-foot-high dummy tulips that are all over downstage, and it's like dominoes. All over, all fall down. Ever try to pick up a three-foot-high wooden tulip while doing the time-step in a lagoon? I tell you, Charlie, it was like Saturday night in Fall River."

> *I know a pretty place*
> *At your command, sir*
> *It's not a city place,*
> *Yet near at hand, sir:*
> *Here, if you can loll away*
> *Two hearts can toll away*
> *You'd never stroll away*
> *If you only knew . . .*
>
> *Here in my arms—it's adorable . . .*

Her voice drew up the different parts of the room, the chair he sat in, the books and lamps, as if it were a velvet sash being unwound from the record on the turntable; no less remarkable that such a large voice, such a vibrant strand, could be contained in those narrow grooves of black plastic as it was that the depth and power of the voice emanated from such a small-figured woman. Her phrasing owed a lot to Mabel Mercer, but that could be said for a lot of singers from those days. It was the resonance and sureness of her range, a lyric soprano, that implored one to listen and then, once listened to, asked for affection. Not begged, but asked; a hands-out gesture when you saw her with that slight tilt of head on the long neck, and the gesture somehow reproduced just by the sound of her voice even in this room in Boston Corners, New York.

Clemmons listened. He had gone to the last show at the Music Hall that night. The backstage repairs had been made, so the Easter numbers were appropriately weathered, and she sang three numbers, "April Showers," "Blue Skies," and "*Ave Maria*"—the pageant closing on the obligatory solemnity that put chorus and Rockettes into fluorescent costumes to assemble into a Rose Window around the singer. She seemed to generate the spotlight that illuminated her, to pull it down out of the darkness and dress herself in its brilliance for this routine extravaganza. Clemmons was no expert on singing but he did recognize her stage presence, this appearance of a unique identity.

He left the theater and went back to his office, only a block from the Music Hall, and typed out a note to Danton Walker, the old columnist on the *Daily News*. He gave him the item about the flooded musical number and then asked him to mention this singer, Jenny Seven, if he had extra space. Walker made an amusing paragraph out of the mishap (he prided himself on his wit), and then in a column a few days later there was this other item.

> Jenny Seven is a lucky number for the Radio City Music Hall's current Easter pageant. A fresh, new singer who has already caught the ear of the knowing.

Clemmons said he cut out the item and left it with the stage-door manager at the Music Hall, along with a bunch of tulips and a note asking her for dinner after the last show, and he further described how foolish he felt standing at the stage door that night dodging the Rockettes who came out in a fast break and smelling of *Aprés Bal*. He almost turned and walked down the block, he said, to become an anonymous admirer rather than a specific figure of ridicule, like all those stage-door Juans he himself had seen, who stood patiently in all kinds of weather like hound dogs that had lost the scent of something they hoped to find just one more time.

"So it's you, Charlie." Her appearance made his decision. "You're the *knowing ear.*"

"Okay, you've got two choices," he told her. "You can come back to my place and I can boil up some Kraft dinner, throw in some peas, a can of tuna and—*voilá*—Tuna Supreme . . . or Dan Walker sent me ten bucks for the piece on the faulty plumbing and there's a restaurant up the street called Fleur de Lis that serves a fair *coq au vin* and I could throw in an extra buck for some wine. I suggest the second choice as the safer one, and it's only fair, since you helped earn the ten bucks, so why not share the spoils?"

He said that the whole time he was delivering this promotion, she looked down the street, tapped her foot as if she had been expecting someone else, anyone else maybe; and he was suddenly aware again, reminded himself that he had just seen her standing on stage in her own circle of light, and—to be more honest, he had also calculated that her salary was probably two and a half times what he was making, scale being around two hundred dollars then. Here he was, playing the suave man-about-town with someone who already had a couple stripes on him.

"I've seen that restaurant on my way home," she was saying, then she turned her head and looked up into his face. "Sure. Okay, Charlie, you're on."

"By the way, my name is not Charlie. It's Andy."

"Sure, okay," she said, and lightly placed her hand on his arm as he had seen her do with a chorus boy to promenade offstage.

Jenny's voice continued to sing to Clemmons in Boston Corners about the city being "a wondrous toy." He remembered it had been, but he had never noticed until now how the Lorenz Hart lyric promoted Manhattan as a place to get away *to*—not *from*—a cozy, secluded haven for lovers. That was contrary to all his promotions, he thought, and he had earned a good living from people like the Walkers today because of these promotions. So now, Clemmons questioned his own memory of those days. Was it true then, with Jenny, or was it only another kind of promotion—something sold to his memory by a perverse agent of his mind? Had it truly been an "isle of joy," to complete the lyric's rhyme, or was this another nostalgia fabricated by a songwriter who, at some point in his life, had to sweat out a summer in Greenwich Village, because he couldn't afford the fare to Greenwich, Conn.?

She was from Cranston, Rhode Island, she told him, and her mother had started giving her singing lessons when she was in grade school. She had won a scholarship to the New England Conservatory, but then her father died and she went to work on a radio station in Providence, singing songs at an early hour between news and weather reports —the "Sunny Singer." She studied with local voice coaches. She did some modeling for a department store, the junior and teen sizes. She had done some musical stock. She had done a little of everything.

"What's this cock dish?" she asked, studying the menu. Her laughter startled other diners like a fall of cymbals.

"Oh. *Coq au vin*?" Clemmons leaned over and pointed to her menu. "It's usually an old chicken in a kind of fricassee with red wine and mushrooms and onions. It's very good here."

"I'm hungry. Is it a lot?"

"Well, let's start with the *paté*." He had leaned back in his chair to give the order to a waiter. "Then two of the *coq au vin, des pommes frites, naturellement,* and then the asparagus looks good. Yes, and a salad. Oh yes, the wine. The *Beaujolais, merci.*"

Jenny had been eating bread, had ravenously broken a roll apart and smeared it with butter, and almost crammed it into her mouth as he spoke to the waiter, though her attention never strayed from the exchange. It was as if she might have been studying his part. "How do you know all this?" she asked when the waiter left. Her voice sounded suspicious.

"Oh, I'm with this firm that wines and dines its clients—they're paying for it but don't know it—and then I was in Europe a little bit . . ."

"In the army?" she asked, breaking open a second roll.

"No, I didn't quite make the war—a little too young,"

he replied giving the disqualification just a shade of meaning, as if to say he had been too young by only a month or even a day, because as he studied her in the comparatively bright light of the restaurant he began to see that she was older than he had thought, that with the makeup off, her eyelids stripped of their fake lashes, and her face scrubbed down to its freckled base, a pale skin that would tan easily, her very plainness suggested an age, a journal of experience to accompany if not to sponsor her manner. This assurance, the poise he had seen her display on stage, must have been something she had put together herself, he would reason, part of her art sometimes betrayed by her own sense of mischief.

"Holy Mary—what's this meatloaf?"

"It's a country *paté*—rougher in texture than others . . ."

"Jesus, Charlie, do you talk like this all the time?"

"Like what?"

"This tour-of-the-rooms bit. You say it's *paté*, I say it's meatloaf . . ." Then she made the most astounding gesture. She sang the word: *"Pah-TAY,"* a clear, round A note, the perfect pitch that other singers were to envy, rolling the sound out over the restaurant and seeming to strike up reverberations in the glassware. Clemmons looked around quickly. The other patrons were caught in a still photograph of wonder and then moved to laughter, to light applause. One elderly diner in the corner even stood to raise his wineglass in a toast. Probably too old to hang around stage doors anymore, Clemmons thought. Jenny laughed, her head back like a child on a swing, and waved to her audience as Clemmons forgot his embarrassment. The chill her impulsive act had given him was quickly warmed by the reception it had received.

"You see?" she said, as if she had just won a point. "So what do you do? You're a press agent?"

"I'm with an office." The name meant nothing to her. "We handle mostly theater. I'm too lazy to go into newspaper work, and it's an interesting job. Lots of free tickets.

It affords me an opportunity to dine well. I am also, from time to time, in a position to help people out. How do you find the *coq au vin*?"

"I look down and it's right here on my plate. Whatta you mean how do I find it? You mean how do I like it? It's okay. There you go again, giving me the tour. Do you know what I mean?"

"Yes, I'm sorry," he replied, though he didn't really understand her meaning at the time. That was to come later, but for now he decided to ask her questions, let her tell about herself between mouthfuls of food; she even snatched the last piece of bread from his dish to clean up the gravy on her own.

Sometimes you think you've lived before
All that you live today
Things you do—come back to you
As though they knew the way.
Oh, the tricks your mind can play . . .

It seems we stood and talked like this before,
We looked at each other in the same way then . . .

By the time they had got into the taxi to ride up to the West Side where she lived, she had told him everything about herself that she wanted him to know. She was only a year older than he, as it turned out. She sat in the corner of the back seat, legs together, the small hand purse she had carried held square on her lap. Clemmons lounged in his corner, pointing out a play appearing at the Century Theatre, that used to be the old Al Jolson, but was torn down in the '60s. His office handled the press. Would she like to see it? He could get her in. No, she didn't like the leading actor. And so it went, up Broadway to the West Side, and finally they arrived at a brownstone in the Seventies with a pet store on the ground floor and an Italian restaurant next door.

"Listen," she told him on the sidewalk. He had dismissed the cab, trying to close the passenger door and pay the driver from the street with a nonchalance that he hoped would disguise his anticipation. "Listen, it's been a wonderful treat. I liked all that dinner. And I do thank you for getting my name in that column. And, you know"—her voice dropped into a lower confidentiality, the elliptical eyes slowly turned up to meet his—"I'd ask you up for some coffee, or something, but I've got two roommates who keep these boring, regular hours and . . . well, thanks again. Call me again, okay?" And she perked up on her toes to present pouting lips for him to touch, rather like the cute illustration on a Valentine card. He walked back to his apartment in the Village. He had only some change left over and payday was three days away.

They would not meet again for nearly two years. At that time, she would confess that her only roommate had been a marmalade cat, and that if he hadn't worked so hard to impress her she would have been happy to have him sleep with her, since no one else had asked that night.

The clockwork sound of the phonograph shutting down, coming to rest, ticked off Clemmons's thoughts as he sat in the large library chair, his reverie running down, memories slowly revolving until they stopped on their own dead weight. Boxer turned on his other side, stretched and resumed his dog nap as if the sudden silence in the room had aroused him. Even the night sounds outside the window had stopped, the chorus of peepers stilled by a great hand and then released.

He reached for the phone on the floor beside the chair. Claire would not be home, probably at the YMHA chatting up Irish poets. But the phone rang first.

"Hi—Andy?"

"Olive. I was about to call."

"Good timing. Hi. You called me? What about the girls?"

"It seems Milly wants to get married."

"When?"

"Your birthday."

"Where?"

"Here."

"Oh my." There was a husky sound like a piece of toffee being unwrapped. It was the way she laughed—though in fact, she had a passion for chocolate, which never added a pound to her but did seem to impart a sweet consistency to her flesh, almost a milky-cocoa coloring. "That child wants a home wedding. She was brought up right, I guess."

"Olive, I don't find any of it funny. Sounds like she wants a circus, not a wedding."

"Are you going to put up roadblocks or somethin'?"

"How is the Governor, by the way? What is this meeting about?"

"Oh, just another frat party these boys still go to—except now they talk till all hours about welfare funds and unions 'stead of girls and pretty things. We're going back home tomorrow. How are you? Have you heard from Daisy? I got a letter from her from someplace in Washington State."

Clemmons told her about their conversation that morning. Olive hummed her response, an agreeable scrim of sound behind which he knew her mind shifted and rearranged all the possibilities. Her eyes would be almost closed, the sensuous, sulky curve of mouth twinned, a sleep-swollen, slightly aroused expression that was not a reflection of her mind. They talked on the phone every week, at least, strangely more intimate, easier with the long-distance connection than any other.

"She's traveling with an apprentice blacksmith. Remember the guy who tied knots in things?"

"What does all that matter to you?" He could tell she had reached for a cigarette, and was reviewing her own question through the smoke. "You've simply got to let them go. You've got to let us all go. You can't make up your mind whether you want us to hang around or stay away. It's not nice on a lady's nerves—or anything else." There was a touch of nugget in her laugh, and he nearly reminded her that it was she who had left Boston Corners, left him to get back to civilization, she had said.

"I saw Earle Hicks today." That would even the conversation a bit. "He's had a bad cancer operation. He's dying."

"That's too bad." Her voice had diminished, lost something of its full throat.

"I'll have to get Benny Smith up to paint the house." He had only meant to change the subject, but as he spoke, another plan took shape. If he could get Olive to come up for the wedding, then he could leave, would not have to have anything to do with it. Olive could run it all. Milly and her musician could perform what rituals they wanted down there in the field across from the house. "Why don't you come on up? Will the Governor let you out of the compound? Milly wants you here."

"There's a reception for some textile people about then," she replies. She has brushed aside his remark.

"Why doesn't he get married or rent a hostess from Hertz? You know, people are starting to talk about him. There was a note in *Newsweek* a while back."

"I suppose he could do without me this one time."

"Olive." The more he thought about his plan, the better it seemed. "Please come up."

"Maybe we ought to talk about it." Her voice had got smaller, as if she had snuggled down into the bed covers. He wondered if the Greenbrier had comforters on their beds. Boxer had walked away to take another place next to the hearth.

"What do you mean, talk about it?"

"I mean, maybe we ought to talk about it." Her voice grew petulant, a tone he used to call her Stepin Fetchit routine.

"I see. You want me to come down there?"

"Uh-huh."

"What about your brother? He threatened to unleash the highway patrol the last time." There was an easy, turning-over-in-bed laugh in his ear.

"I could arrange a cease-fire. You come on down here and we'll talk about my coming up there."

"I don't know if that's possible."

"Andy. Hey, Andy? You're sounding like one of them primmy liberal types. You want something? I want something. If we work together, we both get a little something!" She sounded like her old self, sweating out a delegate, getting a vote. In fact, she had persuaded him to vote for Stevenson in 1956 with such tactics, but he had been relieved when Eisenhower had won.

"I'm going to have to give this more thought, Olive. Meantime, I've got a dog here who has to go out. I'll get back to you."

"Sure thing, Andy. Take care of yourself. Thanks for callin'." She always said that, "Thanks for callin'," as if she were some homely girl alone on a Saturday night, grateful for that single phone call, even a wrong number, though she had initiated the exchange—it was her way of leaving the conversation.

There was no moon and Boxer disappeared into blackness, but Clemmons could tell the dog had stopped at one of the large maples on the lawn, for he heard him blaze the trunk with a heavy stream of urine, as if to put his personal mark upon it even though the squirrels that lived in its top branches were beyond him. Below, in the darkness, was the field where the prize fight had taken place, where two men had beaten each other into bloody pulps. In 1853, thousands of people had left New York City, on foot, on horseback, and in carriages but mostly by way of the rail line just put down by the New York Central; thousands rushing to Boston Corners in the pursuit of violence. Now they took the same route to flee from violence. Lightning bugs seemed to kindle the image of that early host's campfires. That's how it must have looked, Clemmons thought, and listened closely, tried to hear through the screen of the peeper's rasp the old noises made by that multitude.

• • •

"We're gonna recreate the whole thing. All thirty-seven rounds of it. It was before the Queensberry rules, so a round was determined when a fighter went down. Yankee Sullivan would land a few punches on Morrisey, brush against him, and then fall down. End of round and Morrisey hadn't landed a punch. I told you Caan is reading the script? Hey, ever notice how *re*creation and *rec*reation are the same word? How about more coffee?"

This would be the following morning, and Clemmons was sitting in the living room of a townhouse, one unit of a large condominium village he had built in a tract north of Boston Corners and called Dutch Village. The speaker was an energetic man with gray bushy hair and heavy eyebrows, who wore jeans, a denim shirt, and several strands of colored pumpkin seeds around his neck. It was only ten in the morning, and Clemmons was thinking that one strand might have been enough.

A girl of about three turned circles in the corner of the room. She was barefoot and wore a very formal dress with elaborate embroidery on its bodice.

"Here. Cream? Sugar? Saccharine? Take what you want," Clemmons's host invited him to the tray of cups and pitchers set on the butcher block table. The room was furnished like a newly constructed abattoir, one that was yet to receive its first carcass—all heavy wood surfaces, stainless steel tubes, and plain rack fittings. A lone spider plant hung from a blank wall.

"Wouldn't that be a gas, to get Caan and Jeff Bridges teamed up. I know they'll go for it."

"Who's going to play which?" Clemmons asked.

"Well, Bridges will do Yankee Sullivan, Caan will do Morrisey."

"The only trouble there is that Sullivan was smaller than Morrisey, about thirty pounds lighter and also about twenty years older. He was forty years old when he fought Morrisey in Boston Corners. Morrisey was twenty-two. Can Caan look twenty-two?"

"True. True, we've got a little problem with that one," Broome said, nodding his head. His nose wrinkled, his face worked its way around the problem, enclosed it. "Do you smell something?" he asked suddenly. "I smell something. Well, here I am telling you about this fight and you know all about it. But wait until you hear about the train we got. We found it in a museum in Pennsylvania. It's right for that period—1852. And it works! The damn thing really works!" The features of his face had spread apart, a soft explosion. "Listen. What is that I smell? Do you smell it?"

"Have you talked to the railroad company?" Clemmons asked.

"I've got a team of lawyers working there," Sam Broome replied. "It looks good. We only need a few miles of the track. The hard part will be pulling the train by horses out of the city limits. That's how they left the city—horse power. Some fire ordinance about using the engines inside the city. Can you imagine the scene—all those people hanging on the sides of boxcars, on top—anything just to get up here for that brawl. Goddamn it, you build a new house and it smells just like—shit." The smile became the explanation. Both men looked at the little girl humming to herself in the corner.

Broome got up and walked over to a balcony that hung over another part of the house. "Rosé. Oh, Rosé. Someone's done poopie over here. Will you come do something, please?"

Clemmons noted the request was made in the patient, civilized tone of a superior, an employer addressing an underling who was continually at fault yet could not be fired because of family connections. In fact, Broome's wife did look to Clemmons like some bright girl just out of college—she was about Milly's age—who maybe got a job reading scripts and ended up marrying the producer. He observed her slender legs as she bent to change the child's diaper. They were thin and slightly bowed, as if warped by a weight she had been too young to bear. Her hands and arms also were very thin, and one hand moved fitfully to push at long, black hair as she bent to her task.

"You remember Rosé," Broome said, gesturing over his shoulder. "Honey, listen to this. Do you want to tell her? I'll tell her. Listen to this, honey. Andy's daughter wants to be married in the field where the prize fight took place, the one where we're going to make our picture. Isn't that beautiful? A country wedding in May. We can all go. It will be beautiful." There was a sudden shift to business. "There's no problem about your using the field. It won't affect our option. You want me to call the lawyers? We don't need the lawyers. Fuck the lawyers. We won't be setting up until late summer. Hey!" He was on his feet, stiff with an idea. "Listen to this. We get some costumes. We dress the wedding party up, these kids like to get all dressed up in old-time things, anyway. Right? Meanwhile, we shoot some footage of them in the costumes, work it in. How about it? Right?"

Clemmons decided not to answer, for he sensed that Broome was not serious; not that it would be beyond him to appropriate the wedding party, but that the offer was made to prove that he had no objection to the wedding taking place on a piece of property he had already leased. The man's wife had now come to stand beside him, holding the child on her hip. She wore a plain smock of Scandinavian design and her long face seemed drawn and impoverished; her eyes moved foxlike. They caught the light as it came through the wall of glass that framed part of the Harlem Valley, and the light seemed to rinse away whatever color the irises may have had. Clemmons was reminded of photographs of other women with children on their hips, but standing before shacks in Oklahoma in the 1930s, and he wondered at the same pose and expression; a similar misery and hunger, but clothed in the latest boutique fashions.

"You used to work for my father," she said to him. She had looked down, away from the glare, and her eyes became a light green. "Carter Perry," she spoke to his puzzlement.

"No kidding. Carter was your father?" Clemmons looked at her more closely.

"That's right, that's right." Broome nodded his head eagerly. "You were the flack in residence for old Perry's Hall of Culture." It sounded to Clemmons as if the producer were reviewing his résumé. "Here I am trying to tell you about show business and you're an old hand. What ever made you settle up here?"

"Your father was very good to me." Clemmons talked to the woman. "The union had begun to organize off-Broadway theaters, but I was not a union press agent. I tried to join the union but there was a moratorium on new members. . . ."

"Listen. Don't tell me," Broome said with a roll of his eyes. "I got a nephew of mine into the union and the kid doesn't know a fucking thing about public relations. I know what you were up against."

"Anyway," Clemmons continued, "your father came along and offered me this job with him—he had a great idea. He really did." The seriousness in Clemmons's expression made the young woman frown. Then she smiled. Her teeth were crooked and darkly stained, and there was a space where a canine should have been.

"Perry's Hall of Culture with a capital *K*." Broome laughed, his head thrown back. "That was some deal. I guess he was trying to keep up with the Mellons and the Rockefellers. So, you and Rosé probably met." He scratched at something between his shoulders as he looked at them both.

"Sam," the woman said, "I wasn't even born then."

"Oh, yeah," the producer said, still scratching, still suspicious.

"Well, I'm glad you don't object to our borrowing the field. My daughter will be pleased. And of course you're invited to the wedding." Clemmons had spoken to the producer's wife, and then stood up, and shook hands with her.

Outside, he paused at his car door. "How do you like it here?" The condominium units surrounded them like the interior of a stockade. Clemmons had had to locate and tear down half a dozen old barns in Connecticut just to get enough siding for the development. It was a professional inquiry.

"It's a nice little spot for—why should I tell you what it cost?" Broome laughed. "But we got Sheila Hennings in number five—when she's not in a play. Jerry O'Brien is in seven. Then there's that columnist—I never read him—what's his name, Gorman, he's in eight. No, it's like we moved the West Side up here. The best of the West Side. And it's safe. No muggers—no garbage—no dog shit—not yet." Broome laughed and straightened his pumpkin seeds. "Well, really I did it for her. You know, with the kid, she wanted to have a place to get out of the city. Boy, I sure envy you living up here all year round. Fresh air, no pressures, and these wonderful country people. I took a walk in the woods the other day. Beautiful."

"You know, it's a myth," Clemmons said, "about country people. Their morals and teeth are no better than anyone else's. Maybe worse." The producer had smiled absently and looked down at his sandals.

"You've been married a few times," the man said, and continued quickly, ignoring Clemmons's slight shake of head. "Well, you know how it is. She's my third one. It's a long story. A long story. I'll tell it to you sometime. Actually her name is Stephanie. I just call her Rosé because she goes with anything." He had gripped one of Clemmons's arms and looked up, had even winked.

Clemmons would make one more stop that morning,

turning off the state highway above Boston Corners onto a county road, then onto a town road, and then onto a dirt road that was tended by majestic maples on either side. The trees stood tall and hard budded, but the weeds had already closed in on either side of the road, to give the feeling that one was driving through a grass tunnel, a jungle denizened by the shapes of farm machinery, like the bones of extinct beasts, left to rust in the weeds. He would pull up before a large, barnlike building. SMITHTOWN GARAGE. The skeleton of an old-fashioned gas pump leaned against the door, which was quite large and open. The pump resembled a giant toy soldier stripped of its tunic and medals; perhaps it had grown weary of guarding the machine shop, had dozed off, and been court-martialed.

There was no noise when Clemmons turned off the car's engine, other than the tense click-clink sound made by the chain on the big German shepherd Benny Smith kept tied up just behind his house. He knew the dog would be shivering with an impatience to bark, waiting only for the first squeak of the car door to throw itself into a paroxysm of rage, and so, in order to hold the animal on a leash of silence, Clemmons did not move. He also knew that if he looked up and over and around the hulk of a dismantled barrow beside his car, he could see into Benny Smith's front yard, and there would be Little Ben, tethered the same way as the dog but looking more like a balloon tied to the playpen. The child also would be motionless, tense, as he assessed this intrusion into his solitude, then he would recommence the ceaseless back and forth swing of a metronome as he kept time with the refrain he must hear in his head but was never able to sing.

All three of them were held together: the dog, Benny's mongoloid son, and Clemmons; all had come together in their different solitudes, and Clemmons wondered if it could be possible to have a community of solitudes as there were other communities. Claire sometimes quoted to him a poem by Rilke that had to do with two people joining their solitudes, but that was only two people, and specifically the two of them, and usually at four in the morning as they lay on the wide divan in her studio. But a community also implied purpose, not just numbers, a goal beyond the range of its individual members. Solitude withdrew from such an arrangement, it wanted no part of a commune, would not or could not share the work or the pleasures, and preferred something that checked its aimlessness; even a cord or a chain that would keep it safe from freedom and let vanity prosper.

Not many would believe that Andy Clemmons would have such thoughts, to look at him, and especially as he stepped out of his car before the Smithtown Garage. This morning he wore a corduroy jacket and an oxford shirt open at the collar. Chino slacks, red socks, and soft shoes —the perfect picture of a country gentleman, or a gentleman who sold country real estate, and together with the round face, the concentric circles of nose and chin and eyes within that face—the hard radiants of those features only just beginning to soften around the edges—his appearance had been meant to go with attractive though unmeaningful talk, and sometimes he would oblige, the nature of his various occupations had made it necessary for him to oblige; yet, he would always hold back some reflection or observation, like Little Ben tied down on the lawn and restrained from speaking his real angers and hopes by the mask fixed upon his face.

The shepherd grew hoarse with barking as Clemmons closed the car door and strolled into the darkness of the cavernous tool shop. There were two punch drills, a lathe, two table saws, an anvil, welding equipment, hundreds of miscellaneous small tools and wrenches, and the power take-offs to operate the machinery. On the walls were racks that held more tools; the majority of these were hammers of all sizes and weights, from the smallest tack mallet up to a sledge hammer that looked, to Clemmons, as if two men might be needed to wield it. He wondered at all the hammers, if they were to demolish, in a frenzy of genius, what the other tools on the benches and the floor had carefully put together. In fact, all of the tools had belonged—that is, had been *really* used by Big Ben, Benny's father and Little Ben's grandfather, who had operated this garage and machine shop for many years. Actually, if you look at a map you'll find no Smithtown in Boston Corners but Big Ben Smith gave the name to his garage and the half section of land around it, all swamp most of the year. He even got mail, tool catalogues and bills, addressed to the name Smithtown; the Irondale post office had accommodated him.

Benny was probably making a call at some farm to weld a broken plow or tractor housing—he had a portable rig and generator mounted on the back of his pickup. It was about all the work he did, other than odd jobs for summer people; as if Big Ben had died too soon, had only had time to show him how to operate the welding equipment and nothing more in the machine shop. Clemmons walked up a bare wooden staircase bolted to the studs on one side of the interior. He felt that same sense of communion he had in empty houses, for he had climbed to this second floor many times to talk with the old man, to talk local politics, argue about the war in Vietnam. There were units of metal shelving ranked in rows, and on each shelf were cardboard boxes crammed with used parts; everything neatly assigned to its place, voltage regulators here, headlamps there, carburetors below, and so forth, with dozens of old generators arranged on the top shelves, like parts of an invention that never worked. Clemmons wondered if any of the parts worked; if, for example, one could wire up all the generators, voltage regulators, fuse panels, and headlamps together and then plug them in. Would this dingy, cobwebbed loft be blasted by the illumination?

There was also something else. Sometimes in the basements of houses he sold, Clemmons would come across a mess of hardware: small paper sacks of nails, and screws and bolts and washers—purchases made by the previous owner to do a single, simple job; maybe a box of number 8 flathead screws or a sack of ten-penny nails, always torn (perhaps the nails had become restless in their abandonment and had tried to work their way through the paper), and all these odd lots originally purchased so that two or three of their number could be used to repair a window screen or nail down a piece of siding, and then the remainder put in the basement or on a shelf, amassing over the years into a formidable collection of junk that is never to be used again, like events in the past, Clemmons would think, each meant to repair and fashion the present but always with a waste, a residue of memories left over that would do nothing but collect dust. He had a few such stores in his own basement.

He had been looking at a map of the U.S. stapled to one wall. It had been an oil company promotion. Someone had driven a roofing nail into the spot that would have been Boston Corners. Big Ben would have done that; in fact, Clemmons could imagine him carefully fixing the point of the nail not exactly where Boston Corners should be but slightly off to the northwest, perhaps one sixty-fourth of an inch, where he figured his place, Smithtown, was located; though the diameter of the nail head was so large that it obliterated almost the whole county and goes as far as Springfield, Massachusetts, on its eastern radius and Hudson, New York, on the west.

He surveyed the state of Washington, but could not find the Grand Coulee, the map was not so articulated. But Spokane was clearly visible and it cheered him to think that Daisy had made it to there by now, since she talked to him yesterday; the city's perimeter looked large and safe. Many facilities. East of this lay the narrow strip of Idaho like a chimney rising between the two rooms of Washington and Montana or like the central stairway of the old houses built around here. Washington could be the parlor but Montana was a cold, forbidding chamber. His gaze turned South. Milly might be marching through Georgia with her composer. Then to the left, just over the Appalachians, Olive would be rising, preparing to return to the Governor's mansion, which, again, was over yet another ridge of mountains. To the north, in Ohio, his mother would be rubbing some new-found ointment into her joints, loosening them up so she could fold herself into her car where she would spend most of her day, driving from one parking lot to another. And then very close, only about an inch away by the map's scale, was Claire—still asleep, probably sprawled over the poet she had brought home from the YMHA. His eyes returned across the continent, beyond Spokane, the state of Washington, and even beyond the continental limits, the edge of the paper. Jenny was out there, off the map.

The dog had made no noise when Benny Smith had driven up to the barn, the truck's motor being familiar to him, so Clemmons felt a little panic at being discovered upstairs, caught rummaging, one might say; though most of his chagrin came from a self-discovery caught out by Benny's arrival. A different sort of ransack had been in progress.

The man's face was set in its usual pleasant lines, the red cap, with the emblem of a hybrid corn on its peak, was set at a rakish angle across his brow. His eyes were clear of suspicion. "Howdy, A.W. I thought that might be your car. Hey, I'm sure glad you came by. I got something I want to show you." He turned and walked farther into the dim interior of the shop, almost a gesture, Clemmons thought, still self-conscious about being found upstairs, to permit him to step down to the ground floor gracefully so that they would be on the same level and could start over again.

A bare light bulb hanging by its cord from the ceiling had been turned on; it did not illuminate the interior so much as demonstrate how dark it was. Benny had continued to talk the whole time; something about an accident, having just been to a friend's house. "Ozzie's my friend. He lives down on Maple Avenue—you know, in one of them trailers. And he was just bleeding and bleeding and no way could we get him to the hospital. No way would he move. He just sat there bleeding and bleeding with these towels wrapped around his head."

"What happened?" Clemmons asked. He walked across the earthen floor to join the other man.

"He had fell asleep watching the TV and woke up early this morning with one of them horror movies onto it and old Ozzie thought it was a real monster and he just up and ran out of his trailer except he forgot to open the screen door but what's more, it wasn't screen neither 'cause Ozzie hadn't yet changed from the storm door, so he went right through the glass. Cut him bad. He was bleeding all over the place, no telling how long he'd been bleeding, but he wouldn't leave. Wouldn't go to the hospital and we had to get Doc Busch come over from Kline's where he was treating their cows and he sewed him up. I tell Ozzie he deserves to be fixed up by a cow doc, dumb old dog, he is."

"Well, those cuts on the head look worse than they are. The blood's very close to the skin there," Clemmons reassured him.

"I guess so. I guess that's right, A.W. Now lookee here what I got." They stood around a contraption on the floor that looked like a model for a ferris wheel, a rough model made of aluminum tubing arrayed in eight spokes, with beer cans soldered at the end of each spoke, and each beer can divided into two compartments by a flange in the center. A metal trough lay at the bottom, there was water in this, and an arrangement of gears, wires, and a small transformer had been mounted next to the wheel's axis. "Now watch this, A.W.," the man said, with a delighted expression.

He had filled a coffee can with water from a sink on the wall, and carefully poured some of it into two of the empty beer cans at the top of the wheel's perimeter. The weight of the water pulled the spokes around and down, the downside cans scooping water from the trough as they passed through the turn; the whole affair turning jerkily and uncertain, revolving slowly until each can was brought to the apex where its contents would dump into the emptied can below it, giving a startled impetus to the rig that pushed it around. The two men watched the contrivance for several seconds.

"Ain't that something?" Benny Smith said, adding a little more water just as the rig slowed down. "You've heard of perpetual motion? The Minton engine? Well, here's my version. 'Course, I got a few bugs yet. The bearings aren't easy enough, and the shaft here is a little too heavy. But watch this, A.W." He reached over his head and turned off the light bulb. They were in darkness, only the splash of the water at their feet like the sounds of waves coming over a foundering boat.

As Clemmons grew accustomed to the darkness, he picked up a faint glimmer of something, the light of a star so far removed from the limits of ordinary sight that it had to be caught in the corner of the eye and then only intermittently, never seen straight on or for any sustained measure of time. The wires attached to the transformer set near the machine's axis terminated at the base of the small bulb, the size used in a flashlight, and it was the pulse of this small filament that endeavored to lift the dark.

"See that. See that," Benny said. "Isn't that something?"

"It is something," Clemmons told him. "It's wonderful."

"Now, if I could get the right parts, I could build a little pump onto where that light bulb is which would lift the water up to the top, so I wouldn't have to stand here with that coffee can. I could light up all of Boston Corners. When them Arabs turn off the oil, I could wire up the whole country."

"You could, Benny. I know you could," Clemmons told him.

"Well, hell, it's just a gadget," the man said, and turned on the light. He put out one hand and stopped the machine. "What do you need, A.W.?" Clemmons talked to him about painting the house, told him about the wedding. "Gosh, the time goes by, don't it," Benny said, readjusting the red cap on his head. "I remember Milly as just a little girl, I must have been in high school then," he said and colored. "Sure, I can do it for you. About two weeks."

Boxer had been waiting for him, waiting to show him the prize sandwiched by his jaws—the limp body of a small rabbit. The dog ran to him but kept a safe distance, a wary look in his eyes. He had been tricked out of his catch before by a gesture of affection. "What do you want, my permission?" he told him. "Eat it, you monster."

Clemmons leaned against the fender of the car. The earth was in its final thaw and the ground gave up the faint mineral aroma of loosening, of opening. There was water running off the hills, the streams were high—his car had almost had to ford the small bridge in the village—even the liquid notes of robins and cardinals contributed to the flood. The air was warm and blustery and spiced with the raw stench of liquid fertilizer farmers had spread on the softening fields. Part of the balance, Clemmons would think, one side of an olfactory equinox—the other side being the delicious aroma of the timothy that would be cut three months later. The bare earth assembled itself once again. It would go on forever, as far as Clemmons was concerned, and he felt caught up and passed around within this cycle in much the same way he had been caught up in the makeshift arrangement invented for his life. He would have to fly down to see Olive, pass some time with her, if he was to get her to come back and run the wedding; if he was to be free of it. If he wanted to be free of it. He could take Claire somewhere. He turned and walked up the hill to his house. The phone was ringing but it did not hurry his pace. It might be a client or someone in town. The person would call back. It might be Claire, or Daisy or Milly or some other woman who threatened to illuminate his solitude.

Chapter Three

There was a hotdog vendor's cart parked next to the phone booth. Under its striped umbrella, people waited patiently for their lunch and then, as Clemmons dialed Claire's number, two stepped away with buns wrapped in napkins, like diplomas.

"Hello?" Her voice was businesslike. "Yes, hello?"

"Take this down." He looked at the cart. "Medallion number 486-317-C. Nick's Hot 'n' Nice. The sauerkraut looks watery and there's a crust on the mustard."

"You bastard. Where are you?"

"I'm at the corner of Lexington and 48th Street. I'd invite you to have lunch here at Nick's but he's about to move on. You know how these places change once they've been discovered."

"Bastard. Why do you call me like this . . . why didn't you let me know you were coming to town?"

"I did call. Didn't you get my message?"

"There was nothing specific. I suppose you're about to fly somewhere and can't stay. What is it with you, some arrogance that decides we're all waiting for you to call? You should see my schedule. You make me so mad." Her voice had thinned, a fine fabric about to tear. She would sound like that sometimes in bed, as if her vocal cords had suddenly dried up. "I must see you."

"I'm on my way south to see Olive. We have a small family crisis. I'd like to talk to you about it, as a matter of fact. Hear your reactions to it. I'd like to see you, Claire, I really would, but . . ."

"But, you've already bought your ticket and . . . hold it. There's the other phone. Don't go away." The line went blank; the conversation was placed on a siding to give some faster-moving talk the right of way. Cars and taxis advanced sluggishly beside the glassed sentry box. Trucks and buses wallowed like rudderless barges in the congestion. Would they reach 57th Street? "Okay." The other call seemed to have calmed her.

"I have no ticket," he continued. "I'll catch a shuttle to Washington and then pick up a ride with the Governor—he's in Washington seeing somebody and has the state plane. As a matter of fact, I'm not sure when he's leaving; today or tomorrow."

"Oh, this is terrible. Why can't I be better organized?" she said off the mouthpiece. He could hear papers being searched and shuffled.

"You always seem to be well-organized."

"I heard that—seem to be, eh?" The operator interrupted to say the time was up. "What's your number there? Give me your number and I'll call you back," Claire said.

After he gave her the number of the pay phone and hung up, Clemmons realized the call was no longer his, that he had given her the opportunity to direct it, decide when to terminate it. He had heard her use this technique on others. "Call me collect," would be the lure, whether the call was from Connecticut or Australia.

So when the phone rang, Clemmons began to talk quickly; nonsense, anything to hold the conversation. "Nick and I were just talking about when the oil runs out, and you'll be able to see the whole length of this avenue. Sail-powered taxis. Windmills for traffic lights . . ."

"Don't be silly. They've already developed a prototype battery at Carnegie–Mellon to power cars. So, you might as well be waiting here as in Washington. Is that right? Don't you agree?" He said nothing. "Damn it, damn it," she said under her breath. "They can wait. He's tomorrow." She went through her list.

"Did you just get up?"

"Ummn. I suppose if we met for supper, you'd want to squire me and insist on paying for everything."

"Certainly half of it," Clemmons replied. "Did I wake you or what?"

"Or what," her voice caught on half a laugh. "You mean is there someone here?" He had had a flash image of a man dressing hurriedly in a corner of her bedroom as she talked on the phone, as she rearranged her schedule to make room for him. "I should make you think so to punish you, but you would enjoy it too much, I think. No. No one is here. I want to see you, Andy. I had a birthday last week."

"Happy birthday."

"I was thirty-eight."

"Happy birthday."

"No, I mean really thirty-eight."

"And as beautiful as ever."

"That's bullshit and you know it. The other night, at the YMHA, I was standing around with all these people, I've known them all for years; Mark was there and Dan and Stanley. There was a party after the reading somewhere, there always is—but no one remembered to invite me. They all went off with their wives and girlfriends and there I was. I could never imagine being thirty-eight."

"It's better than thirty-seven. Thirty-seven sounds like the number of a streetcar. I can tell you that now."

"Does it?" She sounded amused, soothed.

"Listen, Claire, I'm beginning to cook in this phone

booth. Also, there's a guy outside who wants to call the *New York Times* to place a help-wanted ad."

"What sort of help?"

"A lot of help. I'm serious. I'm going to hang up. I can come there. We can meet somewhere. We have to plan our trip."

"What trip?"

"Ah, you see. You don't know about our trip. Now make a decision and then you'll get to hear about our trip. So, make a decision. I'm counting down right now—ten . . . nine . . . eight . . ."

"Wait, Andy. Andy. Oh, damn you, damn you. Here. There's no way I can change this. You'll have to meet me there—it's a gallery, a photo gallery on Madison and around 73rd Street. The address is . . . well, look it up. It's called The Third Eye. Two o'clock. You're spending the night."

How would a man like A. W. Clemmons spend a couple of hours in New York? Maybe he would call a former friend, someone who had known him in the old days when they were becoming citizens of the city. Or he might tour old sites, and in fact the phone booth was just around the corner from the apartment he had lived in when he had met Olive. But nothing like that appealed to him, though it would be difficult for Clemmons to walk anywhere in New York without crossing a field where an old conversation had taken place.

"Don't you feel like a traitor at times?" Claire had asked once. His departure from the city was incomprehensible to her.

But he had had no choice in the matter, he had answered, and turned on the radio by her bed. Music distracted her when making love, Claire said. Olive had got pregnant, with Milly, and it had seemed a good idea to get out of the city. He tried to find an all-night classical music program. Then the press agents' union had put a moratorium on new members, so he was cut out of jobs. A piano piece tinkled in the darkness.

"That's dopey," Claire had hooted. "Millions of kids are raised in this city every day. I grew up here and there's nothing wrong with me, is there?" She pulled the down comforter up to her chin as if to give him no chance to find a fault. "Blaming poor Olive and the girls and a seedy bunch of flacks for your own selfishness. You were the one that wanted to get out, to set up your little garden. Turn that thing off, Epicurus. I can't stand Scriabin."

He liked the looks of Sixth Avenue, the way human figures charged the monumental buildings with energy. Clemmons walked into a *sushi* counter next to a rare coin shop. He pointed to a plate pictured on the illustrated menu and the Japanese behind the counter began to slice and wrap small packages of raw fish and rice. Across the street is a parking lot and Clemmons thought about the Absinthe House that used to be there. It was a restaurant that specialized in Creole cooking, and it will be remembered as a bar where the smart-money hung out in the afternoons, a spa for sportsmen.

"Well, hello there, Charlie." She had been returning to the bar just as Clemmons and a few pals had entered the restaurant. None of the men at the bar had acknowledged her presence, and had continued to talk of horses, to study their racing forms. "What are you doing here? Looking for some *paté?*" It had been almost two years since that night, but she had remembered.

"We've just come over from Stillman's and thought this would be an appropriate spot."

"What, are you managing a boxer these days?"

"No, but there's a guy, a writer, who wanted to box Ezzard Charles so he could do a piece about it, how it felt to fight the world champion, and some of us went to watch. I see you're down at the Bon Soir."

"Come on down and listen," Jenny said. She stood with her feet squarely fixed to the floor, a pose that suggested confidence until you noticed the eyes move, as if she were checking out the exits; but this movement of the eyes together with the urgent register of her voice gave her a knowing air. "I'll do *'Ave Maria'* for you."

"Is that a big number at the Bon Soir?"

"You better believe it. The waiters go around on their knees." She saw him survey the backs of the men at the bar and she shrugged. "None of them. My accompanist is meeting me here because he's rehearsing a band around the corner." Her sharp laugh marred the bar's concentration. "Well, what can a poor girl do. It's either piano players or first trumpet players. You know about first trumpet players, Charlie?"

She told him she was about to go into a show, a good part with two songs of her own (she was meeting her accompanist to rehearse the music); yes, she still lived at the same place and, no, her roommates had moved out. Her eyes had lighted momentarily on the sway of his question. She was wearing her hair longer so it graced the smooth column of her neck and fell to one side as she bent to sip her drink, the curve an invitation at once as appealing as it was strangely sad. Her talk had loaded up with names, all of whom Clemmons knew he was supposed to identify and fit into particular fames.

His friends have moved on to Chandler's by the time Clemmons and the singer had taken a small corner table. Later, she stood up quickly and walked to the front of the place to talk to a young man with a briefcase. Clemmons noticed her feet. It was late spring and she wore sandals; the toenails were painted a brilliant scarlet and there was an almost prehensile separation between the large toe and the others. She returned with a light step though her face carried a frown.

"There, you see? You can't trust them. He's got a job playing piano at a lounge for the cocktail hour and can't work with me today." However, Clemmons thought he had seen pique register on the musician's face as he left. Jenny sat opposite him, her bare arms on the table with the wrists almost touching. She was deeply tanned, more than the season could allow, and he reasoned she had been south, and in fact she told him she had spent two months of the winter singing lead roles in a music tent near Miami Beach. As she leaned toward him, he could see the slight swell of her breasts and for the first time he wondered how so small a body could mold such deep and glorious resonances. She would refer to herself, sometimes, as *few-titted.* "Okay, your turn to play catch-up," she said.

He told her about the different off-Broadway shows he handled. She nodded. She had read about the union business in the *Times,* but didn't know he had been the focus. Then, his various clients, some singers; how he worked for Carter Perry and his new cultural center. She had auditioned for a show the rich man had backed. He told her about Olive.

"Married?" Several men turned around at the bar, as if to mention the state of matrimony somehow despoiled the place. Yes, he was married, and he told her about Olive, how they had met at the Perry Cultural Center, where she had been an assistant curator. She had come up from the south the summer after college and had stayed on to work in the first Stevenson campaign, and that had led to other similar jobs. Olive seemed to have been raised for a life of volunteer work.

"She was an art history major at Hollins."

"But married," Jenny said again as he looked away. Her eyes had deepened and something flashed merrily through them. He signaled the waiter for another drink. Her legs were crossed and one foot neatly swung time; the low light in the bar became snagged on a thin gold chain that encircled her ankle. "So, married, Charlie."

Like every neighborhood, the restaurant's character changed with the time of day, made over by the citizenry of the hour, and, as Clemmons and Jenny Seven caught up, the horse players at the Absinthe House bar became outnumbered, and eventually replaced, by a pre-theater crowd. "It's getting to be dinner time," he said. "How about something to eat?"

"How about your wife?"

"She doesn't expect me till late this evening."

Jenny recrossed her legs, looked down, and readjusted the strap of one sandal. Her nose wrinkled. "But I don't like fish."

"We could go somewhere else."

"Sure. Like that place you took me with the chicken dish. I know." She sat straight, a mock gesture at primness. "How about spaghetti and meatballs?"

"If you prefer Italian food," Clemmons told her, "there's a spot nearby that specializes in northern Italian cooking. Lighter, not so many spices. We think of Italian food as being heavy with tomato sauce and oregano, but—"

"You're still doing it," she said. Her eyes had become large.

"What?"

"The tour."

"I'm sorry."

"No, it's okay. No one talks to me that way. No one tells me things like that."

"What do they tell you?"

"Ha!" Several people turned at the bar. "Listen, Charlie, I'm really not that hungry. I have a busy day tomorrow. Another time."

So he offered her a ride home, a shared taxi, and she accepted that, but if she didn't mind, he had to stop off at his old office to pick up some material. He still did odd jobs for his former employers and he had to pick up some pictures and take them to the printer's. It was only a short walk from the Absinthe House and around the corner from Radio City Music Hall. He had expected her to say something as they passed the theater, how they had met there, two years ago. But she didn't even turn her head. He unlocked the ground-floor door of the brownstone building and let them into the dark office. He would say later that he had had no other intentions but to get the pictures, and so had not turned on any lights because there had been sufficient illumination from the street for him to find the proper folder. Nevertheless, he found himself saying, "All we have is this leather sofa."

"It'll do," she had said, already barefoot and unzipping the back of her dress.

A very large sedan with New Jersey license plates had pulled into the parking lot and several ladies with bluish-white hair got out. It was Wednesday, Clemmons remembered, the time for matinées. The car stopped just about on the spot where he and Jenny had sat down in the Absinthe House to become lovers.

"You like? Ho-kay?" the Japanese behind the counter inquired about the *sushi.*

"Muy bien," Clemmons said, without thinking.

"Gracias," replied the Oriental.

He took a slow route to the picture gallery, on foot to Madison and by bus from there, because Claire Wolferman was never on time. She did not want to be late for appointments; it was not in her nature to be discourteous or rude, nor was it a matter of too many appointments, but a strange fear of meeting them, a fear that the appointments might reveal some inadequacy in herself, so she would put them off until the last strand of patience had been wound to the breaking point. It was a strange flaw, Clemmons thought; the defect of a chimera, for within her dazzling and exotic exterior she nurtured the suspicion that she had been invented and was not real.

However, when he stepped into the small self-service elevator of the old townhouse that had been converted into galleries, he discovered it was he who was late and that Claire had arrived before him and on time. Her perfume lubricated the air of the elevator.

"Ah, you're here." She held out one hand and waved and then got up from a large ottoman placed in the center of the exhibition room. She was dressed, booted, hair in a scarf, her ensemble in the current mode of a camp follower to a Cossack regiment; even as she walked toward him, her jewelry gave off the tiny clink of distant cavalry. She had taken one arm and leaned against his side to kiss him on the mouth. "Here"—she reached behind her to bring up two young men for introductions—"Andy Clemmons . . . Mr. . . . and Mr. . . ."

He did not listen for their names. They seemed like a team of some sort: one dressed formally, an usher for a high-society wedding, and the other in neat, expensive-looking jeans with the shirt wide open and a choke collar of jade beads around his neck. Curiously, they reminded Clemmons of a pair of cops—one asked the hard questions, while the other offered coffee and cigarettes and perhaps made the handcuffs more comfortable.

"I'll not be long." Claire had spoken into his ear. She was about his height, so with boots she was taller than he and he could look directly into her gray eyes, easily spy into their happiness. She caught him looking, and giggled and squeezed his arm. "Look around. I want your opinion."

She returned to the ottoman, a place clearly reserved for her, while he moved to the near wall. The photographs were small with large mats, and the subject matter seemed to be weddings. They were the kind of pictures that promoted the photographer rather than the state of marriage. Some looked amateurish, like the snapshots taken by a relative of the bride; but these were deliberately off, out of focus. The same couple appeared in one series, flanked on the steps of a church by different attendants, members of a family. Another wedding party had been photographed in what looked to be the lounge of a mausoleum; the lighting in the pictures was flat and with little contrast. The poses seemed arbitrary. There were about a dozen pictures of different brides and grooms, stiff in rented costumes, hands welded to the podium, and standing before the same drop cloth with the same spot of light fixed behind them. Clemmons thought they looked like members of an athletic team who had been given their uniforms only after the season of play was over.

"They are a joy, are they not?" The formal partner had chosen Clemmons. The other seemed to be haggling with Claire.

"Is the photographer related to all these people?" Clemmons asked.

"Bingo!" The young man clapped his hands and turned around to his partner. "Andy just asked if the photographer was related to the subjects. What a profound question," he told Clemmons. "What do you do, Andy?"

"I'm a developer."

"Film?"

"Land."

"Oh." The gallery owner adjusted his cufflinks. "I'll give you a little bio. The photographer received his MFA from Arizona; they have a fine program there. He went to the Guggenheim people with his idea and then he also received a National Endowment. He opened a photography studio in this town in New Hampshire and took nothing but wedding pictures. . . . For a whole year! Think of it."

They had paused before a photograph. "Here, certainly," Clemmons's guide spoke slowly, judiciously choosing his words, "is a return to formalism; here, certainly, is content and, I might say, optimistic content in the nature of the very act represented. A basic human response to life."

"Certainly," said Clemmons. "And the photographer?"

"Exactly," the young man continued. "The anonymity of the photographer is preserved. I think we can safely say that Postmodernism is at an end. Here is genuine self-effacement."

Clemmons had been watching Claire. Her attendant stood close before her, the pouch of his crotch slanted slightly toward her as she sat on the ottoman and probably ready to supply her with more than coffee and cigarettes, Clemmons thought, though he could not tell where Claire might be looking; for the wide-angled field of her myopia encompassed the whole man. He was accustomed to seeing her full-faced in conversation, across a table, or in bed; so her nose in profile almost looked unfamiliar. It seemed thin and sharp, and with no suggestion of the sensual flares at its tip, just then as she turned and smiled at him, or the graceful way it flowed up into her brow as if drawn by Matisse. She had talked of her birthday and he wondered, as she had more of them, if this strong, aristocratic feature of her face would get longer until the tip touched the chin.

For this cruel thought, Clemmons punished himself by turning back to his guide in the pin-striped suit. "There's a documentary quality about these pictures, isn't there?"

"Ah, how very right you are," the gallery owner replied. "The great joy of these pictures *is* their authenticity."

"Would you say an authentic joy?"

"Precisely," the young man said, tasting the suggestion like a rare lozenge. "Yes, that's it. There's a terrible beauty about them, don't you think?"

"What do you think?" Claire had moved up behind them.

"Szarkowski was terribly interested in them," the partner in blue jeans said. "But the Modern is having budget problems, as we all know."

She looked expectant, her face flushed and eyes eagerly waiting for him to say something encouraging, but Clemmons only shrugged and let his eyes drop to the top of her blouse and the line of her deep bosom. "They're unique," he finally said. Her expression became hard, all business.

"This is an important decision for me, and I want to think about it some more," she told them.

"Oh, you're absolutely right," the formal partner said.

"Couldn't agree more," the other said.

"I want them, but this is a decision that I not only must make for myself but, ultimately, for the foundation too, so it has ramifications that must be thought through."

Once the door of the small elevator had closed, Claire turned to enfold him. They kissed wetly, open-mouthed. "Stop the elevator," she murmured against his lips. "It won't take long. There's the emergency button. This is an emergency!"

"We're almost there."

"You're no fun anymore." She shrugged away. "Frigid Wasp." The door opened. "You're a cunt-teaser, Andy Clemmons." Two middle-aged women who had been waiting for the elevator looked at him accusingly. On the sidewalk he steered Claire toward Central Park.

One might first notice the woman, note the saunter and loose stride that seemed to possess the pavement, perhaps even the city, as each booted step sprung complementary rhythms in her scarves and bloused tunic and longish dress; a cadence that would be ungainly on others. Then her companion would be seen. Sometimes he walked in the sidewise manner of an attendant, sometimes with a paternal slant in his posture, or with the wide-armed exuberance of a young lover at other times; the character of his face no more distinguished than the clothes he wore, though there was a quality to the odd jacket and slacks that set their casualness apart. This face was lifted, in fact, to the sky as they crossed Fifth Avenue; as if to take the air but also to inhale the whole moment itself, and they stepped onto the opposite curb with a self-absorbed and easy determination that would make it appear the couple might continue to walk across the park, across the island of Manhattan and on across the continent—arm in arm. But they stopped at a vendor wagon, where the man bought the woman a flavored ice.

"Thank you, I was terribly thirsty," Claire said. Her lips closed around the ball of chipped ice and she sucked the liquid from it noisily. She turned toward a small path that led into the park. "So you're going to see wifey."

"Don't say that," Clemmons said. He dropped a coin from his change, looked for it and then caught up with her.

"Don't use that term. The two of you would like each other. Get on well."

"Ah, you see, that's it. You would like us to get on—get together is more like it." She had no more use for the ice cone and tossed the remnant in a trash basket. "You could start a commune."

They walked more in silence and at a slower pace. Claire seemed to respond to the park, had become less sophisticated in this province. She even crouched suddenly to the pavement to coax a squirrel who had stopped in their path. "I have nothing to feed it," she said sorrowfully as the animal hopped toward her. "But why go? Wouldn't she come to the wedding anyway?"

"But I want her to come up and run it. I want her to take over and run the whole business." He took her arm and they continued to stroll. "I thought we could find a little island somewhere that grows its own . . ."

"So you have to go there to bargain with her, to have her come up."

"Yes, something like that," Clemmons replied. He glanced at her. Her face was a wall painting, the eyes angled and sly.

"You're not even going to give the bride away?" Claire stopped his lips with a kiss. He could taste the sticky flavor of the Italian ice upon them. "You're grinding your teeth again. Look, you've even frightened the starlings. What a terrible man you are."

"I'm only a bothered man."

"Self-bothered."

"What's that supposed to mean?"

"One part of you pretends to be this spirit that cultivates a place of solitude, while the rest of you wants a big campout with all the wickiups."

"There's an image." Clemmons laughed. Claire's fair complexion grew pink, her lips pursed. "I don't get the last part," he added.

"You talk of your solitude, and your freedom"—she

shrugged—"you have neither. Now comes poor Milly who only wants to get married in your front yard—but it disturbs your camp. She's found her way back. Maybe that's what bothers you."

"Maybe you ought to come to the wedding." Clemmons snorted.

"Maybe I will. Oh, that nicked you, didn't it?" She had turned before him and did a little shuffle, a charming imitation of a boxer sparring. Her eyes were bright and her smile generous. "That would disorder your little nest, wouldn't it, if the Babylonian showed up at the temple? And why not? I have a feeling that's what you're doing, that sane, real part of you. Not that layered part you put together at what school was it . . . no matter. But your impulse is to gather us all together. Pull the women in and circle the wagons—there's danger a-comin' in, pardner."

They had come to the meadow where games of softball were being played on the different diamonds. The players were mostly Hispanic, and wore bright-colored uniforms. Clemmons and Claire watched the play from the path. He had placed his arm around her and she leaned her head against him.

"Not to worry," she said soberly. "I may go to Europe about then."

"I had hoped we could go away, spend some time alone."

"There's someone I must see," she said simply. Then, "Andy, what do you think of me? Tell me something special, something unusual."

A long, high fly arced in the air, looking as if it might carry to the roof of the Metropolitan Museum but then, its velocity spent, the ball dropped to the earth. "You are," he finally said, "suspended in my consciousness, suspended in my life like a little red circle in a Miró painting."

For a moment, Clemmons thought she had not heard him. He wondered if he had spoken the words aloud or had only thought them. Then she slowly turned and faced him with a timid smile.

"Where did you get that?" she asked him. "Did you read that somewhere? Did you really make it up? Look at you. Look at that smile. That's why you drive us crazy. I see you smiling like that when you're asleep. It makes me want to mother you and then I want to fuck you. What are you doing? Where are you going?"

"It seems a good idea to get a taxi," Clemmons told her.

In Claire's apartment, Clemmons waited as she changed. The living room was no different from when he had first seen it three years before; it resembled the attic of a museum; even the deep-cushioned furniture had an artifactual quality. Paintings on the floor leaned against three walls; some had been hung. Stone and ceramic objects abounded, quarried from Claire's generosity to the artists. Two large tables, one the length of the three windows that overlooked East 77th Street, were piled with stacks of books, most of which Clemmons knew had never been opened. They resembled chips for a game that had become so boring to the player that she had left the table, even left her winnings, to move on to another table where the stakes promised more.

"You don't think much of those photographs," Claire said. She spoke through the half-closed door of the bedroom, across the foyer from the living room. "I don't want them," she continued, her voice muffled in clothing. "But I'm in a position where I almost have to buy them."

Clemmons imagined her changing clothes as he heard her talk about her father; how the pictures had interested him, or so the pair at the gallery had told her. She seemed to be in competition with her father for these collections. He traced in his mind's eye the long column of the spine as she raised her arms to let a garment fall down over her. He enjoyed the sounds of material moving around her; the quick, light steps, and the silent hiatus in which she might be choosing a sash or a comb; then the impatient rush of her entrance.

"There." She appeared in a linen caftan, barefoot and her hair up. A heavy braided cord of purple was fastened at her waist. She settled into his lap like a large cat.

"The Governor is leaving at eleven tomorrow morning," he told her between kisses. "So I have to catch the nine o'clock shuttle."

"What luxury," she said. She rubbed against him. "We have all that time. All that time. I have food in—some *pesto,* not mine, but some I ordered, and we are sufficient."

"Self-contained."

"Yes. Self-contained."

"An island. A garden."

"Yes. A garden." And then the phone rang. "Damn," she said, and stretched across him to pick up the instrument to listen in on her answering service. "Yes, I'm here. What's this about?" It was someone important to her; apparently a member of her family. She often would talk for hours to a sister or a brother; plans that had to be discussed and evaluated, it seemed, in the early hours of morning.

So now he sat in the light of late afternoon, a fulcrum to her long body as she lay across him to discuss with a relative some matter that involved second mortgages, zoning appeals, or foundation appointments. He found it irksome. He never minded sharing her with other men, his lack of claim to her perhaps an ingredient of her attraction, but he had become very impatient with these interruptions that fractured the time he wanted to spend with her; particularly when they came to no purpose and were only clusters of busyness within her leisure. She had become very heavy upon him, and permitted herself to be folded up and turned to one side like a large doll, so he could stand up.

On the smaller desk, one that she used for her correspondence and business, was the exact evidence that supported the case he was making—several stacks of letters, all as unanswered as the stacks of bills he knew were unpaid. It was an untidy portfolio tossed among brass figurines, and Mayan clay lamps, and the new translations of Villon and

Octavio Paz. Clemmons had long ago deduced that this ebony lacquered tabletop held more than a clue to Claire's personality; it also explained her continual failure with men, her inability to sustain a lasting relationship, not to mention marriage. The sort of men she liked were drawn to her because she gave the appearance of being in command of complex matters. Clemmons had seen her quick mind and laserlike conclusions, together with her startling good looks, pull these men across a reception, an opening or after a reading; hounds on a rich scent, their faces soft and eager to be stroked, to be taken in hand and modeled.

But there would be mornings after the nights of love-making when each might wander about the apartment to come across this table with its horrifying surplus of negligence; a frightening, if not unmanning, sight for anyone who had hoped to hand over his own accounts to Claire Wolferman to manage.

Claire sat on the edge of the sofa and continued to speak into the phone, her face concentrated and supported in both hands, her elbows resting on her knees. She had the solid quality of a Maillol statue, Clemmons thought. He sorted her bills and arranged them in chronological order determined by their postmarks. Some were three months old. She hung up the phone.

"What are you doing?" she asked darkly.

"I'm putting order into your life. Get your checkbook."

"I don't know where it is." He looked at her. "Well, all right, I know where it is, but let's not waste our time like this. I'll pay them tomorrow. Please, Andy." She had risen and encircled his neck with her arms to nuzzle him. "I promise. I'll pay them tomorrow."

"Your phone will be shut off and then what will you do? No. Do it now." She walked away flatfooted, rummaged in a chest drawer, and returned with the checkbook.

"I'll pay everything but the Saks bill. They haven't given me credit for a suit I returned, and I'll be damned if I pay them."

"Okay," Clemmons said, sensing a bargain. She sat down at the table, folding one leg under her, and began writing checks.

"This is some sort of Calvinist principle, isn't it?" she said as she licked an envelope flap. "The least you can do is tell me a story. Fix yourself a drink and tell me a story. There's some wine in the fridge, I'll have some of that."

A cozy ambience settled upon the room as the man sat on the sofa to browse through journals while the woman leaned over her bookkeeping and accounts at the desk, and were it not for the sophisticated collections of art objects in the place, the sounds of the five o'clock traffic outside on Third Avenue, the scene would have suggested a suburban domesticity, an old and peaceful partnership.

Claire had put on an oversized pair of glasses to make her computations and they gave her a studious mien, rather like the schoolgirl she must have been, who crammed at the last hour for a final examination. However, the business on the table had also aged her; there were somber lines across her forehead, her nose had become thin, and the two impressions formed a third in Clemmons's mind: the figure of a well-educated, intelligent woman who would settle into adequate endeavor for the rest of her life. He looked away.

"That's his book there." She had directed his attention to a volume of poetry on the floor beside the couch. Though she had asked for a story, Clemmons would listen to hers. It was a medium-sized volume from a good publisher, and the picture on the back looked familiar; but then, poets all looked alike to him.

"He's from Arkansas." She chuckled and tore off a receipt.

"You'd rather be with him than with me in St. Martin."

"I love him," she said, and sealed an envelope.

"Does he love you?"

"I don't know. That's the problem. He's in Italy on a Guggenheim. If I go to him that will seem like I'm pushing, forcing him to a commitment. He's younger. About six years younger, and . . ."

"Nervous," Clemmons supplied. He had been reading the poems. Most of them seemed to be about the man's childhood, his father a sharecropper, and how the grime of poverty had mixed in his food to be consumed by his soul.

"Yes, maybe that. But if I don't go, I also wonder if I shall lose him, not to another woman, but really lose him. You don't like his poetry." She sealed another envelope.

"I can't tell." Clemmons shrugged. "I'm put off by the snobbishness. The redneck pretensions. They all jump too quickly into upperclass beds."

"That's unfair." She looked over her glasses at him. "You're jealous." Her smile was sweet and a coil of dark hair had slipped from the bun fixed atop her head. "How easy for you to talk like this, the Voice of the Middle West. A member of the great majority. You think you're egalitarian because you treat everybody alike. You even try to dress the part, but it's phony."

"What do you mean?"

"That jacket you have on."

"What's the matter with this jacket?"

"Stand up." Clemmons stood up. "Turn around. See, look at the way it's together at the shoulder. The pockets don't match. It looks like something you might have got at the J. Press outlet in Columbus, Ohio."

"As a matter of fact I did buy it in Ohio, but not Columbus."

"There, you schmuck." She laughed. "Not even the capital." The envelopes of paid bills outnumbered the unpaid. Clemmons took off the jacket, his tie, and loosened his shirt. He walked to the windows. The trees below were already full-leafed, their season far in advance of those that grew farther north in Boston Corners.

"You said something about my gathering everybody, all of you together."

"Did I say that? I don't remember saying that." She put a check and bill into an envelope, licked the flap, and sealed it. She chased the taste with a sip of wine. "It sounds very *andante,* very heavy." Then she whistled a few bars of something that was probably the *andante* theme of a piece of music he could not identify.

"You said I wasn't free." It came out more thoughtful than he had intended. Her soft laughter cut the moment.

"Ah, poor baby," she said. Then her manner became professorial. "It's a myth, I think; all those people going west to freedom. There's no freedom in the wilderness. *Polis.* That's where there are choices. What are they all running away from? Sound familiar?" Clemmons was watching a police officer write a parking ticket, fix it under the windshield wiper of a car parked in the street below.

"The fewer choices, as in Boston Corners, say"—her voice dragged its burden of irony—"the less freedom. Man was not made to eat bread alone—by himself. Epicurus was wrong."

"Let me write this all down." Clemmons turned back to the room. "Sounds like those boys at the gallery. Modernism is dead."

"Modernism is dead. So is Epicurus. And I'm done with these goddamn bills." She abruptly closed the cover of the large checkbook, and neatly stacked up the envelopes. "According to your principles—I've done the business, so now I get the pleasure." Her smile was silky and she rose from her chair like a scarf unfolding.

"Amor con amor se paga," Clemmons said.

"What's that?" she asked, coming toward him. "Something to do with love?"

"It's an idiom, one good turn deserves another."

"You're awful. I hear you talking to my answering service. What do you say to that girl? You are teasing her, aren't you? Fucking her ear?"

"Generally, I'm trying to find out where you are." They

had been embracing, the woman attempting to shape her body to his but never quite satisfied with the fit.

"Thank you for making me do the bills." She kissed him. "Hungry?"

"It's dinner time."

"That hungry."

"No."

They walked through the apartment's small kitchen and into a room that was more of a greenhouse than a studio. The floor was set with small Spanish tiles and a large skylight cast an even, otherworldly light upon a small glade; tubs held a bamboo, jade trees, a small orange bush. Claire had begun to take the combs from her hair as she walked ahead of him, and when he had turned from removing his shoes, she was already lying nude upon the squarish sofa, her arms above her head, one leg slightly over the other, the pose of Goya's Maja. With a half smile, she watched him undress. The sofa was an antique bed with endboards of equal height, very high and curved at the top.

"You look like Cleopatra on her bark," Clemmons said. He pulled off his shirt. She made no answer but pursed her lips. She inspected him.

"You look pretty good yourself. You're amazing. How old did you say you were? Have you been running?"

"Not bad," Clemmons admitted, as he looked down on his body. "But lately I've noticed some slippage of the Herculean girdle."

Her laughter seemed to begin underneath the bed, and come through the mattress to shake her. "The what?" The luxury of her heavy breasts rolled and tossed, her belly quaked, even the tonsured pubis lifted as that part of her came up for air to laugh all the more. "The Hercu-what?" She rolled and seized a corner of the cotton throw in her teeth, like someone in a delirium.

Clemmons was by now laughing too; though with one knee on the bed, he still tried to explain how he'd seen a diagram in an ancient anatomy book and about the different names given to the muscular systems. "It's right along here"—he was determined to explain and even outlined the angle made by his pelvic bones and a slight swell of flesh.

"You idiot." She gasped and reached for him. But the mood had changed. She would start to giggle and then he would laugh, so their play was more sportive than passionate; not without its pleasure but somehow unsatisfying, not fully testing the urge.

They woke in darkness and ate by candlelight without looking at the time; the pasta was served on the large table where she had worked that afternoon. She told him she wanted to get married, wanted to have a child before it was too late, and he told her about the film being made about the old prize fight, about meeting Carter Perry's daughter, and about listening to that old record made by Jenny Seven. The *pesto* was flat and Clemmons deduced that she had forgotten to add the cheese, but said nothing. They drank a lot of white burgundy, and became very drowsy.

When they returned to bed, she turned away from him, on her side, and hugged his right arm to her breasts, to fall asleep quickly like a child with a doll. Later she woke him, her thighs pressed against his face like hot silk. She had done something to him while he was asleep, for his erection was almost painful, but she would not let him move and held him to her.

After a time, they moved apart and then joined together, their energies falling and rising as the sky grew light, but a continuous charge from those energies gave off aromas that overcame those of vegetation until their bodies' sweat rendered all tactile sensation nearly impossible. At last, she clung to one of the tall endboards of the couch and he hung over her, the two of them resembling survivors in an open boat. He watched over her shoulder, through a window, as the outlines of a water tank became defined by the dawn. Lights burned in several of the windows of the apartment building in the next street. People were preparing for another day. Claire had put a hand to one breast to caress, pull at the nipple. Another light went on in someone's kitchen, and then another. Her hand was now between her legs, touching them both at once. Her fingernails pricked the thin membrane that held their release. "An-dee."

Clemmons woke with a start, the heat of a full sun beamed through the skylight onto his face and Claire's weight athwart his legs. He found his watch. If he were lucky he could make the ten o'clock shuttle, and he struggled to his feet, neither showering nor changing the shirt he had worn the day before, nor even shaving. Claire stood at the door, still drugged with sleep, her face puffy and sullen-looking as she kissed him, tried to hold him back with kisses, but he got out the door. When it closed behind him, her phone began to ring.

There were no empty taxis on Second Avenue, so he had to squeeze into a bus for the trip downtown to the East Side Air Terminal. Fortunately, when he put his hand into his pocket, he found the exact change for the fare. Clemmons took this to be a good omen; that he would catch the plane at LaGuardia and make the connection with his brother-in-law in Washington, and perhaps be able to convince Olive to manage Milly's wedding. The bus was crowded, standing room only; people going to work. Mostly women. As Clemmons edged through the crowd, they seemed to make way for him—even stand away from him when he finally took up a position by the rear exit, one arm up and hand fixed to the metal support, in a small clearing all to himself. Clemmons, still groggy and anxious, was not certain of his perceptions, but it seemed to him that the women all looked at him curiously, some smiling, others grim, and he wondered if they could smell Claire's aroma upon him—smell themselves upon him.

The forty blocks downtown to the airline terminal would be a long journey, and Clemmons would keep his eyes on the graffiti before him the whole way.

Chapter Four

Clemmons would disappear, sometimes several days at a time, and no one would know where he had been; not so much that his pals kept track of each other but they seemed to move together through the city to different jobs and better apartments, an informal society and mobile, so that when someone didn't show up at a regular haunt, it would cause a little wonder and a few questions. Someone would ask Red down at Louie's on Sheridan Square if Clemmons had been around and he would say no, he hadn't seen him for several nights; then someone would say that he hadn't shown up at Chumley's or the San Remo either, while another would mention that Clemmons had missed the opening day at Belmont. So a concern would be raised that he might have a problem.

This anxiety would sometimes shift into resentment when Olive's name was mentioned, for though some had married by then, her "foreignness" cast her as the agent of Clemmons's mysterious behavior though she tried to harden her syllables to talk like the rest of them; and what some called her "plantation manner," others called classy. To be honest, Clemmons had begun these unexplained absences before he and Olive were married, assisted by Carter Perry's generous paycheck, the high wages paid by a rich man who wanted to be accepted, as it turned out, only for the great wealth left him by a grandfather who had had something to do with condensed milk.

Clemmons would say later that he had come across the sale notice for a farm in Boston Corners by chance, but it's safe to say that no one reads the classified section of the *New York Times* by chance, especially the real estate columns. It is a bulletin that demands a persistent audience. True, he may have seen the name Boston Corners *by chance* in a list of properties and remembered it as the place he had visited with his father.

So he would board a train on the old Harlem Valley Division of the New York Central and travel the same route north as did those fight fans a hundred years back. It's a particularly beautiful route of escape from the city, even today, though most of the tracks have been torn up and the remainder poorly maintained. Indeed, Clemmons would sometimes say he thought he might be riding in some of the same square, wooden coaches as those used by the mob that rode to Boston Corners—the railroad was notoriously bad about equipment; but they were, at any rate, the same that carried him as a boy to visit his father, who had spent his last years in the Berkshires writing a book about the Morrisey–Sullivan fights. This, then, was the fortuitous part, the chance of it all—how on the train going north to look at real estate, the straight, rigid lines of track somehow bending round a curve in his life, he had been brought back to the place he had forgotten.

As for that first trip, the farm advertised was beyond his means, but he was able to purchase a smaller lot that another farmer was anxious to sell to pay a feed bill. More small parcels were acquired; ridge land or rocky ledges that shelved the slope of the Taghkanic Range, property no one wanted and for which no use could be foreseen. Nor would Clemmons claim any foresight, but only a peculiar urge to possess some place that would take him away from his city routines, a caesura in his rhythm. Then it became a game. He applied practices he had seen work in show business, never completely buying a piece of property but controlling it with an option and then trading or selling this right for larger interests until, through a turn of chance, a shift in people, events began to fall consistently upon the squares that bore his name—a shopping center, condominiums, several developments; then Irondale, a hamlet restored to meet the demand for a past that no one remembered. His speculations, the developments, coincided with a time when all hoped to escape to a simpler, gentler past.

Olive had known none of this, and even after their marriage was as mystified as others were about her husband's irrational absences, often suspecting he might be having an affair, or trying to end an affair that might have preceded their marriage; and in fact the appointments Clemmons kept in Boston Corners did take on all the devotions required for such liaisons: the alibis, the two-journal bookkeeping, and the rest. However, when he took her to visit his domain in Boston Corners, to witness the sale of a house he had built in partnership with a local contractor, Olive accepted the success of this Monopoly game, and would continue to do so with an equanimity that dismayed him.

Her attitude suggested that she did not appreciate what he had done, or was not aware of its financial rewards, but this was not the case, and he was to understand that in the dull and dulling comfort of her upbringing, she had never learned the risks or hard chances that went with real achievement. Success for Olive Chase was the magical yeast that went with the palace; it rose overnight mysteriously and wonderfully and, just in time, turned into a sumptuous breakfast. Ironically, this alchemistic interpretation may explain her passionate espousal of Adlai Stevenson's candidacy, which went against the rest of her family's expectation, because, just to remember, the Illinois governor's voice did seem to rise magically from the convention floor in Chicago, rise just in time, it seemed, to feed the imaginations and tease with its wit and taste, only to fall flat with the first cut.

So A. W. Clemmons's travels continue on this morning after he leaves Claire Wolferman's apartment, though to be truthful, his visit with her was a passage within the same trip as his trek through the large, tacky lobby of the National Airport on his way to the men's lavatory, on his way to see Olive; was all part of the overall journey; a gathering together, as Claire called it, that had begun with that first train ride up to Boston Corners, that first absence from his life's routine that he could still not explain satisfactorily to anyone.

He had forgotten his electric razor at Claire's apartment, and he cut himself with the cheap plastic substitute purchased at a newsstand. Several patches of toilet tissue were required to staunch the blood, so his face acquired a frayed look. Clemmons was amused by the idea of his ragged face about to meet the stern and proper mien of Governor Wendall Chase, the next Republican candidate for the presidency, so some said. That he was about to enter this realm of power after he had changed shirts and washed up in the airport's lavatory like some nameless transient with no place to stay further defined the joke he shared with his image. When he changed shirts, he discovered the ambiguous mark Claire had left upon him, a strawberry imprint beneath his left breast; either a stamp of approval or point of vulnerability, maybe both.

He located the old Convair at the far end of the terminal's parking apron. The plane was painted a flat white and bore the sovereign state's seal just behind the cabin gangway. The artist had been careless so that *brunensis rampant* in the rhododendrons looked awkward, even quizzical, rather as though the bear had been discovered relieving himself upon the state's official flora.

"Good day, Mr. Clemmons," a steward greeted him at the top of the steps. "The Governor is on board and will join you for lunch as soon as we are in flight." The young man took Clemmons's valise and returned to the small pantry. Fixed to the floor of the cabin were several large armchairs, similar in design to those that used to be in railroad parlor cars but of much lighter construction. A bulkhead cut the cabin in two halfway back, and Clemmons imagined Governor Chase behind it, immersed in some meditation that went with the office.

"How's it going?" The speaker was a black man who had just entered the plane; another passenger, Clemmons assumed, but he turned out to be the pilot. The man's smile was broad and knowing. Clemmons smiled and nodded, and buckled himself into one of the chairs. "We all set?" the man asked the steward, and received an affirmative. He removed his suit jacket, handed it to the steward, and opened the small door into the control compartment. A copilot was already at the controls, and the black pilot spoke casually with him as he rolled up his sleeves and then eased into his own seat. "Let's go," he said as he reached over his head and set a couple of switches, punched another. The starboard engine started, the propeller began to fan.

The steward had closed the entry door and brought Clemmons several printed documents to read as the plane taxied out of the runway. They were forms that absolved the Commonwealth of any liability for his injury or death should either occur. He signed them. Another piece of paper turned out to be a ticket form with his name and destination, time of departure, and date all neatly penciled in. There was a charge of $72.33. "Will you take a check?" Clemmons asked the steward over the roar of the engines.

The man nodded. "It's our department of transportation," he said with apology. "They go over the Governor's expenses with a comb. If you were on business, it wouldn't be a problem. Also, you're family."

"I guess we all have to be careful," Clemmons said, and wrote out a check. They moved swiftly down the runway, the engines a harmonious drumming that abruptly lifted them from the earth, and the plane climbed and turned lazily toward the west. The air was so clear that Clemmons could see the swell of the Blue Ridge Mountains ahead, and on this "expanse of floor," as someone once described it, were laid out the precise lines of different communities, all the counters and pieces of occupancy, set down. Clemmons could spot the smallest details: the articulation of automobiles, tricycles beside driveways, items of clothing fixed on laundry lines, flower borders.

But it was the shape and placement of the communities that interested him, most of them—he could see from three thousand feet—not put in a good place, but yet there they were, and he inspected these towns as he might review a plat for one of his own developments. The access to main roads, the restrictions inherent in the topography and those maybe imposed by zoning regulations, problems of drainage and water tables; it was easy to analyze every aspect from this altitude, easy to spot the wrong usage of land, easy to identify the expedient shortcut toward profit. One village was placed in a lowland between ridges that would surely channel spring rain into its streets to flood basements. Another was stitched over by so many concrete expressways and interchanges, its one small dominion cut and sewn up into a straightjacket, that its citizens could not move within it though outsiders could move through it very easily. A third community had been established against the eastern slope of the Blue Ridge Mountains, and Clemmons could imagine the dark shadows that would begin to wash over it by early afternoon so that it would lie under fathoms of night long before the day had turned.

"It looks easy from up here, doesn't it?" Chase's voice startled Clemmons, as did his appearance, because of the optical illusion presented by all celebrities, who look one way in magazines and on television but appear completely different in the flesh. Their images come from a two-dimensional source, and when seen in the round, the third dimension seems inauthentic.

"I wish I could rearrange some of those klunks back there." He nodded toward the rear of the plane but meant the Capitol they flew from. He slumped into the chair across from Clemmons and pulled down the tie from his shirt collar. He wore a cardigan sweater.

"It sounds like you may get the opportunity," Clemmons replied.

"It is a noble challenge," the Governor said with mock sobriety, and lifted his face. Wendall Chase resembled the sharpwitted, ambitious clerk in a small-town drugstore; someone who might know all the answers but none of the questions, a face that may raise doubts as to the accuracy of a filled prescription but to which Americans, all too often, entrust more important remedies.

"You wouldn't believe the nutty ideas I've been listening to for two days," Chase continued. "They're talking about transporting all of Washington, D. C., over the Blue Ridge Mountains and into little towns like that down there. Where you are, you're going to get New York City in your lap. Forget Philadelphia. Philadelphia has no place to go. Somebody asked, how much time for all these evacuations. Oh, about a week, was the answer. Can you believe that? We're going to check with the Russians and say, Don't hit Chicago until Thursday because there's a breakdown in the right lane on the road to Peoria. The whole thing can be directed by those guys who fly around in helicopters reporting on traffic conditions."

Chase paused and turned to the steward with that authoritative manner made familiar on TV interviews but which was due, Clemmons knew, to an old football injury that forced him to turn his neck and shoulders together. "Do we have any of those gherkins on board?" the Governor asked.

"I had a client this week," Clemmons told him. "He's buying a house just to build a bomb shelter in the basement. I remembered those bomb shelters Rockefeller promoted during the Cuban crisis. The state commerce department put out plans for a shelter that you could build in your basement for four hundred dollars. Olive and I thought about doing it—for a little bit. The girls were just babes then. But we bought four hundred dollars' worth of wine instead and put that in the basement."

Chase turned his face to peer through the small window of the plane's cabin, but he had smiled slightly. "Old Nelson had some silly ideas and few of them included people. But he had one idea—we learned from it, you might say—take care of your own people yourself. It must have come from being raised on those big estates. Anyway, not to worry about Washington. Washington will always screw it up. On the other hand, Nelson put up that pile of junk in Albany that has nothing to do with people."

"I kind of like those buildings."

Clemmons's taste did not seem to surprise Chase, for he merely nodded and continued, "The only way to look at those buildings in Albany is from six thousand feet high, as if they are sculptures in a museum. Nelson liked museums, not people. They're colossal tombstones. Bomb shelters and tombstones. I went with him the last time down to Brazil and we went out to Brasília. He ran from one view to another, looking and waving his arms. 'Jeez, isn't this swell,' he kept saying, and then someone asked, 'But Governor, where are all the people?' He was amazed by the question. Never occurred to him. Put the people all underground, out of sight. In a museum. Out of the way."

"The people, no," Clemmons replied. His brother-in-law looked across at him with a curious cast in his eyes. It could signal either anger or amusement or even an attack of stomach gas. "What are your philosophies of government, anyway? *Time* calls you a Dixie-Pop."

Chase seemed to wince at the expression. The steward had brought two small trays that contained cartons of milk with straws and sandwiches wrapped in cellophane. He put a small jar of pickles on the executive's table. "You want some of these," the Governor offered. "I find them extra good. Well, whatta we have here today? Hey, it's ham!" he said with a forced enthusiasm. It was a pallid scrap of meat pressed between two slices of white bread. Governor Chase took a large bite and chewed lustily, sipped from his milk carton.

"I got no one idea, A.W., but a whole potful. But basically I believe that there is a measure of goodness in every human being and, as I see it, it's the duty of government to let that good come out—to give it a safe arena, you might say. And nothing more than that," he added sternly with that special look in his eyes. "Being President don't interest me none, anyway—look at that poor devil in there now. The only thing different he has from me is a few buttons to blow up the world. Who needs that? Nossir, I like it down here. All that talk about me going for it is—just talk. To keep some others honest. You want the rest of your sandwich?"

"So you're not running?" Clemmons handed him the remainder of his lunch.

"Now, I didn't say that, did I?" When Chase smiled, it gave him a sly, sensuous appeal, much like his sister's expression. "Oh, I suppose if some old boy came up and tapped me on the shoulder, I would rise and take my place at the bar." He had nodded to the terrain below, as if to acknowledge the Virginia earth that contained the remains of others so chosen. "But it wouldn't be no fun, you know. I like it here. I'm down on road level. And that reminds me, that if the purpose of your trip is to set up a divorce, I'd like to talk it over with you and Olive first. Just for the timing, you know."

"No divorce, but a wedding."

"Of course, I don't understand why the two of you are still married anyway," Chase continued as if he had not heard the other. "I barely understand how or why you got married." He looked out the window, presenting his statesman profile. "Poor old Olive. You know, she's part of a generation of Southern women we seem to breed down here who—it seems like they've been conditioned by fraternity weekends; that is, they learn to be interesting, affectionate, stimulating, and otherwise responsive human beings —but only on weekends. The rest of the week, they're not good for much. Then as they get older, become wives, they can only be all those good things on weekends in hotel rooms on conventions or on vacations away from the domestic community. It's not their fault, no one told them how to act during the week. She should have come home after her year in New York running that museum. But then came Adlai—and then you. So, who's getting married?"

Clemmons told him briefly while he thought about Olive. It was true, he told himself, she had seemed to go sour when they had moved to Boston Corners. At first, he had thought that it was because she had given up politics, but it was the social side of that life, the dinners and benefits and parties, that she missed rather than the cause. One evening—Clemmons's memory opened—the girls had been tucked into bed, there was a fire in the library hearth, and he had anticipated a quiet meal; just the two of them, candlelight, some Brahms on the phonograph. Olive had been busy in the kitchen, and Clemmons—the practical side a second to his romantic nature—had even taken a quick washcloth bath in the small commode under the stairs. But it turned out that Olive had only been doing the dishes, those from breakfast and the night before, and when she joined him in the library, she lofted a thick peanut butter and jelly sandwich, almost held it out as a challenge to him. "Lookee here, Andy," she had said glumly. "I don't feel like fixing anything and, as we know, there's no Chinese take-out around here. So, you're on your own." There had been the shadow of an ultimatum in her voice.

"Well, these girls today have all this feminist stuff going for them," Chase was saying. "I like it. I got the ERA through down here, you know, and we got the first pussy attorney general in the Republic. She's goddamn good, too. You ought to be more caring with little Milly."

Clemmons was offended by Chase's offhand manner. The Governor had turned to face him, a sorrowful suffering in his eyes; the sharp edge of the man's face seemed ready to splinter Clemmons's denial.

"You know, you're a hard man," Chase said. "You don't know how hard you are. And it's funny that you don't seem like that, which is where Olive and Milly and these other women make their mistake. I think you ought to open your arms to this girl."

Clemmons smiled, even laughed at the folksy admonition, and turned to the window, thinking it was easy advice from a confirmed bachelor, a man who seemed to live almost a monkish life.

"But I want to tell you one thing." Chase leaned forward and placed a hand on Clemmons's knee. "You treat Olive nice, d'ya hear? If I get any notion that she's been made unhappy, I'm going to take your pants and throw them on the first truck out of town. Get me?" Then he smiled and sat back in his chair and closed his eyes.

The two men said nothing more. The plane droned smoothly westward and over the velvet fold of the Great Valley that opened to Clemmons's weary inspection, to pull his perception down within it. He felt like part of him was falling out of the plane, not all of a piece or even frighteningly, but like a slow draining of some chamber of his personality that flowed into the soft contours of wilderness below. Then the steward was shaking him awake, telling him to fasten his seat belt, that they were landing. The seat opposite was empty, the Governor had apparently retired to his command post behind the rear bulkhead.

Clemmons made the mistake, a mistake he always made, of trying to talk casually to the driver of the car Olive had waiting for him at the airport. He felt a special kinship with the old black man. A little over twenty-five years ago, the same man had driven him and Olive to the way station where they caught the midnight C&O sleeper that had started them on their bridal journey. But the old man, who seemed to chin himself on the steering wheel, withstood Clemmons's attempts at intimacy with clucks of the tongue, some nods, and a couple of "Yassuh, that's right." He drove the station wagon with a transient care as if, once he had delivered Clemmons to Sycamore Hills, both he and the car would go their separate ways—even disappear—until called up again.

Sycamore Hills had been built by one of the large coal companies in the eastern part of the state with surplus profits that might have otherwise caused them embarrassment with the federal government. It was a compound consisting of a thousand acres with well-stocked streams, man-made lakes, and a golf course that hosted a major PGA tournament. Set into third-growth timber were new houses of every style and gross exaggeration, as if the wealthy who had settled this province had done so in order to escape the sensible proportions sometimes demanded outside the pink brick gates. The guard who signaled them through the entrance wore a bright green trooper's uniform.

"Miss Olive's staying at the Governor's cottage," the driver spoke a carefully rehearsed message. "But she down at the club pool right now, and I'll leave you there and take your case on up to the house. You need anything pressed or cleaned?"

There was a high stockade fence enclosing the pool and clubhouse, a perimeter of last defense, perhaps, though the frail rough-barked shafts enclosed a seraglio of children presided over by greased madonnas. The scene was brilliant, the reflection off the azure blue pool water so polished by the chrome and tiled appointments that Clemmons had to stop while his eyes adjusted. He made her out at the far end of the long patio. Olive sat on a chaise longue, several other women around her, and then she saw him, raised an arm into the air.

"Andrew Wing," she called. "You come right over here and sit on me."

Clemmons walked awkwardly across the tiled pavement,

his hard-soled shoes moving uncertainly on the wet slickness, the layers of his clothing catching and bunching around his limbs. Olive was making space for him on the couch as the women around her seemed to part a way for him, eyes lowered, like conspiring handmaidens, Clemmons thought, though most were of Olive's age. She had maintained an appearance, a physical neatness, that they had not, an opulence of shoulders and breast that rose above the top of her swimming suit, its straps lowered, that was at once soft and tempered.

"Sit right down here and give me a big smack." She pursed her lips. Her face gave some lines to the truth of her age, but with an interesting effect, for it suggested a looseness in her expression, a worldliness encompassed by thick black hair, but Clemmons knew this sensuality only rested lightly, tantalizingly, upon the features of the face. "You remember Mary Belle, and Sukie and Lilly Mae. And this is Lilly Mae's daughter, Cindy, just home from school." Cindy was a young woman who looked as uncomfortable as Clemmons felt. In fact, he had just become aware that, with the exception of some small boys playing in the shallow end of the pool, he was the only male within this chlorine-scented sanctuary of women.

"Why, honey, what have you done to yourself?" Olive had raised the oversized sunglasses to her forehead to inspect his face. Her eyes were the same as her brother's, though it was the only characteristic they shared. She touched the healed cuts on his cheeks. "Some mean old pussy cat has scratched you, I bet," she said with a laugh, though he heard the tenseness underneath. The entourage had begun to break up as each of the women excused herself to "get wet," each sliding off different edges of the pool to cruise its dappled waters. Clemmons explained about the razor and Olive laughed once again, obviously preferring her own interpretation. "You want to take a dip? It's almost time to leave and Bubba has a suit in my locker."

"No, I'll wait. Maybe tomorrow," Clemmons replied and

moved to a chair beside the couch. He noted her legs were smooth and evenly tanned. "You look very trim."

"Well, I don't do nothing but loll around down here, play a little tennis, and swim. I heard from our eldest last night, and I got a postcard from Daisy a couple of days ago."

"Where was she?"

"Someplace in Iowa. You really are not going to take part in this wedding?" Her voice had lost its heavy slur, as if now that her peers had left, she could speak differently. "It would be such a little thing for you and would mean so much to Milly. Why not?"

"Because I am not going to be sucked back into that whole role, playing the happy husbandryman with his bower of rosy kinder. Especially not for her."

Olive pulled back, and then leaned forward to vigorously rub her legs. "She is her father's daughter," she said. "She's been giving an A-Number One imitation of you since she turned puberty." Then she straightened, holding up the top of her suit. "Well, we certainly wouldn't want to inhibit you, repress *your* free spirit." She started to rock in the seat, as if something burned her. "My God, the way you talk about Milly. I'm the one that should be offended! You know something?" Her voice slipped into a syrupy inflection. "They had a musical touring through here a while back, it had been on Broadway, and they had a big musical number about people doing it with their mouths. I mean, a whole bunch of people singing and dancing about sucking! Can you believe that?" She had paused breathless, almost looked at him covertly.

"It's a big hit," Clemmons told her.

"I guess I was never very good at it."

"You were always hopeful," Clemmons told her.

"But I mean, that's my upbringing; yet, I'm the one that accepts Milly and not you. Why is that?" She shrugged into a towel jacket. "I bet that Jenny Number could do it real good."

Clemmons looked perplexed.

"Well, she was a singer." Olive stepped into a pair of high-heeled sandals.

"That doesn't make any sense," Clemmons told her and stood up, but he decided not to go further. "Look, I don't want to get into this, to have an argument or bring up all this again, particularly over someone who is long dead. I came down here to try to arrange for our daughter's wedding, and to meet everyone's requirements to permit everyone to do what she wants."

"You mean, *he* wants," she said over her shoulder, and clip-clopped toward the gate in the loose sandals. "C'mon. We got to get up to the house. I hope you brought something decent to wear. There's a supper tonight over at the club."

"I wasn't planning to dine out," he told her. They walked along the neat roadside and across an expanse of green lawn, a continent of lawn already taken in the name of golf —a small flag staking the claim fluttered in the afternoon breeze. Beyond was a cluster of buildings composed of four condominium units that Clemmons admired for their architectural snugness, but their interiors he knew were similar to highway motels.

"Don't you want to know anything about Milly's beau, your son-in-law to be?" Olive had walked through to the bedroom. Clemmons stood in the cushioned setting of the living room. "Fix a drink. I'll have a little Scotch and water."

"He's a musician of some sort," he yelled back. He wondered if his voice would carry in this room; it seemed to have no atmosphere.

"Oh, you're so arrogant." Olive laughed. He heard a shower turn on. "He already has two records. That's one of them on the cabinet. He's booked a whole concert tour to Australia for their honeymoon." Her voice became muffled in vapor as Clemmons picked up the glossy record album. FIND STANLEY LIVINGSTON. No jungle, just a garish abstraction that didn't look at all like Africa.

He walked to the open French doors that looked out on a bunker; the green lay to the right. A small clump of birches, set artistically out of the way, sifted the gold light of the afternoon sun. He felt as if he had been traveling for days, and had left Claire's apartment weeks before, rather than only that morning. The order and regularity of his life in Boston Corners seemed even farther away, and the neat, planned expanse of the golf course before him, even such a huge enterprise designed for a sport, called up the symmetry of his own routines, routines that had been thoroughly set apart. He could accuse Milly and Olive, all women, for their irrational disjointed behavior that, unaccountably, bumped and jostled his schedule. What he did not realize, would perhaps never realize, was that what he considered to be irrational acts were really logical steps toward definite goals but planned so far ahead that the intervening segments he encountered, that he identified, seemed to have no connection. It was Clemmons, and not the women around him, who took each day as it came over the Berkshires, responded to it, and thought nothing more. The order to his life could only be claimed in retrospect.

"It amazes me," Olive said, coming into the room, "that you do not see that the girls are cutting their lives from your pattern. No, you don't see that, do you?" She had wrapped a large purple towel around herself, a smaller one of the same color around her head as a turban, and she looked very fit.

"No, I don't see that." He brought her the glass of whisky and water. She had settled, feet tucked beneath her, in the corner of a large sofa that seemed to be covered in what looked to be sackcloth but which was soft to the touch. "They have no purpose."

"Lordy, don't you think if they wanted to, they couldn't find something to do around here—there's just all kinds of interesting jobs could be found for them around here. Honey, reach me one of those cigarettes in that box there. I only have six of these a day, and this is my second. I'm saving the rest for tonight. Thank you kindly." Clemmons held a match to the end of the extra-long cigarette, and Olive pulled on the flame, blew the smoke toward the ceiling. "But they all struck out on their own, just the way you did. You know you weren't supposed to be a success. I never did understand how you did it. It's just a wonder." She had paused and her eyes seemed to grow even rounder. "What do you think of my getting a few wrinkles taken out, Andy? Just a little tuck here and there." She pressed her fingers to the corners of her eyes and then just under her jaw. "Lucy Crowe Miller had it done last year and she looks just fine."

"Look, Olive." Clemmons had sat down beside her on the edge of the great sofa, and her expression turned sly, but he ignored it. "I'm down here to ask you, to hope to convince you to come up to Boston Corners to take care of this wedding for Milly. It's for Milly, I ask. I've talked to Benny Smith about painting the place. I've arranged with this movie producer who's rented the field to let her use it for the ceremony. I've made all the arrangements for it to go smoothly. But it needs you."

He touched her as he concluded, his palm pressing and stroking the smooth roundness of her knee. The fading light slanted through the large windows to illuminate them like actors in a stage piece. The woman continued to smoke and observe the man who sat—as if ready to get up and leave, but held there by the one hand on her knee. From outside came the small concussion of a golf ball being hit, and the sound seemed to push through the transparent gel that enclosed them. The ice in Olive's drink rattled as she lifted the glass to her lips.

"You know, the wife of that movie producer turns out to be Carter Perry's daughter," Clemmons told her quietly. "I haven't thought of him, of all that, in a long time. She remembered me by name."

"Why shouldn't she remember you? You got her daddy's name in all the newspapers. Even *Life* magazine! You almost made Carter Perry into an interesting human being. But then, you gave all that up, moved up to hicksville where people go to retire or fail. I was prepared for failure. Down here, we're raised to take care of husbands who are not quite able to do things on their own, except with a little family help. You know? You still don't know how you did it. See? If you were a pro, you could tell me exactly how it happened." Her laughter turned lazily in the dark, and she stretched her legs out, across his lap. Clemmons felt his joints soften, as if the glue that held them were being dissolved as the tidy weight of his wife's legs pressed him into the cushions.

She turned on a floor lamp, a column of marble entwined by a plaster vine. "We must be at the club in an hour. You smell like something the cat brought in. Take a shower. Get dressed." He let her pull and push him into her schedule, let her incorporate him into her rounds and routines so that he would complete the picture she had of herself in this society. This was the bargain, and he knew it.

It would not have surprised him if she had organized this particular dinner dance in order to pull him through the doorways of the country club, doorways always jammed with women, to introduce him to these women friends and to the men who stood just behind them. She had, at the very least, timed this visit to coincide with one of the scheduled fetes. "You remember Andy, don't you," she would say, her face luminous and the eyes like darts. "Oh, Andy, here's Hattie Still Webster, a real fan of yours. And of course Dr. Bob."

He remembered their wedding reception, being pulled through what seemed like whole counties of relatives and friends in a similar fashion, though it was a different country club—an older and more traditional place, not this Sycamore Hills Club, which was an enormous building whose interior appointments, carpets, moldings, and even furniture seemed to have been sprayed on the corrugated steel of its bare walls.

When there seemed to be no one else for him to meet, Olive turned into his arms, and they danced. Clemmons was touched by her crisp posture, by its formal eagerness, reminiscent of other dances when they were younger, and she hummed with a high-pitched breathlessness that sometimes lost the melody sawed out by the four-piece band. Her color had become high, her round cheeks pinked so that they looked unnaturally rouged. She had even begun to pant.

"Slow down," Clemmons said. But she pressed his hand to twirl her around near the bandstand. The tempo behind her eyes beat faster than the one kept by the drummer of the small orchestra. "Take it easy, Olive." He stopped; then moved into a slower rhythm, and she followed. "The Governor talked about divorce today," he said to her.

"You don't want a divorce, do you?" She had almost snuggled against him. "I like it this way. It's like we're having an affair."

"It seems unfinished. Loose ends."

"Oh, pish-tosh. You always want everything tied up. I can't think of a better arrangement. The kids like it, I like it. You're so conventional sometimes."

"Sometimes I feel borrowed, like a tuxedo, rented out for the junior prom."

"Why Andrew Wing, I'm surprised at you. Here you are in the nostalgia business. That old-timey village you fixed up just to sell houses to all those West Side types in New York—you borrow a whole past, a fake past. All I want is for you to make a visit now and then. It's a fair deal, isn't it?"

Clemmons did not answer. Then, "Why don't you stay in Boston Corners this time. For a little while." The music had stopped. "After the wedding," he added.

"Now that won't work. We've been through that. I'd have to take up something if I lived up there with you. I'd have to be one of those ladies that take up photography or some kind of good works, do something *creative* while their husbands are being successful."

"There'd be no competition to . . ."

"Andy, I don't care about none of that." One hand still rested on his shoulder. Dancers left the floor to sit at small tables set up around it. Clemmons saw a couple circle them, like scouts, then bear down in their direction. "Don't you know, by now," Olive said, "that I don't want to do anything? If I lived with you, I'd have to do something. I'd have to be *busy*. I don't like to be *busy*. Besides, I have no place up there."

"Hey, you two," the bright-eyed woman said, "we'll buy you a drink." Olive hurried the introductions as if she were now anxious to leave the dance floor, to remove them from view, so Clemmons did not catch the names, but that would not have mattered to him since all the names down here seemed to be interchangeable. The two husbands followed their wives off the floor.

"Do you have a sport?" the man asked. "Golf?"

"I keep a dog who is a vegetarian," Clemmons replied. The man nodded to accept the category. His face was richly fleshed and very red, as if he had only come off the course; even his eyes seemed hot and turned slowly. "Golf?" Clemmons countered.

"Yes," the man said.

"It's not what it used to be, is it?" Clemmons said. "I mean, not much exercise anymore with all those golf carts to ride on." They had come down to a lower level and into a barroom paneled like an English pub. A game room adjoined, and the ping-ping of pinball games gave off an electronic excitement, if not a pulse, to the music that seeped from hidden speakers.

In fact, Clemmons and Olive had driven to the club from her condominium on one of these golf carts; every dwelling in the compound had a similar vehicle. Nor were they the only ones. He had counted over a dozen battery-powered wagons advancing slowly across the scrubbed turf of the golf course, heading toward the huge metal barn of the clubhouse from different points of the development. It was like the remnant of an armored patrol returning after a disastrous mission, but with couples singing in their summer finery. At the terminus, near doors convenient to the locker rooms, each cart was plugged into a bank of electrical receptacles so that the batteries could be recharged while its passengers danced and dined.

"No, not many of us walk around anymore," the man had replied to Clemmons. He had laughed good-naturedly, and waved to the bartender. There was a gracious, restrained manner in the man that Clemmons liked. "It's quite a different game than it used to be," he continued in a soft voice. "I miss the caddies, you know, chatting with them between shots. Some of 'em had good stories, and it made it more—somehow more sociable, you might say."

"They were all black, I suppose," Clemmons said. "On the other hand, it's probably cheaper to plug in one of these machines."

"Then there's another thing," the man said, ignoring or not hearing Clemmons's remarks, for which he was grateful; it gave him the chance to take them back. "There's widespread moral corruption these days," the man almost whispered, his hard eyes fixed on the two women, Olive and his own wife, who sat on bar stools behind Clemmons. "I mean, you wouldn't believe the widespread cheating that goes on. People move the ball around all the time. Better position on the tee. The emphasis is to get to the shot on the wagon. Make the shot. The carts make getting to the shots easier. You can't talk on those machines; it's like sitting on a Mixmaster. No, just get there and make the shots." The man had stopped talking as softly as he had begun, without a trace of anger or regret in his voice, almost as if these feelings had long worn away in him, had been worn away by the promiscuity of the incidents that provoked them.

Someone in the next room had scored on a pinball machine—a flurry of small chimes. Meanwhile, a silence had settled between Clemmons and the man next to him, a quietude that Clemmons was not sure was not his own doing, had not been caused by his own inability to speak to people like him unless, of course, he was selling them real estate. It was a fault in which he took no pride. Olive had no trouble talking with these people. She was one of them, he reminded himself—again unable to focus the several images he carried of her into one sharply defined portrait—and she was now almost head to head with the other woman, a matronly exchange of thoughts, gossip, whole paragraphs of social data disseminated though they had probably been with each other at the pool that afternoon.

On the other hand, Clemmons might consider that many whom chance places in the path of the gentle juggernaut of wealth may suffer crushed spirits, so that they are definitely marked, changed from the rest of us; a kind of flattening of the soul. Even the most generous among them, the most responsive to human natures (such as Claire; Clemmons would sometimes be confounded by her sudden shifts, withdrawals, and flights of introspection), even these will exhibit a strange vacancy during the simplest human exchange, as if such ordinary matter cannot pass through the barrier in their spirit, a blockage pressed by their circumstance. So, Clemmons fell into his own resources.

A large mural behind the bar depicted a hunting scene with all the usual pointing riders, dogs, and wild-eyed horses. The dogs, imprisoned in the cliché of the mural design, reminded Clemmons of Boxer, locked up in the cage of the boarding kennel and at this moment forced to eat the chickpeas and cabbage that were his punishment for being a dumb animal in a changing environment. Or the animal of a changeling environmentalist, Clemmons chuckled. His eyes moved to the doorway of the gameroom and there, as if she had been waiting for him to see her, a young woman abruptly turned, head back and eyes whited like the horses in the mural. She stepped one, two, three paces into the room and leaned across the glass panel of one machine to follow the game on another; another game of bump and tilt, Clemmons would think and smiled in such a relaxed, round fashion that Olive reached over to squeeze his arm, for she would think he had begun to feel easy in her homeplace at last.

"There's one thing *can* be said," the man beside Clemmons spoke evenly. "More holes can be made. With the go-carts. Thirty-six holes is nothing anymore. You just get in, ride around, make the shot, and keep going. Really something. Listen, I better take a dump before dinner. Excuse me." And the golfer slipped off the stool and walked through a swinging door.

Clemmons let his glance lie lightly upon the curved and tense figure of the girl who leaned over the pinball machine and, as if she had felt this play of eyes, she shifted her feet, perhaps to avoid it, but only to set off another roundness beneath her light dress. Finally, she stood straight, stiff-spined, and walked into the room and out of his line of vision. It was curious to Clemmons how women, especially American women, seemed to have developed a photosensitivity in their flesh, so that they were conditioned from an early age to feel the eyes of men upon them. One afternoon, sitting at a café in the Piazza del Campo in Siena, Clemmons had watched a man take pictures of his daughters. The little girls coaxed pigeons, gawked at vendors, ran and chased each other, while the father recorded every gesture, every move they made until the eldest put up her hand and in a weary voice said, "No more, Daddy, no more." But the man was not to be stayed; he merely retreated, fitted a longer telescopic lens on his camera and continued to poke at them from a greater distance.

"We hope your stay will be a pleasant one," the woman at his right said. Olive looked happy; her expression implored him to say something nice.

"That's easy to do," he replied. "It's a generous place you have here." His words, bare as they were, seemed to be sufficient, for the woman turned to Olive and both women nodded and smiled. Olive's large eyes lowered with suffused delight. "I was just saying to your husband, what a handsome golf course this is," he added.

"Oh yes." The woman laughed and pulled on her cigarette. "Old Joe likes his golf. Well, so do I. We golf together. Just get on our little go-cart and tootle along. Stroke for stroke."

Clemmons watched her lips close around the end of the cigarette. In the seductive light of the bar, Olive looked some years younger. The smooth flesh of her fine shoulders and arms—she even raised an arm now as if to expose more of herself—seemed buttery soft and liable to be cut by the sharp line of her dress. The sleepy expression in the dark eyes set in the round, androgynous countenance, and the rather full flesh under her chin (she had that little double chin when she was twenty) gave her a babyish look; but, in fact, if in the old days one had reached out to chuck her under the chin, a few fingers might be lost.

He found his wife had somehow skipped over the scrapes and skins of middle age; there was even something sensually provocative about those years in her, though he might not be unwilling to admit that this line of interest may have been stimulated by the firmer, younger haunch he had observed earlier in the gameroom. It was at that moment the bartender announced dinner was being served upstairs.

A. W. Clemmons found that he was the unannounced guest of honor, the sought-after table mate for dinner; not so much because he was good-looking, which he was not, but because he was different-looking. In the old days, sometimes, as he walked along 44th Street in the theater district, he would be approached by autograph hounds, their books and pens thrust under his face. "Are you famous. Are you famous?" they used to cry, and sometimes Clemmons would pause and soberly sign a name, usually that of an obscure ballplayer, then walk on. It was this look of "being someone" that may also have angered his friends then, for people dislike the look of success that shows no effort, no trace of struggle—even if that look is due to chance, a face for which its owner was not responsible. All the more reason to dislike him.

In addition to this look of celebrity, actually not such a great feat in this bland room full of insurance agents, bankers, and gynecologists, there was the simple matter of his being a guest and the husband of Olive Chase, and a not too frequent guest at that. Moreover, she had assured his glamour by her accounts of his real estate dealings: how he had bought an old village, termed a "ghost town,"and hired two dozen painters to paint every building in one day; had completely restored the village almost on live television—a sparkling image of a country town that promoted the sale of land around it.

So for all these reasons, Olive was forced to surrender him to others, almost bestow him upon a table—one, Clemmons noted, that seated the oldest women at the party. He took his place. The chair on his right was empty. Silently, the diners toiled with their fruit cups. Now that the table had won him, none of its occupants seemed to know what to say to him, and they talked among themselves in low voices, as if their conversation might offend him.

She must have waited until the last metal ball had dropped into place and the lights on the panels had gone dead, for she arrived flushed and artlessly apologetic. Clemmons rose and pulled out the chair beside him, thinking she looked thinner in full light than she had in the pulsing gloom of the game room. Then, he made a second identification; she was Lilly Mae's daughter-at-home-from-school that he had met at the pool. No doubt it was acknowledgment of this connection that she had given him in the doorway downstairs, and not the tossed Frisbee of a nymph's glance as she turned into the thicket of gadgetry. Clemmons went back to his fruit cup. On the other hand, as he had stood above and behind to place her chair, she had taken a little more time than seemed necessary to arrange and settle herself, looked back at him over her shoulder as if to see the effect as the scalloped front of her dress fell away; even leaned forward a bit more—a fold of dress not quite right —as if to prove that her breasts were free of support and uniformly tanned.

"Well, I hear Milly's getting married," the girl said. "I declare, they're just falling like flies all around me."

"You know Milly?" Clemmons asked.

"Um-huh." She had pushed aside her fruit cup without touching it. Her manner suggested that she would eat none of the meal, was only there to satisfy some required credit in a social curriculum. "I met her and Daisy a couple of times when they visited their mama. Is it true that Milly's marrying Stanley Livingston? He is *some* musician. *Some* wild man. Easter break some of us cut school and went down to Virginia Beach where the band was playing and we just had a ball. That was *some* party, I tell you." She paused to let a plate of chicken be placed before her. "We must have been stoned the whole time we were there. All the comings and goings: I'm afraid I don't remember but half what went on." She laughed and played with the garniture on her plate and then pulled an olive off a toothpick and placed it between her lips. "Old Stanley Livingston came to one of our blasts. At least, I'm told he did. I can't wait to talk to Milly about him. I have a recollection of some of the goings-on, and I just better check it out with her." She laughed, leaned toward Clemmons as if the two of them were in a conspiracy at this table of old women, though Clemmons had been straining to listen to a conversation on the other side about cutting back chrysanthemums.

"I don't guess some of them got back to school at all after that party. That was some party. I just barely managed to get through finals myself and even then I had to take a couple of incompletes. Milly must be about two or three years older than me, I guess. That sure is hard to believe. I mean that you are her daddy. I suppose you could be somebody's daddy but not with daughters that old. My goodness. I bet that's what you were smiling about when I saw you downstairs. You were just sitting there smiling away."

"I was thinking about Daisy's dog," Clemmons replied. The chicken had been broiled with a lemon sauce and tasted better than it looked.

"Well, my goodness."

"His name is Boxer and he's a vegetarian. Well, he doesn't want to be, but Daisy thinks it's better for him. But he hunts down woodchucks and rabbits for himself."

"Getting a little on the side, huh?"

"He brings them back and eats them whole on the front lawn. I can hear him all night long chewing and crunching their bones."

"Oh my."

"But what's even more interesting is the way he eats them." Clemmons turned in his chair toward the girl and paused. She pulled away. "He eats them from back to front. That is, he starts chewing on the hindquarters and the tail and works his way up to the head. I can tell you, it is some mess sometimes when he starts pulling out the intestines and starts chomping on them. Some mess." Clemmons took a bite of chicken and a little sauce dribbled down his chin. He caught it with his napkin, and continued to chew and talk at the same time. "You can imagine the smell sometimes. Yes. I keep thinking the woodchucks and rabbits are vegetarians, but they smell just as bad, you know, down there. Now why does Boxer eat them that way, starting with their rear ends? I asked that question myself and a vet told me he thinks it's some old animal instinct, to start at the end that has no teeth, the end that can't harm you—in case the animal is not completely dead—so you start on the harmless end—the smelly one, it's true, but it won't bite, will it? Yes, thank you, I would like some more wine." Clemmons leaned away to give a waiter room to refill his glass.

"That's disgusting," the girl said. "I think that's the most disgusting thing I've ever heard." Her voice had risen. "That's the most disgusting thing anyone has ever said to me. Ooh!" She stood up quickly as if something had been spilled on her linen dress. Clemmons looked at her blankly then sipped his wine. At the table, a small audience had formed around the scene. They would assume he had made some outrageously obscene proposal to the girl.

A scream went up, but it came from the far corner of the room, followed by muffled cries. Chairs were pushed back, a commotion rose and fell. Heads swiveled and turned from table to table, toting the word, passing half-filled sentences around the room.

"What . . . dead?" ". . . Dead . . . Joe Stone, dead? . . ." "Here? . . ." "Dead? . . . Who? . . ." "Dead?"

Olive's hand rested on his shoulder, squeezed his neck slightly. She sat in the empty chair beside him and her eyes were very round. "Joe Stone, Jr. just had a heart attack and is dead."

"Who is Joe Stone, Jr.?" Clemmons said.

"You talked with him at the bar before dinner. About playing golf? He didn't come up for dinner and so they went looking for him and they found him downstairs. In the men's room. Sitting . . ."

"Don't tell me." Clemmons stopped her and, in spite of himself, began to laugh. He coughed and drank some water. Olive had also started to laugh, then wiped a tear from her eye.

"You're a bastard, you know that?" she said, crying and trying not to laugh at the same time.

"Do you want to go?" he asked.

"I think I better, before you make me disgrace myself."

By the time they unplugged the golf cart, she had regained her composure; and as they drove away from the clubhouse, the accordion in the small orchestra started to play "Auld Lang Syne." A half moon made the bunkers and hollows of the golf course look treacherous, a manicured no-man's land, and Clemmons turned away from them, driving the sighing vehicle across the terrain as Olive gripped his thigh to her, held it tight above the knee as if she were afraid she might fly off of the cart when it slowly passed up and over a slight rise.

"Turn down here," she directed.

"The condo is that way."

"I know where it is. I want to go this way. There's a pretty little sand trap down here, just before number six."

"Oh," he replied, an old accomplice to her whims and frankly aroused by his familiarity with them.

"Here," she said as they came to a sand trap but then, "Oh, pish-tosh," when she saw the other golf cart. It was parked beside the silver-plated bowl of the trap and the couple who had arrived on it already shadows moving in the pit.

Clemmons looked at his wife, saw in the moonlight the bemused almost expectant expression in her eyes, as if she were observing or listening to some review of themselves rather than eavesdropping on others. She sat stiffly beside him, her head slightly inclined. "We can find another one," he whispered. But Olive only shook her head, then again shook it, a rueful set to her mouth. She relaxed, slumped in the seat beside him.

"No, let's go back to our place," she replied in a normal, flat voice.

It might have been a mourning dove that woke him, or it could have been an owl; Clemmons could never tell them apart. In fact, he had never learned to distinguish one bird from another by its song, and only knew a few by sight even with all the time he had spent in the rural confines of Boston Corners. In any event, he lay in the bed beside Olive and listened to the bird call coming from the golf course outside their bedroom windows. The moon had long since set and the night was dark.

Yet, he wondered, it may not have been the sound of the bird that woke him but the weight of his half-erect phallus as it brushed against his thigh. Olive lay on her side, her back to him and her breathing resonant with the depth of the sleep that embraced her. As with the birdcall, Clemmons could not distinguish in his memory, in his dreams, what had inspired this awkward hardness that, even as he tried to trace its stimulus in his half-stirred consciousness, grew harder, as if to launch itself from his body, to fly into space. When they had returned to the condominium, Olive had lavished upon him, and he upon her, the most tender, the most loving of caresses and, though there had never been in their sex life the intricate or prolonged passions that he had known with others—Olive had always seemed to reach her satisfactions too easily, too quickly—there had been a generous and responsive character to her appetite. "Getting cozy" was one of her euphemisms for sex, always drawled with a lowering of lids over the heavy, protuberant eyes, and even as her shyness disappeared in their time together, she would accompany the phrase with some gesture, such as unbuttoning his shirt and slipping her fingers across his chest.

Yet now, as he turned carefully in the bed so as not to disturb Olive, so as not to brush against her, this traitor to his satisfaction rose beyond his control. He had read in a magazine at Ralph's Barbershop in Stout Falls that the male continued to perform sexual functions automatically, to insure the continuation of the species. It had been a letter to the editor in a column concerned with some aspect of human sexuality. It was that sort of magazine. A woman had written a letter about the number of erections her husband had while he slept. She had stayed up one whole night, she wrote, and watched her husband's erections come and go while he continued to sleep peacefully, innocently. She asked the editor of this department, a former call girl and a star of pornographic movies, if she thought her husband was being unfaithful, perhaps dreaming of his affairs with other women. How should she handle this problem, she asked.

The answer was unexpectedly scientific. All male animals, she was told, generally have full erections every ninety minutes during sleep. Scientists, anthropologists, and sexologists were not entirely sure why this is so, but it was generally thought that it was a residual response left over from the time when *"homo erectus"* (*oops,* the editor apologized) only had connection with the female while she slept —when she was most accessible and least able to defend herself from a sexual connection. The female, in most species, usually has to be forced or caught off guard. But, the editor proclaimed, "not us up-to-date, modern pussies. So, my advice to you," she concluded, "is not to question what inspires that gorgeous hard-on but to get down on it and ride, baby, ride."

Idly, Clemmons reviewed this advice as he listened to the plaintive call of the unidentifiable bird on the golf course. Where had all those females gone who had been so inaccessible, so reluctant that they had to be taken while they slept? He knew that if he turned toward Olive, pressed against her, she would open to him without breaking the rhythm of her snore, and would wake happily to his penetration. Just then, as if the thought had been the deed, her snores abruptly halted. She turned to him fully awake.

"What's the matter?"

"I was thinking of that girl at dinner tonight," he answered. He had only meant to select some answer that would cover his real thoughts, but as he spoke the lie, he realized that there was some truth to it also, some part of his mind had been reviewing his earlier conversation with the young woman.

"I saw her. Cindy Hill. I was about to come over and scratch her eyes out when the word came about Joe Stone, Jr."

"She wasn't doing anything. Just a young kid, but I was mean to her."

"Why?"

Olive had nestled against his shoulder and he stroked the fine texture of her hair. "I guess she reminded me of Milly."

"You will break my heart, Andy," Olive said softly. "Milly and Daisy are strong enough. I'm not."

"It's this place. The waste of it."

"You're a bully." Drowsiness sweetened the epithet. "Taking out your hypocrisy on that poor girl."

"I'm not the hero you thought. No club foot; that was all a lie. Club head is more like it. My dentist says I'm grinding my teeth down to the nub. Can you imagine Byron toothless? I can only dog paddle. I'm sorry about the girl. About Milly. I'll try to do better, Olive. Olive?"

But Olive had drifted back into sleep and Clemmons lay beside and partly under her, listening to the cry of the dove or owl, now joined by the chirps and trills of other birds just as unknown to him. He lay expectantly in wait for the dawn, while Olive, asleep, held him by his limp penis, as comfortable and comforting a grip as taking his knee on the golf cart, as if this tether of his flesh would keep her safe on the surface of the earth.

Chapter Five

More than birds singing on the fairway outside Olive's condominium had awakened Clemmons. It was a sound that would ring in his head for the next several days so that his behavior became strange, distant; rather like the preoccupied attention of a hunting dog tuned to a whistle that only he can hear.

"If you don't stop being so uppity," Olive had joked, "I'm going to call Baby Bubba and have him pack you over the mountains."

But her jest only seemed to deepen Clemmons's melancholia. He'd read somewhere that Schumann's last compositions had been keyed to A by a syphiloma. So Clemmons thought of himself, trying to shake a similar sound, this A note, from his mind, and in fact its source was no less venereal than that of the malady that took the composer, for it was the clear, resonant memory of Jenny Seven that made all around him seem discordant.

He would blame Olive for striking the first note, there at the pool on that first afternoon when she referred to the singer, but he had been thinking about her, had been rounding her up, since coming upon that old record album in the house he had sold in Boston Corners. In all probability, without Olive's ironical reference to Jenny, Clemmons would have summoned her spirit anyway, to chastise his idleness with Olive at Sycamore Hills, to put—with that peculiar primness—the one's hard work and devotion against the easy play of the other.

"Sunny Singer—ha!" Jenny's explosive pronunciation of the aspirant had always seemed to give new meaning to the word "hoyden." "Sunny sucker is more like it. This old guy and me had the studio to ourselves every morning. He was the engineer, played the Hammond, and read Robert Service, and I sang and blew him while he read the commercials. He said it was good for my voice. It is, isn't it?"

She would be in a show trying out in New Haven and they would be in a room on the fifth floor of the Hotel Taft, next door to the Shubert Theater. Clemmons would have come up from New York.

"I guess it isn't true, is it?" she said and sat up in the bed. Her smile was pained, a residue of chagrin disappearing from her lips as she considered how she had been tricked again—even years before, tricked again—and as she held her hair up and away from her neck (they were in a room without air-conditioning) Clemmons caught in the jellied light a quick-winged fleck of anger in her eyes.

"I'm not so sure it's not true," he said, stroking her back. Her spine rose smooth and neat to flourish in that peculiar curve of neck, that downcurve that suggested both weakness and resilience, and which was even more shaped toward the last quality as she turned to look upon him with a speculative expression. "I mean, I've read about it—semen containing protein," he added.

"The boys in the chorus talk about vitamin C." She laughed again. Clemmons had caught on early that there was little humor in her laughter; one more rough timber raised against the world. "You're just telling me that." Clemmons had to look away from her, her smile had been tremulous, prepared to break open, the first to laugh at her own betrayal, her own ignorance, and thus another coarse defense. "You're such a liar, Charlie."

"Don't call me Charlie."

"Why, you are my Charlie," she said and leaned above him. "You think I call everybody that, don't you. Some sort of a handle to use in the morning when I can't remember the guy's name. Yes? Don't look away from me. Isn't that so? C'mon, 'fess up."

"Yes," Clemmons finally said and laughed for no reason.

"But that's not true." She had become serious, absorbed in her contemplation of him so that he became uneasy with this close scrutiny, but it would be an expression that he would become used to—this sober, almost studious composure that came over her features when they were alone talking, or even sitting in silence somewhere, a museum or park bench, a look that he would, in time and perhaps too late in time, feel privileged to see. "You are my Charlie. My Charlie Boy."

She had slowly lowered her face and kissed him, not full on the mouth but precisely at one corner of his lips and then pulled back to once more study him, as if to evaluate the effect of this chaste kiss and then hopped off the bed, stretched with her arms high and walked to the bathroom. The brief exercise had diminished her small breasts even more, so that only their blunt nipples remained in relief.

"How old were you when all this happened?" he asked.

"You mean Providence? The radio station?" She had sat down on the toilet, the door open, and he could see her knees, her hands holding some tissue, and her profile.

"Yes."

"Maybe sixteen."

"Christ!"

"Why Christ? Oh. Well, he never fucked me if that makes it better. Thought I was too young for that. Even talked to me about saving it for the man I married. He was a sentimental old fart."

"He did nothing?"

"Oh, he fooled around. You know. When he'd plug into the network he'd fool around with me. I'd lie there listening to Arthur Godfrey. Jesus, there were some bums on that show."

"Godfrey's show?"

"Yeah, some of his girl singers. What were their names? One sang sharp all the time and had no rhythm. He was probably screwing her." She flushed the toilet and bent over the sink to wash her hands, throw water on her face. "Speaking of abstention"—and she suddenly made a small aria of the word, the mellow sounds bouncing off the bathroom tile—"*Ab-STEN-N-N-N-shun.* Wait until you see this turkey tonight. Do you know what it's about? Are you ready? It's about the Shakers. You know those people who didn't believe in doing it at all? How can you make a musical about that? Even *Oklahoma* had a little screwing. But I got a couple of songs. You heard one of them last night. Not bad. Then there's a big number on making chairs . . . fitting the little dowels into the little holes. I sing it dirty."

As she talked, she had rummaged through a small kit bag, opened and closed the mirrored door above the sink, then finally walked back into the room holding the round diaphragm case and the other accouterments of birth control. It amused Clemmons that Jenny always prepared herself for their love-making in his full view, even now laying out the tube of jelly and the diaphragm at bedside, rather like a precocious Girl Scout preparing for an overnight hike. Olive always did this behind closed doors, and far in advance, as did most young women of that day—that is, if anything was used at all, for birth control was usually the man's responsibility, with some reliance on luck.

As he watched Jenny carefully squeeze a worm of spermicide around the rim of the rubber diaphragm, Clemmons wondered, not for the first time, if she demonstrated this technique to him so that he would be able to do it in case some sort of an emergency arose; say, if both of her arms were broken and they found themselves in a remote motel far from medical assistance. On the other hand, Jenny Seven was one of the first of those women, sometimes referred to these days as "a modern woman," who felt it necessary if not natural to involve the man in all the workings of her body. If he were to take pleasure of it, then he would not do so in ignorance.

During all these preparations, she kept up the conversation. The show would close in New York, but Dick Rodgers wanted her to audition for a part in his new musical. Julius was opening a new place and had asked her to be on the opening bill. She could always go back to the Bon Soir. Frank had called her, he stopped off to see her on his way back from Spain, and wanted her to make a screen test. There was an industrial show being put together that paid very well, but it meant being out of New York for several months. Meanwhile, her preparations had been done routinely but no less exactly, and she had stretched out on the bed, her head to its foot, knees up and apart, to insert the folded diaphragm into her vagina. It was much the same position in which she would soon receive him, and Clemmons, always fascinated by this gynecological display, speculated how others might respond; these phantoms who only had first names and who called her on their way through town. Did she conduct the same sort of birth control workshop for these celebrities as she did for him, they being more worldly than he and certainly more accustomed to having everything done for them? On the other hand, did Frank Whatever-His-Name really look at her if he had this opportunity? Did Frank (once Clemmons had almost asked, "Frank who?," but was afraid the answer might be something like Sinoma or Smith), but did old Frank know, for example, that on the edge of the outer lips, in about the eleven o'clock position, just under a crisp copia of blond hair, lay a small, nut-brown mole?

"There," Jenny said with the happy satisfaction of a master craftsman who had prepared the workbench for the next project. But they lay quietly, unmoving, and listened to the midday traffic outside their window. "I'm sorry about last night. It seems pointless to you, I guess, to rehearse into three in the morning when you know the show's a flop. You made a lot of arrangements to get up here, I bet."

"It wasn't too difficult," Clemmons lied. He idly caressed one of her feet. It hadn't been easy; another one of those sudden, unexplained absences. "And I don't think it's pointless. It's the profession. It's what you do. It's to be done right."

"How's your wife? I'd like to see her someday. Maybe you can arrange something, Charlie, say like when Vivien Leigh looks down from the steps and sees the girl that Robert Taylor is going to marry. I'd just like to see her—from a distance."

"She's in Hyde Park today. At Mrs. Roosevelt's. With Stevenson."

"Big time."

"She's only the chauffeur; somebody had to drive him up there for lunch."

"The money says he's going to lose again. Why does he do it?"

"Why do you rehearse until three in the morning in a show you know is going to fail? Olive talks about Dulles. She doesn't worry about Ike so much as men like Dulles."

"You know, you have great legs. I love your legs."

"I like yours," he replied.

"Have you bought any more property at that place, Boston what?"

"Boston Corners. I have a binder on an old farmhouse that—remember that little cabin near the falls? Well, the farm is just . . . What are you doing?"

"I'm blowing the hairs on your thighs. Close up it looks like a wheat field in the wind."

"What do you know about wheat fields? You're from Rhode Island."

"I played Lincoln, Nebraska."

"I bet. Wait a minute. Not this morning."

"It's the specialty of the house." She looked up, genuinely perplexed.

"No. Come up here," and he reached down and pulled her up to lie beside him. "Here now."

"Ah, Charlie," she would say. "Are you truly my Charlie? Truly my friend, Charlie?"

The prepared, sylvan complacency of Sycamore Hills could not compete for his attention while this sort of commotion continued in his head, continued to turn aside the gentle gestures of affection that Olive offered him, for they had become devalued by the hard currency of Jenny's strident figure. But it was more than a physical comparison. Jenny's appeal to him was in her professionalism, her art, her dedicated and rigorous schedule of rehearsals, voice lessons, and performances that formed a paradigm of hard work as mysterious to him as it was illuminating. True, the routines of theater people were not unfamiliar, but the performances out front—the finished acts—were his concern, and his job was to attract an audience to them because of their seemingly effortless grace rather than to call attention to the arduous labor that had produced them. So he had put this part of the business aside in his consciousness, if it was not entirely forgotten, and Jenny called it out.

One more thing. Even with the sexual exploits, or exploitations, Jenny's was an oddly Spartan life—a life on the run, and this quality appealed to Clemmons, struck a chord in his own nature, so he would never think she might want something else, a more permanent place. Her footloose existence was only a part of a hard apprenticeship she must endure so that she might come on stage and sing one song so right that it would always be hers. "The way Jenny Seven sang it," people would say.

But this solitary life, the opportunities it offered them as lovers, would sometimes sour him when he sensed the purpose that fueled her every waking hour. Clemmons would feel his own life being weighed like a cork against Jenny's dedication, and then he would put upon Olive and her way of life the judgment he felt Jenny's life made of his.

One afternoon, he met Jenny in the Automat on the south side of 57th Street near Sixth Avenue. It's no longer there, but it used to have excellent beef potpies and one could eat reasonably well for very little. It would be winter and her face was plain within a cocoon of wool scarves. There were heavy galoshes on her feet. Her plaid skirt, a trifle long even for those days, had been pearled by droplets of rain about to turn to sleet.

"Hiya, Charlie," she would say and put down a worn satchel that bulged with scores, music. She had been working with a voice coach in the Carnegie Studios up the street. If he opened it up, turned to the middle of the packet, Clemmons knew he would find a piece of cheddar cheese wrapped in wax paper and grooved with the precise marks of her front teeth. It had been her lunch.

"You look exhausted. Are you sick? Do you have a temperature?" He put a hand to her brow and she pressed against it, turned her face, and closed her eyes like a cat being caressed. "I'll get you some tea."

When he returned, she had loosened and unwound her outer clothing, and she seemed to get smaller, more childlike, as the thick wrappings fell away. The image was enhanced by the ponytail that kept up her hair. "Umm!" She leaned over the hot cup and breathed deeply. "I'm pooped —or should I say, poo-payed."

"Where were you last night? I called you until very late."

Jenny sipped her tea, her eyes closed.

"Where were you?"

"What did you want?"

"I just wanted to talk."

"Oh. Well," she spoke quickly, as if his answer had determined the one she chose to give him. "Jimmy Van Heusen was in town and called me, and we went to the Blue Angel to hear Johnnie and closed the place up. Then Jimmy said come to his place, so a bunch of us went up there—he's borrowing this fabulous penthouse from some character—and he played the piano and we all sang. He's got some new songs. Fabulous."

Clemmons watched the woman making change in the glassed booth near their table. It seemed as if the coins poured from her fingers, a peculiar bleeding, and she moved stiffly, never smiling; as she turned from right to left to right again like one of those mechanical gypsies that used to tell fortunes in penny arcades.

"I was hoping we might go to a museum. There's a show on. Matisse at the Modern."

"I would like that," Jenny replied. "Yes, I would like that."

"That's why I called. But it's too late now." He drank the last of his coffee. "I have to go with Carter to New Mexico the end of the week. He's bought a pueblo of Navajo rugs and is bringing them back for a show at the Center."

"Oh, yeah." She had loosened her fall of hair and forked it with her fingers, and then combed and gathered it together again and wound a rubber band around it. Plates rattled at the steam table. The doors of empty food compartments snapped shut and the silvery turntables revolved and returned with the food items restored. "So what else is new?"

"Olive is pregnant."

"Ah. That's why you called."

"She says it was a mistake."

"Sure."

"Well, I don't think she wants it, really. We're thinking of maybe moving up to Boston Corners. I could still do jobs for Perry from there. Come in for a few days each week."

"You think Olive will like living there? Out in the sticks? Doesn't seem like her place, if you know what I mean. Why move? Why leave the city?"

"It's getting dark, but it's still early," he said. "Why don't we get some of those chicken sandwiches, pick up a bottle of wine, and go have a picnic. At your place?"

She made a face, as if there had been a bitterness in the tea. She shook her head. "I'm really exhausted, Charlie. I have an early call tomorrow."

"What's wrong? Something's wrong. We've been off like this—since you came back from Vegas."

"It has nothing to do with that." She had reached out and taken both his hands in hers, and the strength in her grip surprised him. Then she as quickly let go. He almost expected her to slip away, to slip off the table, disappear. "Do you know, Charlie, that you have a way of putting your right hand against your neck, just under your right ear? Like now."

"No," he said.

"You do it when you're confused about something. Like me. How long has this show been running?"

"Off and on? Almost five years."

"Amazing. That's a record of some sort," she said and hunched over the table. She seemed to grow cold and hugged herself. "What do you want of me? If I knew that . . . there's no question about what others want. Right? But you make me jumpy; I can't settle you in my mind. You keep coming at me from different directions. These little picnics of yours, for example. And the museum tours. The weekends at Boston Corners, tramping around the woods. The books, the movies . . ."

"The bed . . ."

"Sure, that too," she agreed soberly. Again she had taken one of his hands in hers and brushed at the hairs with her fingertips. "I sometimes think I'll quit. Throw it in. I never was much of an ingénue, but the character parts are coming up more and more. I'm too young to be playing a madam or the old maid school teacher. Too old for the kid sister."

"What would you do?"

"I could get married," she replied and stirred her tea with one finger, then sucked it. "I get offers all the time."

"You're joking." Clemmons laughed, then saw she might be serious.

"You think, Charlie, that I'm like some character in *All About Eve*—all that bullshit about waves of love coming over the footlights. That's bullshit, Charlie. Like W. C. Fields said, 'Don't let the posy fool ya, bub.' "

"But what about all the work you've put in? All the rehearsing, and all the time and all . . ."

"I'm tired, that's all. I'm just tired. The big part never seems to come round. There are all these young broads coming into town by the dozens, by every Trailways bus, and all of them can fuck and some of them can sing and some can even dance. And that reminds me, I've got to call my dance teacher. Hold the seat."

Clemmons watched her lean against the marble wall of the restaurant to talk into the pay phone. Feet crossed, the open tops of her galoshes seemed caught together. She looked like a schoolgirl calling home to say she would be late for supper; something had come up; extra lessons, a Coke with her girl chums, or a horny teacher, Clemmons thought. For even as he watched her, he began to doubt she was calling her dance coach but rather one of those single-named celebrities, or a friend who had been told to look her up when he came through town.

"Jenny, how about some supper?" he said when she returned. He watched her closely. "I know a place . . ."

"You always know a place." She laughed and took his hand. "That's your solution for everything, isn't it, Charlie? Have a good meal. Well, maybe you're right. But not tonight. I'm not up to it tonight. You ought to be home with Olive anyway. I sometimes feel bad about her. Not the screwing part, but the fact that we have no future, you and me. That's long past, and it seems . . . wasteful for us to use her time up. You know?"

"What do you mean, we don't have a future?" he asked, though he was afraid she was right. Their relationship had become not so much a consistent passion as a renewable intrigue to be picked up at different intervals, intervals that seemed scattered through the run of his life like parentheses in ordinary prose to give it distinction.

Meanwhile, she had finished her tea. They sat in silence, the tables around them slowly being taken up with those who dined early at the Automat. Clemmons sat leaning over the table to look up at her attentively, as if he were trying to pick up the melody she might be humming under her breath, and Jenny slumped away, down into her chair, her head forward and figure concaved, a tension between them as if they had been posed by some artist who sketched from the restaurant's balcony, say a John Sloan or an Edward Hopper. Clemmons knew there was no future for them. If he had ever thought of leaving Olive before, he would not do it now, with a child on the way. More important, if he broke up one camp, he might only establish another; so, perhaps he would try to incorporate them all to enlarge the perimeter of the general community around himself.

"No future." Jenny shook her head. Nor, indeed, would there be an immediate future for them after this night—over a year would pass before they met again. "Will Olive have to quit working?"

"Perry is a generous man. He'll think of something. Also, she's been getting calls from some politicians. She built up quite a list in the Stevenson campaign, phone numbers, contacts. She has a good sound on the phone. She's got two senators after her, their people are calling her—presidential hopefuls."

"I need a rest," Jenny said softly. Then wrinkled her features and fiercely rubbed at her nose. "There's this guy who's been after me to go to the Bahamas with him. He's got a yacht. A ya-chet. I could use some sun, some nothing-to-do." Her eyes had been looking lightly over the room as she spoke, from table to table and then lightly came to rest upon him. "Whatta ya think about that, Charlie?"

Clemmons shrugged and looked out the large window that faced 57th Street. The early evening traffic moved carefully through the frozen slush. Chains on the tires of buses and taxis slapped at the underbodies of the vehicles as if there were cogs beneath the pavement to turn the scene on cables.

"How about another cup of tea?" Clemmons said.

"Was her name really Seven?" Olive is asking him. She is behind the wheel of a small sports car and they are going to a tennis party. She handles the car expertly and with flair, almost nosing it down into the hollows of Sycamore Hills rather than driving over the pavement. Clemmons has a momentary sense of weightlessness.

"It was some sort of German name that sounded like that. Siebener or something." Small yellow flowers bloom in the marshland by the road. They are the kind that Benny Smith calls cowslips but Clemmons had found them in a book described as marsh marigolds.

"Genevieve, I suppose," Olive says almost to herself. "You had a record of hers around the house. I used to play it sometimes when you were gone—probably with her." Olive chuckles and stabs at the cigarette lighter on the dashboard. She holds the lighter to the cigarette between her lips. "Judy Garland she was not."

Olive had no reason to be fair, Clemmons would agree. The crisp, abbreviated whiteness of her tennis outfit snugs around the smooth tanned flesh of her arms and thighs, and a billed cap is set low across her brow. "It was a poor recording," he finally says.

"Maybe." She nods. Time had softened her verdict. "But I knew all about you and her when you took me to that club where she was singing." It sounded as if the low wetland they passed through has affected her voice too coincidentally; just as the car swiftly tops a hill, her speech regains a firmer timbre. "I confess she gave me a little buzz."

"You?" Clemmons says, a little surprised.

"Oh, I don't mean that, but she made me feel sexy, made

me feel special, important, like the slightest movement I made, taking a drink, lighting a cigarette—it had some big meaning to it."

"It was the lyric of the time," Clemmons says, but Olive continues talking.

"Let me finish. I've thought about her. That night. It was at Julius Monk's place. He came over to the table. Carter and his wife, us, that ass of a writer and his girl. We had come in for a long weekend."

"It was your birthday," Clemmons says.

"Happy birthday. What a birthday present you gave me, sugar. Took me to hear your old mistress sing."

"Slow down. You're going too fast."

> UPSTAIRS AT THE DOWNSTAIRS . . . 161 West 55th St. The elite style of Miss Jenny Seven reminds us that the lyrics of Cole, George, and Larry were written for the rich in heart. The Len Green trio admirably supports and the impeccable Julius polishes the Steinway during intervals.

Six of them had crammed around a table only large enough for drinks and a few elbows. The lights abruptly went down and Jenny was introduced. "May I dai-wreck your attention and ah-plawse—" The combo swooped into a crescendo that seemed ready to blow its instruments apart; then Jenny was there, in the spotlight, already singing, snapping fingers—tempo up.

How's your romance?
How is it go-ing?

She would string out the word, give it a hard, ironical turn that suggested that she already knew the answer and was happy for it. Though the small stage was close to their table, she seemed tall. The perspective was all off, as if the darkness were that of space where all rules of earth were invalid and the spotlight that burned her face was a star about to explode.

By the time she had reached the bridge and gone into the song's release, she had set the room into a stir. Would she be able to keep up the pace? Then she cut the lyric in two and gently introduced the verse. The room was put off balance and the audience had to reach out, as it were, to touch the world she had put together.

Olive had turned and leaned against Clemmons, giggling, her eyes sly and happy. She had seemed to fill out, plump with delight, the moment they had driven onto the Henry Hudson Parkway and seen the George Washington Bridge. He knew a long weekend would not be enough, but he wondered if he would be able to get her to return to Boston Corners at all. She was a native of this excitement, the hush and chatter, all its gestures adorned her like jewelry that caught and magnified the luster of her own self-awareness.

"I'm having a good time," Olive whispered in his ear. As the lights came up, her expression became almost demure. There was a pinkness under the light umber of her skin and her mouth seemed swollen. "Let's go back to the hotel. I'd like some more of them conjugal rights."

"Is she a friend of yours?" the writer had asked him.

"Jenny Seven?" Clemmons replied. Carter Perry looked at him across the small tabletop with a grasshopperlike inquisitiveness.

"He did the promo on her album," Olive replied for him. Clemmons shifted in his chair. Perry tried to get a waiter's attention.

The writer continued. "A friend of mine is a writer on the Garry Moore Show and he said she's a hot number."

The small table between them was not large enough to hold the slippery innuendoes the man dumped out. He seemed to have a dossier on Jenny; the famous men who had had her. Even a syndicate figure—this was for sure—would send her air tickets to Miami or Las Vegas or wherever the mafioso happened to be when he got the urge. Olive looked with hooded eyes upon the writer. She hardly breathed.

Clemmons could not recognize the Jenny he knew in the crude profile drawn by the other, for it was a caricature, a negative print. But, he listened with more detachment than he thought possible. Then he stood up. He had had no intention of speaking to Jenny; however, the quick way Olive turned to Carter Perry, the quickened way she started talking to the producer, seemed to okay his seeing Jenny if it did not give him the idea to do so. It would, he told himself, somehow be an apology for the biography he had just listened to.

She saw him first, his reflection in her dressing room mirror, as he came down the narrow hall backstage, and it was as if she had been patiently sitting before the mirror, the door open, waiting for him to materialize in the glass. "Don't smear me, Charlie," she said and tilted her face toward him. He kissed her awkwardly, his lips tasting the medicinal patina of makeup and perspiration on her cheek. "I was thinking of you this week, all safe up in the country while the rest of us were about to be blown up. I bet you have a bomb shelter at that. How're you going to keep all of us refugees out?"

"It seems to be over. There was a late report tonight that Khrushchev is backing down."

She had removed her blouse and he noted the pale angularity of her shoulders. "I know but Jesus, what a week! Missiles. Blockades—Stevenson freezing hell over. Oh, you remember Mel Stein, don't you?"

It was such a small dressing room that it seemed impossible for another person to be in it and yet remain unnoticed except for the fact that he stood within the closet enclosure, a small corner of the room with a pole fixed diagonally across it and curtained, and that Mel Stein was able to fit within such a small corner, almost to hang there like some piece of wardrobe Jenny had put off wearing for the time being; even the pained, lopsided expression on his face when Clemmons turned around conveyed the idea that he might be suspended on a hanger.

"Hello, Clemmons," the man said, and laughed but with no humor.

"Well, hi, Mel," Clemmons said and put out his hand. He was happy to see the man, one of the old gang, and his enthusiasm pushed aside any question, for the moment, as to what Stein was doing in Jenny's dressing room, as it obscured the flint in the other man's eyes.

Someone more cynical might say that Clemmons always assumed everyone liked him because there was no one he himself disliked. However, it was really that he had lost that native, animal capacity to recognize danger in another being's expression, an ability that is still functional in those who have made it through the grove all in one piece. On the other hand, Mel Stein always looked like that, "a malevolent George Washington" someone once said, the large carpenter-square nose and broad forehead laying the foundation for the description.

"Sweetie, run out and get me some soda water with a lemon squeezed in it. I've got a throat like a taffy pull." As she spoke to Stein through the mirror, Jenny had motioned to Clemmons to sit beside the dressing table. Stein left the room, one shoulder lowered like a running back hitting the line.

"Which one is she?" Jenny said when they were alone. "The one with her hair piled up like one of those little laundresses? I remember asking you to bring her somewhere so I could see her, but Jesus, Charlie"—her laughter barked at her reflection in the mirror—"you really are something else, to bring her here."

"It's her birthday and we're with the Perrys and a writer he's funding. Carter wanted to see you. I couldn't put him off without seeming—you know. How are you?"

"Oh, going along. I've got a neat spot at the fair in Seattle. Lots of pennies."

He sat with his back to the mirror, almost facing her. Her face had changed subtly, even under the makeup he could tell it had somehow been altered, as if the pores of her skin had increased in diameter, an infinitesimal enlargement but whose sum exaggerated the complexion and features. She had become coarse-looking, Clemmons thought, and looked away.

"It was a good series," he finally said. "But Terry was just too good."

"Stein took me to the fourth game here. He asked me how I learned to keep a score card." Her eyes shifted from their study of herself in the mirror—she had been repairing her makeup as she spoke—and rested upon him. The effect of their gray stillness, the only feature about her that suggested contentment, softened his opinion and even urged him to appreciate what had first seemed unattractive.

"I told him," she answered his question, "that I went with a ballplayer who taught me how."

"Like you used to tell me about all those trumpet players." He had taken one of her hands in his.

"Listen, I'm always discreet," she replied. "So you have another little girl now."

"How do you know?"

"Stein." She shrugged. "He's still plugged into the old network and I guess you must have told someone."

"Yes. We call her Daisy." He watched her redo her eye liner. "How about Stein?"

"What about Stein?"

"I mean . . . Stein?"

"He's very gentle and not jealous. You introduced us, if you remember. He's away a lot," she added. "In fact, his magazine is sending him to Italy next week. Do you get into the city much?"

"Yes, there's usually something almost every week that I have to come in for. Perhaps I should go?"

"Oh, Mel? Don't worry. He won't be back until you leave. I gave him an excuse to get out; my throat's fine, or hadn't you heard, Charlie? He's shy around other men. Comes from being the runt on the block, maybe."

"Well, I also meant . . . those at the table."

"*Those* at the table. My, aren't we being formal."

"I mean . . ."

"You mean, you mean. What do you mean, Charlie?" She leaned forward, to get even closer to the mirror as she applied powder to her face.

"I want to apologize," he said. Clemmons pushed aside an assortment of cosmetics and cotton swabs to make a small space for his elbow on the corner of the dressing table. "I think sometimes of that formal declaration of separation I made to you that night at Chumley's—what an asshole I was. It was like the Versailles Treaty."

"Well, I thought it was a little much, Charlie. I thought, Gee, we're just having a friendly hump now and then and you sounded like you wanted to hire lawyers and draw up papers—to divide property. I get the cat."

"I also realized how it must have made you feel," Clemmons said. "And for that I apologize."

"You must do a lot of thinking up there, like Thoreau or somebody." She had turned slightly in her chair and now faced him so their knees almost touched. Her bare arms and shoulders seemed unnaturally pale, as if she were recovering from some long illness. Her head leaned to one side and toward him. "So, how's it been with you, up there in the country? In your bomb shelter? No, don't move your hand. Leave it there under your ear and tell me. Don't cover your mouth—just tell me straight out."

"It's been fine for me, but not for Olive."

"And that's trouble. Well, that's what you get for taking her away from all the bright lights." Jenny laughed and got up. She took a fresh blouse from the rack, slipped her arms into the sleeves, and buttoned up the front. Her movements were methodical, crisply done, and he knew she had already begun to think about the songs in the next set; she had begun to put on her professional personality.

"You say next week?" he said.

"Uhmn, help me with this," she said and held out a large cuff link. Clemmons fixed it into the cuff of the silk blouse. Then he did the other. "I've got to talk to Lenny about one of the numbers," she said.

"There's a show on Flemish painters coming into the Met," Clemmons said. She had begun to hum under her breath as she brushed her hair. "How about Wednesday?"

"How about Thursday?" she replied. "Two o'clock on the Egyptian side of the entrance hall."

"Okay," he said and reached out both hands to her, but she had picked up a can of hairspray and used it around her head, as if she had been attacked by insects. When he walked down the narrow corridor and back toward the club's main room, he heard her vocalizing, warming up. She sounded a perfect A tone: *"Pah-ta-a-a-a-y."*

The car slows down as Olive lightly presses the brake pedal. Clemmons admires the agreeable line of muscle that runs the length of her bare leg and thigh. "I've never seen you act so peculiar," Olive was saying. "I never dreamed you'd agree to come down here like this, just to get me to come up there for Milly's wedding. Andrew Wing, do you think our first-born is going to get married without her mama standing beside her? But you were so eager to get me up there that you'd do anything. Anything." She chuckles, and turns into a drive lined with brilliantly flowered azaleas.

Clemmons sits low in the seat of the convertible and sights the shape of the approaching clubhouse over the car's hood. It resembled a prefabricated Monticello: a lot of columns with nothing to support. His face feels warm, burned by the wind or Olive's remark. He is anxious to get back to Boston Corners; to leave tomorrow. There were two closings and the general store in Irondale had some problems.

Olive pulls into a parking space and brakes abruptly. "Scrawny but serious. Yes, that was it. She was serious." And she turns off the ignition.

When they recommenced their affair, Jenny generated another sort of heat in him even more powerful than the sexual. Its source lay in the area that Olive sardonically pointed out: she was serious.

It was like some strange variation on the Puritan ethic, Clemmons would say. Her rounds and routines, recording dates and rehearsals, auditions, classes; the whole rig of continuous work that kept her in tune, gave her a composure, put a serenity in those large gray eyes that could almost drug Clemmons with their tranquility.

On his way into the city (it took two hours by train), he would put aside the *Times* and look out the window. He would be traveling the same route, down the Harlem Valley, even the same roadbed, that had been traveled a hundred years before by the thousands of people who had come north from the city to watch the fight in Boston Corners. Overnight, the small community had been ravaged; a no man's land, a place of brutality and waste, dedicated to a brawl between human beings. As the train stopped at each small station on the way—Dover Plains, Wingdale, Hartsdale, Chappaqua—his tension seemed to let out one notch at a time. He tried not to contrast the two women, though he found it curious that Olive was usually exhausted and cantankerous at the end of a day—a day with few tasks; whereas Jenny was almost always fresh after her day's rehearsals. So he would escape to the calm arena that Jenny seemed to offer; a one-man, wrong-way replay of the raucous excursion of a century before.

"She's got the Betty Crocker syndrome," Jenny told him once. They had met again at the Metropolitan Museum, for as lovers and other undercover agents know, secrets are best kept in public places. "All of us these days are born with a diaphragm in one hand and a cookie cutter in the other."

She had been waiting for him among the Etruscan funereal figures and went primly on tiptoe to offer her lips. "She needs something to do."

"The girls are in school all day," Clemmons said. "I've tried to get her interested in the Irondale restoration. Seems like it would be a natural for her to manage; it would be the same sort of thing she did for Carter Perry. She's bored, but she won't do anything about it."

"That's what I mean," Jenny said, taking his hand and leading him toward the main hall. "She's finding out that the cookie cutter don't cut it. It's all made up; like that phony village you're fixing up. I bet you're going to have everybody running around in sunbonnets and bib overalls. Listen, are you ready? I can give you a list of actors who need jobs."

"Where are you taking me?" Clemmons asked. They were walking up the wide marble stairs to the museum's second floor. "I thought we were . . ."

"We are, we are, Charlie." Jenny laughed shortly. "Don't worry, I got the cookie cutter in place."

"That's not what I . . ."

"Sure it is," she said quickly and stopped to embrace him on the steps. She had fixed her hair in two braids this day and wore a sweater and slacks. Clemmons wondered if those who saw them might think he was a teacher with his young student, an uncle with his niece. The idea intrigued him. "Sure, it's what you meant," Jenny continued after they had kissed. "It is soi-tain-ly what I mean, bub. But I want to show you something first. Something I found while I was waiting for you." Even though she was taking the steps two at a time, he knew the breathlessness in her voice was due to something else.

"You can't expect her to be satisfied with all these made-up doo-dads," she said when they reached the upper floor. "She's finding out they're not natural for her." She had stopped before a small painting by Giovanni di Paolo. "Look at that," she said, almost as if this picture of Adam and Eve were her work. Then she skated away on the smooth marble floor, leaving Clemmons alone to study the painting. The archangel Michael was escorting the unhappy pair from the Garden. Paolo had managed to plant an incredible amount of vegetation within that small frame, Clemmons thought.

"Yes?" he said finally.

"Do you see—down there." Arms out, she slowly turned in a far corner. "The angel has a daisy."

"Yes." Clemmons saw. The angel's genitals were hidden by a bright yellow flower, each petal meticulously formed. What looked like the marsh grass that sprouted from hummocks around Benny Smith's garage covered the groins of the First Couple. "Obviously some sort of class system. Angels get daisies and ordinary folk get weeds."

"Or maybe everybody had daisies once," Jenny said. She had sat on the wooden bench in the center of the room. Her mood had suddenly sobered to a curious self-absorption, as if she were studying and arranging a patchwork of thoughts before trying to sew them together.

Clemmons sat on the bench beside her, though he faced the opposite direction; a love seat. He had grown very fond of these Sienese faces. The heavy-lidded madonnas with the bags under their eyes—full of tears, he supposed—all seemed to incline their piteous heads from left to right; whereas, if he remembered correctly, Botticelli cricked Venus's neck from right to left. A secular bend.

"I almost stopped singing last night," Jenny said after a little while. "I had done the first set and was sitting in the dressing room. All of a sudden, the songs sounded silly to me."

"Stein has been talking to you again."

"No. It's not Stein. I wish he were here. He's on the Coast. It's a lot of other things I've been thinking about. It's hard to do bright little lyrics about naughty couples living in sin when people are getting killed just trying to go to school. You ready? Last night, in the middle of a number—

in the middle of 'Just One of Those Things'—I got the feeling that no one was listening. They weren't noisy and they looked like they were listening, but they weren't. Cardboard cutouts. They were closing in and I couldn't get through. It needed a Presley to get through. Chubby Checker could get through. Ha!" The harshness of her laugh was strangely softened within the hard, marble-edged perimeter of the museum room.

"They were listening," Clemmons said. "Your voice carries farther than you think it does." Her severe expression startled him; how it aged her face and deepened the lines, and bleached her complexion. "Jenny," was all he could say and put his arm around her waist.

"You know what, Charlie? I want to quit."

"Quit?" Clemmons was genuinely shocked.

"Sure, why can't I quit? What if Stein asks me to marry him. Why can't I just quit and marry him. We're the same size." She had almost sobbed. "Oh, don't worry, I'm not going to quit." She had turned to face him and spoke as if to soothe him, as if he were the one who required comforting. Her eyes were bright, unnaturally sharp in the diffused light of the museum, and for a moment Clemmons wondered if he had glimpsed something in them that he had never seen before, something like a blindness that came from staring out over footlights into darkness while pretending to see into that darkness.

"Too good," Olive is saying. "You're just too good." But she is talking to one of her opponents who has just made a passing shot down the line. Clemmons sits by the court and watches this game of doubles made up of three women and the club pro, for the game is to be a lesson also.

"That was a nice stroke," the man says.

"Thank you, Bus," the woman across the net responds.

"Yes, I could tell from the way you moved into it that it would be a good stroke." Clemmons judges him to be in his early forties, stringy in thigh and neck, though the face is glazed by the sun with a permanent, youthful pink. "Just let it flow," he's telling her. "Let it go naturally."

The three women are all about the same age, though Olive has a compactness the other two have allowed to go soft. Clemmons admires her self-contained, stiff-spined cadence as she marches to the corner of the court to retrieve a ball. Perhaps that is why the pro had chosen her to be his partner, Clemmons muses; for that efficiency at small tasks.

"Okay, serve it up," the pro commands. "Really throw yourself into it now." He crouches, tense, expectant, to receive the serve. The shorts are pulled higher on his left thigh. Blond hairs stand out on his deeply tanned legs like prickly filaments.

"Ouf," the server exclaims. It was a good serve, flat and neatly placed in the corner. The pro returns it to the near court. The player at the net smacks it smartly to Olive's feet. She has pulled herself in tight, as if the ball were something to be avoided.

"Ah-ha, what'd you do wrong, Olive?" the pro asks with a crooked smile. "What'd you do?"

"I didn't get set up in time," she replies peevishly.

"And what else?" he coaxes her.

"My racket wasn't back?"

"And what else?" he continues patiently as he comes toward her, casually picking up balls on the way.

"My feet weren't loose," she says and looks furtively toward Clemmons, like an anxious child.

"That's right," the pro says. "You've got to keep those feet loose, so you can move. Now watch this, ladies." The two on the other side wander up to the net to observe, a rather forlorn curiosity in their contemplation, Clemmons thinks, as if the net were a fence that would always keep them apart from the real world.

The pro has stood close behind Olive and reaches around her to grip her racket, his hands next to hers. "Now just try to follow my steps, try to anticipate my movements, the direction I'm going to move. Ready. Go!" Olive and the pro skitter about the tennis court in a sort of fast shuffle, back and forward, side to side, as the man curves his body around Olive's. Sometimes she trips, stumbles over his feet, and falls against him, but for the most part she is able to match his movements, the direction of his quick changes of pace. It looks to Clemmons like some old dance pattern, say, a gavotte or an unusual polka.

"There." The pro straightens up and releases Olive. "Feel the difference? Do you feel the difference?"

"I feel the difference, Bus," Olive says and readjusts the sweatbands on her wrists.

"Do you see the difference?" he asks the women across the net.

"We see the difference, Bus," one of them says. The other one nods, seemingly dazed.

It was this sort of bland good time he had failed to give Olive, for which he still felt a little guilty; guilty for thinking she had wanted something else, and that he had not read her right. All that time in New York, he had seen her poised and balanced with important men, artists and politicians, whose maneuvering seemed as easy for her to follow as her own breath; all that time, what she had really longed for was this sorority of aunts and cousins and old school chums, an oral history society that met in continuous session to quilt the endless narrative of family histories and that, if the need arose, could find a man for an hour or two in order to "feel the difference."

It would be easy for him now—even now looking back as Olive waves to him from the base line with that same sort of broken-wrist flap of hand that Milly had either inherited or adopted and that signalled happiness—easy to identify from this distance the various warning signs she had given him in Boston Corners.

"So, she's leaving you," Jenny said.

"Not leaving me," Clemmons told her. He had called her from the pay phone outside the general store in Irondale. Across the road, in the post office, he could see Ernest Miller sorting the mail and eyeing him curiously: why would A. W. Clemmons be using the pay phone and not the one in his office or at home? "She's not leaving me. She's only taking the girls down to her family's place for Thanksgiving. Just a family reunion."

"Oh, yeah?" Jenny replied. He had been lucky to find her in, and this luck was a good omen, something not to let slip.

"We'd have three or four days, Jenny. Just the two of us."

"I'm supposed to audition for a part, the Wednesday before."

"A good part?"

"Not so great. Then Mel wants me to have dinner with his brother's family."

"Fuck Stein!" Clemmons was surprised by his own emotion, and looked about the compound of the old village. He half expected to see the word slashed on the freshly painted siding of the Methodist church.

"You've got to be kidding," Jenny had drawled. "So where would we go? If you think I'm going to stay there and do the cooking, you're crazy. I'm no different than— she is."

"We could come . . ."

". . . and I don't want to be there," she continued, anticipating his suggestion. "I wouldn't feel right. Anyway, I've seen that dump. I don't blame her for wanting to get out of it. I bet you all sit around and guess the number of seeds in a pumpkin. Big deal. Are you ready? Ha!"

"Wait a minute, wait a minute," Clemmons said. "We could go to the Cape. To Provincetown. I'll have the car. I'm taking them to Newark for the plane. Then I can pick you up, and we can take off right then. That's where the Pilgrims first landed, you know. Not Plymouth Rock. They landed on the Cape first, looked around for water and food. Found some corn, as a matter of fact, in some Indian graves. Then got shot at by the natives and pushed on to Plymouth Rock."

"Oh yeah," Jenny said. He could tell by the sleepy sound in her voice that he had intrigued her. He needed a few more embellishments, a few more bright bits to catch her.

"It's off-season. No one will be there, no tourists, no summer people. The light is wonderful. Wait until you see the light. That's why painters have always gone there. That's a curious atmosphere because of the sand, water, latitude, I don't know what. And the beaches. Great sand dunes, cliffs over the sea."

"What will I tell Stein?" she said. He had won her.

"To hell with Stein," Clemmons said, always flushed with the other man's loss. "Tell him you're having your period."

"Ha!" said Jenny. "I will be."

It's about a five-hour drive to Provincetown from New York City, but Clemmons would take the old U.S. Route 1, going through the small and large towns to Providence, and then Route 6 from there on out. Some city people gravitated toward Provincetown for the summer while others went to Fire Island, almost as if the season made up two camps: the anthill of Fire Island attracting the active and ambitious—operators like Mel Stein, for example, who wanted to stay close to the action—while Provincetown drew the more passive observers, one might say, dedicated to true light and beauty.

As they drove through Connecticut and Rhode Island and then into Massachusetts, Clemmons told Jenny about the painters who had been attracted to the light. In the summer, Hans Hofmann or Franz Kline or Mark Rothko might walk down Commercial Street, maybe to a sandal shop or out on the wharf to pick up some fresh fish.

"But none of them will be there," Clemmons told her. Jenny sat in the corner of the seat, knees drawn up under her chin. She had dressed for the occasion: wool cap, scarf, slacks, heavy coat, and mittens; in fact, she was almost too appropriate, almost as if she had been newly costumed.

"All the galleries will be closed, too," he continued. "The town will be pretty much deserted. Maybe no restaurants open, even." He had to laugh at Jenny's expression, how her eyes had rolled up. "Don't worry, you'll love it. The light, the dunes. It's the best time to see the place, this time of year."

"Light-smight," Jenny said, and looked out the window. They would have just worked their way through New Haven and crossed the bridge where the Quinnipiac River empties into the harbor. The light here was flat, weighed down with smoke. It would be late afternoon. "Isn't there some easier way than this," she said. "We've hit every red light since New Rochelle."

"It gets better from now on," Clemmons assured her. "It will also get prettier, Jenny, old girl. You'll like it." But the succession of small towns along the old road only made their journey more complicated, and Clemmons knew he had been wrong to take this way. Perhaps the whole trip had been wrong. Leaving Manhattan, they had given up the anonymity that gives lovers refuge, but here they stood out, even the license plates on the car were different, out of state. Clemmons sensed there was a logistics to adultery outside of a large city that was difficult to solve. He had put them in an exposed position, their relationship clearly on view, clearly illuminated by that very quality of light that he had been so anxious to show her, and which would reveal them to themselves if to no one else.

"Does the radio work?" she asked.

"It's a fine radio."

Clemmons had begun to have misgivings about their trip the moment he pulled up before her apartment (the same brownstone, incidentally, he had returned her to that first night). He saw her standing on the sidewalk. Even when she saw him, her expression did not change, she did not smile, and barely said hello as she threw her case in the back seat and got in. She looked like someone's spoiled kid sister that he was giving a ride, as a favor, but who had already gone moody because he was a few minutes late.

"Listen to them," she said. It was a record by Peter, Paul, and Mary. "Maybe I should learn how to play guitar and come on like Minnie Pearl."

"You're still worried about that?"

"I'm going to end up singing for fags. Also . . ."

"And?"

"Well, I lied to Stein. He knows I lied. He knows I'm with you."

"So what?" A light rain began to fall and Clemmons turned on the windshield wipers.

"So, I don't like to lie."

"What is this with Stein? What's he doing now—still hacking for that scandal magazine?"

"He's also food editor for another one and gets a lot of free meals."

"Food editor? What does he know about food?"

"In fact, we went to the Fleur de Lis the other night. Remember, you took me there. He was supposed to be incognito but he couldn't help implying too much to the waiter, the owner, about his connection with this men's magazine, so we got the best of everything." She giggled.

"That's his style," Clemmons said and laughed.

"I would like to be incognito," Jenny said quietly. "And rich. Incognito and rich, that would be nice."

"Is he jealous?" The traffic had melted away, and they were alone on the highway.

"No. Not that way. In fact, he sometimes asks me to tell him about—about men."

"About me?"

"Yes . . . and others," she added. Clemmons did not take his eyes from the road, but he could feel Jenny's eyes upon him, feel them evaluating his response.

"What does he want from you, then?"

"I don't know. He keeps bringing me little bouquets of

roses. Little pink roses. I don't know what he wants. It's not the old body, that's for sure."

"Jesus! Wants to hear all about your love life. That sounds like him. It fits in."

"You know that he hates you," Jenny said, but she had smiled.

"Hates me?" he replied, genuinely amazed. "Why should he hate me? We hardly know each other."

"Because you know things about him," she replied. She had moved close, leaned against him and stroked his hair. "And because you have no opinion of them," she added. "You only think they're an amusing story."

"Well, they are funny," he insisted.

"But he's ashamed of them," she continued gravely. Her fingers pulled gently at the hair over his right ear, arranged and rearranged it.

"I don't get it," Clemmons said. He liked the way Jenny sat close when they drove somewhere. She had done it those times they had driven to Boston Corners, and sometimes they would pass another car with another couple snugged up the same way, and Clemmons would think, "high school sweethearts." Olive never sat this close and never fooled with him, or touched him.

"Look," he said, "that's Providence up ahead."

The weather turned around the next day, and seemed to pull Jenny's mood with it, for they woke within the crisp, brilliant bell jar of the small motel cabin they had rented in Truro Center. Jenny sat straight up in bed and began to sing, her voice vibrating within the shell of light that enclosed them—fortunately the other cabins seemed to be vacant. She pulled the covers over her head and then pulled them and herself down over Clemmons so that he was twice warmed, only his face left cold and exposed as Jenny moved under the covers to, finally, because of "her condition" she said, take him in her mouth. He felt as if he were being drawn into the center of the sun.

But as the sun went higher in the sky, as the light became

more and more like crystal, it became clear that Jenny felt awkward in this stringent landscape. The bleached sand and graying grasses of the back dunes seemed to scrape her composure, and her good spirits faltered. She had worn the wrong kind of shoes but refused to let Clemmons buy her a pair of sneakers, and she viewed the panorama from Pilgrim Heights with suspicion, as if there were something unnatural about the ocean appearing on both sides of the land at once. The high bluffs at Highland Light frightened her, and she clung tight to Clemmons's arm, shivering either from the cold wind or fear—probably both, he thought—though she did not turn her eyes away from the slate-blue expanse of the Atlantic that fit the horizon like a tough membrane. Clemmons put both arms around her, readjusted the scarf she had tied over her head, and let her look and look and look like a child seeing disaster for the first time.

But the actress in her created a role around this sense of insecurity, her feeling of being "out of place," and she gave a performance that was meant to entertain him while it protected her feelings. It was the role of a petulant child who had been promised a good time, with a few worldly embellishments.

"Jesus, what a dump," she said. They walked down the middle of Commercial Street in Provincetown. Most of the stores were boarded up. There were few people on the street. "No wonder the Pilgrims didn't hang around. I bet they don't even hump on Sunday in this town."

"It's the off-season," Clemmons told her, for the fourth or fifth time it seemed. He had noted that most of the restaurants were closed or were only serving on the weekends. A couple of bars were open, but Jenny hardly drank and the atmosphere didn't appeal to her. "There's a nice view of the harbor from down here, just a couple of blocks down."

"View-smew," she said. "That's all they do around here is look at the view. Look at the light," she mimicked him.

"Turn on the light, Laura." She had even begun to hang back a little, walk slightly behind him.

Or else he had begun to walk faster, as if he were determined to finish the obligatory tour, get it over with quickly. He had given up trying to point out to her the different angled planes of weathered shingles, or the houses where certain artists and writers lived. When they passed the site of the old Provincetown Playhouse, where O'Neill's plays were first done, he remained silent.

The sun seemed to have passed behind a filter that permitted all of its brilliance to pass through but none of its heat, for it had become very cold and the stiff breeze off the harbor drove this cold through the fibers of their clothing. Clemmons had become desperate, like a man suddenly trapped in a hostile environment, or in one that suddenly had turned hostile. The motel room was warm but bleak; its swaybacked bed and old television set offered limited options and surely not ones they had to come all that way to choose. No one he knew was in town, and he frantically combed his memory for any name, however slight the acquaintance, he might look up in the phone book. He could think of some story to explain Jenny. But no one was around.

"Ooh-ooh," Jenny said, as she stamped her feet and held the muffler over her face. She scrootched herself in behind him to huddle like an orphan. The cold wind seemed to have frozen his brain, so it worked sluggishly, turned over the different possibilities slowly, even as another part of it rang alarms. "Do something, Charlie," Jenny cried through her scarf. "Do something."

He started to run in the direction of their parked car, pulling Jenny after him by one hand. Her mitten came off in his hand and she screamed, holding up her exposed red hand before him, and he hurriedly replaced the mitten, pulling it on backward, but it would have to do. They continued running, their limbs working jerkily but still working, and finally made it to the car. The car felt like a meat locker, still and cold, and their frantic breathing froze on the inside of the windows. Miraculously, the car started.

"Where are we going?" Jenny asked. She hit her feet against the floor.

"There must be a restaurant open farther up the Cape," he said. As they drove, the car gradually warmed, though Jenny continued to shake. She seemed unable to control herself. Clemmons kept scraping the small hole of vision in the frosted-over windshield.

"What kind of fucking place is this, Charlie?" she asked. But she had unwound her scarf, and by the time they reached Eastham, the car's heater had gained the advantage. They had loosened their outer clothing and the windows had become clear. "Now what?"

"There might be a place in the old village," Clemmons said. He turned off the main highway onto the old road that cut through the small town.

"Lookee-dat." Jenny pointed ahead. "It looks like the kind of place Cary Grant used to bring Katharine Hepburn." The vision warmed her spirits. It was a pure white inn by the side of the road, with a wide, graceful porch that, even in this cold, seemed to offer the indolent pleasures of summer. There was a bright light burning in each of the large curtained windows on the first floor, and an arrangement of Indian corn fixed to the front door, a red door, freshly painted it looked, and of such massive carpentry that no wind could ever pierce it. "Do you think it's open?" Jenny asked as he stopped. There were no other cars in the parking lot. "You go in, I'll stay here," she said.

Clemmons would be glad to go in alone, and then had felt bad about feeling this way as his hand closed around the large brass doorknob and turned it easily, the door swinging effortlessly inward on its hinges to admit him to a rag-rugged foyer. Yes, the friendly woman told him, they would be serving dinner in two hours, and yes, they had a table for two. He heard, but could not see, the crack and pop of a large hearth fire, probably in the taproom to the left, but the dining room was just beyond. It sparkled jewel-like reflections off glass and silver. The aroma of sage and nutmeg was overpowering, and almost brought tears to his eyes.

"Let's go back and change," Jenny told him. "We have time to go back and really get dolled up," she said. She almost bounced on the seat, like a child jumping on a bed.

"You will be a touch of class to the Ye Olde Village Inn," Clemmons told her. He tried to make up for his previous feelings. And she would, he agreed with himself. He could already visualize her taking her seat in that proper New England dining room, her hands carefully realigning the silver and the glassware ever so slightly so that the setting would be really correct.

As he drove, he imagined her looking at him across the candlelight of that setting. The small, sharp nose was given its value, and then the baby mouth, the downturned line of lips caught in a surly shadow until she smiled, and finally this light rose to flood the serene depths of her eyes. Sometimes he would catch her looking at him as if from a long distance, like a face on one of those ancient vases at the Met.

"How much time we got?" Jenny was saying. "Two hours? We have time to stop on our way back to the motel. That antique shop that was open in Wellfleet."

The place housed junk—old magazines, unrepairable radios and appliances, and a few pieces of secondary interest. But Clemmons was eager to humor her, so they pulled up and stopped at the old house with the sign ANTIQUES nailed over the bald door. Clemmons could see that there had been a small porch over the door once, but it had been long removed, even sold, he thought. The proprietor was a very fat man whose flesh seemed to ooze the same kerosene that burned in the space heater in the center of the front room. Assorted scrap was piled almost to the ceiling and seemed ready to be set ablaze by the heavy vibrations of heat sent out by the stove. They had begun to sweat almost immediately upon stepping through the door.

"You folks take your time," the man said. Even his eyes seemed to swim in some kind of oil.

Jenny found a pile of shellac records and began to sort through them. From time to time, she would call out the names of old bandleaders, singers from a bygone era, sometimes with a footnote of her personal knowledge. Clemmons looked through a pile of old books. Complete editions of Kipling and Hugh Walpole. A novel titled *New Hope* by Ruth Suckow. A double-figured edition of *David Harum.* Benét's *Western Star.* A phone rang in the back of the house, where the kitchen might be if it had been an ordinary house; Clemmons imagined the fat man heating up canned soup there over a used hot plate—one that still worked and therefore had not been brought out front. He leafed through a copy of *Walter Reed, Doctor in Uniform* by L. N. Wood.

"No kidding," he heard the man say. "Machine guns," the man wheezed. "I'll be damned. Well, I hate the sonuvabitch, but I wouldn't have gone that far. Yeah. Yeah. Yeah. Okay. Yeah."

Looking back to that moment, Clemmons would remember that he had begun to button up his coat, pull on his gloves—even though he had no sense of doing it then, no idea he was preparing to go back out into the cold even as he heard the ponderous footsteps of the store owner approach them from the rear of the house.

"Whatta you think of that?" the man wheezed. "They just bumped off Kennedy in Dallas."

He would remember how they left the place and got back in the car and then, still some sense of survival quick in their numbed instincts, they found a café where Clemmons had several hamburgers put up in a bag along with containers of coffee. Truro Center looked deserted when they got to the motel, as if it had never been peopled or perhaps those remaining had fled to the beach to push off in a boat for the safety of the open sea.

In the motel room, they ate the hamburgers and drank

the coffee as they watched the flickering horror on the old television, a set that Clemmons was certain would soon end up in the store they had just left, perhaps be trucked there as soon as this particular program came to an end.

Jenny had begun to weep. She cried openly and childlike, as if something inside her had been broken beyond repair. She sat on the edge of the bed, a half-eaten sandwich in one hand as the other fisted a paper napkin. From time to time, she would softly strike one thigh. Clemmons put his arm around her and kissed her face, tasted the salt of her tears and gradually her sobbing quieted, submerged beneath this other, more vital, no less important need. He began to make love to her as they sat on the edge of the bed, the gray hearth of the television set limning their gestures.

"Oh, wait," she said, suddenly remembering. "Get a towel." But he was not to be delayed, not for a moment; and even gently pulled her apart like overripe fruit to taste the hot, slick pulp. "My God, Charlie," was all she said and groaned and went slack. The somber commentary on the television became as inarticulate to their hearing as the steady language of the sea.

When he rose above her, ready to enter her, Jenny opened her eyes and lightly laughed. "You look like a fucking Indian," she said. She reached up and traced the blood over his cheeks, his forehead.

"I am a fucking Indian," was all he could think of saying.

"Sweet Charlie," Jenny said and enfolded him. He kissed her eyes where tears had once again begun to appear.

The next morning he told the motel owner, "We had a little accident." The man looked stunned. "My wife's period came on her suddenly and the sheets got blood on them. I want to pay for it."

"It's a terrible time," the man said and turned away.

On the trip back, Jenny tried to find a radio station that played music, but all carried reviews, and reviews of reviews, of the assassination. It was like listening to the slow, gradual countdown of some experiment that would launch them into a different atmosphere. So they listened and rarely spoke the whole time back. When they entered Manhattan, it seemed as deserted as Truro Center had been. Perhaps everyone had left to celebrate Thanksgiving outside the city limits. Another colony lost in the forest. The streets lay empty and the intersections expectant, quiet, and Clemmons felt that if their car stopped at one of them and they waited long enough, they would witness a dreadful incident. He even turned west on 82nd Street, going the wrong way, and drove the whole distance to Fifth Avenue without meeting another car. No police in sight.

When had he grown old? Clemmons looks in the mirror in Olive's bathroom. Had it all happened last night as he slept, or lay awake beside Olive? He would be glad to leave this morning, to get back to Boston Corners and a good night's sleep. But these gray hairs at the side? Perhaps if he cut his hair shorter, they would not show. His whole face looks baggy; the circles under the eyes and the way his nose seems to have become thicker, almost spongy. Nothing could be done.

"It's the mirror," Olive says behind him. "It's a special magnifying glass that makes everything look more so. Now hurry up, because I want to get in here." She shoos him out and closes the bathroom door.

"It was nice to talk to Milly, don't you think?" she speaks through the door. "I want to compliment you for being so easy with her."

"I didn't say much to her," he says. He dresses.

"That's what I mean. If Daisy's in Kansas City, she should be in Boston Corners very soon."

"What is she doing in Kansas City?" He closes up his suitcase, looks around the room.

"Visiting friends."

He had always wondered where Daisy had made all these

friends she seemed to visit perpetually, a far-flung network of hostels franchised by her sociability.

"Milly's young man sounds nice," Olive continues. He hears the toilet flush and then more water running. Then, the shower starts.

Nice and flat. Nice and bored and boring, Clemmons thinks. Like the music they play. "Yo, Pop," this boy's voice rang in his ear. Pop. They had only just returned from the tennis game. "Yo, Pop." Olive had handed him the phone after speaking with Milly, as she had begun to remove her tennis costume. "You guys are just terrific," he heard his daughter say. He knew what she meant. She meant that she had caught them in the bedroom, Olive had made some slightly suggestive allusion to that fact, and Milly thought it was just terrific that the two of them, at their age, were in the same room where certain events might occur. She probably told all her friends, especially this boy who kept saying, "Yo, Pop," in his ear.

"Yes, hello," he said finally. Olive moved about the room naked, moved with the same determined stride with which he had watched her march after tennis balls. Clemmons wondered if he should call Milly's fiancé Stanley or Mr. Livingston or the whole name.

"My real name is Paul," the boy said. "Stanley Livingston is just the name of our group. I took it from an old movie with Spencer Tracy where he plays this guy in Africa who's lost. Hey, man, you got a great lady here. You must have done something right, man." Olive had made an obscene *moue* with her lips, turned into the bathroom and the shower.

"Hey, Pop? Pop?" It was Milly's voice.

"Yes."

"I'm very happy, Pop. I want you to know."

"That's good, Milly. I'm glad."

"And I'm real happy that you're letting us do it in Boston Corners. It means a lot to me."

"Yes. Sure. Fine." He kept saying these same words,

it seemed, and only these same words until he had hung up.

Olive is back in the room, rosy brown from the shower. "Want a quickie before I dress?" she says, but she was already pulling up her panties; he knew that if he said yes, she would have made herself available; though her offer was part of a larger convention, part of the social contract she kept in her head along with the names of all those people she was always introducing him to in splendid doorways.

Even at the airport, she manages to locate a couple of people to whom she introduces him. "I'll see you in a month." She pecks him on the lips. She has always been shy about showing affection in public. What she offered was more like a necessary recognition. Clemmons sometimes wondered what Olive recognized in him beyond his attendance at specific functions—social functions, sexual functions. He was necessary, at certain times, for some of these. There were few occasions in Boston Corners that made him necessary.

A woman takes the seat next to him. He's made wary by the way she says, "Pardon me, please," as she reaches for her seat belt—the emphasis put on *please* as if it had taken great effort to push the word through her unyielding lips and out into the congenial air. No small talk with this one, Clemmons thinks. One false word and the attendant would be summoned. He sees himself—A. W. Clemmons, Country Real Estate—being hustled off the plane in Baltimore. He lets his thoughts ramble over the landscape below.

One evening in Jenny's apartment, he fell asleep while reading on the sofa and awoke with the understanding that he must never see her again. How long after the trip to Provincetown he could not remember, for the homey details of that evening made it no more singular than any of the other times he had been there. It had been cold weather. She had turned on the gas grate set into the marble-faced hearth and its hissing warmth had casually undone him; he let the book slip from his fingers and closed his eyes. It had been a biography of Amelia Earhart, an unusual book for Jenny to have, for her tastes were bracketed by Ayn Rand and Kahlil Gibran, so he supposed Mel Stein had left it. Other strange books had appeared recently.

Then the muted sounds from the street gradually woke him. It had grown dark though it still may have been afternoon. He lay with his eyes closed, feigning sleep, and tried to place her by the hushed sounds of her movements. She had been knitting in the winged chair next to the sofa when he fell asleep but now he put her in the small closet of a kitchen opposite the apartment's entrance. The gas grate gossiped cozily. There was the scrape of metal against a tin can. She talked softly to the cat, a distant relative to the one that she had claimed for fussy roommates years before. The cat mewed and purred. Some water ran; was shut off. The old-fashioned scent of her perfume passed over him as she walked behind the sofa and into the bedroom that overlooked 72nd Street. Who had helped her fit that large bed into that little room? The bedlamp switch was clicked. He heard the doors of the closet fold back and clothes hangers scrape along the metal rod. He imagined her inspecting each garment, holding it up to the light to see if it needed to be pressed.

It was more than eavesdropping. It was as if he had left the apartment and had somehow returned to watch her perform the simple tasks of her private life, those chores she saved up to do when she was alone. She dialed the phone by the bed and spoke in a low voice to her answering service, they had let the phone ring several times earlier, and he heard her repeat names both new and familiar to him. Her voice was different, flat and mechanical. It sounded all business. He felt like a burglar, a thief waiting his chance.

As Clemmons lay there with his eyes closed, his conscience stumbled blindly over a fact that he had not wanted to recognize but that had been there all along, had become unrecognizable because it had been there all along. But with his eyes closed, he was forced to see it as his ears strained to pick up Jenny's movements in the small place.

He intruded upon her life. He had never lied to her and, she said, he had been kind to her, and he could still make her laugh—sometimes intentionally—and for these and other reasons she would always invite him into this small apartment, into her life, but he woke to the thought on this winter afternoon that he no longer had the moral right to accept the invitation. She had talked excitedly about the assignment Mel Stein had given himself and how he had asked her to join him; she had mentioned it several times. Clemmons sensed her earnest interest, that it meant something to her, though he also knew that he could have swept the scheme from her mind, thrown it out with the books by Camus and Simone Weil and the others Stein had brought her. Then what? Her life would continue in this apartment. He would continue to visit her in this apartment, but come as an intruder, someone to take up her time between rehearsals, between the selection of a dress and the filing of fingernails. He would have to leave her; leave her alone. For if he did not, he would become only another of those who would call her when he came to town, another trumpet player, one might say, who had found her special accomplishments recommended on the sheet music that came with the traveling show.

"Ah, Charlie. You're awake." She smiled down upon him. Her head inclined gracefully to one side.

"Yes," he answered.

When he changes planes in Baltimore, Clemmons tries to call Claire Wolferman, but she would not be back until late afternoon, her answering service says. He leaves no messages. He had been watching a man and a woman standing outside the phone booth in the air terminal. The man carries a small briefcase and is conservatively dressed. The woman wears rumpled slacks, a turtleneck blouse, loafers with no socks. Some of her hair has come loose from the pinned coils on the top of her head and her hands are clasped together. They stand very close to each other, though Clemmons sees a great distance between them; the way the woman's eyes stare vacantly at the bank of luggage lockers behind her companion. They do not speak. The man studies her face intently, as if he hopes, expects her to say something, to say it first, yet there is a whippet alertness in his expression that suggests he would look away just as quickly if the woman faced him. He tries Claire's number again from Grand Central station but she is still out.

The rail service was cut back years ago, so no train goes as far as Boston Corners anymore, only to Dover Plains; so he must drive the rest of the way. He had parked his car at a service station. Boxer hangs over the back seat and tries to lick his face during the trip from the kennel to the old farmhouse on the knoll with the red sign out front: A. W. CLEMMONS, COUNTRY REAL ESTATE.

But there's another car already parked in the small bay by the front steps. It is a medium-sized, foreign-made sedan, though it still looks much too large, too much for its driver to handle, for her head barely comes above the steering wheel. There is a wispy magenta scarf tied around a small white head.

"I'm so happy to see you, Andrew," his mother greets him. "I've been sitting here almost three hours."

"Three hours?"

"Don't talk, get me out of here. My joints have froze up and I can't get out and I'm about to wet my pants. Hurry."

Clemmons opens the car door and lifts the old woman out. She is very light and he thinks how curious, as he carries her up the slope of the front lawn, that such delicate hinges could collect such thick impediments. Boxer runs around and around them, then disappears to reestablish his domain. Clemmons walks up the terrace toward his house, carrying his mother in his arms. He can hear the phone ringing.

PART TWO

Chapter One

So now, coming up around the small plateau that hangs above Irondale, that is divided by the county road that goes through the village, A. W. Clemmons puts one foot down neatly in front of the other, arms and elbows working like the driving rods of the old Erie four-wheelers that used to haul the ore out of the local mines, puffing up and around the same grade—the old roadbed is still visible on the left side of the highway—puffing as he neatly places each of his blue-and-cream-striped Korean joggers down in the narrow track of dust between the hard-surfaced highway and the graveled shoulder, putting them down straight and neat as he remembered Choo Choo Justice used to run, because he had made the mistake once of looking back over his shoulder as he ran and had seen the waffled text of his passage printed in the dust like a duck's track. Did he also walk like that, he wondered?

He would attempt to run this route twice a week, a distance of about five miles from his house in Boston Corners to Irondale; but run it only one way, for usually someone would give him a ride home at the end of the day after he had completed his calls and met his appointments, sometimes even making a sale because of his attire, the old gray sweatsuit and wool cap and jogging shoes being enough to swing a client into the buyer category because of the quaint value he would have in some further, oft-told narrative of how this local real estate agent had jogged over to close the deal. But now on this morning, coming up on the Moegler farm at the crest of the hill, he gets winded, is out of condition, because the week's stay with Olive had put him off running for yet another week after he returned, so that the transcendent high that sometimes lofted his pulse and breath at this point in the route did not come and he felt his thigh muscles knot and a sharp pain cut into his lower abdomen like a surgeon going after his appendix without anaesthesia, except it was on the wrong side, and so he negotiates a new finish line and makes it only about fifty yards ahead, a line stretched between a highway marker on the far side of the road and a large oak inside the pasture fence under which some of Moegler's prize Holsteins innocently take the air. He's even more conscious of how his feet meet the ground, to finish the race with grace and style before the approving gaze of the black and white heifers; and then he breaks the imaginary tape. And then he stops.

"Good morning, ladies," he says to the cows.

The cows bunch at the fence, jostle for position to thrust out their great, delicate faces, and their soft nostrils dilate, the ears perk as if to shake the yellow plastic tags that certify their pedigree. They follow him as he begins to walk, follow him like an awkward but timid mass of fans following some celebrity, pushing against the bare wire fence, and putting down their own hooved feet miraculously without entanglement. The bolder ones thrust forward while others seem to hang back, though these same ones look at Clemmons roguishly over their sisters' rumps; but it is the eager question that glows in all their beautiful, dark eyes that makes him pause once more, put his hands on hips, and laugh.

"No, don't look at me that way," he says. "I'm not the

one." He looks away. There is wild columbine in bloom on the shale-set hillside across the road. Olive had tried to transplant many of those plants but they never took in the well-prepared, enriched soil around their house. "I'm not the one," he repeats.

The heifers seem not to believe him. They snuffle and murmur among themselves and stretch out their necks as if to identify him by his smell or as if they were not sure they had heard him right. "You'll get yours from Barney Waldor and his magic straws." He continues his walk.

Though the frozen sperm in the long plastic tubes would be warmed from its hundreds of degrees below zero storage temperature, warmed and then liquified, the process always reminded Clemmons of those old folk tales that described Satan's frigid ejaculate. "You'll never know what it's really like," he tells the cows, though he would not be sure that he had spoken the words aloud, for lately he sometimes caught himself only thinking what he may have spoken; say, an observation prompted by some remark of Claire's, but which had never ventured forth from his mind's seclusion; then her silence would surprise him as he waited for her to speak, to answer him, though she would look at him with eyes much like those that now regarded him from across the wire fence and at that point he would realize that it was the other way around; that she was patiently, almost amusedly waiting for him to speak and what he had thought he had said, he had only thought.

"You'll never know what it's really like," he shouts, to be sure this time, and the cows seem to receive the message amiably as they amble along, apparently resigned to the platonic relationship enforced by the fence if nothing else. Perhaps it's for the best. The hard thrust of the bull's cock was not all that it was cracked up to be. "Ah, excuse me, for that." But if many could do without it, why not all? The old pizzle causes dissension in your ranks, ladies, quarrels where there should be unity, the very maul that splits the heartwood of sisterhood and turns daughter against mother. But who would be jealous of that slim, anonymous plastic tube, who's going to fight over the frozen sperm of some old bull who has long gone to join Ferdinand? Who's going to do that? "Why, warmed up to one-oh-one-point-five, you won't even feel it," and his voice halts the group of heifers, so that the cows bringing up the rear bump and crash into those before them, highbred muzzles sliding up on sleek haunches, complaining as those who are awkward or too slow always complain when they suddenly catch up.

There's something else. Clemmons waves to a ton-and-a-half pickup that has just rattled past him. The loose tools in the back of Benny Smith's truck are sifted by the vehicle's racketing progress, as if the final value of the hammers and chisels and clamps were being assayed during the trip. The pommeled handle of the heavy vise welded to the truck's bed turns back and forth in a half arc like some part of the vehicle's motive power.

"There's something else," Clemmons says aloud. You girls are in the milk business. If you want to be fucked then you're grazing in the wrong pasture. The cows have stopped, struck dumb by his thoughts. You're the third generation of cockless wonders. All desire should be bred out of you by now anyway. Clemmons has started down the other side of the hill, past the small green highway sign with the white letters, IRONDALE. The cows watch him pass on, held back by the boundary of the fenced pasture, a forlorn group suddenly made aware of its limitations while one or two of them, perhaps the duller ones, already turn back toward the tree, though most still watch Clemmons intently, patiently, as if they are waiting for him to return and return to them in some more appropriate form, some form they guess to be carried undeveloped if not unborn within the baggy, stained folds of his gray sweatsuit. Then he does stop and turns around to face them once more. The yellow-tagged ears pitch forward, the scarves of tails pause in coquettish flight. "Ah, but I could tell you stories about your great-grandmothers," Clemmons shouts. "Those were real cows," he shouts, and the animals respond huskily.

He continues toward the village as his breathing resumes its normal measure, and though the picture-postcard prospect of Irondale is prettily laid out from this elevation, Clemmons no longer sees this crossroads complex of post office, general store, church, and old hotel as a clipping that might be carried, transferred from one wallet to the next without explanation; but which, accidentally dropped during some exchange, might prove an extraordinary curiosity to a stranger who came across it lying in the road.

In the same fashion, people who may have taken this county road by mistake, or for adventure, would come across the village of Irondale, the buildings all painted in muted primitive colors (Claire Wolferman had referred to the paint as "recycled Williamsburg"), and they would wonder about its history, be interested in who had painted it this way and why anyone would have wanted to maintain this dilapidated outpost of the old Livingston Manor. The buildings were commonplace, were more like those found in cow towns and mining towns and the poorer farm villages of the South and Midwest, and not at all like the neoclassic façades that could be admired only a few miles across the border in Connecticut and Massachusetts. But here were these homely frame structures put together with a minimum of architectural detail, as if they had been put together from an elementary plan book and were not supposed to last from one century to the next, when at such time a more current plan book with designs just as ordinary would be used to replace them. But they had lasted, and they had been preserved and repainted these peculiar faded colors, so that travelers would delay their passage to take a closer look, to take a turn around the tiny round park set in the middle of the confluence of roads where an enormous common cottonwood grew, unusual for these parts, whose great root system seemed about to suck up the small plot that sustained it, turned past the wine-red post office, the white church, the dark green general store with its numerous outbuildings, barns and sheds, all painted various hues of ochre, russet, and indigo, and then perhaps thinking to stop for a cold drink of something at the store, the travelers would be pulled mysteriously into the parking lot as if their car were running on tracks laid down beneath the road surface, a parking lot shared by the old hotel, a grandiose term given to the two-storied building that had been used as a flophouse for railroad crews and supposedly had been built by one of the Livingston hellions as a place where he could eat raw oysters and entertain doxies, both brought down from Boston on the Salisbury turnpike.

The sign fixed above the door of the old hotel—A. W. CLEMMONS, COUNTRY REAL ESTATE—affected a kind of lettering associated with quaint shops in a London mews, though it somehow did not seem out of place on this square building painted a flat plum color with sky-blue trim and gray shutters. The travelers, now stopped in the parking lot, would look at each other like people awaking from a dream, trying to relocate themselves, how they had gotten there; then, to assume a human decision for the direction their car had taken, they might turn to each other and say something like, "Well, it wouldn't do any harm to look. It wouldn't do any harm to see what they have."

It had been that easy. Clemmons was tired of hearing from Olive or Claire or Rita Pickens, his office manager, how easy it had been for him to save the village of Irondale, to become its new manor lord as it were, and to keep it from the fate that had erased the village of Hammertown from the map. Old man Hicks, Earle's father, had needed quick cash to prolong his Florida vacations, hold the sun a bit longer above him, which was curiously much the same attitude the Livingston family had had when they surrendered the whole domain in the 1840s to the tenants rather than fight the takeover, as the Schuylers and the Van Rensellaers did. The Livingstons gave it all up in order to keep those verandas that looked west over the Hudson, to keep the sun, even a cooling sun, in their faces a bit longer.

Clemmons sometimes wondered if his negotiations for Irondale had not been assisted by a habitude inherent in the land itself, planted there by the Dutch, nurtured by the English, and sustained by the American Livingstons, so that it became like the genes of some species, slightly altered by a historical or environmental fault and then passed generations on down; though in this case it would be like an unwritten restriction or proviso put into the deeds to the land and buildings that demanded all subsequent owners must be distant, *in absentia* in manner if not in actuality. Even Jenny and now Claire would chide him sometimes for his superior attitude, and with the self-awareness these women had given him, he would wonder if the local bankers had advanced him the mortgages to buy the whole village because they thought they recognized him—they, the descendants of those tenant farmers who had seized the property from the Livingstons over a hundred years ago, had seen in his bearing that same pose, a semblance of the original, rightful ownership.

Benny Smith is waiting for him at the post office. The man leans back against the rear fender of his pickup, the long bill of the farm hat almost over his right ear and the large smile on his face going the other way. He looks to Clemmons like some old-time aviator who has miraculously landed his aircraft in the village square, but who has no idea of how he did it or how he will get it off the ground and into the air again. As Clemmons walks across the small park, around the great stile of the cottonwood, Benny's smile gets broader and there is an intense glee in his eyes, as if he has been waiting for him all this time in order to prove to Clemmons that even passing him back on the road, in the truck, he has still somehow beat him here to the post office.

"Hi there, A.W.," Benny says. "I was just thinking I should get up to your place and start that painting. You want the same colors or what?"

"Same colors," Clemmons tells him. "We have only a couple of weeks. How's that friend of yours—the one that got cut, that wouldn't stop bleeding?"

"Oh, he stopped bleeding all right," Benny replies. The man rolls up some advertising circulars that were in his morning mail and blows through the paper tube as if it were a pipe. "But old Clinton Hoyt got tricked."

"What happened to old Clint?" Clemmons thought he knew who Clint Hoyt might be.

"He went over to Copake one day and some kids there dared him to put this firecracker—it was an inch-and-a-half salute—they dared him to put it in his pocket and light it, and he did." Benny suddenly stops and pops his eyes. He folds up the circular and puts it in his back pocket.

"Well, what happened?"

"Oh, it blew his whole pocket right off his pants." Benny snorts. "Blew it clean off his pants."

"Was he hurt?"

"Naw, he wasn't hurt, but it sure tricked him good."

"I guess so," Clemmons agrees.

"You been running, huh," Benny says, and opens the door of his truck. "Me, I like to drive. See you later, A.W." The engine turns over, starts, and he pulls the truck into a U turn around the cottonwood and then, as if to prove his statement, he accelerates and takes the corner by the hotel almost on two wheels. The heavy tools shift perilously to one side of the flatbed like loose cargo in the hold of a foundering freighter.

Ernest Miller turns from the small black-and-white television propped up on a postal regulations manual that rests on the post office safe, turns only his head and not his body, for he has no intention of missing the answers on a morning quiz show even though this particular customer might be the owner of the building the government rents for this U.S.

Post Office, third class, Irondale, NY, 13582, because being civil service, Ernest Miller knows that he could be postmaster of Irondale out of the trunk of his Vega if he had to be, so A. W. Clemmons gets the same treatment any other citizen gets—it makes no difference to him.

"She's picked it up already," he tells Clemmons and then goes back to his program. "Think of that," he exclaims. Some answer has surprised him.

"Any problems?" Clemmons asks. "Is the new septic tank okay?" The postmaster nods. "Any interesting Wanteds?" Clemmons has picked up the collection of FBI flyers hooked together and hanging above a small table routed and grooved for inkwells and pens. There are cardboard coin boxes for the heart fund and muscular dystrophy, and the hand-lettered advertisement for a bake sale at the church that had taken place a month before.

"Here's a good one," Clemmons says. "Wanted for mail fraud. A postmaster."

Ernest Miller laughs. "Wish him luck."

Outside, Clemmons must wait for a large milk tanker to go by before he can cross the road to the store. The trailer rig makes only a slight pause at the intersection where a full STOP is required, and Clemmons thinks there is an insolent hiss to the truck's airbrakes, as if in the brief hiatus it sized up the town's insignificance and then passed on through. He would buy the aspirin for his mother now, because he would surely forget to do so if he went first to the office where Rita Pickens waited with her legal-sized yellow-page pad of memoranda, notes, and suggestions she had kept for him since only yesterday. He looked up at the second-floor windows of the old hotel, half expecting to catch her watching him, perhaps timing his perambulations.

On the other hand, he wasn't sure the store would even have aspirin. It carried so few items these days; most of the bins and shelves and counters built to offer complete lines of hardware and fancy groceries were empty, like bare choir lofts, all the way up to the stamped tin ceiling, unreachable even if stocked with goods because the mechanical arm that had been invented to extend a man's reach twelve feet to neatly pick up and pass down a jar of Crosse & Blackwell's pickled walnuts had broken long ago. There had been no need for it anyway. Clemmons sometimes wondered who bought all the lighter fluid and for what purpose. And the pet foods—several flavors for both dogs and cats were ranked in three shelves above the lighter fluid; that also interested him, for he had always thought house animals in rural areas were fed from an endless and natural supply of farm scraps, but it gave him, he felt, a special insight into his neighbors' lives to imagine these contemporary stadtholders opening tin cans to feed their cats, the same as in any city kitchen. But the staples that paid the store's rent were bread, milk, cold cuts, and beer. Naturally, there were cigarettes to go with some of the lighter fluid.

There are yet a few old-timers around who can remember and tell about the fine teas and coffee beans, the great wheels of cheeses sweating on marble counters, and the bins of spices that still smelled of the sea that had borne them from their foreign climes, and there was yet a residue of these aromas inside the place, just as you first stepped inside the door as Clemmons does now, and before the basic odor of damp cardboard boxes takes over these delicate memories. It somehow heightens the disappointment with the place, a cruel flick upon a nostalgia that reaches something it had never known, that perhaps had never even existed. Clemmons felt it whenever he entered the store, so he knew those travelers who were passing through must have felt even more cheated when they stepped into the store expecting to find gingham and ginger snaps, and finding only garlic loaf and Genesee beer.

True, there had been several opportunities to rent the place to young couples, all from the city, who proposed to invest the store with those effects and kinds of merchandise, prefabricated these days, but which the oaken cubbies and shelves had been built for, seemed now to call for in an empty referendum, but Clemmons knew they would have not lasted long. From the beginning, the week after he had had Benny Smith and his relatives paint the whole town in one day, he had rented the store to the Springer family, who began to turn a profit immediately by selling lighter fluid, milk, and beer; for though none of them could appreciate the ingenious mechanism that could precisely lift down something from the ceiling, they innately understood what the community required, the entire inventory within easy reach.

So, though he always felt this sense of betrayal and knew tourists might feel even more, Clemmons would think that their disappointment came not with the store they entered but with the time they could not, and there was nothing he could do about that.

He is the only person in the store. Radio music plays somewhere in the back. The cooler packed with soda and beer on the right purrs, and the fluorescent light within the small meat case casts a shadowless illumination around the hunched rolls of salami and boiled ham. He walks to the center of the premises, even looks behind the counter to see if someone might be there, rearranging something on the lower shelves, and then this tow-headed girl comes from behind the curtain tacked across the rear alcove. She moves behind the counter quickly, almost with a stealth seconded by an anxious expression, as if he were some stranger there to do her harm rather than the landlord who had only come in to replenish his mother's supply of aspirin.

"I do for you?" Her voice is flat and lacking in any expectations, as if she had never in her life heard anything more than the basic signals and requests, and, looking closer, Clemmons realizes she is not as young as he first thought. She has self-consciously smoothed down the material of a blue apron worn tight over blouse and jeans, and he sees that her hands are fully shaped, already reddened by laundry and dishwater, the longish nails cracked and painted a reddish brown.

"Aspirin." She moves behind the large, old-fashioned cash register, the one attribute from the store's earlier era still in service, almost to put it between them, and regards him steadily. Her eyes are the color of tortoise-shell combs. "Aspirin?"

"I'll see," she says, and turns her back on him to walk to the end of the counter and reach up to a shelf next to the lighter fluid section. It is only the third shelf up, but she must go on tiptoe and reach high to feel blindly along the wooden ledge. The whole exercise compacts the lines of her figure, almost hardens the womanly body within the clothing, Clemmons thinks, so that it looks sculpted out of something more than flesh.

In contrast, her face is laid down in horizontal, soft lines, puffy around the strangely colored eyes and the wide mouth; even the nose seems to have been pulled between the two high-placed dashes of her cheekbones, to give her a somnolent expression, still warm from bed and had only wakened, or had overslept, or had been just punished for either. She hands Clemmons a small, flat tin of aspirin, one that contains twelve tablets.

"I'll need more than that," he says and makes a quick calculation. "Do you have about six more of these?"

She shrugs and looks furtively to one side but goes back to the shelf, this time with a small footladder so that she can climb up easily to the level of the shelf without stretching. So, Clemmons thinks, she must have felt his eyes upon her, perhaps even thinks he's buying more aspirin only to get another look. "There's ten more," she says.

"I'll take them all," Clemmons says quickly to prove his sincerity, then changes his mind. "Maybe not all. Maybe someone else might need some," he adds, thinking that his one purchase could wipe out the entire aspirin supply of Irondale and no telling when it would be replenished, if at all. He imagined people staggering under the oppression of splitting headaches, unable to get across the mountain to the Rexall drugstore in Green River because of the blinding pain, then tumbling back into the hollow like the heaps of machinery Jack Marshall junked by the roadside.

"Well, how many then?" she asks, still standing on the small ladder, able to look over his head to some point at the rear of the store, a sullen recognition in her eyes; men were always putting her up on ladders on some excuse, and keeping her up there while they decided what they wanted of her.

"I'll just take the six I originally asked for," Clemmons replies, releasing her; though a certain self-righteous tone got into his voice when he said *originally,* as if to imply his original instincts had been correct until she had stretched up that way.

"I know you, don't I?" she says. She begins to ring up each of the aspirin tins on the antique cash register. She jabs the tabulator keys with the reddish-brown tipped fingers, and her eyes are focused so intently, so close to the panel that Clemmons thinks they might cross.

"Do you?"

"You're the owner. Mr. Clemmons. You wouldn't remember me. That time you had that class at the community college on real estate selling, I took it." She pulls the cash register lever. "I had darker hair then." She fluffs the straight tungsten-colored hair with one hand as she reaches out for his money with the other. "Leroy likes me to fix it this way and it don't take much."

"Who are you?" Clemmons gives her a bill.

"I married Leroy Springer, but I was a Turner before that." Clemmons remembers the youngest Springer, of the same family that has leased the store, had married a girl from Gallatin. Her eyes have become crafty, slitted, as she carefully counts out his change. "Want a bag for these? I been working here a few days only."

"What's your name?"

"My name is Betty." She looks at him directly now, as if

she were no longer afraid of him though she still squints slightly; but Clemmons guesses she had never been afraid of him, or perhaps of anyone.

"People call me A.W."

"Do you have a few minutes?" she's asking him, as she unties and then reties the blue denim apron around her middle. "Dad Springer was talking the other night about butchering deer for hunters this fall and maybe hanging other meats, but that the cooler needed fixing and he was going to ask you about it."

"What needs to be fixed?" Clemmons asks, already turning to follow her. He might lose sight of her and never be able to find her among the piles of six-packs and bags of potato chips.

They pass the curtained alcove behind which the radio plays softly, and he thinks he smells fresh tobacco smoke. Then they turn right, down a short flight of steps, and come to the cooler. It's a large walk-in with a heavy door on immense brass hinges, a cool repository—so the legend goes—of some of the best steaks and loins ever carved in the Harlem Valley, but now dank and empty, brushing them both with a musty, almost tropical warmth as she pulls back on the door.

"It needs all new wiring," she starts to speak immediately, the mechanical register in her voice indicating she's repeating a list she's heard. "And this floor has got to come up and all new planking laid down, the kind that lets water flow through, like latticework, and the compressor might have to be replaced entirely if parts can't be found for this one, it's so old, and then these hooks up here—for hanging the meats onto them—they's something about them not being right for the new health rules, though it seems to me hooks are just hooks." And as if to demonstrate the efficacy of the old equipment, she reaches up and grips one of the large metal hooks in both hands and bends her knees so her feet are off the floor.

In the warm semi-darkness of the old meat refrigerator,

Clemmons is suddenly chilled; he feels the sweat turn to icy rivulets on his flesh underneath the warm-up suit, where he is completely naked, he remembers, save for the jock strap that makes him feel even more naked as it becomes tight and heavy—as if by stepping into this old abbatoir, the two of them had stepped out of time, disappeared from Irondale unnoticed and only for a moment, and into this dark closet where once meat had been routinely prepared, casually handled.

"It's something to think about," Clemmons says and steps outside. He breathes deeply of the old, waxed-over odors in the store. "Tell Springer I'll think about it. I've got a daughter who's getting married soon," he says.

"Is that a fact?" she replies, now following him back toward the front of the store. "How old is she?"

"She's about twenty-five, but what I mean is, is that I have a lot on my mind and I may not be able to get around to it soon."

"We'll be here," the woman says. "Twenty-five? I'm twenty-three. Do you have your aspirin?" she asks by way of parting, for Clemmons has opened the front door and stepped through.

He pauses for a moment and looks back between the various commercial posters plastered to the front door windows. She has turned, and walks back toward the curtained alcove, untying and then retying the apron around her slender waist.

"There are some of us who wonder if you really are in the real estate business or whether this is some sort of a CIA front." The voice seems to come from nowhere, to fall from the sky; but unlike the rain, it has not been softened by the conversion, though its hard mineral composition contains elements of humor.

"Good morning, Rita," Clemmons says. He has walked to the edge of the store porch and looks up at the hotel's second floor. "I'm sorry, I'm late."

"I suppose it would be possible to conduct your business

this way," the voice speaks through the screen of an open window, "but I would get a permanent crick in my back, and all of Irondale—that is all two or three of them—would know just how shady a dealer you are."

Clemmons believed that Rita Pickens hated him, even from the first day he hired her, and oddly that was why he had hired her. He climbs the steps to the second floor offices—they never had been able to rent the first floor of the hotel—climbs with all the mock solemnity of a man mounting the scaffold. How felicitous this same ascent must have been for that Livingston rake—a belle on either arm, a bellyful of oysters—and to what glories he rose; but how worn the steps were, the treads dished by decades of humdrum tripping toward assignments as commonplace as what awaited him at the top of the stairs.

He is given a temporary reprieve because Rita was talking on the phone when he enters the office, the instrument cradled between her long jaw and shoulder to free both hands to strike a match and hold it to a cigarette already stuck in one corner of her mouth, saying, "But of course," and then coughing as she lights the cigarette, saying *But-of-course* in a wise, knowing manner, the edge of the words slightly rasped, to imply that she had known the information all along. She would say it to him, *But-of-course,* as if what he had just reported, something that had only just happened—say, the decision to extend a town road, which would, in turn, affect the property value and this information only just phoned him by the town clerk, a favor for a favor, and Rita Pickens would exclaim, "But of course," as if it were old news, published on page one of last week's edition of the *Green River News*.

On his soft-treaded jogging shoes, he eases into his own office, wondering who it is she talks to, who it is who calls her; is it one or several different people that call so that she can give these enigmatic one-liners as she lights cigarettes like some woman reporter in an old movie? Sometimes she would never say anything, but only start to laugh after answering the phone, laugh and choke on cigarette smoke, and then continue laughing as if the caller had immediately begun the conversation in some ludicrous dialect and continued to tell one joke after another, never giving her a chance to speak, like those phone services where you can dial a number and have the recorded voice of some comedian entertain you. Perhaps, Clemmons thought, Rita had made some arrangement whereby she would be called by this service. Once he asked her who had just called her, who had just sent her into a fit of choking laughter that had left her panting and breathless over the calendar blotter on her large antique desk.

"If it is the policy of this firm that the employees cannot receive a few personal calls, then I'll arrange to take them at the pay phone on the porch of the general store," she replied, moving the pencil from behind her right ear and inserting it behind the left one.

"Sugar, you do it to yourself," Olive once answered his complaints about Rita Pickens. "You always want to lie down with the she-wolf, offer your hand to the rattler. Don't you know there's a thing called 'natural enemies' that you should stay away from? You always try to change them, like a missionary, or something." She had caught his amused expression. "Even me, honey. Look out —I bite."

In the middle of the mail, most of it disposable junk, is a card from Daisy, mailed two weeks before from Richmond, Indiana. "Fantastic," she had scrawled across the back of the advertisement for a motel whose parking lot, at least in the picture, was barren of cars, which made Clemmons wonder how successful it might be unless it catered only to hitchhikers, such as Daisy, who came on foot or were dropped off by motorists who had made arrangements elsewhere. But Indiana—he looks at a map on the wall; she might arrive at any moment.

"Well, how are things down at Tara?" Rita asks from the doorway. "Is Miss Scarlet tearing up the pea patch?"

"You've left me all the junk mail," he says. "How come you get all the good stuff to read?"

"For the simple fact," she replies, "that someone has to keep a semblance of business going while the elite meet to eat."

"So, what's new this morning?" he says, sitting back and submitting to her review of his business. She sits across from him, lights a cigarette, and looks down at the large yellow pad of paper. "What about unit seven at Dutch Village?"

"We have a buyer. I read and proofed all the contracts last night, if you wonder why my eyes are red. Also, it's possible the Donaldsons are selling out. The barn's not much, but the house has possibilities and there's a hundred and eighty acres."

"All along the state road."

"But of course."

"I'll go by later and see what's up." He makes a note on a small pad of paper.

"I hope you'll change your clothes first. I don't think it would mean much to the Donaldsons to do business with Roger Bannister." Her smile is a valiant attempt but it does not transform her plain unattractiveness, and perhaps had only meant to draw approval for the attempt, for the courage in that attempt. Clemmons knew there would be pictures of her, still kept somewhere, school pictures or at camp, showing her pudgy, hearty self crouched in the front row, on the end, that same smile thrust toward the camera to prove to someone that she was having a good time, was part of the group—at least when the shutter clicked. If she had only been ugly, Clemmons often thought, it would have given her some distinction.

"The plat description for the subdivision on Kruger Lane is ready for the planning board. . . ." she has continued. Clemmons only half listens for he trusts her efficiency, her expertise. In any event, his business is set up so that it only need be managed by someone like Rita Pickens, with a few things now and then for him to personally attend to; and these would often be identified for him, without her knowing it, by the use of the word "tiresome." He would listen for it, knowing that when she used it in respect to some personality or some transaction, this would be someone or something that he personally would have to take care of. She has just used it now. It reminded him of Milly and Daisy when they were young girls talking of boys or of school classes and they would use the same word, this boy was "tiresome" or history was "tiresome," and it always meant that they were unable to answer the challenge posed, and so would label it "tiresome" and pack it off to a category of boring subjects, unworthy of their consideration. It was difficult to imagine Rita Pickens's girlhood, if she had had one; maybe she had emerged fully formed, tubular and sarcastic.

"Just a minute," he interrupts her review. "Sam Broome is tiresome? He seems rather interesting to me. What did he want?"

"Oh, the big Hollywood producer—thanks to his wife's money." The large, almost aristocratic nose wrinkles.

"Well, what did he want?"

"Oh, something about needing to change the usage permit for the old fight site. It seems he wants to produce a rock concert now as well as make a movie."

Clemmons adds another line to his notepad. He carefully draws a large question mark on the paper. Then he leans back and puts his feet on the desk. Rita has returned to her list, a long list and padded, he knows, with incidental if not insignificant decisions she has made in his absence; but the longer the list, the more the attention and, possibly, the more the approval. Clemmons would know that too.

Olive had always accused him of hiring Rita because he felt sorry for her, because she was unattractive and because the bookstore she tried to run in Green River had gone broke, and that he felt responsible, having sold her the small house she lived in as well as renting her the space for the bookstore. And it *was* because of how she looked—not because he was sorry for her, but a little afraid of her as he was always uneasy around unattractive women, not knowing how to respond to them—that he asked her to join him in the real estate office, as if to force himself to polish this awkward part of his nature. Then, also, he had sensed that one more failure in her dossier, such as the bookstore, would be the reference that would at last expose the forgery in her smile, show the surprising frailty within that dowdy sturdiness. It would have been too much, and, anyway, he was in a position to give her a little success. Moreover, he needed someone.

"Well, which is it?" Claire asked him. She had been watering the plants in her studio greenery, holding the long spout of the can high above her head so that water spilled along her upraised arm into the vale of armpit and down along the sleek velvet of her side. Her flesh pebbled and the large nipples had thickened. "You're a phony bastard, you know that. All this humanitarianism is nothing more than the voice of a feudal prince talking. You really are a manor lord. You don't want this woman to leave because she's now a part of your domain. Olive was smart to get out when she could."

"There's no one answer to things," he remembered saying. "You always want one answer to everything." She had turned and come to where he lay on the couch and dumped the rest of the water onto his groin, and this memory makes his position, feet propped up on the desk, uncomfortable, just as the phone rings to interrupt his reverie and Rita's itinerary, and to dissemble his change of position to answer it—all in one.

"Where are the day lilies?" the voice says in his ear.

"The what?"

"The day lilies," his mother repeats. She sounds like a young woman to him. "I planted all those day lilies around the wall in the back terrace, and I can't find a one."

"It's too early for them, isn't it?" He remembers the day lilies and that she had planted them almost twenty years ago. Boxer had dug a lot of them up in fits of hunger, but most had come to their natural end. "I have your aspirin," he says hopefully.

"Oh, I'll surely need it," she replies. "I've been on my knees all morning. You've let this place go to hell, Andrew," and she hangs up, not angrily but with nothing more to say.

"And that reminds me," Rita says. "I'd like to have a little party for the bride and her consort. It won't be as elegant as the others do's I'm sure, but I would like to know a good date."

"You shouldn't . . . don't do anything fancy," he tells her.

"I can assure you it won't be fancy," she says, straightening up and presenting the high, smooth plateau of her bosom. Clemmons always imagined that there would be no separation there, that there would be not two breasts but one large mammilla that grew across the whole width of her chest. "I don't wish to present a conflict."

"Check with Olive when she gets here. She's running the wedding. I won't be here."

"I see," Pickens says, receiving the information with studied gravity. Then she abruptly looks at her watch, for there are footsteps on the stairs. "They're here early. Last on my list. Movie people. Want to use the square for a location. Television commercial."

She rises quickly and walks to the outer office to meet them. He hears her talk with an easy, hard familiarity, and the rapport which Rita obviously strikes with these people, though perhaps only having talked with one of them by phone, reminds him of her real value to him, why he would have hired her if for no other reason—and he would tell himself that he had sensed this quality all along, this abrupt, abrasive manner of hers, so wearing and negative to a long-term relationship, which was ideal for the short, quick intimacy of a real estate transaction and which, in its semblance to wit and sophistication, attracted prospective clients, particularly those from the city who were put at ease by her manner, as if they were on familiar ground in this rural back area where they hoped to escape the very same tone of voice they welcomed in Rita Pickens.

"As you can see"—she has been guiding them toward his office—"Mr. Clemmons has just run the perimeter of his land holdings. Not quite all of it goes back to Queen Anne." There is much laughter and exclamations, handshaking, and Clemmons is standing, nodding, and shaking hands. "How about some coffee? Cream? We have the real stuff up here." Rita has become the efficient executive secretary, the good office help, willing to play at a camaraderie even at the cost of her role as an independent woman.

"It's just ideal," the second man says to Clemmons in the square later. They had already settled the terms upstairs.

"What's this ad for again?"

"Pickles." A brand name is mentioned. "That's why it's perfect. You can smell the pickle barrels from out here. We'll do the interior shots at the studio in the city."

"Isn't this a sensational place?" the woman says as she joins them.

"Fabulous. Truly fabulous," her colleague agrees. "What was the history of this place?"

"It was a community built because of the ore mines. The Livingston family owned it all, a grant given them by the Continental Congress—"

"This is some place," the man with the camera interrupts.

"Fabulous, truly fabulous. How's it look?"

"It's going to be perfect." Polaroid pictures, test shots, are passed around. "What's the history of this place?" the cameraman asks.

"He was saying they had mines here since the Revolution and it was all owned by one family."

"How long have you owned it?" the woman asks brightly. Clemmons judges her to be in her early thirties.

"About ten years. You're the director?"

The woman nods. She wears large gold loops in her ears and her dark hair is fluffed out full around her face.

"This is for me," the cameraman says. "I'm going to get out of the city one of these days and find a place like this." His companions snicker.

A large John Deere tractor pulls through the intersection, the man on the seat looking back over his shoulder at the large manure spreader he pulls. A trail of manure is left on the highway. Clemmons returns the man's wave.

"Yuck." The woman makes a face. "I've just given up milk." Her two companions laugh. Clemmons turns away and looks toward the curve of the road that comes from behind the post office and enters the small junction. He thinks that Daisy might trudge around that curve at any moment; that if he stares at it intently enough, perhaps the force of his gaze might ignite her presence there on the road, her long blond hair spread wide around her face, and the sleepy, dark brown eyes that are her mother's slyly recognizing him. She would raise both arms to wave, one arm would not be enough for Daisy.

It would surprise his old friends to see him turning in the center of this tiny hamlet, prickly skinned within an old pair of warm-ups, turning momentarily away from these film makers who, on their drive back to the city, would talk about how aloof he had been, how out of touch with reality this yokel had been, though in that very moment he had touched something close and painful enough to satisfy anyone's description of reality.

The pain made him stagger slightly and he moved away from the group to get a better view down the road, perhaps to catch a glimpse of a light-crowned head in the distance, like the glint of something moving on a far shore; and then to ease this disquieting probe within his mind, his body—he could not tell which—Clemmons grabs at the pod supported in his crotch and fiercely scratches as one might make one-two-three taps on the diaphragm to relieve some gastric discomfort, though it does not help. There is no remedy for what hurts him now—certainly nothing acquired in neat tins—but in any event, he continues to scratch, almost thoughtfully and unaware of the raised eyebrows and the shaped, silent exclamations on the lips of the three people nearby.

Moreover, he almost asks them to give him a ride home, so as to deliver the aspirin to his mother, and also to take a shower and dust himself with antiseptic powder, to relieve this itch, but he lets them go, not wanting to share any more of himself with them, not wanting to become part of their fiction, a tidbit broken over a drink at some bar that evening, perhaps a bar around Rockefeller Center, a bar he once knew and where, even now, if he were to walk into, the bartender might recognize him but not quite make the name. So he waves them good-bye but remains in the center of the square, without a ride and too tired now to walk not to mention run back to Boston Corners; somehow suddenly a vagrant in his own village, marooned somehow in a familiar place and with no way to get out of it.

He hears the phone ring in his office, and he hears Rita answer, laugh, and then say something. He faces the front of the old store and its large dark windows veneered with cigarette placards, illuminated by beer signs, almost completely shuttered by announcements for church bazaars. The post office is behind him, and within it Ernest Miller continues to watch the old flickering television like some full-size sculpture, one of those contemporary pieces that pretend to illuminate life by reproducing an exact replica of it. He knows this place to be his: A. W. Clemmons, sole proprietor and owner. But he also feels like a stranger who has only just come into the small square, to lean now against the ribbed bark of the cottonwood, already warmed by the late morning sun, a stranger who had some little knowledge about the hamlet, who knew for example that once it all belonged to someone named A. W. Clemmons, and that it would yet abide for a while though the man had become a memory.

It is like double vision, he thinks, with all of its advantages and discomforts; and he looks around him, at the three roads that come like spokes into the hub where he stands, hoping to see Daisy on one, Claire on another, or perhaps coming along together with Olive on the same road, and then Jenny and all the other women he has known. Even Milly, that girl who has hurt him with her likeness to him; he would keep the last road open for her, the one from Green River, from the south. But it is a small, compact car of foreign make that comes down this road, that makes one slow revolution around the tree where he stands, and then stops.

"Hi-ya, squire." Sam Broome seems too large for the small car's compartment. "I've been hoping to talk to you. We got a problem."

Chapter Two

The itch was worse. The hot shower has spread the prickly flush over his scrotum and around the base of his penis. Clemmons takes a fresh towel and with almost a perverse pleasure rubs the affected parts, which only speeds the irritation; he can almost see the rash advance as he feels its heat cover his flesh like a warm breath to stimulate his cock. He douses the area with antiseptic powder, instantly aging the pubic hairs, and puts on clean undershorts.

As he continues to dress, he can hear Sam Broome's voice rise and fall in the kitchen downstairs like a prayer chant of some sort, speaking to Julia Clemmons as she busies about the cabinets to bring cake and teacups to the table. She probably has not yet removed her gardening gloves, Clemmons thinks, her haste to serve Broome suggesting his importance, as if he were her son's most honored friend rather than only someone who had a bit of business to transact. Julia Clemmons always overdid these social amenities, always brought a person another cup of coffee when one really didn't wish another cup of coffee, though Broome would not recognize the real nature of this concern, even as a creature of sham himself, but would ascribe the old woman's behavior to some elemental female instinct to serve the male.

This was not the case. It was to control even this brief exchange. She would set the table for it, in a ladylike manner to define the limitations of this one meeting and order its events. On the bureau in the guestroom across from his bedroom, Clemmons has checked and seen the familiar pictures she carries with her everywhere. One is a framed engraving of the Brownings she had clipped from an old *Harper's Weekly*—as a young girl she often said—and carried with her since. This staid and formal portrait of poets at ease was another kind of definition—laid down for her in Vincennes, Indiana, as surely as the engraver had limned the strands in Robert Browning's beard.

Clemmons used to study this engraving for hours as a boy, knowing it was important though not suspecting its iconical nature, even thinking it was a picture of his parents for a time; however, that illusion waned for he could not match up the frail, dry-voiced Herb Clemmons with the imperial presence that stood behind the overstuffed chair, loomed over the poetess like a supervisor over a balky clerk, though the glint in Elizabeth Barrett's eye—if it were not a slip of the engraver's stylus—indicated that textual exegesis was quite unnecessary, thank you very much.

On the other hand, Julia Clemmons did resemble Elizabeth Barrett, in gesture more than physical detail: the patient turn of the head and the placement of one finger in the pages of the book the two poets had been reading (as much to mark their place as to point to the civility of their evening, their life). *Sonnets from the Portuguese,* of course. Clemmons knew the picture by heart, had identified the jasmine and laurel that seemed ready to overgrow the poets, and had become less frightened of them as he grew older though he still had dreams of giant begonias and slithering lilies, even after his father had left them, had driven off and out of the picture, one might say, in the high-walled Packard that was a backdrop in the other picture on the bureau.

In this photograph, a young Julia Clemmons perches on the running board of the car, knees together, staring into the camera. She leans, almost tips forward, into the camera, as if Herb had just nudged her off as he slipped into the half-open door on the driver's side and behind the wheel to drive off—just after the shutter clicked.

These two pictures would always establish Julia Clemmons's residency, whether in motel room or freighter cabin —or any of the other stops along the route of her restless vagrancy—put down like the flags of some old Arctic explorer and now put down in the room across the hall, to chill Clemmons a little because they signaled her nearness and sounded an old relationship of mother and son that he could no longer play—or no longer wished to play and certainly would feel awkward playing—as if she had brought with her a pair of his old corduroy knickers and told him to try them on.

"Hey, she's a little sweetheart. A little pearl," Sam Broome exclaims as Clemmons joins them in the kitchen. The producer is wearing more beads than usual this morning and when he hugs Julia Clemmons to his breast, she almost becomes entangled in a scrim of beans and shells, but she seems amused. She still wears her garden gloves.

"You didn't tell me you got this little sweetheart for a mom," Broome continues.

"Why don't you give her a contract?" Clemmons says.

"Listen to that, will ya?" Broome releases the old lady. "And here you are keeping all these secrets from me." Broome seems to pursue Clemmons though the latter only moves to the breakfast table. "You never told me—in all the times we talked about the Sullivan-Morrisey fight, in all the dealings for renting the field down there for the film—that your old man wrote a book on the fight. That your old man was Herbert Clemmons."

A. W. Clemmons looks down along the kitchen floor and up at his mother who is busying herself with some cut flowers at the sink. The expression on her small, puggish face is as if she has lost her hearing—suddenly. "You've heard of Herbert Clemmons?" he asked.

"Who hasn't?" Broome explodes.

"Nobody has," A. W. replies.

"John Vandercook thought very highly of your father's book, Andrew," his mother says, her hearing miraculously restored.

"Is that right? Think of that," Broome says, slapping his thigh. Clemmons would have bet his last dollar the man had never heard of John Vandercook either. "Have you got a copy of it? Could we put an option on it? You have the rights?"

"I have the rights," Julia Clemmons says. Her voice has become motherly, and she even brings another slab of dark chocolate cake to the table. She gives it to Broome. "You really should look at it if you're going to make a movie about the fight. My husband was very thorough."

"Listen," Clemmons begins, then stands up to rearrange the material at the front of his pants. Then he resumes his seat.

"What's the matter with you? Are you nervous about something?" Broome asks. "Hey, terrific cake. Did you make this?" Julia Clemmons laughs at the question.

"I got some kind of a jock itch," Clemmons says. "Prickly heat." He notes his mother's gloved hands rise to her chest, press lightly, a slight defense against the "man" talk, the male afflictions. She leaves them, taking up her trowel from the counter on her way out.

"So, let's get back to this rock concert," Clemmons continues. "How did you know about my daughter marrying this guy?"

"Stanley Livingston? Your partner down at the store told me. That Rita Pickens is something else."

"How do you know they can do a concert, want to do a concert? It's supposed to be a wedding. And twenty thousand people? You think you can get twenty thousand people here?"

"Sure, twenty thousand. I've already talked to their manager." Broome sucks cake icing from several fingers. "But your local politicos say I only have a permit to shoot a movie down there, not run a rock concert. It's just a matter of definition. I thought you could make a few phone calls. You know the buttons."

"Twenty thousand! It's short notice, isn't it? To promote the thing, sell tickets?"

"With their name? They're high on the charts. Got a big record right now. No problem."

"What happened to the movie?" Clemmons sips coffee and looks down at the field across the road. He would have to get Benny Smith's cousin over to mow it before the wedding. The light in Broome's eyes had taken a frantic cast.

"Oh, the movie is still on," Broome replies. "But this could generate a lot of interest in the movie—think of it"—his voice gains energy. "A rock wedding—we could film it! The same location as the old fight. Hey, it could be a feature. Fantastic!" Broome has stood to accommodate his excitement.

"I don't know if I have the sort of pull you need," Clemmons says. "I'm really not all that important. But—well, I'll see what I can do." He stands, being more comfortable on his feet.

"You ought to see somebody about that." Broome gestures toward where Clemmons has just scratched. "That's one part you have to keep working, you know? Hey, how about your dad's book? You going to loan it to me?"

Broome follows him on his heels through the house, even to lean over his shoulders at the bookcase in the library, and almost takes the book from A.W.'s hands before it can be offered. *"The Champion of Boston Corners,"* the producer reads the cover. "Well, that title's got to go—we can do better than that."

"He put in a love story."

"While this big fight is going on in the background, right? I get it." Broome had begun to look around the room, pick up and inspect books, pictures, different articles, as if he were sorting through a batch of goods prior to an auction. Then he leaves without saying good-bye to Julia Clemmons, though A.W. points her out as she crouches in a bed of iris in the side yard. The old lady continues to dig, resembling, even in green slacks and one of her son's red sweatshirts, an animal that had prematurely risen from its winter hibernation and is trying to get back underground.

"These iris should have been divided up years ago," she says, knowing A.W. has come to stand behind her. "They get choked up and get stunted, stop blooming. That will be nice if your father's book is made into a film."

"No movie will be made," Clemmons says. His mother continues to ply her trowel, as if she had not heard him.

"He worked very hard on that book, I remember."

"How do you remember? He wrote it here, alone. We were living—where were we living, then? In Ohio. In Akron, Ohio, we were still there." Down in the field across the road, wild sorrel and anemone were already in bloom, fresh white and yellow eyelets stitched into the season's worn cloth.

"He wrote me about his job on the Berkshire *Eagle*," Julia Clemmons continues, the rhythm of her cultivation unbroken. "How he had found out about this old prize fight and said it was the idea he had been looking for."

"I found him here, by accident, wrote to him when I was in New York—just before he died. He sent me a copy of the book."

"No, I gave you the book," she says.

"No, no . . ." His mother had a way of appropriating the past, of rewriting it.

"Now you listen to me," Julia Clemmons says, almost scrambling to her feet. She waves the muddy trowel under his face. "You don't know anything about taking care of this place. Here, carry these iris. We'll have to transplant them. Come on. Pick them up," she commands and strides off toward the field.

"Wait," Clemmons says, but grasps the bulky package of damp plants, holds them away from his clean clothes. He follows her.

"Here," she says and falls to earth, to dig and dig. "They'll make a nice border for the ceremony."

"But—" Clemmons begins to say the field is too large, the plants too few.

"There's lots more we can move," she says, guessing his thought. Clemmons sees himself trailing behind her the rest of the day to offer dripping clumps of vegetation.

"I have a couple of appointments this afternoon," he says.

"It won't take long to move them," she replies. It would take a week, he thinks. "We can make a nice bed around the sign here," she says with a sprightly pride. It is the state historical marker designating the field as the site of the Sullivan-Morrisey contest. It gives the wrong date for the fight, and Clemmons had given up trying to get the authorities to correct it.

"I really can't help you too much, Mother."

"That's all right," Julia replies airily. "It won't take long."

The field almost simmers with the first growth of spring. A quiet expectancy prepares the meadow for the great rush that boils just beneath the surface, and Clemmons falls into a familiar reverie often visited during the lull of long summer evenings: the peace that now fills this old arena where two men had stood toe to toe for thirty-seven rounds as thousands of screaming, brawling spectators looked on. The village must have been ravaged; not a chicken, pig, or egg left untasted, not a virgin left untried. The heat of the sport, the flush of bloody combat had drawn them by carriage, on foot, horseback, but mostly by train. Supposedly the trainmen had stopped a mile below Boston Corners and disconnected the cars, and the horde had walked, run the rest of the way. It had been a riot, lawless where now only robins sang, and cardinals feinted in the light.

"I'm not really wearing the right sort of clothes for yard-work, Mother," A.W. says patiently.

"That's all right," the old lady answers and plants the last bunch. She stands up, a bit shakily, though she heads for another flower bed.

"Well, at least let me get the wheelbarrow," he says.

By the time he returns from the toolshed, pushing the barrow before him, she has dug up more iris, the green leaves stacked on the ground beside her like the cutting blades of disassembled machinery. "Here," she directs him. "Put them in the barrow and cover them with the newspaper, so the roots won't dry up. I put these in, I remember."

"I think Olive planted these here," Clemmons says.

"No, I remember distinctly putting this bed in—they're a dark purple bloom."

Actually, Clemmons now remembers that it was Milly who had planted this bed of iris and that the blooms were yellow, flecked with dark brown, a common variety. She had brought a whole bushel basket of plants back from somewhere and had spaded them into the ground. Then she had gone to bed for two days, leaving the shovel and empty basket on the ground beside the newly made flower bed.

"These will look nice for the wedding, next to the others," Julia Clemmons is saying. The wheelbarrow is heavy with the transplants and she precedes it, her gloved hands turned out and held away from her body, like a figure on an ancient vase. Clemmons brings up the procession, trundling the barrow with measured steps.

"You're being silly. Not giving her away . . ." She shakes a stand of iris away from the mass and squats. "What will that do? Does it matter? Is that so important?" She pats the soil around the transplant. "Don't you even like her?" she continues. "These will be very nice here. Your father liked iris—he called them flags, I remember." Clemmons moves awkwardly beside his mother, his movements made more awkward by a sudden rage over the reason for their move from the city. His separation from Jenny. It had been the new baby, Milly. Twenty-five years later she was again disrupting his life. So he told himself.

He turns away to see Boxer run onto the lawn, a groundhog in his jaws. The dog sits down and vigorously shakes the animal by the neck, though it is clearly dead. Then he drops his prize and pants, wide-mouthed and fat-tongued, a happy-go-lucky, gooney smile that Clemmons finds himself returning. As his mother's infirmities seemed to come and go, so did her mind's direction; subject matter dissolved almost whimsically, and then just as arbitrarily would resume a solid dimension. He sometimes wondered how she could find her way about on highways without maps, without getting lost, save that the routes she traveled had by now almost been printed in her being like the delicate blue tracings of veins in her slender arms.

And like knowing where to turn off the interstate highway, where to find the right junction of county roads, his mother's accusation had correctly marked his disaffection, something he had been trying to pass by. He just did not like Milly, but there was no way he could escape his mother at that moment. No excuse turned him away from her and what she made him admit—he had arranged so cleverly for Rita Pickens to run the business that he was not needed at the office, and something in the sounds of the field convinced him a sibilant spell had been cast on the telephone. It would not ring. There was no escape for several hours, until Benny Smith would arrive to set up his painting rig. Clemmons was fated to troll behind his mother, pushing loads of flowers before him and feeling like some figure in a local legend; some character, say, in a Washington Irving story who had been hexed and must carry about the ludicrous punishment for his misbehavior for all to see.

There must be other parents who did not like a child. Why was affection a part of the contract? It could not be that unusual; he could not be the only one, and so why should he be singled out and marked down? It just happens, he thinks, and looks toward the dog for support. Boxer had begun to gnaw the groundhog—hindfirst—and eyes him warily.

Milly seemed to go through her life like one of those seasonal workers who follows the harvest, always moving but never getting ahead. She had run through several cycles of meaningless jobs, meaningless love affairs; a wasteful schedule that sometimes seemed intentionally designed to embarrass his sense of order, save that it had no design—and even that would anger him. If she had consciously taken an adversarial role, he could have at least respected that, but her opposition was inert, a dead weight like the animal in Boxer's mouth that the dog would shake to pretend a companionable resistance.

The havoc of the time may have helped their estrangement, but the division came before—as if it had been born with Milly. In his mind's eye, he could see through the walls of the house above where his mother tamped down the transplanted iris, see through the thick insulation of years past and into that large armchair in the library where the two little girls would climb on his lap for a story after their bath. Pink-kneed and rosily damp, they would arrange themselves in positions hardly changed from the fetal, their nightgowns primly stretched over chubby backsides and mouths thumb-plugged. Even then, even then, he thinks, there had been something about Milly, something that would make him grind his teeth while trying to smile. As she grew older, of course, the girl would see behind the smile.

"There's more," his mother is saying and points with her trowel up the hill. She leads a slow attack up the gentle terrace and around the side yard as Clemmons brings up the rumbling wheelbarrow.

Olive used to blame herself for the disaffection, for getting pregnant when she did to edge them out of the city and Clemmons away from his urban haunts—but Olive no longer thought that way, no longer cared to assume any responsibility for their past lives; and, in any event, it had never been true. Nor could the estrangement be laid out for psychological interpretation, as Claire would knead the problem even as she would massage his back and shoulders while he stretched out in her bed. No matter what discipline she would apply, his relationship with Milly would not bend to analysis, until she would pummel his shoulders. "You think you're some kind of a primitive," she would say. "Like some old Greek. It flatters you to feel archetypal. Without a reason. So you won't feel any guilt or even have to question it."

"Well, answer me this then," he would say to her. "Here's a question Milly asked me the other day. She said to me, 'What about Daisy? What's the difference?' " The girl's face had been swollen with hurt and the soft Sienese symmetries had become gross, sullen-eyed.

"There's no difference in the way the two of them live," he had said to Claire. "Daisy wanders about like a TV comedy about flower children, picking up jobs and men indiscriminately, interchangeably. It's a cliché. They're both clichés. Nothing serves them but clichés. But I like Daisy—I enjoy being with her. So it's not the so-called life style. I tell you there's no reason for it—I've never liked Milly. Say we had been separated at birth, never knew our relationship, and then met—would anyone be critical then? Is it necessary to like everybody? I'm sorry, I can't feel close to her. There's a dumbness she has about ignoring the way I feel, or forgetting about it if she does. She keeps coming back. She gets that from my mother—but she ignores things—passes over them to something more pleasant."

"I don't like you when you talk like this," Claire said and shrugged away from him. Her face had become pinched, older; she stood up and slipped on a robe. "You become hateful and dry." She had walked into the front of the apartment and made some phone calls, leaving him alone in her bed.

"Stop grinding your teeth," Clemmons's mother is saying. She lifts a last clump of plants from the wheelbarrow and drops them into a prepared hole. "What are you always thinking about that makes you so angry? I can see your jaws working."

"I've always been fortunate, I think, to be surrounded by people who can perceive my feelings through my jaw line."

"Now you look here," Julia Clemmons says softly, though he is a little cowed by her gravity. "I'm an old lady and that means that I've put up with a lot of crap. That means I don't have to put up with any more crap. If you want other people to take care of this wedding for you—you just mind your tongue. Do you understand me? Get the hose. These have to have a lot of water on them."

Clemmons struggles with the coils of garden hose that seem to have slithered and bred more kinks since Benny Smith had dumped it in the toolshed last fall. He starts to laugh with frustration as his arms become encircled and strung up, as the irritation in his groin heats up, and his flesh is nipped by a hundred little sawtoothed mouths. Then, just as quickly, he is flushed with a rage against the hose—against the carelessness that had merely thrown it down, so that it had almost lain in wait for him to step into its rubbery constrictions, step into its tangle while neatly dressed and prepared for the orderly pursuit of business and not to wrestle in the hazardous confinement of a toolshed with a hundred yards of recalcitrant garden hose—even at this moment he scrapes his forehead against a wooden shelf, to jostle a small can of stain to the floor where the lid pops off and spatters his fresh chinos, so that he throws himself through the narrow aperture of the shed's doorway, pulling behind him the tangled mass of hose like the entrails of a beast that has tried to swallow him up, has tried to digest him, the whole mess pulling with it the chimera's other internal organs: cans of paint, a rake, a pickax, several flower pots, and the brittle dried-up plasma of last autumn's leaves. Clemmons looks back on the butchery, festooned in gore.

"How you doing, A.W.?" Benny Smith's merry question is asked with no recognition of the circumstances; Clemmons could just as easily be standing on the lawn dressed in formal wear. The handyman had appeared more than arrived, his truck parked below.

Clemmons hands over the watering duties to him, almost strand by strand, and returns to the house to change his clothes. He was moving too fast, too jerkily, knocking over paint cans, thrashing about, becoming more entangled in a mess he had not made. As he changes his pants, he thinks back to this morning, to that solitary figure jogging over the horizon, carefully and neatly placing one foot down in front of the other, breath and thoughts all in order. The day's agenda had been neatly titled. He blames Sam Broome, whose desperation had infected him on the drive home from Irondale.

"You're a success," Broome had told him. "You've made a whole town. Look at you. You've put it together, man."

"But what's happened to the movie about the prize fight?"

"Listen, we're moving into a new era. Violence is no longer the thing, you know. We have to bind up the wounds."

"With a rock concert? Twenty thousand people overnight in Boston Corners?"

"Right. It could be another Woodstock," the promoter had said. There was something in the man's voice that caught Clemmons's sympathy, something different from the usual clangor. The financial backing for the movie was slow coming in, he said. High interest rates. Inflation. It was to be put on a back burner. But a concert with Stanley Livingston would go.

"But there's not much time, is there?" Clemmons had asked. His question seemed to tap another vein of energy in Broome. The time factor would lend to the excitement. The compression would generate momentum on its own. The more he talked, the more Clemmons wondered how much of his scheme was worked out as he talked. How much was on paper? Signed up?

"It's funny about time." Broome gestured with both hands momentarily off the wheel. "I can feel the rightness about this concert. We got the band, the occasion, the old history of the place. It will be symbolic." His hands were off the wheel once again, as if in supplication.

Clemmons had turned to look out the car's window at the slate-sided ravines around Black Rock where the old mines had once been. The collapsed chutes had been grown over long ago, absorbed into the terrain like healed wounds. It was like coming across old tools piled in a heap; the worn spots on the handles could almost identify their former owners. Almost. Broome could not see him smile.

So A. W. Clemmons may have told himself that he saw Broome's concert scheme as another means by which Milly's wedding could be managed without him, and that could be partly true; but he also would seek out Earle Hicks later in the day to talk to the planning board chairman about the change of permit because he had recognized an old urgency in Broome's voice.

He would contact Hicks after several business calls, after a time browsing the shelves of the Rexall Drug Store in Green River for some remedy for the itch, and after telling the Donaldsons that he wasn't interested in taking over their mortgage, a decision he had only made when he turned down the dirt road to their place and saw the laundry strung out in the breeze between the house and a shed, a festive dressing of random colors that would have gloried a yacht club.

Old man Donaldson worked his jaws, chewed his gums, and looked off into the feedlot behind the barn where some mud-sotted Holsteins steamed against the fence posts. Clemmons told him about high interest rates, about the market drop in real estate, about anything that came into his head that would give the man some excuse for the life he had chosen to live, and for the loss he would now have to take for that choice, for being broken like some of the old machinery that now rusted in the weeds of the low ground, strangely worn out and made junk, both man and machinery, by the soft-eyed, dumb creatures, behind the barn, which continued to take dollops of spring air on their spongelike tongues.

"That's it, is it?" was all Donaldson said, still looking toward the cows. He was only a couple of years older than Clemmons, though he looked ten or fifteen more. He had said the same thing, *"That's it, is it?"* when Clemmons had brought over the army sergeant who had come down from the recruitment office in Hudson to deliver the medal, awarded posthumously to the youngest Donaldson boy for his courage in Cambodia.

"Why not give it another year," Clemmons told the man. "Things could be a lot different in a year's time. Meanwhile, the land will keep its value, maybe even increase."

Donaldson smiled and pinched his nose between his fingers. He leaned over and carefully spit, almost drooled, a strand of tobacco juice between his rubber boots. "The missus needs a rest," he said. "She's got ailments," he added, a slight emphasis on the word to suggest their mystery, something his simple husbandry could neither understand nor treat.

"I'll list the place. Do my best to move it," Clemmons said. "I wish I could do more. I do." The farmer then shifted his eyes so that their slanted gaze cut across Clemmons's face like an edge of broken glass, a look honed on suspicion and disbelief.

The Glenview Hotel was neither in a glen nor was it a hotel except during deer season when hunters from the city were sometimes laid out drunk on the floor upstairs like pieces of checkerboard in their red-and-black plaid jackets. Nor was there a view of anything but the junkyard across the road, and even then not of the junkyard proper but of the high plain fence that the state had forced its owner to erect around it, thereby overruling the local zoning and planning boards, both run by Earle Hicks, who had felt this cosmetic protection of the community's sensibilities was somehow an infringement of the junkyard owner's rights and freedom. Moreover, the final argument used by the state authorities to defeat the local opinion was a perverse interpretation of that same local opinion, as if to rub the grievance in even more—that is, the fence would protect the patrons of the Glenview Hotel from the unsightly tangle of junked cars and machinery; whereas Earle Hicks, who spent most of his afternoons at the Glenview, had argued that to sit there and look out on the acres of boxed engines, pyramids of wheels, and the ranked shells of old cars was a damn sight more interesting than to sit there and look at a bare wooden fence.

There was almost what might be called a spiritual diminishment, a closure put around more than just the visual (though Clemmons knew Hicks would never think of it that way, because he could never put it into words, never find a way to express his frustration, which could anger him even more), for sometimes Clemmons had heard Hicks and his cronies sit a whole afternoon before the fence and pick over the junkyard from the windows of the Glenview, recognizing an old pickup or a corn picker or broken combine, with a memory or a story to go with each. It had been like keeping watch on a family plot.

Then too, Clemmons often thought there had been an unintended irony in Earle's appointment as chairman of the zoning and planning boards, that the power had been given to him by the town board as an example of native wisdom, for who better knew how to determine the usage of land and buildings than the disinherited heir to most of it? Nor did it matter that the tax maps now mostly had the name A. W. Clemmons printed along the boundaries, because the town fathers thought—and the way they thought Olive had taught him—that a kind of democratic principle was maintained when Hicks was given the authority to tell Clemmons what he could or could not do with the property. But as most principles and theories melt in the harsh rain of events, so on almost every occasion the state or some other higher authority would overrule Earle Hicks's decisions—usually in favor of Clemmons or some other newcomer, for what Hicks and the other locals had not reckoned with, as they retreated farther into the gloom of the Glenview Hotel, was that these higher authorities not only encouraged men like A. W. Clemmons but, as political entities, were usually owned and operated by men like A. W. Clemmons.

On this afternoon, the Glenview is deserted, and Earle Hicks sits alone at a table in the far corner near the shuffleboard game. His face is the color of one of the tomatoes he will be selling in late August, if he is still alive in late August: tight-skinned and of a red so dense that parts of the skin look blue. His eyes slowly take in Clemmons as he enters the place, as if hardened by whatever cooked inside him.

"Can I buy you another?" Clemmons says by the table. He had brought a glass of beer for himself from the bar. The man shrugs and smiles as if to say he didn't care one way or another, so Clemmons sits down. They have the place to themselves except for the owner, who stands at the far end of the bar, face raised to the television set. Hicks begins to laugh, a silent rolling of shoulders. He shakes out a cigarette from the pack, sticks it in his mouth, and flips open an old Zippo lighter. He sights down the cigarette, through the flame, at Clemmons. He snaps the lighter closed, takes a long, death-defying drag on the cigarette.

"What do you care about all this?" he asks through a stream of smoke. "You already got your rent from Vosburg's Field, whether that Jew does his movie or not."

"The concert could bring a lot of money for the town," Clemmons replies. "Even jobs."

"Sure." Hicks laughs again. "We could all get dressed up in bonnets and bib overalls and sell fried chicken. Real picturesque, don't you know." His face pulls together, almost puckers around the cigarette in his lips that he sucks on deeply. There is applause and music from the far end of the bar.

"What does it matter to you?" Clemmons asks. "You've already given him permission for a motion picture location. Why not change it for a concert?"

"Sure, why not? Well, it will take some consideration," the man says. "We got to worry about drugs and about crowd control and about undesirables. We got to give all these things consideration, don't you know." He looks wisely at Clemmons across the table, to suggest the real consideration need not be expressed. "No, I tell you, A.W., we got to do things here in an orderly way; can't just switch around whenever one of your city people change their minds."

Clemmons wonders how long Earle Hicks has been waiting for him at this corner table. He settles into his chair; it will be a long afternoon. Hicks would preside importantly, would wheel, cut back and forth through the dust-mote hours, and Clemmons would give him his head, a horse gone feisty allowed to run out its balkiness. It could take an hour—maybe more. He looks around the bar and out the window at the board fence around the junkyard.

"There probably won't be a concert anyway." He is surprised by his own voice. "Not a movie either," he adds to the instant's premonition. Earle Hicks's red face goes crafty, as if he were preparing a look that would go with anything Clemmons might say. But Clemmons says nothing more.

"There, you see?" Hicks says after a while. "You see what I mean? We got to give it some thought. My daddy may have sold you the town, don't you know, but he left me in trust of it. And even though you're turning it over to trash like Springer, I still will have a say about some of it." He winks one eye and smiles almost wickedly, so that Clemmons felt some joke had just been played upon him, though he knew that was how he was meant to feel; it was a trick the natives around Boston Corners played on outsiders—a nearsighted sense of humor that allowed them to make fun of those who succeeded where they had failed.

"No, sir," Hicks says emphatically and gets up, goes to the bar with his empty glass. "I'm buying a round." Clemmons knows he could leave then and the end result would be the same, but he remains in the chair, looking out the window at the plain board fence across the road. A milk truck goes by. The dank, sour air in the place seems to support a wisdom that Clemmons, for the moment, is content to breathe—sit back, relax, and take what comes down the road.

Chapter Three

Like three pink moons, the three views of the human heart look down upon Clemmons as he lies on the examining table: anterior, posterior, and a cross section showing the valves and arteries, each one fixed to the white firmament of Buddy Ray's office wall, hanging above a metal bench on which were arranged a canister of cotton swabs, several trays of surgical instruments, beakers of antiseptic, and the half-finished plastic model of a building. D-R-Y-G-U-L-C-H S-A-L-O-O-N. The model is at Clemmons's eye level as he lies on his side with his naked posterior raised like a fourth moon, a white one and far more controversial, that is to say, open to examination, than the other three that seem to illuminate the scene.

He could look right into the small building's interior—the swinging doors had yet to be glued on—to see along the tiny bar, beyond a table with several spindly-legged chairs to a staircase at the rear that ascends nowhere. There is a pinpoint-sized spittoon by the rail of the bar and a diminutive "painting" of a nude female hanging on the wall over the bar's tiny bottles. Clemmons wonders, as the doctor pokes and scrapes the skin around his genitals, if there were cards even, lying on the small table, a poker hand flung down that took the pot, the loot already squandered at the bar or in one of the nonexistent rooms upstairs, or perhaps the cards would be specifically rendered—tens and eights, the last full house held by Wild Bill Hickok.

"What have I got?" he asks over his back. If not the playing cards, Doc Ray would have put down a small paintbrush, a razor knife, or tube of glue when Clemmons arrived for his appointment, for the doctor worked on models between patients, and Clemmons knew that when its swinging doors were finally fixed, the saloon would be put down in some little town within the wilderness of the large diorama being settled in the basement under the medical clinic. Originally, the layout had been for a model train, and though the tracks were still in place and occasionally a small engine would jerk its string of coaches around a bend to grind down the main line, the doctor had long ago become more interested in developing the towns and villages that lay along the route than in operating the miraculous invention that had sparked their growth.

"Well, what is it?" Clemmons asks again, thinking of photographs he had seen of the whores from that day, women like those who might be found lolling about upstairs in the Drygulch Saloon, and wondering how or why anyone would catch any sort of disease from them, why anyone would ever get close enough to catch anything from them. If it was from Olive, then probably she had got a little something more from that tennis pro than tips on her forehand smash. If from Claire, it was probably a poetic strain of spirochete, or maybe a long-tailed narrative of a disease passed on from a rowdy novelist. Doc Ray says nothing, perhaps not wishing to address that end of him, and Clemmons feels the sack of his scrotum being lifted and laid to one side, feels the faintly pleasant scratch of the doctor's scalpel, perhaps the same one used to trim the flashings on the model's plastic parts. It scrapes the area of the rash, Clemmons's own imperfection.

It would not be fair to put suspicion only on Claire and Olive. There had been others; a young woman about Milly's age, a stranger met at a party in Albany whose name he could not remember now. She was a legislative aide, studying law. But she had never returned any of his phone calls. She had always "just stepped out of the office." Once had been enough, apparently. Casual, pleasurable, but enough.

Perhaps it had been more than enough; but that had been about a month ago, he reckoned, and some symptom should have shown itself by now. On the other hand, he wonders if it was a condition accountable to any time limit, a cumulative thing. Perhaps it was a synthetic disease composed of organisms pumped into him from Olive and Claire and the girl in Albany—Cynthia? What was her name? No matter—and from every woman he has ever known; each one contributes a wriggly fiber, a particle of herself that had swum aimlessly in the currents of his being until, by chance, it had encountered another of its kind, and then another, in turn joining up with more, until finally like a swelling school of fish, they jostled and dashed against each other in the narrow channels of his balls. It would be a lovely disease, he thought.

"Turn over and spread your legs," Doc Ray says.

Clemmons does so, eyes moving from the three moons to the blank cosmos of the ceiling, and finds himself remembering the old man he would see on his way to school who would sit by the sidewalk, in good weather, in a straight-backed chair with his legs spread wide as if to expose the enormous bulge in his pants to the warm and healing sun, sit widespread because the huge growth that ballooned in his crotch and strained against one pant leg as far as the knee had wedged the legs apart. He and the other boys of the neighborhood had guessed darkly about diseases caught from elephants, but Clemmons now wonders if it had not been some malady similar to what he may have contracted and that the old man had been a kind of omen for him, an ancient whose message he had not understood until now, until too late.

In fact, he remembers how the old fellow would wave and smile at them as they rushed by, always late and juggling books of geography and spelling; smile like an imbecile or what in their boys' language they would term an imbecile but what really may have been a profound and kindly wisdom, while waving them on to a knowledge from which no lessons could save them, welcoming them and bidding them good-bye all in one motion.

"So, what do I have?" he asks Doc Ray. "Is it fatal?"

"It's all fatal," Ray answers. "You can get dressed."

The doctor has turned his back to him and bends over a counter, carefully sifting something from a filter paper onto small glass saucers. He leaves the room with the specimen plates, closing the door as if now Clemmons deserves some privacy.

Before he puts on his shoes, he steps onto the scales and taps the counterweight to balance the beam. He adjusts the height stick and stands straight. Five-feet-about-eleven. One hundred seventy-five pounds. That's with clothes, with change in one pocket and his billfold in another and in that billfold, various cards and some ID that give his height as six feet. He used to be six feet tall, or nearly so, and somewhere had lost about a half inch. The girls had got their height from him, he had always thought.

He had left the long length of Daisy lying on the living room sofa undisturbed. An idling in the night had wakened him as it had abruptly stilled the peepers, a car door closed, and he had heard her cheery voice say *thanksalot* and then he had turned over against a cool spot in the sheet and slipped under once again. He had watched her sleep this morning, bent over her, moved by the trustful elegance of her exposed neck, her face solemnly closed, lips pursed as if to receive a kiss. He had almost kissed her.

On the floor by the sofa was a large backpack and a smaller nylon satchel beside it, and then next a pair of high-topped, heavy shoes neatly aligned at the toe. Daisy's feet seemed too small for such boots, her delicate arches would surely crack against the unbending leather soles. Were it not for the long, single blond braid that lassoed one shoulder, she resembled a weary boy, one of those sweet youths enchanted in Shakespearean idylls about to waken for the happy ending. Or another image: she looked like one of those Civil War photographs by Brady of a young soldier sleeping or dead by his equipment, and Clemmons had turned away quickly, angry with himself for even thinking this, for this self-inflicted punishment, and left his daughter on the sofa, sleeping and alive.

"Okay." Doc Ray darts into the room. He sits down on a low stool. "I'm going to grow a culture, but it looks to me like you have a touch of monilia. It's a kind of fungus, a yeast infection. Nothing serious." He had not spoken to Clemmons directly, but turned away as if embarrassed.

"How did I get it?" Clemmons asks as he buttons his shirt.

Ray looks at him over his glasses. "Surely, A.W., I don't have to explain that to you." He revolves away again and takes out a pad of prescription blanks. "It's a very natural condition. Sometimes a woman's system will go out of balance, maybe she's taking something to treat another ailment —or there might be a chemical imbalance during menopause, could be a dozen reasons. In any event, the bacteria that normally live in the vagina are killed off and this fungus develops." He tears off the prescription and hands it to Clemmons.

"Well, what about the male? Can I pass it on?"

"You can give it a try," Ray answers. "But I'd lay off the stuff for a little bit, until the rash clears up. That ought to take care of it." He points to the prescription. "If something different shows up in the culture, I'll let you know. It won't hurt you to take a rest."

The man's primness always surprised Clemmons. Not even the hard-boiled mannerisms could disguise Ray's attitude, almost a resignation that must have come with his diploma, that there would be moments in his practice that would turn him away, patients he could not face. Clemmons always expected doctors to be more worldly, Olympian; but maybe it went with Ray's hobby, why he made models of the real thing.

Though that wouldn't be fair, Clemmons will think later as he waits for his prescription to be filled, for the train set in the basement under the clinic was an authentic domain to be managed and not a facsimile, even if the doctor's wife had told him, as he related to Clemmons, that if he wanted to play with toys he had to do it somewhere else—not in her house. Sam Broome would understand the importance of those miniature communities glued to plaster hillsides. Maybe Clemmons would introduce the two men.

The shopping mall is busy and the enclosed arcade echoes with shuffling footfalls, the cries of children, and the bland hum of piped music. Clemmons sits on a bench near the pharmacy and across from the Easter Bunny Hutch, where a huge white rabbit lounges in a high-backed chair. Behind Clemmons is a small plantation of real and vinyl plants watered intermittently by a fountain that seems to have pump trouble. The shallow basin of water, set in a bed of crushed stone, has been loaded up with pennies and scraps of paper; reefs of pink chewing gum lie just beneath the surface. Clemmons waves to the rabbit but there is no response, and it is difficult to tell whether the person inside the costume had seen him, where the real eyes had been looking, though the large, pink, plastic pupils sewn on the face stared directly at him. He wonders if it might be the same person inside who also had been Santa Claus and who would be Uncle Sam and Jack-o'lantern later on. As for Sam Broome, maybe Clemmons would delay telling him about Earle Hicks's decision, or lack of decision, as long as possible—somehow keeping the bad news unofficial by not saying anything about it.

He is joined on the bench by two old men. Clemmons moves away a little to give them room. They are dressed sportily and both wear caps with long visors. When they sit down, they carefully cross their legs, each putting a hand between his thighs, and there was a synchronous rhythm in their movements that suggested an old routine of brothers.

Clemmons is thinking about Florence and Venice and how he would like to see those cities again before they crumbled, before they were melted down by fumes, overrun. Perhaps he'd take Claire there. Or Siena. He knew a *pensione* in Siena, an old palace built into the town's walls, that had long, dark corridors and rooms that seemed to generate their own blazing light, a surplus of brilliance, that overflowed the tall, open windows to splash upon the Tuscan countryside, and rise above it in a steamy haze. Just opposite the *pensione,* a small necropolis had been settled on a hilltop where candles kept the dead company at night, offering a replica of life and the same sort of deception played by the unattended lights of prairie towns where, when you got there, the streets would be empty and the houses dark.

A little girl has just climbed into the Easter Bunny's passive lap. A photographer dressed in striped tights and a belled doublet looks through a camera on a tripod. The costume would be suitable year round, Clemmons thinks, a utility page that could be slipped into any part of the shopping mall's calendar though not an androgynous page, for he observes a viola swell to the hips within the tights. PICTURES WITH THE EASTER BUNNY—3 FOR $1.99. Several examples of the camera's work are pasted on the placard. All the children look puzzled, the bunny startled. In fact, it seems to him that the camera had surprised the Easter Bunny and the children in some activity that mocked the whole pretense of innocence, gave new meaning to the myth.

"She's got no feel for it anymore," one old man is saying. "Now you take mashed potatoes. You'd think they wouldn't be much to do with a little gravy and some ground meat. I put that kitchen in myself. Nice counters with real formica tops onto them. Everything electric. That's the best. That's the best way. Why'd I do all that?"

"We found a nice spot down in St. Pete," the other replies. "Everything's taken care of. Then there's a lot of activities for them, don't you know. Cards and different clubs. And the rest is all taken care of so they don't have to worry about it. There's a workshop for making furniture."

"Do you have your own tools?"

Clemmons does not hear the answer for he has left the bench, an abrupt departure that sprung his step so he momentarily lost his balance and staggers, causing the men on the bench to regard him with curiosity. His order number has yet to be called at the prescription counter, so he returns to the glassed-over *paseo* of the mall. There's another child on the Easter Bunny's lap.

"She's adorable," he hears the photographer say.

"She's my sister's little girl." The other voice sounds familiar. "I'm just minding her for the afternoon, then I had some appointments to myself, but she don't take much."

"She's adorable," the photographer says again and bends forward to focus the camera. Clemmons steps back to appreciate the womanly ass within the striped costume. Lights flash. The picture has been made. "Just one more, honey," the woman says and pulls the tab on the film pack.

The little girl looks uncomfortable on the Easter Bunny's lap, looks suspicious, Clemmons thinks. The Easter Bunny hasn't moved. All seven feet of rabbit, one ear brokenly folded over, is parked at an angle in the oversized chair and hasn't moved the whole time.

"Hey, is there someone really inside that rabbit?" he asks. "You couldn't get away with that if it were Santa Claus. He's the real thing." When the photographer turns around, the face does not match her nether perfection, a disappointment Clemmons has encountered before, though it sometimes goes the other way.

The other woman has also turned, on cue almost, and the knowledge bursts within Clemmons, with all the swift clarity of strobe lights, that the girl from the Irondale store, Betty Springer, had seen him sitting on the bench with the two old men, probably had seen him give his prescription to the pharmacist before that, had been watching him all that time and then had staked herself out on the worn red carpet of the Easter Bunny's hutch.

Her smile was one of long acquaintance. The photographer looked desperately beyond his shoulder, offstage you might say, as if to summon a recalcitrant member of a PTA pageant. A man in the uniform of a policeman appears at Clemmons's elbow.

"What's the trouble?" he asks.

"No trouble," Clemmons replies.

"What are you doing here?"

"I'm waiting for a prescription." Clemmons nods toward the pharmacy.

"Let me see some identification," the policeman says.

"You mean to say, you don't know Mr. A. W. Clemmons of Boston Corners?" Betty Springer says. She has come to the braided rope that sets off the Easter Bunny's hutch.

"You know this man, lady?" the policeman asks.

"I certainly do." The girl smiles. A green blouse, open at the neck, compliments her smooth throat. She tucks her hands into the jacket pockets of a jeans suit.

"We've had a lot of trouble," the photographer is saying. The cop has walked away. "Some men seem to think that I'm here for their special kind of amusement. They make remarks."

"I'm sorry," Clemmons tells her. As he looks at her, she pushes a strand of hair beneath the fool's cap. "You do good work. These pictures are very good. Have you ever exhibited?"

The woman does not answer, but looks at Clemmons as

if she might call the policeman back. However, Betty Springer returns, with the little girl by the hand. She pays the photographer and receives the pictures. The little girl hops from one foot to another. "Now mind yourself, Linda," she says to the child with a glance directed toward Clemmons. The little girl regards him with the same gloomy distrust she had given the Easter Bunny.

"Does Linda like ice cream?" Clemmons asks.

"That child will eat almost anything," Betty Springer replies. "She's my niece. My sister's little girl."

"You came to my rescue. Let me set up some treats," Clemmons offers. "First, I have a prescription to pick up. I think it's ready."

"You sick?" she asks. She peers up at him from under heavy, dark eyebrows. It's almost one long eyebrow that passes straight over both eyes, uninterrupted by the bridge of the nose, to underline the sincerity of her words and suggest an unexpected soberness to the thoughts behind that brow. "Are you all right?"

Yes, he will tell her, he was all right. It was only some kind of a pesky virus, one of those going around and nothing to be worried about. Nothing catching. The little girl had run before them directly toward a lunch counter—a swift and practiced vanguard, Clemmons felt—as he and her aunt strolled through a grove of tubbed ferns. All the real and unreal vegetation around him, the light filtered through the smoked-glass dome above, made him think of walking through a rain forest. Then he thought about *Green Mansions*. It had been a favorite book, read and reread, and the girl in it, who also had silvery hair, had starred in many of his teen-age sexual fantasies. He couldn't remember her name, but he thought she came to a bad end.

"I was just going to call Dad Springer, because Leroy had let us off on his way to work—he's on the third shift now, don't you know—and I had this doctor's appointment, so I was just going to call and say, 'Come and get us,' and there you showed up and about getting arrested, so I guess it was real fortunate all the way around."

"It was indeed," Clemmons agrees. They would be driving back to Boston Corners.

She sits beside him in the front seat, legs neatly crossed, a crimson sandal dangles from one foot. The little girl dozes in the back.

"That sure was something, to see you about to be arrested." He expects her to laugh, but she does not.

"Well, thanks to you, I wasn't."

"I guess there's all kinds of randy old devils sniffing about," she says primly. There's a shift in her tortoise-shell eyes, a flash of something. Clemmons looks at the little girl through the rearview mirror. The child sleeps, a thumb in her mouth, and her dress thrown back, so the other hand rests on her exposed belly, over the navel. "Women have to be careful these days," Betty Springer says.

"It's always a problem," Clemmons says. Her face had been made up to follow a diagram for beauty that must have seemed credible on a magazine page. Outside the artificial lighting of the shopping mall, it has become a mask. The eyes were edged in a dark substance, orange pollen brushed over the high cheekbones, and the whitish-pink lips look as if the mouth has been peeled off the glass of a display case. He preferred the older woman, the photographer. There had been something appealing about her harried expression, something sensuous in the worn lines about her mouth and eyes. She had seemed understanding, forgiving, even as she called the cop.

"Honestly," Betty Springer says as she leans over the front seat to pull down the child's dress. When she smiles, it seems to deepen her scowl—one part of her face pulling on another part to cancel all expression. "She's a sweet little thing."

"You say you've been to the doctor, too?" Clemmons says. They are now on the open highway. He imagines her lying upon Buddy Ray's examination table, under the three hearts. She would be pink like those three hearts, he thought, but a translucent pink as if the doctor were showing light through her, from within. But it would be a different doctor.

"Only just to pick up my examinations and to talk to him," she replies. There's a leap in her voice. "We been married two years now and no sign of any little ones on the way. Lordy knows we've tried—we surely do try. Leroy just wears me out. Dad Springer says he wants lots of grandchildren and he's getting them too, but not from Leroy and myself. So, I go to this doctor to see if there's something wrong with me. Leroy says it's not him. He says he's got more sperms in his little finger than most men have down there, and I said to him, 'That's just the trouble, Leroy—you got yours in the wrong place.' But I go to the doctor anyways. Dad Springer says we got to produce and multiply. So I'm at the doctor's. And he does all these examinations. You should see some of the things he makes me do—good thing that policeman wasn't standing around in his office when I'm taking all these positions, don't you know. And him peering and poking around." She chuckles and hugs herself.

"So, what's the verdict?" Clemmons asks. They pass through Claverack, under the branches of old maples that line the highway. The leaf buds are a green about the color of her blouse.

"Well, I'm okay, that's for sure. There's nothing wrong with me, that's for sure," she replies and sits up against the car door. Clemmons pulls up at a traffic light and stops.

"It's probably just nerves," he says. "It takes time, sometimes."

"You've had two children, haven't you?" Betty Springer says.

"Yes, that's right. Two."

"I still can't believe that you've got daughters who are about my age. I mean, you certainly don't look that old."

"Thank you," Clemmons replies and moves the car as the light changes.

"That comes from all that running, I guess. You stay in good shape, I guess. I tell Leroy that if he sits around all weekend drinking beer, how does he expect to do anything."

"You said you were in that class I had. You're interested in real estate?"

"That was only because Dad Springer was thinking of selling off some of that place he bought down by the old railroad yard, you remember, and he wanted someone to know how to do it so he wouldn't get tricked out by some of them New York City people. So, I volunteered. But that don't mean much." She reaches into her shoulder bag, takes out an emery board, and touches up the edges of her nails. The polish is the color of oxblood.

"What that old man really wants is something I can't seem to give him." She tosses the file back into her bag. Evidently not with Leroy, Clemmons thinks, picturing young Springer, a thin boy with the complexion of raw milk. How about the old man? Why doesn't old Springer do the job himself?

On the open highway, Clemmons lets the car run freely, lets it run smoothly over the speed limit to sixty miles an hour. He imagines the bearded, Old-Testament figure bending over the delicately built woman beside him. He imagines her face turning away, lacquered and set; expressionless, though the stench from those broken teeth would be foul.

In the old days, a Livingston might have the privilege. They would come to the manor lord or the word would get around that one of the tenant women seemed to be barren and arrangements would be made. Perhaps upstairs in the old hotel. Or extra help might be brought into the manor house to prepare for a summer fete, and this girl would be given some rooms to do up in the far wing, up near the eaves where mourning doves cooed. It would be summer, windows open to air the bed linen, the deep feather ticks.

Her skin would be slippery with perspiration. She'd have one of those frilly white caps on her head.

"I guess spring has sprung, the rabbits run," Betty Springer says. "I surely do like spring. Leroy's already got in his peas and lettuce. Do you garden much?"

"Only greens . . . some tomatoes." Such rites or rights of the manor lord were reprehensible; he had been told so enough times by Claire and others, even by Jenny though she had apparently given herself to similar usage, but A. W. Clemmons, driving through this countryside once ruled by such men, felt a curious sadness for them. Though they had seized both the land and its people, held them both in a peculiar bondage, and, he supposed, used some of the women badly, ultimately they had been taken over by them, had disappeared into the land as surely as they had passed into the women, leaving only their names behind at crossroads and then sometimes with the wrong dates or spelling on the historical markers. "It's still exploitation," he can hear Milly say. "No matter how you dress it up—somebody's being worked over."

But he often thought there was a kind of negative capability at work between men and women. It was not only sexual, for there were women, such as his daughters and mother or Rita Pickens, who took a part of him into themselves, part of his imagination or a prejudice or some other part of his character, and transformed that item so that it became part of their consciousness, their fabric, so that gradually the original disappeared into them in much the same way the Livingstons had parceled out their features among the local gentry. Earle Hicks boasted of Livingston blood being injected many generations back and Clemmons had learned to look closely at others, to catch in a certain light a line of nose that might claim the old patent.

"We're still eating on things I put up last year," Betty Springer says.

By the flick of resentment in her voice, Clemmons knows what she leaves unsaid. It was the same faintly sarcastic preamble Olive would use just before she had said something like, "Another garden?" when the new seed catalogues had arrived. Or later, "What am I supposed to do with all this?" when he brought in the first harvest; a litter of yellow and green squash that rolled and played about their feet. Maybe, Clemmons thought, the next time he encountered Leroy Springer at the Glenview Hotel or at the Sunnyside, maybe he would buy him a beer.

"It saves money. The vegetables do taste better," he offers.

"I guess so," she replies. Her tone backs him off. Having already imagined her nude on the doctor's examining table, he transferred her easily, projected a pink-and-white image onto a bed, perhaps the cramped bedroom of a trailer made even more confined by tasseled comforters, satin-covered pillows. Even with the cement blocks Leroy had used to snug up the footings, the whole trailer would quiver with the vibration set up by the fringes over their heads.

But he was put off by her ambivalence, an expression that would acquiesce to anything, give equal value to every opinion; his thoughts idled, then turned back to the photographer in the mall. She had been an older woman. She had looked put upon to Clemmons, but her eyes, rimmed with anxious moisture, also showed a glimmer of knowing within them. She was aware why men harassed her; she knew and enjoyed pleasure, had that old-fashioned moral capacity to enjoy pleasure that men could sense, that almost sent out waves to pull them to her. But this same quality also let her set the time and place, and call a cop when otherwise bothered. Betty Springer, the same age as his daughter, was not so complicated.

"They're always working on this road," she says as Clemmons brakes before a flagman. A road crew with a large truck has blocked one lane of the highway. She looks at the sleeping child in the rear seat, and settles back against the door, partially facing him as if prepared for a long wait. "I just read a very interesting book, about some men in a plane that crashed in mountains down in South America, and they end up eating each other. And it's true, too. Have you read that one?"

"No. I've heard about it, but I haven't read it," he tells her. He's entering a dangerous area now. He only half hears her account of the book, only half observes the county highway workmen, for he reviews the patch-and-fill operation that has been his relationship with Milly. He sees her face gone white, the eyes blanked and sealed up as the two of them abruptly discover they have unwittingly taken the wrong turn in their discussion, the same sort of discussion he's just been having with himself.

"How dare you tell me how to live," she would say imperiously. "You phony son-of-a-bitch. Moral choice, my ass. Where's your moral choice, selling people something that never existed? You two-bit Walt Disney."

"So what am I going to tell Leroy?" Betty Springer asks as the red flag drops and Clemmons eases the car around the dump truck. He knows she does not expect him to answer. "Barney Waldor has this artificial insemination business for cows, and Dad Springer tells me that some of them bulls is long gone. I mean, they're dead a long time ago but their sperms is still doing the trick, don't you know, just like they was alive. I guess they got something like that for human beings too, don't they?"

"Yes," Clemmons says and turns at an intersection, heads south toward Boston Corners.

"I bet I could sign up for some of Einstein? Or some of Errol Flynn? Wouldn't that be something? Leroy would never know the difference."

"No, probably not."

"Well, I think my sister's home by now. If you wouldn't mind, we can drop Linda off there first." She directs him down a familiar road, though he had never known who lived in the mobile home parked on blocks beside the small creek. As he sits in the idling car to wait for her to return without the child, he's conscious of being looked at. There was a push of curtain at the trailer's window.

Betty Springer returns on the paved walk from the trailer with the stride of a much taller woman. The spiked heels of her sandals seem to put her ankles to an ultimate test, make them more fragile than they are. She gets in quickly and gives him more directions. They bump over the abandoned rail lines and cross the small plain of the old staging yard. Not long ago, several trains a day, several different lines, would junction here, lay off freight cars, hook up with more. Now there was nothing but a bare, grassless field, and a sign—LOTS FOR SALE with a phone number he figured would be old Springer's.

The road wound up behind, toward state lands, and at one curve she guided him down a dirt driveway. "It's a pretty little house," Betty Springer says.

"It is indeed," Clemmons agrees. He is stung by his earlier snobbery. The afternoon sun slants through a pine wood to illuminate the neat cottage like lights from one side of a stage proscenium. Brick, shutters, shingles, the prickly sides of yew are all edged by a golden light that is caught and almost woven on a loom of white strings fixed to a board fence by the kitchen door. Probably for sweet peas, Clemmons thinks.

"Leroy will just about finish the barbeque this evening when he gets home from work," she says. "He's always building something." She has opened the car door and put one leg out, pauses to look down along it to where the red sandal is about to contact the earth as if she were about to step out onto unfamiliar ground rather than her own front yard. "Would you like to come in?" she says.

Clemmons is surprised that she does not add, *It won't take much,* and then is once more ashamed so he says, "No. No, thank you. Maybe another time," he adds. There's an amused mote swimming in the yellow-brown eyes, caught by the lowering sun. Her cheeks are pink, almost an unnatural color. He's tempted to tell her about his condition; instead, he says, "One of my daughters arrived late last night and I haven't had a chance to talk to her."

On the way home, he thinks about how the young woman's face had closed in around the sullen horizontals of its usual expression and he pulls to the side of the road. He almost turns around and goes back. But the impulse is accompanied by its own regulation. He imagines how she would greet him at the door; puzzled, coolly curious, as if he were a stranger. She might even call the police, the sheriff's number was probably tacked to a bulletin board by the kitchen phone for just such emergencies. After all, she had been shown how to do it by the older woman, the photographer in the mall. On the other hand, perhaps they were all born knowing their options, their rightful timing, and these different choices were tacked onto their natures from the beginning. They were the ones with the options.

The melancholy call of a field owl summons his attention to the view before him. He had parked on a small rise that overlooks the vale of Boston Corners. The top of the tall cottonwood in the center of Irondale pokes far up on the left. He can not see his house because of some old maples, but he can pick out the field where Yankee Sullivan and John Morrisey over a hundred years ago had vainly gone thirty-seven rounds for the possession of a title to that field, and to that day. It looks like any other field.

Chapter Four

"Daisy, what is it you do?"

"Do, Pop?"

"Yes, do. Do for a living."

"Oh that," she says and swings a heavy hank of wet hair about in the sunlight that warms the terrace. She has just shampooed it, for the twelfth time as far as Clemmons could reckon; in fact, she seemed to have spent most of her time in the bathroom, attending to some part of her personal hygiene. He wondered how she could maintain such care on the road, if at all, and if during these pauses in her journeys she attempted to soak up cleanliness, even store it someway.

"Well, I and a couple of friends have this trip-guide business. When I'm bopping around, I have this little tape recorder, battery-powered, and I tape my impressions of places, my thoughts about how things look. Famous sites. Also, good places to eat, where to camp or ask for fresh water. Things to look for. Then I interview local officials sometimes or just people in the area. Then we edit this and put it on cassette tapes and sell them to people who might want to make the same trip. Mostly, we sell them to people who just want to listen. They don't go anywhere."

"You're a businesswoman," Clemmons says. The young woman smiles and pulls a comb through her hair. She sits on the flagstone near the lawn. Clemmons slumps in a sling chair. To one side are paint buckets and parts of scaffolding. Benny Smith has already painted half of the house, and the evening air is laced with turpentine. A pot falls to the kitchen floor inside.

"I better go help Grandma," Daisy says.

"Stay. She'll call if she needs help." He wants to have a quiet moment with his daughter, for such moments would become rare. Milly and her entourage could arrive at any moment. Olive was scheduled to fly in on the weekend. His place was being taken over. Boxer trots up from the field below and Clemmons is reminded of the quiet mornings they used to share, their horny fellowship. All those woodchucks gloriously chomped up.

"He looks terrible," she says. "What have you been feeding him?" The dog lies down by her bare feet. Daisy wears jeans and an oversized flannel shirt, probably borrowed from someone between here and the state of Washington. Borrowed, not bartered, he thinks, then is angry with himself for making such a qualification. She looks healthy, tanned, and loose-limbed. The plum-shaped eyes shift and glisten. "Milly will be very hurt if you don't give her away."

"Will she? I doubt it very much," Clemmons says.

"But you won't even be here."

"No." He had been trying to reach Claire, to make their arrangements. "When you sign on as a parent there are certain duties to perform. I've done those. From there on, it's friendship, maybe the best kind. But if not—then it's better to just leave it."

"She says things she doesn't mean," Daisy says. Her head turns, one side of her face blanked by a fall of blond hair. "You know that," she adds softly.

"Daisy, simply because I put some paint on some old

buildings doesn't mean I cheat people. And I'm not a sell-out because I feel responsible for a kind of community that doesn't fit her high level of sophistication. I wonder why she wants to come back to this hick place at all to be married."

His daughter does not answer, though he can almost see the words forming behind her brow. She picks shoots of grass and feeds them one at a time to the dog. Boxer chews them up, one at a time. The dog has a look in his eye that seems to recognize retribution.

"She wants to set herself apart from me, like where I stand the piano drops," Clemmons continues. "Even in pictures. You've seen those pictures your mother insisted we take the last time. Did you look at Milly in those pictures? She looked into the camera like a wooden effigy, eyes of glass. Everyone else smiling, if only for the occasion, but she wasn't going to be caught on the record with a pleasant, human expression. Not sitting next to me, anyway." He has become worked up, his feelings hooking him unawares, and he stands then turns to look up at the house's roofline. This afternoon Benny had cleaned out some wasp nests up near the center beam. Clemmons could count three or four insects hanging in the air opposite the spot where their colony had been. He wonders if a wasp could look confused, dumbfounded, distraught. Probably to other wasps.

Daisy speaks soberly. "It's never made sense to her, you living here. She knows how you like the city, how you used to be part of it. She feels cheated maybe . . ."

"Listen, we've been through . . ."

". . . maybe also responsible for you leaving the city."

"Oh Christ, now it's guilt." He sits down again. "I can't bear being guilty for her guilt. No more."

"Milly is greedy," Daisy says smiling. "She wants you to have a city pad and a country platz. Both."

A burst of swallows attack the air over the field below, turn in a tight chandelle, and disappear. The transplanted iris seem to be doing well around the freshly mowed field.

It resembles the lawn of a large estate, as in fact it is, Clemmons thinks, or at least used to be. "This fellow Broome wants to do that," he says. "He wants to put together a package of nostalgia, wants to film it."

"He can't do the concert. The band doesn't want to. They have contracts that forbid it." Daisy spread her hair so it lay like a golden cowl upon her shoulders.

"Yes, I know, but Broome was desperate. The film on the old fight has been held back for some reason. He needed something to take its place. You move around a lot, Daisy, and you tape these reports on the places you visit—have you come across any yet that were started by women? Any towns? Settlements?"

"No. Well, I see what you're saying, but until now women haven't had the opportunity to start a place. It hasn't been safe for them, maybe."

"Or maybe they don't want to. Men like Broome need a place. Need to make a place." Boxer continues to chew mournfully on the grass fed him by his owner. "I used to see men like that in the city—and this explains why I could never satisfy Milly's aspirations for me—but I would see these men wandering up and down; say, Madison Avenue. They would have come in for a quasi-business appointment, or to have lunch with an old pal—some guy who hadn't left the city yet—and they'd sit and talk about the old places; where this bar used to be, or that landmark had been torn down, and finally the other guy, the one with a job, would have to go back to work and the visitor would have nothing to do by midafternoon. No place to go. All the old places he remembers had been torn down. So you see him walking up and down Madison Avenue, Lexington, Fifth, whatever. Dressed too well for slumming. They always carry a briefcase of some kind. They walk as if late for an appointment, or they might stop before a window with cameras and calculators—gadgets, or they watch themselves on the screens of the closed-circuit TVs in the window. I promised myself I wasn't going to join that troop. I cut all ties."

"Milly says the country is for retired people and dilettantes," Daisy says. She smiles.

Then why does she want to be married here? Clemmons is offended by Milly's opinion—even by way of Daisy. Peace was all he had wanted. So, you're running off with Claire, Milly would answer. You call that peace? You don't understand, he'd reply. Claire has her own kind of solitude. Ha! You like her because she's a loner with no place to go. Milly's voice would be harsh, and just imagining the snap of its lash makes him grind his teeth as he sits on the porch steps. Why can't I clear out? Everyone else is planning escape routes. Balls, Milly would say. That's not the reason. She would be cool and patient. A maddening girl. Be honest, A.W. Say it. You just want to be away from all of us.

"Hey there, Big Julie," Daisy has greeted her grandmother, who staggers out the door of the house like a seaman escaping an engineroom fire. Even the old lady's face is pink and she fans herself with one end of an apron. It is amazing to Clemmons that neither have heard his mind working. His teeth ache.

"The cheese soufflé is in," she says, out of breath, and sits down on the top step of the porch. "And I made it just the way you like it," she says to Daisy. "With no bacon or ham in it."

"Al*right,*" Daisy says.

"And now, Andrew, I'd like a little something," she says, still fanning herself.

"Candy time," Clemmons says.

"It's candy time," his mother says and blows air up over her cheeks.

"White wine, Daisy?" he asks and the girl nods. Inside, he fixes their drinks on an old wooden icebox that serves as a bar. He had refinished it himself, years back. He pours himself a bourbon and water. He fixes his mother a vodka and tonic, her usual, except with no vodka. The placebo always satisfied her; sometimes she would even become a little tiddly on the tonic water and lime wedge, saying the first drink had been a little strong and, please, make the second lighter on the vodka. A real drink would make her maudlin. She would sometimes cry. Other times she would become very argumentative. On the other hand, Clemmons wonders, maybe he's the one that wants no arguments, but only the casual agreements of strangers.

When he returns, the two women are sitting chummily side by side. It pleases him to see his daughter sitting next to his mother, one arm around her, and her round full eyes steeped in affection. The many years that separate them seem to vanish in this intimacy, a womanly intimacy from which he was excluded but which, at the same time, he felt he had arranged.

"What are you talking about?" he asks, handing out their drinks.

"Whether the wedding ceremony should be at one end of the field or the center," Daisy answers.

"I think it should be in the center," he says.

"What do you care," his mother says. "You won't be here."

"No, that's right," he says. "But for the sake of history, it should be the center."

"Where the fight was?" Daisy says. "To balance things somehow."

"That's the theory," he says and sits down, remembering it was Sam Broome's idea, the pledge of love on the same ground where brutal blood had been shed. It was a sentimental notion; ground was ground.

"It would make a good movie," Daisy says. "Someone like Stallone or James Caan."

"They weren't all that big," Clemmons says. "Morrisey weighed about one fifty or sixty and Sullivan was twenty pounds lighter and much older. But he was a deadly boxer, smart. He made a fool out of Morrisey for thirty-seven rounds. Beat him to a pulp. He'd come out, box around, deliver a punch, and then intentionally slip to the canvas.

The round would be over before Morrisey could land a punch."

"Then there was that lovely girl," Julia Clemmons says. Her speech slurred slightly.

"What lovely girl?" Clemmons asks.

"The one who was courted by that young man who worked in the grocery store."

"No, Ma, that was in Dad's book. That wasn't true."

"I don't know about that," she says, and rattles the ice in her drink.

"What happened to Sullivan?" Daisy asks. Her hair is dry now and floats around her face like a golden weaving come undone.

"Where's that book of your father's?" Julia Clemmons asks.

"I loaned it to someone. Why?"

"I just want to check something," the old lady says knowingly. "Just checking something." She rattles her drink again.

"Listen, Ma. Dad put a lot of people into his book that were made up." Clemmons looks at his mother. "We should keep our facts straight."

"I'm pretty sure that girl's name was Laurie," Julia tells Daisy. "Her father was a carpenter and he helped build the ring they fought in." She nods, and her granddaughter smiles and nods. Clemmons feels he's the dupe in a conspiracy, that he's been given a bogus message to deliver, and each word draws him closer to an unjust fate: destroy the bearer of this information. That's the information!

"Sullivan was murdered in jail," he says thoughtfully. "In San Francisco. Vigilantes, they think."

"But he won the fight?" Daisy says brightly. She was a good child.

"Not on the record book. By the thirty-seventh round, he had Morrisey beaten to a pulp. Years later, Morrisey became a state senator. Rich. Started the track at Saratoga. So who lost?"

"It was terrible," his mother agrees. "I remember your father telling me."

"It's for me," Daisy says and jumps up. The phone has rung.

"Her name was Laurie, wasn't it?" Julia Clemmons says. "Wasn't it Laurie?"

"Yes, Laurie," Clemmons says and looks down. "Her name was Laurie." The passing sun sharpens the pointed leaves of the iris plants along one edge of the open field.

Jenny's voice had become lost down there, as if she had gone beyond the field and through the woods on the other side; lost just as he told himself he had found her for good.

"You only say that, Charlie," she had said.

"Where are you calling from? I tried to call you, and your line is temporarily disconnected. You sound far away."

"I played San Francisco." Her voice turned clearly in his head. "A turkey called *Carnival in Flanders*. So, if I come back, what's the difference? Even with Olive living down South, it would be no different. What do you want, Charlie? Do you know?"

"Yes, I know."

"You *vant* to be alone, Charlie. Olive saw this and that's why she moved out. Oh, you like us well enough, maybe even love some of us, but we're only supposed to use the guest towels."

"Does Stein actually believe he's going to find Amelia Earhart alive?"

"Of course not. But he thinks he knows where she landed. He's been interviewing old admirals and pilots out here all week. We leave for Hawaii tomorrow. Then Australia. Then New Guinea. From there it's everyone into the canoes."

"Why do you go?"

"I'm not sure—well, don't laugh. Okay? The idea of her running out of gas with no place to land bothers me. That would be awful, watching that gauge get lower and lower and no place to set down. If we can find the place she landed, that would be something. You might even get me back, Charlie."

"Yes, come back."

But it is Claire on the telephone. Daisy has called him from the kitchen. "I've tried to call you for days," he says to her. "Didn't your answering service give you my messages?"

"They don't take you seriously," Claire replies. "I told you to stop speaking Spanish to them. They only record messages in English. How's the wedding coming along?"

He tells her about his mother and Daisy, about Olive coming on the weekend. "We don't know about the bridal party. It may be a hoax. Or perhaps some plot, some sort of guerrilla plot to assemble us here all at once and then hold executions."

"You're terrible. Why must you always wipe the bottom of the plate with shit."

"What is that, some kind of old folk expression you brought from Russia?"

"We didn't come from Russia. We came from Hungary."

"Well, anyway, when last heard from, Milly and the Stanley Livingston were in South Carolina. So, I want to talk about our plans. Is it to be St. Martin? Georgetown? How about Barbados? None of the above?"

"That's why I want to talk with you. I don't know if I can get away."

"What? What do you mean?"

"That's why you like me, isn't it?" Claire laughs lazily. The image of her sweet smile cruelly came to mind. "You like my being a transient. It saves you from feeling bad when you come and go, because you know I might be leaving for somewhere, too. I'm not here waiting for you all the time."

"But I thought we talked about going somewhere to . . ."

"Something has come up that I have to deal with," she says evenly. It's her business voice. He had heard it often enough, usually in the middle of the night as she talked to someone on the phone. He wondered if, right then, some lout lay over her legs as she talked on the telephone to him, some fourth-rate versifier who waited patiently to rhyme a couplet.

"Who's there?" he says, then is immediately chagrined.

"I'm not home," she answers. "Hold on a minute. . . ." The line goes dead. In the kitchen, his mother and Daisy were setting the table by the window. His daughter waves for him to come to the table. Familiar with Claire's telephone perambulations, he wonders if he should ask them to bring him a plate of food so he could eat standing up at his desk in the back room as Claire finished her thought, her idea, whatever. A sound like ruffled cloth, a clump-clump, followed by silence again. He becomes a little angry. He had seen her do this with others, put the phone down, sip some wine, kiss him; it was a demonstration of her power that he did not think he deserved.

"This soufflé is only good just now," he hears his mother say. Daisy looks at him imploringly.

"You there?" Claire's voice returns. "Listen. I can't talk now. Can you call me back? Call me back at exactly nine-thirty. Okay? Do you have a pencil? Here's the number."

"What's the area code?" He takes down the number.

"Same as yours," she giggles. "I'm very close to where you are. That's what I want to tell you."

"Where are you?" He looks out the window. Maybe she's standing in the road with the phone held to her ear.

"Call me back. Nine-thirty," and she hangs up.

His mother's cooking was always evenly good, if not extraordinarily imaginative, and normally Clemmons would have enjoyed the cheese soufflé, the spinach salad, and the macedonia she has made for their supper; but it all tastes flat, the same. He wonders if the last meals of condemned men were as flavorless, made flavorless in spite of careful preparation because the diners had lost their capacity to taste anything. The taste buds went first, someone had told him.

"Who was that?" Daisy asks. "One of your little pals?" Her expression teases him.

"A good friend whose opinion I need from time to time." He pours some wine.

"I bet," she says, taking a mouthful of soufflé. "Do you still carry rubbers in your wallet? I came across a couple of Trojans in your billfold the last time I was home."

"Stop that, Daisy!" he says. He looks quickly at his mother. She seemed not to hear them, bent over her plate with a preoccupied air like some member of a bridge club testing the dessert. "What were you doing going through my wallet?"

"You told me to," she says. "I wanted to borrow a few bucks and you told me to look in your wallet. What's wrong with that?" The girl persists, "I think it's nice. It means you take some responsibility. Most men these days dump it all on you."

"You look more and more like your father, Andrew." His mother's words surface, rise out of a deep conversation she has been having with herself. "You have more hair, of course, than he did. But your face has settled like his. He had the sweetest mouth, and his eyes were like yours, never knew whether he was serious or making fun."

"You had good times, Grandma?" Daisy asks.

His mother has become animated, her eyes glow and there is a youthful sway to her body. "We had such good times, Daisy," she replies. Julia Clemmons was the only grandparent the girls would ever know, and they eagerly sought information on the others they had missed. They liked to hear stories, and when his mother was in the mood, if her joints were not too painful, she would oblige.

"Sometimes, we'd pack a picnic and get in this Packard car we had and just drive down along the Wabash River, through little towns like Beal or Orville. Sometimes we would go all the way to New Harmony, where those people had started that colony—it was all deserted by then. Sometimes, Herbie would fish there in the Wabash and I'd gather berries for us. . . ."

"What berries would that be?" Clemmons asks.

"Why strawberries, of course. Wild strawberries," his mother answers calmly. "And then we'd have our picnic there, on the banks of the Wabash." Clemmons hums the tune that goes with the words. His mother doesn't hear, but Daisy silences him with a look. "Or we'd go to New Harmony. It wasn't fixed up then the way it is now, no state park. And we'd go from house to house . . ."

"Oh yeah," Daisy says happily. "I was there. It's nice."

". . . one time we even spent the night there, in the meeting house. I remember the moonlight. The whole village was lit up, like day. And we were the only people, had it to ourselves."

"Far out," the girl says. The old lady has stopped talking, like a record that has abruptly ended. Even her pose and expression are suspended. She looks disengaged. To oblige Daisy, to oblige both women, Clemmons nudges his mother back into the groove.

"You and Dad had many good times. What happened to that old Packard?"

"My husband did many articles for the *American Mercury*. Mr. Mencken paid very well. They were undercover articles, mostly about labor unions. He'd always sign them with an X. Or that's what Mr. Mencken did. It made them more mysterious, I guess . . . by Union Leader X. Something like that."

"And he bought the car with the money from the magazine articles," Clemmons says. Daisy's eyes were like beacons.

"One day your father just got in that car and drove off. Left you and me there in Vincennes. I guess that car was more than just a car for him. It was a location. Men need their space."

"So do women," the girl replies.

"That's how he got up here. In that car. Then he built that cabin, the one you knew, Andrew."

Except it wasn't a cabin, and his father had not built the small Colonial house he used to visit. Why would his mother think of it as a cabin? Why would she think Herb Clemmons had built it? By the time he got to know him, the older man could hardly lift whisky to his mouth, let alone a hammer and saw. He'd be all right when he met the train at Copake Falls, sober and cheery, but in an hour he'd cry, and in another he'd be incoherent. The mornings would be the worst; the way he apologized. By then he was only doing stringer work for the newspaper, an irregular column. He also wrote annual reports for local companies—that's how he lived. That was the place he had cut out of the woods for himself, Clemmons thought. His getaway.

If Sam Broome had whined, he had done it out of his wife's hearing. That afternoon, Clemmons had finally put his courage together and gone by Broome's condominium in Dutch Village, but the producer had already left for the city.

"He heard about it yesterday," his wife had said when she opened the door to Clemmons. "He located that Mr. Hicks who told him the concert permit had been denied. Come in. Can you come in?"

"So what will he do?" Clemmons had asked. Stephanie Broome had been refinishing furniture. She wore heavy work gloves. A dungaree shirt hung loose over shorts.

"Do? What do you mean do? He's gone to New York to see some backers for the movie. He still has the permit for the movie." She had led him out to a balcony off the duplex's living room. A small table—it looked like a copy of a Shaker design—had been set upon newspapers spread out on the deck. "I think it's cherry," she had said. "Do you think it's cherry?"

The wood beneath the layers of paint had a faintly reddish hue. "It looks like cherry," Clemmons had agreed. The young woman had retrieved a pair of sunglasses next to a pile of rags, a paint scraper, and a tin of remover. The glasses were oversized, and when she put them on they called attention to her retroussé nose, its pert and piquant sensuality within her thin face.

"I wear these to protect my eyes." She smiles. "From the paint remover splashing." Her smile was small and neat, which made the stained, crooked teeth even more disturbing. Clemmons wondered what the priorities had been that determined this girl's nose be operated upon, be surgically reshaped, but had left the teeth miserably intact. Perhaps she had been meant to move through society showing only a tight-lipped smile; a musing, haughty ingénue. On the other hand, it would have been typical of Carter Perry, the culture entrepreneur who had been her father, to have ignored such basic flaws as long as something could cover them over, a dazzling surface effect.

The view from this balcony, from this side of the complex, looked south, and Clemmons could see far down the Harlem Valley. To the right, the Catskills were so clearly outlined that it seemed as though they were on this side of the Hudson; say, over around Clermont, and not miles away. Just below where he stood, across the highway, a farmer was disking a field. Corn would go in soon, if it got dry enough.

"I'm sorry about this," he had told Stephanie Broome. She bent over the table, carefully scraping, scraping. "It's my fault. This man Hicks has held a grudge against me for a long time. A while back, I managed to option the whole town from Hicks's father, and took it over bit by bit, as I could afford to. It was just luck. Also, the old man was greedy. But his son felt left out. Earle thought I had cheated. Cheated him. He eventually inherited some of the money—but not the village. So there's been this thing between us. He's always wanted to get back at me."

As he had talked, Clemmons had turned from the view back to the young woman working over the table. Her long, dark hair had been fetched up in a disorderly pile on the top of her head and speared by a couple of brass pins. As she bent over her work, the loose shirt fell away so Clemmons could see her bare breasts sway and jiggle. With no sexual curiosity, nor the slightest whim of desire, he had observed how well-modeled they were, how they issued from a rather bony thorax and how the aureoles formed delicate pink halos. He awoke to the fact, standing there on that balcony, that he was looking upon her as kin more than as a woman, someone with whom he had more things in common than not. It was very peculiar.

"So what will he do?" he had asked. Stephanie Broome had begun to whistle to herself as she scraped the old wood, as Clemmons talked. Then she straightened up, repositioned the big sunglasses with one gloved finger.

"He'll just have to cut it." It sounded as if she had referred to a delicious dessert. "He's run through all my money. His last two pictures lost a bundle. He can't even sell them to television. He's been playing producer ever since we married and now he's going to have to produce. Really produce. Do a number." She had dabbled more remover on a corner of the table.

Her voice had that open, laid-back drawl of Eastern finishing schools, the sort of accent that used to be heard on Saturday afternoons at the Jumble Shop or P. J. Clarke's. Stephanie Broome could have been just as casually selecting salad greens at the grocer's. Clemmons looked into the living room of the duplex, now thinking its chic barrenness might be attributed to something besides style.

The little girl trudged around the corner of the bookcase–storage unit, her bare feet sinking deep into the pile of the carpet. She wore an exquisite white pinafore over a pretty dress, and the front of the embroidered material was darkly spotted with the juice from the large peach she held in both hands. Her mouth and cheeks were similarly stained, a sumptuous wetness. She stopped abruptly, seeing Clemmons on the balcony with her mother, and brought the peach to her mouth. She contemplated him, no doubt reviewing the different possibilities this strange man's appearance might present. Then she advanced toward him on shaky, pudgy legs. She had a crazy grin and a maniacal look in her eye as she held out the peach to Clemmons. "Eat?"

"Just today, I got an offer," Clemmons is saying to Claire Wolferman. "She was very young and she offered me a peach."

"I bet."

"Hold on a minute," he says and puts the phone down to step to the door of the library. He hears his mother and Daisy laughing upstairs, the sound of the television rising like surf around their voices. For a moment, he is tempted to look through a magazine before going back to the phone, to leave Claire hanging on the line as she has beached others. "I just wanted to close the door," he says. "Now where are you?"

"I'm at Axel's Farm," she almost whispers.

Clemmons is shocked. "What are you doing there? Why, you're right up the road from here." He's quickly suspicious. She is probably visiting someone at the writers' colony. She's surrounded by poets affecting cowboy boots and silver Navaho belt buckles. She has even chuckled meanly into his ear.

"It bothers you that I'm so close, doesn't it? Like I said, it would mess up your plans if the Babylonian strolled into your wedding party."

"Why are you here—there?"

"I'm on the board of this place. One of my family's foundations funds it. They've got an administrative problem and there's a board meeting."

"Are you staying there?"

"Hmm. I have a nice little room, all to myself. On the

ground floor of the old gatekeeper's cottage. Why don't you come up and see me?"

"You mean now?"

"Hmm. I'd leave a light on for you, and the window would be open. They have a funny curfew system here, guests have to leave at midnight, but no one would know. Andy. Please?"

She has never sounded so winsome and the urgency in her voice provokes the same need in him. "Listen, Claire, I've had a problem but it's pretty much over. Nothing serious. But I wondered if you've been to a doctor lately."

"Yes, I have," she says matter-of-factly. "He says it's okay for me to have a baby. Everything would be normal."

"That's not what I mean."

"What do you mean? Oh, Andy, this is too good an opportunity to let go."

"How long will you be there?"

"I don't know how long I'll be here." She begs but not seriously. "I'm here now. Tonight. Oh, for God's sake," she cries into his ear. "Loosen up that tight Wasp asshole of yours and get up here. Who's there? Why can't you leave? Is wifey there?"

"No, just my mother and Daisy."

"Well, tell them you're going out for some pizza."

"No one goes out for pizza in Boston Corners."

"Nor for anything else, it looks like. What a dump. No wonder you like to come in to see me."

"That's not true . . ."

"Are you coming or not?" The imperious tone of her voice carries an ultimatum. More. It sounds as if she were already activating Plan B. Claire always had more than one plan for every whim, or she made them up as needed. He can see her getting out a flashlight, preparing to make a bed check of contemporary American letters. "Andy?"

"Yes. All right," he says. "I'll be there as soon as I can."

"You're leaving now?"

"Yes."

"Now."

"Yes . . . yes."

When he shouts upstairs, Daisy asks, "How long are you going to be gone?"

"I don't know. These meetings can sometimes drag on. Why?"

"I thought maybe you could pick up some pizza on your way back. Peppers and mushrooms."

"Can't be done," he shouts back, wishing someone would let him in on the joke. He seemed to have stepped into a tangle the last few days; odd that this would be so, as he remembered how carefully he had put down his feet when he jogged into Irondale that morning several weeks ago.

But now he drives toward the writers' colony with reckless speed, the thirty or more miles seem to double even as the car's wheels roll over them, the highway passing under the headlamps like an endless belt. Stands of new burdock and sumac grow at the roadside, catch the car lights, bend and release the darkness. Some locals would pick the tender burrs of burdock now and cook them before they hardened into spiky musket balls. The weeds still seem manageable, deceptively domesticated, growing along the road in the simple harmony of a spring night.

But the dance goes faster and faster, *allegro molto,* as Clemmons drives faster. He is eager to lose himself in the luxury of Claire Wolferman's arms and to forget, for a while, the tangle grown around him.

Chapter Five

It used to be said of Americans that we can be recognized by our good teeth and decent footwear, but if nowadays this observation can be made of others, there is yet something else we might claim as singular, and that is the luggage we carry. From the beginning we have been a nation of travelers, within and without our borders, and an American with a suitcase or a trunk in tow is as familiar to station platforms as he is to the pages of literature.

Survey any air or train terminal; our luggage is usually set down into one of two groups: an array of matched cases or mounds of bulging rucksacks. It is curious that in a nation where choice has been constitutionalized, we limit ourselves in our variety of luggage to either the formal or the informal; no practical alternatives in between. So it is, as travelers, we either resemble a casual military on some quaint maneuver or a staff of servants accompanying garments for which the owner waits impatiently in the Capitol.

The luggage belonging to Olive Chase Clemmons falls into this last category, her husband thinks, even as a powder-blue suede overnight case pops out of the baggage chute and onto the moving track. A larger valise of the same color comes next, almost shoulders its way through the opening, though without losing its feminine essence. There would be more, Clemmons knows as he looks around the Albany Air Terminal.

It was somehow right that Olive's luggage should precede her, a sort of honor guard clearing the way, he would think, though in fairness, he had been late meeting her plane—he had to run Benny Smith over to the clinic—so she had already deplaned and disappeared into some part of the terminal when he arrived. But her luggage is here, and she would eventually show up to claim it. Another suitcase—for a set of cymbals, perhaps—has just appeared and moves majestically toward Clemmons.

He often wondered how many pieces of luggage she owned; or what different ensembles or particular articles they had been designed for.

Clemmons had discovered that luggage made Olive feel secure, and she always took a lot with her, even though she might not open half of it. Just to know she had it nearby made her feel good. He could never reconcile this characteristic with the liberal political causes she had championed when they first met. The two somehow did not go together.

So now, here is A. W. Clemmons, piling all this blue suede luggage on a baggage cart as a porter says, "Sure is a lot of stuff."

"Sure is," Clemmons agrees, thinking the porter had only been challenged up to now by the attaché cases and "over-niters" of state politicians who pass through the Albany airport.

In fact, Olive is escorted by one of this kind. Clemmons sees her in the orange shirtwaist dress almost as he recognizes the species that accompanies her across the terminal. The man walks a half step behind Olive, the look and pace of an attendant—and a hack attendant at that, Clemmons would think.

"Here you are, A.W." Olive embraces him. She smells of

many good things, including Scotch whisky, and her eyes lift slyly to his face. "I was getting worried about you. You remember ol' Pres Simmons from the Governor Stevenson days. We met on the plane. Imagine that."

The two men shake hands. Clemmons almost asks ol' Pres to help, when the man stoops and, without breaking his stride or conversation with Olive, picks up the last bag.

"You think we can get all this in the car?" the porter asks.

But they do, with a couple strapped to the rack on top. Almost before the car is out of the terminal's parking lot, Olive has kicked off her shoes and curls up on the seat, massaging one bare foot. It is a disarming pose; the country girl kicking away the confinements of the sophisticated lady. But her eyes are dark, they have that "unhappy look," and she makes several *humfps* before she says, "You didn't have to say that."

"Say what?"

"I'll just relieve you of that, ol' Pres."

"Was I supposed to tear the bag out of his hands?"

"It was the way you said it. Your tone. If you're going to be all pokey, Andrew Wing, you can just turn right around and take me back to the airport and I'll just fly back." She knew she had him there.

He had planned meeting her in a more cheerful frame of mind, because not only was he genuinely glad to see her but her arrival meant that he could leave. Or it had been supposed to mean that. But so many things had begun to go wrong. The latest being Benny Smith's accident.

"But how did it happen?" Olive asks.

"He had cleaned out this wasp nest up under the eaves, near the ridge pole. Today, he was there painting and a couple of the wasps came back—looking for their nest, I guess—and took out their frustration on him. He slipped trying to get away and fell. Fortunately, it only looks like a dislocated shoulder."

"Well, get another painter."

"Impossible. You have to line up house painters a year in advance. I'll finish it."

"A.W., you shouldn't be climbing around rooftops at your age. You look terrible anyway. What have you been up to around here? Or down to? You look like you've been doing it too much."

"I'm fine," he says. "I feel fine." However, he is exhausted. Only last night, as he was getting ready to climb out of Claire's window at the writers' colony, he caught a foot on the casement ledge and tumbled to the ground. It was only a fall of about three feet, but if he had been as high as the dormer windows of his house, if tired and distracted as he was, he were to make the same mistake, it would be serious.

Claire had just been telling him how wonderful he made her feel, how she felt "set up"—that was her term—the day after one of his stealthy visits. "Yesterday," she had whispered, "someone said I glowed." And just then, he caught his foot and fell backward into the Wagnerian mists that seemed to seep up through the grounds of Axel's Farm.

"Listen, that reminds me"—he eases the car into four-lane traffic—"have you checked in with your doctor lately? I seem to have picked up a kind of fungus, maybe from you—nothing serious and I'm okay now," he adds quickly.

"From me? From me?" Olive blurts. "Well, I like that."

"It's possible I may have given it to you, I don't know . . . "

"Well, shoot. Aren't you the one? I'm okay, you can believe that. Anyway, so what? You have to learn to take the pain with the pleasure."

"No pain, just a little itch," he said. She sprawls over the seat to plant a wet kiss in his ear.

"I am a little down, I guess," he says. He feels a comradeship with this handsome woman, the mother of his children. He wants to tell her about Sam Broome and Earle Hicks, but then decides against it for there would be too much to explain about the producer. She doesn't know him. "Maybe I'm going through some kind of midlife crisis," he says, gunning the motor to get around a truck on the highway.

Olive's laughter comes out like sorghum on a cold morning. "Honey, you've been going through a midlife crisis since I've known you, since you turned twenty-one." She cranks down the window and lights a cigarette. "Well, have you heard from Milly?"

"No."

"I did. Just before I left. They were in D.C. and planned a couple of days there. Her man's daddy is some sort of a high-powered lawyer it turns out, with some agency down there."

"So when does she arrive?" The logistics were becoming more complicated with each day. If Claire were still meeting with the other trustees of the writers' colony when the wedding took place, how could they go anywhere? How could he go away—anywhere? Moreover, it was slow work getting Claire to move from anyplace once she settled in. He remembers how she would stay on at restaurant tables long after the waiters had retired, the lights all but turned out on them; she rarely had any immediate plans, no other location that immediately required her presence. A bad characteristic? Clemmons wondered. So even after her administrative duties were done, she might just stay on at the writers' colony. Maybe, Clemmons thinks, he could apply for a fellowship. He might write his memoirs; it seemed a time for memoirs.

"I'd say in about a week," Olive has just said. "She told me what she wants. How's Daisy? I'm anxious to see your mother. How is she? It's going to be a simple wedding. You'll like it, A.W.," she says.

"I won't be here," Clemmons replies.

"Oh, that's right. I forgot about that." Olive's large eyes slant, and she puffs on her cigarette. "Where you going? Do you know where you're going? It's shameful, I think, for you to cut out, take off from your own daughter's wedding." Her voice is not angry, but is even slightly amused. "I guess you got some sugar baby stashed away somewhere."

"I have no . . ."

"A.W., this is Olive you're talking to." She tosses out her cigarette. "I know all about your proclivities. I bet she's in the arts. You go for the arts. Like that singer."

"Cut it out." His fatigue has made him vulnerable; she has got to him. He looks at her. She has changed her position and sits with legs crossed, one foot swinging quickly to and fro. She's having a good time. "You always bring her up."

"You're always thinking about her, so I always bring her up. I don't care if she's been chewed up and digested by every savage in Timbuktu, I can still be jealous of her. You ought to be happy for that, on both our accounts. Hers and mine."

"Let's change the subject. There's this man called Sam Broome who wants to make a movie about the fight." Clemmons talks in clusters of information. Carter Perry's daughter. Sam Broome. The local opposition. Earle Hicks. Broome's cash problems.

"Does he know what he's doing?" Olive asks. "Why are you so het up about it?" She turns to the open window and the turbulent air seems to perk her up. "He sounds like another one of . . . you're always picking up these people. Don't you believe in natural selection? That woman in your office, Rita Whatever, and I could name others before. This guy. You get put upon all the time by this sort, because you think you've had the good breaks and they haven't. I tell you something—you know why Rita Whatever didn't make it with that bookstore? Because she was too dumb to realize that nobody around here reads books. That's why." Olive straightens her dress, pulls it even to her knees with a prim impatience, and then falls back against the seat, arms folded across her bosom. Her eyes are closed. "They're not pioneers, Andy. I expect most of them, one reason or another, had no choice in the matter. You ever see a fox move around a chicken house?" Clemmons wonders when it was she had last witnessed such an encounter. Olive's cheeks have flushed beneath their tan. "Why, he pretends he just likes it out there, tippy-toeing in the moonlight, and that funning look on his face, but he wants to get inside there with all those chickens real bad. Real bad. I'm telling you."

"So you're saying I'm dumb—not able to tell who wants to get in with the chickens." He laughs. In spite of himself, Olive has raised his spirits.

"Nossir, you're not dumb," she says, leaning back again. Her eyes close. "You're good. But sometimes that amounts to the same thing." She smiles, as if she reviews a silent film clip that features A. W. Clemmons, good and gullible, virtuous and vacant. He sees himself swinging long ladders into china cabinets. Falling out of windows at two in the morning as beautiful, nude women lean forward to kiss him.

The word "pioneer" had made him smile. But then as she warmed to her subject, heating to a revival pitch, her description had become right and he had smiled from this recognition, out of embarrassment, from being caught out. Olive always had this effect upon him. Her eagerness to barter ideas, to pick through the remnants of a conversation or a problem until—and you could always tell when by the excitement in her language—she pieced together an ensemble that would dramatize the truth of the matter. It used to be said of her, in the old days, by those politicians who had either been helped or hurt, that she talked "like a man," and it had been meant as a compliment. But they had known no other way to put it, their own language being deficient.

At this moment, she looks very pleased with herself, Clemmons thinks. She seems to nap, smiling, but she could be humming under her breath for all he knew. A plump double chin cups her round face as the orange material of her dress stimulates the tanned flesh tones of her neck and arms. He wonders if she's touching up her hair, because its Oriental blackness is deeply lustrous, almost blue. Milly had got her coloring from her. The years had compacted on Olive's small bone structure, but tennis and swimming have smoothed and modeled her so she resembles one of those physical education teachers who, though much older, are far more attractive than their younger, more lissome students.

So now he's surprised by a sudden urgency. Surprised, for the last several nights with Claire would seem to have left little to urge—though there is a sensuality that will often accompany exhaustion, a thin line between the two and sometimes one is even taken for the other. Looking over at Olive, he wonders if in her wily knowledge of him, a scholarship polished in their marriage and parenthood, she has not deliberately spoken the way she has, talking directly to the fears and doubts in his mind, knowing the intriguing effect it would have on him. Olive Chase had that instinct that seems to be given to some Southern women, passed on to them along with the old stories, which held that though the way to a man's heart might be through his stomach, the way to a man's mind was through somewhere quite different. Olive never cared much for cooking.

In other times, he would probably have pulled off the highway, or even checked into a motel using an alias, probably the name of a baseball player, since the owner might recognize the real name and wonder why Mr. and Mrs. A. W. Clemmons of Boston Corners are checking into a room at one in the afternoon, and then only a dozen miles from their home. They had done that before and, in fact, here is the Half Moon Motel coming up just ahead, a place where he and Olive had abandoned their captained selves on more than one exploration, and he even takes his foot off the accelerator, considers, then resumes speed. The slight variation in the car's motion pops her eyes open, almost audibly, and she sits up and smacks her lips.

"Of course, A.W.," she says, watching the Half Moon

Motel pass. "You know I like you for it. I love you for it. I respect you for it. I respect you like hell for it, but—sugar —don't ask me to live with it."

So here's the problem. The house is half painted. Before he fell from the ladder, driven off by the wasps he had alienated, Benny Smith had done the front, two ends, and the porch steps. The easy part. Left were all the dormers, the trim, and the triangular vents high up under the eaves. Where the wasps were. Moreover, the moment Olive walked into the house, after kissing Daisy and hugging Julia Clemmons, she had declared that all the drapes, rugs, and slipcovers had to be washed and cleaned. At this moment, Clemmons can hear her inside the house giving orders on where to put things. The whole place is being rearranged. "Push, Grandma," he hears Daisy say.

Then, this morning, he checks in with the office and Rita Pickens tells him the movie people have shown up to film the commercial at the store and that maybe, just maybe, he ought to be around, if only for the sake of form, since the sheriff's deputies are a little put out because no one had informed them, and they were having just a jolly time redirecting traffic through Irondale. But, of course, she had finally straightened things out, but not without some effort —her back pains were killing her—but could she, since he has deigned to call his place of business, could she speak a moment with *"la chatelaine,"* so he hands over the phone to Olive who speaks to Rita Pickens with a loquacious warmth, an intimacy that summons the atmosphere of sorority reunions.

Then, Claire Wolferman is still at the writers' colony. Her committee was still arguing over the new director, and when he called her last night, she had become petulant and almost belligerent.

"Why not?" she had asked.

"Well, I just can't," he had said, keeping the other ear open. The women were in the kitchen talking. It was after dinner.

"You could, if you wanted to," Claire said, her voice going sour.

"I really can't tonight. It's difficult to get away."

"Think of something," her voice challenged. "I'm all alone here tonight. They've all gone over to Pittsfield, bar-hopping. We could have the place to ourselves. I've thought about it all day." Her voice was that of a child who had been promised something special for dessert.

"I tell you, I can't tonight. Tomorrow."

"Maybe I'll just come down there," Claire said. "It would be very normal. I'm here after all. On business. We know each other. I'd like to see what you're like in your cave. All your women around you."

"Oh, yeah," Clemmons replied, trying to smile. Even talking on the phone, he tried to smile. Just then, Olive materialized in the doorway. She hadn't been trying to eavesdrop, but had padded through the house barefoot. She looked for something. "Well, have to look at the plats first," Clemmons said evenly.

"Someone's there. Olive's just come into the room?"

"Yes, that's right," he replied, all brisk business.

"I've been thinking about you all day," Claire said sulkily. Olive had paused at a bookshelf, then picked up the cushions on the sofa. "I've been thinking about sucking your cock."

"Uh-huh," he said.

"I'd take a long time. Very slow."

"Yeah, sure," he said, and smiled at Olive. He made a desperate gesture, rolled his eyes, as if to say "damn business." She looked back, a flat stare, as if to say "damn liar."

"Is she still there?"

"Listen, let me call you back. I need to give it some thought."

"Oh, c'mon, Andy. Damn it. I need to talk to you. Also I want to hear about the wedding. Just for an hour. You can think of some reason to be away for an hour. Don't you go out to local bars to talk with people?" Olive had found whatever she had been looking for and had left the room.

"I really can't. You have to understand."

"I understand that I need you now. You've needed me times and I've been there. I've been sitting all day with these old dopes who don't listen to me. They all think I'm just a rich twat, playing with daddy's money. Well, I may be but I'm smarter than they are. My ideas are better. Is she still there?"

"Tomorrow night. Leave a light in the window," he said. "I'll stand beneath your window and sing *'mi canto del cisne . . . por puro gusto.'* "

"Oh . . ." Her voice had melted. "What's that mean? Something sweet? *Gusto* means 'pleasing'?"

"I'll be Robin Hood climbing to your balcony."

"Will you?" She sounded mollified, then added, "It's only a couple of feet." But he had soothed her.

But this morning is a different matter. Clemmons looks up. The lapstrake siding under the eaves looks flayed where Benny Smith's departing brush strokes had left a ragged edge of paint: a moment in time brushed on that place where Benny Smith and nature had collided. To fall from such a height, Clemmons thinks, might well be a swan dive and not so graceful a one at that, so he has fashioned a halter of sorts out of nylon line and has fixed it about his waist and shoulders and thrown the bight of the line around the chimney nearest the unfinished job. Benny Smith holds the other end of the rope.

"You look like one of them mountain climbers, A.W." Benny Smith giggles. The handyman reaches into the sling that supports his left arm and pulls out a piece of a wasp nest. "I saved some of this, like for good luck," he says brightly. He holds it close to Clemmons's face, so close and so demandingly that the gesture might look hostile though Clemmons knew this was not so, that Benny rarely showed anger but sometimes his motor reflexes would speed up, in spurts, and the abrupt movements give the appearance of anger. It disturbed him, Clemmons knew, when this happened; but there was nothing he could do about it, and it was a condition that would become more pronounced as he got older. In time, he might duplicate the ceaseless bobbing and weaving of his son, Little Ben, who, even as they stand here talking on the terrace, Clemmons looped with rope like a lineman, sits rocking to and fro in the cab of his father's pickup truck down by the old fight field. The boy moves ceaselessly, like some part of the truck's mechanism that has been left idling, and Clemmons imagines the two of them, father and son, swaying back and forth like buoys marking a harbor entrance. Or perhaps, in some magical transfer, some reverse placement of fault, the father alone would bob and weave and the son would become still.

"You know how many sides they got?" Benny asks. He still holds the brown, dry comb before Clemmons's face. Then he inspects it himself. "They got six sides, and all even, like they was stamped out. Each one just like the next. Look at that."

"It's amazing, isn't it?" Clemmons says. The section is feather light. It is approximately two inches in diameter and with about forty-five hexagonal compartments, each one nearly identical to the other and all precisely constructed, interlocked. Clemmons squeezes the papery construction. The hive has great strength in the direction of its chambers but the cells are easily collapsed if compressed laterally. The slightest pressure will wreck their symmetry. Some scientists, Clemmons thought, could reduce this difference in stress to a tic in the wasp's nervous system, a relay point in a set of impulses that moves the insect to engineer these identical geometric perfections over and over and unknowingly.

"You can keep it," Benny Smith tells him happily. "I got lots more. Hell, I knock 'em down all the time."

"Thank you," Clemmons says seriously. He puts the fragment in his pant pocket. "Now, you just keep your foot against the bottom rung of that ladder and hold on to this end of the line. If I slip, it will break my fall."

"You bet your life, A.W.," the man says.

"I do, indeed," Clemmons replies and picks up the bucket of paint and a wide paintbrush. He feels like a man mounting the gallows as he climbs the ladder, already hitched to his final adventure. Nor does he climb the scaffold alone or unnoticed.

"Be careful, Pop," Daisy says through a living room window. The screen door slams; light steps scruff the porch.

"Oh, Andrew." It's his mother's voice from below. "Should you be up there? Don't fall. Be careful, now."

I'll be careful, he thinks, because such warnings and precautions had caused him to fall too many times before. How many apple trees, garage roofs, or playground jungles had he fallen from because she had warned him to be careful, even waiting underneath the tree, walking back and forth in the play yard, with a patience weaned on the sure expectation that he would fall. It had been like a last juvenile perversity that urged him to fail, hard to shake loose even as an adult; to unthinkingly shrug away her advice, her cautions, he would sometimes find himself walking on empty air. So he had learned to take advice calmly. Very carefully, he wedges the paint bucket and brush into a joint of the house and roof, and pulls himself up on the steep shingled surface.

He lies at a sharp angle to the horizon, along the inclined plane of the roof. The composition soles of his work shoes slip, then catch, then slip again on the worn and cracked cedar shingles. His left arm is jammed beneath his body.

"Once you get by that," Benny Smith says from below, "the rest is easy."

Moving crablike, Clemmons inches his way up and away from the edge of the roof, getting higher and higher, holding the paint can and brush in his right hand and pulling himself up with his left. He remembers the old movies about commandos sneaking up on some enemy post. Some of the rope tied around his torso enwraps one leg and he pauses to undo it, then eases up onto the ridge of the house section next to the center part where Benny had been painting.

Cautiously, Clemmons stands up and balances on the ridge pole. Actually, it's more than wide enough to walk on comfortably, and the roof that he had just clung to, had almost tried to grow on like moss, seems to have leveled out now that he's standing up. It is still cool, and there are no signs of the insects. The outline of the old wasp settlement is directly over his head, like smudged erasures. With a heavy brushful of paint, Clemmons wipes out the last of the ruin. "Drunken archaeologist," he says to himself.

"You okay?" Benny Smith asks from below. He is inside the angle of Clemmons's sight.

"I'm okay. Do you have a good grip on that rope?"

"I got it, I do, A.W. I'm holding it and I also got it around my belt, too."

This is not the highest part of the house; the roof that supports the four dormers of the upstairs bedroom is another three feet higher; another height, he thinks, to master tomorrow. But even from where he stands, there's a clear view in all directions except at his back, where the mountain ridge rises above and almost over the house like a great wave of green water. The morning sun was still on the other side of the mountain, perhaps cautiously creeping up the sharp, slate-loosened incline as he has just done the roof, but its light already warmed the fields in the valley beyond, sparkled on metal and glass, etched fenceposts and the wires that connect them. His vision has become meticulous, high-powered, and he can see all the details of the barnyard in the farm almost a mile down the road, toward Copake. The iron bands that hold the silo together, the bolt heads on a tractor's wheel parked near a shed. The broken windows in the barn's ground floor patched with chicken wire. As he paints and looks, then dips the brush into the can and applies it once more, he sees the farmer emerge from the barn, step to the tractor, mount it, and back it up to hitch into a cultivator.

Clemmons breathes deeply, feeling a kinship with that farmer, and also with the someone cutting wood way off the other way, the sound of the chain saw like a model engine. He imagines all the others he cannot see, a host of husbandry engaged in the morning light. Where the town road turns into the state highway, Clay Moore's green sedan comes into view, its U.S. Mail sign on top erect. Clemmons pauses, paintbrush dripping on the shingles, his work shoes, to count the stops the toylike car makes as the mail is distributed—his interest disengaged by the distance that permits him, at the same time, to observe who gets mail this morning and who does not. It was like making a catalogue of the view's contents, a reference of the community for the time it might no longer exist so that its places and features could be called up from such remembrance and given the immediacy of memory—if there would be anyone around to call these things up.

He knew well enough that the good weather stretched such illusions, put him within the same frame as those who actually grew from the land. He always thought of it that way: not lived *on* the land but grew *from* it, like the corn they raised for their winter feed. He and those to whom he sold old houses, the rundown farms and tenant shacks, they all lived *on* the land. The preposition was important. His easiest sales were always made on days such as this.

But then poor weather set in, or hard winters, when the limitations of rural life would close in upon the new owners of these old country places. Those who belong, who grew from the land, welcome these wet or cold intervals, for there are chores enough to do inside the house or barns—repairs, mendings, all set aside for just such bad weather. But in bad weather, those who live on the land are kept inside with nothing to do, save to walk from room to room of their refurbished old houses, putting up busyness that preserves their illusions of belonging.

Clemmons is thinking this as he squats to paint some lower strakes, neatly outlining the frame of a window set at a 45-degree angle into the siding parallel with the pitch of the roof, that same window just opposite his bed and through which he can see the Taghkanic Range. He handles the brush with a flourish, a casual expertise, barely getting any paint on the window frame, which looks pretty good, doesn't need to be touched up, and, anyhow, he isn't going to come up here again with a can of trim to do it. He stoops and peers closely at the smudge on the windowpane. It is the greasy shadow of that queer dollop of paint that had looked like a question mark, except from this side of the glass, it resembles a worm, one that has coiled and reared, ready to strike.

"Look out!" yells Benny Smith because Clemmons stumbled slightly as he straightened up, the muscles in his legs cramped and stiffly responding. The rope that connected him to Benny has lost its slack.

"I'm okay," he replies. Talking to Benny this way, with the man under the roof line and out of sight, made the exchange even more otherworldly than usual, he thought. It was as if the man's voice passed up through the maple tree that hung over the roof and was amplified through the new green leaves. "I'm going to move down this other side now," he says. Slowly but with confidence, he steps down the other side of the roof's slope. There was this section to do. Then they could move down to the back of the house. That would be the afternoon. Tomorrow, he'd come back up and do the dormers. "So, what else is happening?" he asks.

"I went to Bucky Waldron's layout last night," the voice says.

"That's right. I heard he had died," Clemmons says, carefully laying down a path of fresh paint along the back eave. "He died up in the woods, isn't that it?"

"I guess they must of had to busted his legs to get him straightened out," Benny's voice now seems to come from a louvered panel set like a keystone just under the roof's peak. "They didn't find him up there in the wood back of the old mill until days after. His sister reported him missing."

"Jacking deer to the very end," Clemmons says. "You got to give him credit. I like that."

"Wasn't just deer, A.W.," the voice replies. "He was shooting everything in sight, I guess, from the way they tell it. They found all around him: rabbits, groundhogs, squirrels—it was a shoot-out, you might say. I guess there wasn't much left of them squirrels after that old 32–40 of his got to 'em. I guess not."

"That's crazy. Why'd he want to do a thing like that?" Clemmons looks up and around. There has been a noise somewhere behind his right ear.

"I don't know, A.W. I surely don't know. Nobody could ask him, because he was as dead as them squirrels and that one deer he bagged—they say it was a neat shot, right back of the ear and at two hundred yards—because he was just sitting there, deader than one of them groundhogs he'd blown apart, and like them getting full in the face, but mad, they say. Heart attack, they say. He looked madder than hell, somebody said. Just sitting there leaning against that tree and that old Browning across his lap, ready to go. Had the safety off and a shell in the chamber. Ready to fire. Don't you know they had to ease that out of his grip. Don't want to be shot by no dead man, no sir."

Clemmons is sitting down to paint, but the roof angle is too sharp, and he feels his behind slowly slipping down to nudge against his feet; so, he stands up and bends over to apply the brush awkwardly but more safely.

"He always felt like that place was his, don't you know." Benny's voice now comes from the creamy depths within the paint bucket. "He'd jacked deer onto it since he was a boy. The wardens just gave up trying to get him. One year, I know, he had the cooler down at Hicks's store packed in like sardines or something." It was natural for Benny to refer to the Irondale store by the name of its previous owners. Its rightful owners, Clemmons thinks.

"He gave me some venison a couple of years," Clemmons speaks into the wall before him. "I guess he had taken them up at the Muller place."

"That's for sure, A.W. He come into the garage last week, don't you know. All mad. He'd been all afternoon at the Glenview Hotel, I guess. He talked about them machines, the bulldozers and all, being parked down onto the slough —how they's already drained the swamp and cut a road right up through the old cornfields. You hear old Bucky talk, you'd think they'd come on his land, like they were doing the trespassing. He was something." The man's laughter bounces from roof to siding and back to roof and then spills off into thin air.

The sun has now risen above the mountain line and Clemmons can feel its heat on his back. A trickle of sweat runs down his neck. The glare of fresh paint dazzles his eyes. There's a buzzing around his head but he does not look up. Perhaps if he does not acknowledge them, the wasps will not bother him. He had read somewhere that if one encountered a lion in the jungle and did not meet the beast's eye, then the animal would pass by, just as happy to avoid a confrontation. He wonders if the same principle might apply to wasps.

"You still there, Benny?"

"I'm here, A.W.," replies the voice from the other side of the house.

"You don't think he would have shot any of those men on the crew, do you?"

"Oh, no. He wouldn't do that. He was a hunter, A.W., he wouldn't have done that. He was just a hunter."

Clemmons pulls his safety line clear of a small lightning rod, and takes one-two-three steps down the back side of the roof. He's on the very edge, and the last section of unpainted siding is just before him. In spite of everything, he's enjoying the simple task of painting. The instant success of every brush stroke painting over, if not brushing away, all his problems. Just for a time, anyway. This morning, he knew it would only be temporary when he woke up refreshed, with a calm mind and a light heart, and he inhaled the sweet prospects of the day. Now every swipe of the brush soothes him.

Sugary and spiced aromas had lifted through the house from the kitchen that morning as mother, wife, and daughter worked at cakes and soups and breads. This evening he would play Natty Bumppo in the dark woods of Axel's Farm, darting from tree to tree toward the illuminated window above the small balcony. He wondered if there were actually a night watchman or whether that was only a persona in Claire's fantasy. Perhaps he didn't have to come through the window either, but could enter by the front door of the old mansion, maybe nod to the poets engrossed in their poems, and pass on down the hall to her room. She would be capable of such a ruse, and it amused him, so he laughed as he got out of bed. Later, after a shower, as he stood before the bathroom mirror, he was suffused with a sense of well-being that was both kindly and all-powerful. The term *Jovian* had come to mind. So it is easy to see why, at this moment on the roof, in the hot sun, and dazed by the glistening wet paint, A. W. Clemmons not only can ignore the wasps that whirr about his ears but imagine their noise to be the weaving of halos.

He also hears the clump and hiss of a well-digger's drill, putting down a trochee to meter the morning. Someone must be building a house, he had sold a couple of lots recently; or maybe putting in a trailer. Somehow he had held the place together long enough, saved it long enough so new fresh wells could be sunk.

He had done it haphazardly—catch as catch can, to use his mother's phrase—and maybe that's why it had worked. Julia Clemmons had talked about New Harmony the other night, and he wonders now if the problem with such settlements, all their streets laid out around an idea, is that they were only an idea and better left in the mind. Only the ideas remain, uninhabitable, visited by tourists but not lived in. Like the Shakers in Chatham. How can you make a musical out of people who don't do it, Jenny had said.

He dips the paintbrush into the creamy paint and generously spreads it on the strakes before him. He would go back to old man Donaldson. He could cosign a note or even give him enough of a binder that would get him and his wife down to Florida.

The morning swells around him, grows luminous as it expands, pulling on the fragile resources of light and air and spinning them like a membrane that balloons around him and his house and the women inside it, around Benny Smith below and Little Ben in the truck below that, and then around all the fields and woods, the streams, roads, paths, the livestock, heads down and almost stationary: the tractors and farm rigs moving faster, more directly and around the silos and houses; this canopy getting larger and larger to encompass Irondale—he can feel it happening as he stoops over to paint, does not need to look up to see the glistening curvature high around him, and even hears sublime vibrations as if he were within a huge bell where all the sound was strangely muffled inside the clangor.

Then it stops. Silence. Nothing. It is like all colors coming into whiteness, like all elements of an explosion reaching that null point just before the explosion, just before all noise breaks loose around a parenthesis that sucks time and place into it. He even feels something press down upon him.

The screams begin in the kitchen. Clemmons moves instinctively. He has a picture of his thigh muscles stretching and contracting as he slips and scrambles up the smooth shingles. Also, he visualizes flames. Women with their hair on fire. Burns blistering and crackling fair arms only lightly protected with flour. He reaches the peak of the roof, legs in an easy stride now, and the paintbrush has been thrown aside, the paint can just behind, but both seemingly fixed at their different radial points along the down-falling arc, or so he sees from the corner of his eye, for at this apogee of his own flight, all action seems to have stopped—all action but the frantic, screaming race down the lawn of daughter, mother, grandmother, some sort of generational processional he has time to observe, running not with hair on fire but with hair wildly outspread, blond, black, and white hair, and arms outspread—six arms, he counts, outspread like those of figurines—all running toward the tall, dark-haired young woman who stands like another votive with her own arms outspread beside a purple van pulled up behind Benny's truck.

Clemmons sees all this in the interval of blessed weightlessness given him, and then he puts one foot down and lands blindly on the slanted plane of the roof, which propels him, catapults him higher, and even then his mind carefully reviews what is happening, for he thinks how lucky to have the rope, to be tied down, so he won't fly too far up. Just then, he passes over the edge of the roof and looks down into Benny Smith's upturned face, as always, fixed in wonder.

Chapter Six

"But how did it happen?" Claire is asking.

"Nobody's sure," Olive replies. "Apparently he had become despondent over this film about the fight. Nobody knows why."

Claire does not respond. Clemmons has been lying in bed listening to the two women. They sit together on the short sofa at the end of his bed like the women he used to see in New York sitting on benches to wait for a bus, or to rest halfway home from a market; a chatty acquaintanceship, at once close and impersonal. The taller woman turns toward him. Claire wears large-framed glasses that give her the expression of a serious student. "Did you have any idea this would happen?"

He shakes his head and then says, "No," but his voice comes out in a croak because he hasn't used it much lately, since the cracked ribs and bruised muscles of his chest and neck hurt when he talks, so he squeezes out sounds with difficulty, like working out a cramp in a muscle, exercise made for fluency.

"A.W. saw her—about a week ago, wasn't it, sugar?—and says everything seemed all right. I didn't know them at all." Olive straightens as if to pull herself away from the subject.

Claire had kept him company while his wife and the other women had gone to Rita Pickens's party. She wears sandals and a boxy cotton dress, and she had read to him, the whole while, stories by a new Scandinavian writer who seemed not to use verbs. Or perhaps the translator had omitted the verbs. Clemmons feels he deserved better.

"There was a little girl, too?" Claire says, as if to repeat the facts would somehow elicit different answers, answers that would wake them to reality, bring them all back to life, as it were, and out of the nightmare that Olive and the women of his family had encountered at Rita Pickens's. Rita had just heard the news and told them all about it as she had mixed drinks.

In as much pain as he had been, with all the discomfort he now suffered, Clemmons wished for more pain. He wished his injuries had not been so slight, that he had not been so lucky, so that instead of resting on his bed, his bruised ribs taped and the rope burns under his arms treated and healing nicely—instead he wished that he was encased in a body cast from head to toe, a shell that roughly approximated his form but within which he could shrink, even disappear. A story from Čapek comes to mind, about an accident victim lying unconscious and unknown in a hospital and how the hospital staff make up the person's life, fabricate an identity for the man just as he slips forever into anonymity. It would be better to lie there all but gone, and hear himself recreated in the women's words—and the more erroneous the information the better, he would think —than to suffer his own full presence and the total awareness of irrevocable facts.

He tries not to think of the little girl, her face smeared with peach juice, and the way her eyes had shone. Nor could he block the image of her mother's breasts—smoothly plump and oddly inappropriate for the bony rib-cage, but all the prettier for the disparity—how they had moved. Then he tried to recreate something different for Sam Broome, some other way he would have him return from the city, develop a successful settlement for him, so to speak. Perhaps to think about what actually happened made it part of something told, something that would never be over as a moment can be over, because the story can be repeated over and over and over and kept alive. He had shot them as they slept. Then, he'd taken himself into the bathroom. To be neat, Clemmons figured. Had he worn all those beads or had he gone in a simpler vanity?

"Well, I'm just going to change my clothes," Olive says, standing up. "I do hope you can stay for supper. I think it was just a lucky thing for us that you called up." She was using her fruity voice, a ladylike modulation that Clemmons had learned to be wary of. "So fortunate that you just happened to be in the area just now."

"I think so too, and thank you, I'd be delighted to stay," Claire replies. Her directness, sweetened by the charm of someone who has always got her way, strikes a responsive chord in the other woman. Clemmons can see Olive refocus her regard, look differently at Claire.

"We're going to have a wedding rehearsal this evening. A party. Perhaps you can stay for that, too?"

"Thank you. I will." Both women are now smiling frankly, a mutual recognition of sorts. Clemmons looks away, fusses with an afghan laid across him. It doesn't surprise him that they have felt out their compatible qualities, or that they even share certain similarities, but in the meantime, they seem to have forgot all about him. This new relationship has nothing to do with him.

Meanwhile, Olive has left him and Claire alone. She's been using the rear bedroom that had been Milly's. On the way to the airport, and that seemed a long time back, he had rehearsed an awkward suggestion that she use the back bedroom, to be "more comfortable," but she had saved him the embarrassment. She had claimed the room herself, pulling her bags into it and unpacking some of them, leaving the rest about the room like the sections of a stylish barricade.

"Tell me something," he says to Claire.

"Yes."

"How come you never got your nose bobbed?"

Her face darkens. "I ought to come over and jump on your chest."

"I didn't mean it that way. That's not what I meant."

"How did you mean it? You don't like my nose?"

"I love your nose."

She looks at him over her glasses, her smile tentatively returning herself to him. Then serious once more. "My father wouldn't hear of it. He thought it was bourgeois. See this little bump and then the sharpness of the tip?" She turns sidewise and traces her profile with one finger, a gesture as spontaneous as it is beguiling, as though he had never studied her, seen her from this angle. "This is supposed to be an aristocratic configuration." She laughs. "Why all this with noses?"

"I was just wondering if a nose that's been fixed would grow old with the rest of the face. You know, would it never change, but always remain pert; twenty years old while the rest of the face turned sixty." Her eyes had deepened as she followed his thought. "That girl," he adds.

"Oh." The bedroom becomes smaller. It's as if the woman's height, when she stands to come to him, has somehow lowered the ceiling, and he reminds himself that he is virtually helpless. He can move his arms only very slowly, as if the muscles in them had been stretched beyond their elastic capabilities by the wrenching jolt in the rope harness that had stopped his fall, pulled him up safe. But Claire has sat down carefully on the edge of the bed, raised her glasses to her forehead and leaned forward, as if to study the pores in his skin. "Does it hurt if I kiss you?"

Gradually, her lips took his, as if she were blindly feeling her way around his mouth. "Were you surprised to see me? I almost think you hanged yourself just to get us all together." She kisses him again.

"Is this some sort of a reward?"

"It's not enough?"

"Do that again."

"What? This?"

"Hmm. Somebody's coming. I mean—up the stairs."

Claire sat back, not believing him, though just then she heard the footsteps. It's a short hallway, so Rita Pickens is upon them almost as they draw apart.

"Well, I just wanted to see how Quasimodo is doing," she drawls, turning red. It's as if she has caught them naked, though Clemmons wonders what part of the color comes from anger. "Is it true that you and Benny Smith are putting together a circus act to replace the Flying Wallendas?" She continues to talk through her awkwardness, putting up a quick screen of associations to hide her discomfort. "It's been described as a kind of pageant, some kind of reenactment of the scales of justice. There's even talk of putting the two of you up on the Methodist Church, so you can ring out the hour"—and here she begins to cough and laugh simultaneously—"like those figures that bob up and down and go around on townhall clocks in Europe."

"What happened," Clemmons talks to Claire's bewilderment, "is that when I fell, the rope looped around the chimney broke my fall, I bounced up and then dropped again, and this time, the man who was helping me was pulled up, so he was hung up too. He had the other end wrapped around himself. So, we were both dangling there until Paul . . ." he couldn't remember his prospective son-in-law's name, "Paul cut us down."

In fact, he couldn't remember if Milly had made more of an introduction than a quick, "This is Paul," though to be truthful the confusion and hysteria of the moment had precluded anything more formal, and Clemmons could imagine the story told to the family's future generations, if there were to be any, of how he had met his prospective son-in-law while hanging from a rope, trussed up and eyes popped like a duck in a Chinese butcher shop.

"Certainly nice to meet you," the young man had said. His voice was light, but his hands had worked surely over the knotted ropes.

Clemmons had felt all of his blood rise into his brain. He even saw red and was afraid the membranes that kept the fluids of his body separate would burst. He remembered illustrations in ancient texts of certain tortures that had made improvised fountainheads of the victims, all the body's liquids spouting from the different orifices. But what disturbed him even more, at that moment as he still swayed and vibrated like a cocoon about to give birth, was the way Paul looked. Not the way he looked, but how he looked.

As Clemmons had swung and twirled, slipping again and again from the young man's grasp like an elusive piñata, he endeavored to get a closer look at Milly's intended, catching vignettes, you might say, of the youth as he spun first this way and then that way as his vision raced another way into darkness. But the view clips began to assemble into a composite picture; the long auburn hair glimpsed during one orbit, the thin lips on another, the delicate nose as he revolved once more until the whole fit together in Clemmons's whirled mind. It's Jesus, he thought. He was being rescued by Jesus. He'd seen those Vandyke features on calendars and the fans handed out by funeral parlors. He'd seen that same face in the illustrations of motel Gideons and on the billboards advertising some Biblical motion picture. It really was the way he looked, Clemmons was thinking, and here he was reaching up to try to undo him, to release him from this strangulating bondage. As he passed out, he had heard Benny Smith say, "Well, I'll be."

"You poor man," Claire is soothing him. Rita Pickens has left them, has gone home. "And all that time I thought you had forsaken me, had picked up some young chick somewhere. I waited three days. Then I called. After all, I have a legitimate reason for being around here. I said that you were selling a house for a friend of mine."

"It doesn't matter," Clemmons says and moves.

"You mustn't get up."

"I can walk, get up. The more the better. I'm just sore that's all."

"But let me do it. Is it something I can do for you?"

"All right." He lies back against the pillows. "The second drawer in that chest. Inside, you'll find a box."

"Right, with papers, letters?"

"Yes. Look through them. You'll see a photograph of a couple with . . ."

"This one?" She holds up a picture.

"Yes." He motions and she brings it to him.

"He's some kind of a great white hunter?" Claire holds the picture close to her eyes, as if the glasses perched on her head were forgotten.

"He was a guy named Mel Stein," Clemmons says. "A hack writer I used to know in New York. He bought that outfit at Ambercrombie & Fitch, I remember. Even had a 'correspondent' patch sewn on one arm, but he worked for skin magazines. Exposé stuff. He was looking for Amelia Earhart."

"And the girl?"

"His wife, I guess."

"The natives look hungry."

"I think they were." A peculiar blindness has affected Clemmons; he can no longer see the details of the picture. Several guitars in the field below ignite into a furious flamenco exchange and, just as quickly, subside. There is laughter. Clemmons has been trying to tear the picture in two but his numbed fingers are not strong enough.

"Can I help?" Claire asks, taking the photograph. "Who's Charlie?" She sees the brief inscription on the back.

"Search me," Clemmons says.

She tears the photograph into smaller and smaller fragments, drops everything into a wastebasket. "Listen. I think

I'll go downstairs and see if I can be of help." Her manner is briskly attentive, like that of a nurse going off duty. "Want anything?"

Clemmons is now alone. There is no one upstairs after Claire joins the others in the kitchen. He can hear the murmur of their voices, a laugh or exclamation occasionally surfaces and then falls back into the general swell of talk. The dormer windows are open, and there is a scent of May on the cool air, as well as the sound of guitars being strummed in the meadow. He knows there are several vans pulled up down there, almost in a circle like the old wagon-train days. Milly's friends had set up camp in the field below the house. He had been restless last night, and he had got up and stood for a long time at the front window. They had built small fires and these were still glowing though all was quiet. He had imagined them all curled in their sleeping bags, toed out from the fire like the spokes radiating from a sun dial. He imagined Milly curled into her young man, Paul. He had stood there for a very long time, imagining them sleeping, breathing.

The cockeyed window by his bed was almost dark, but only because it faced east with the screen of mountains before it, for there was yet plenty of light through the front windows that faced south for the sun was still setting. Because of the darkness outside this window, the white splatters of paint stormed against the panes. When he had flung everything to one side in his abortive flight, the paint can had sprayed its contents over a wide range, some of it dousing the windows so it looked like a blizzard, an obstinate and perverse last stand of winter that refused to give over that part of the house, even though the rest had already been warmed by spring, hived by wasps, and nested by returning phoebes. Perhaps a change of seasons would be of help.

Or it also looked like confetti, Clemmons is thinking just as he hears laughter on the stairs. He can hear their lovers' heckle, pause then resume, then more laughter. There is a faint tinkling noise that turns out to be a drink Milly has brought for him, along with a small tray of cheese and crackers; there is wine for herself and Paul. She is bringing an offering, Clemmons muses.

Always, on first seeing Milly, Clemmons felt something in her manner that gave him a start, even if she were only returning to a room; something in her look made one suppose she was about to lay down an ultimatum, give orders, command one's life or at least a portion of it—which she usually tried to do—but at the same time, her expression could be very winning; and with her dark coloring and tall graceful figure, she would pose a contradiction, be both attractive and bossy at the same time.

"Candy time, Pop," she is saying and hands him a highball. Just now, even, Clemmons recalls another mental snapshot he had taken the other day. As he had balanced on the fulcrum of his flight, he had looked down on Milly standing by the purple van, arms outstretched to the others, and he had wondered why her feet were still.

"That's not as funny as it used to be," he answers. "I feel ready for Sunnydale Manor."

"C'mon, Pop. You're just fine," she says eagerly. "We thought we'd keep you company." She sits on the end of the bed and motions Paul to the small settee. It seems to Clemmons that neither of them has changed clothes since they arrived, though he knew they had. It was just that they wore the same kind of Levis, sweaters, and boots all the time. The only difference between her get-up and Paul's was an artist blouse or smock worn over a turtleneck sweater.

"Was that you I heard playing the guitar earlier?" Clemmons asks Paul. In the half-light of the bedroom, his resemblance to Gabriel Rossetti is startling.

"No, that was some of the boys just—playing around." Clemmons gets the idea that Paul had almost used another term, that he had exchanged it for language he felt the older man could understand.

"It's very pleasant. The sound of music coming from the

field down there." Clemmons stops short, stopped by the look on the other's face. It seems his own language has been confusing. The word "pleasant," for example, may have been inappropriate, maybe was even pejorative these days. Paul even looks sick. "Are they rehearsing something? One of your numbers?" Clemmons tries again, but matters only seem to worsen. The young man's expression has grown fierce, as if compliments were offensive, as if any kind of talk, forget compliments, were offensive and angered him.

It was the same mien reproduced in the pictures on his record album; photographs taken during a concert. Milly had presented the family with several copies of the record, *Find Stanley Livingston.* He looked like one of those angry Hindu deities, eyes focused on some metaphysical point in the temple wall. Perhaps some terrible energy was generated in the guitar, passed through his fingers when he touched its strings to transform this rather pretty, passive young man into a mythical warrior. Maybe by now the metamorphosis had become automatic; the mere thought of his music could trip it, even to have it mentioned by a well-intentioned ignoramus would be enough to excite this curious ferocity.

"They were just playing around," Paul says once more. Then he stands up. "You got a bathroom I can use?" Clemmons gestures to the door, wondering if the boy is actually going to be sick, because Paul leaves the room, abruptly shuts the door.

"So, looks like you'll be here for the wedding?" Milly says brightly. There's an appealing challenge in her eyes. They are his mother's eyes, set wide and gray and with a contemplative fold of lid.

"Looks like," he answers and accepts a piece of cracker and cheese. "You're looking very pretty. Paul must be good to you."

"Paul's been married before," she says. "He's written this beautiful poem for the service. Then we got Mr. Quincy from the church in Stout Falls to do the rest."

"He's a nice man."

"Pop?"

"Yes."

"I'm pregnant." She sips some wine, looking at him over the rim of her glass. "Does that make you mad?"

"No."

"I just want a baby. Paul liked the idea. We'll always have the baby, even when we split." She notes his expression, had expected his look of surprise for she continues quickly, "Well, I'm not going to get locked into that old trap. Just because I have a baby. No, thank you. We both agree on that. As soon as the baby is big enough, I can lead my own life."

"What's that mean?"

"Just what it says." Her voice has thinned and two white lines trace the sides of her nose—familiar danger signals.

"You mean this marriage, this living arrangement with Paul is only meant to last long enough for you to have the baby and to raise it to a certain age."

"Sure. Why not? That's more honest, more open than the usual shit." That her babyish lips could pronounce such words so easily had always surprised him.

"But what about the child? Won't your theory deny the child a home?"

"I don't have a theory," she snaps. She had almost flinched when he spoke. "Home?" she repeats. The tutorial tone of his voice had stung her. "What the fuck good is a home? You know what a home is? It's a fucking box to package you. It's a fucking . . . shooting gallery and you're the target, like that woman and kid in that condominium village."

"That was different."

"How was it different? Fabulous hairdos in five minutes. Twelve ways to fix hamburger. One way to die. Bang-bang. Fuck that." She is standing over him and Clemmons is a little apprehensive. She would not strike him, but she could become so irrational sometimes.

"Wait. Wait a minute." He speaks calmly, holds out a hand to her, pats the counterpane. "Sit down now. How do we always get into this? We're talking about happy things." He coaxes her down from her wrath and she sits again. Then, he says, "It should be a beautiful baby. Paul's a handsome man."

"It will be very beautiful." She sniffs, her face averted. It's as if he's agreed to something she's been petitioning for all along.

"I suppose you selected him partly for that."

She puts a hand over her eyes and he's afraid he's said the wrong thing again, but then he hears her giggle. "Partly. More than partly, right." She looks at him sideways and he wonders why he doesn't like her more. "Also, he's on the track. He's really cooking these days. We've got a contract, went to lawyers and everything, so there are already trust funds set up. Just for the baby. Not me. It's all legal."

"You amaze me, Milly. I mean you impress me." Something like pride rises within Clemmons though he also feels a loosening of his limbs. It's as if he's become an invalid all at once, and he pulls his legs together and puts them over the side of the bed, not to sit beside her so much as to prove to himself he can do it. But she gently avoids the arm he was slowly lifting up and around her and faces him squarely. Her face is sunny and eager.

"You see, Pop, how I've planned all this. It's not just a whim. I've spent a lot of time, going over all the details. It's all worked out. I gave it a lot of thought. I didn't just want to do it here for—well, I had my reasons. You know?" Then she leans toward him, in much the same way Claire had done earlier. "Everybody has a part in it." He expects her to say more, but she does not. Then the bathroom door opens and Paul enters the room.

Clemmons had almost forgot the young man, and only on his return from the bathroom did Clemmons reflect that he had made silent use of its facilities. He had expected the sounds of nausea, a disgorging of anger and frustration—

at the very least some flushings of water. But he couldn't remember any noise whatsoever.

Milly has jumped up to greet him, even hugs and kisses him, but Paul is strangely unresponsive, does not attempt to touch her and, in fact, holds his hands out before him and away from her, like a surgeon all scrubbed up and trying to avoid contamination. That, Clemmons suddenly knows, is what he's been doing all that time in the bathroom. He's been washing up. The bathing facilities in his van are limited. It's been a thorough cleaning, the young man's ears still glow pinkly from the washrag's friction, and Clemmons imagines the meticulous care with which the musician inspected and flushed out every crevice, every pore of his skin. Groomed his auburn beard.

The bridal pair take the settee together, side by side, though looking not so much like two people on the brink of matrimony, as like a couple waiting to see a specialist. Siblings, Clemmons thinks.

"Well, Paul, in any event," he continues, or tries to continue whatever he had been saying to the musician earlier. He sips the diluted bourbon and reviews the limited repertoire. "In any event, it's good to have you all here," he finally says, thinking there were other phrases he could have also used such as, *no matter what* or *under the circumstances,* or even *despite everything,* but then he chides himself for these thoughts even as he chuckles over them.

"It's really weird being here," Paul says, as if this thought had come to him in the bathroom, as if he had divined this message in the peculiar consistency of the basin water. "I mean, to get married where that old fight was and to come here to this place that's got the same name as my group. You know? That old family that ran things. Mil's told me about it. The Livingstons, you know."

Clemmons observes them both for several moments. His daughter clutches Paul's arm and looks proudly upon him. The musician looks straight ahead, at a place above Clemmons's head. The plain sobriety of the youth's face, so different from his earlier expression, strikes Clemmons with an insight into that former expression. It was not anger or disgust being shown but fear—fear of him. With all this young man's fame, his growing fortune, and with all the attention given his life by the media (Milly had made sure everyone saw the press book she kept)—the boy in this room and at this moment was put in the humble role of a young man meeting and talking with his prospective father-in-law. It was the same sort of reduction, Clemmons reminds himself, he always felt when Julia Clemmons came to visit.

But with all that, he continues his other thought, picks up what Paul has just said and prepares to answer it, aware of the consequences it will have, even as he gropes for another way of imparting the information so that it will not crash through the precarious harmony and understanding that has enveloped them, smash through like one of those apocalyptic chords that the Stanley Livingston Band seemed to favor—the detonations had started coming from the record player downstairs. It was like the flight from the roof again. Clemmons has time to think, a hiatus in which he can survey the past, present, and future, before it becomes all one blur. "Of course," he says after a deep breath, "it's not the same name. I mean," he continues to their blank, uncomprehending stares, "the Livingston Manor family spelled their name differently from the Dr. Livingstone you named your band for. He used an 'e' on the end."

It was as if he has just told them the earth would stop, and deer would turn vicious. Paul had fallen back against the sofa with a winded look. "Wait a minute," he says. "There was this movie and Spencer Tracy played this guy named Stanley who found this other guy, and he said, 'Dr. Livingstone, I presume.' That's what he said. Livin-*stun*. Livin-*stun*," Paul repeats the name. "Not Living-*stone*."

"Yes, that's right," Clemmons says. He finishes his drink and puts the glass on the floor by the bed, out of the way. "That's the way it's pronounced. Without the *e*. It sounds like Livingston but it is spelled L-i-v-i-n-g-s-t-o-n-*e*. Livingstone."

"Holy shit," Paul says brokenly. He almost puts his hands to his face but then remembers not to. "Holy shit," he repeats. "Everything we've put out is spelled like that. Holy shit," he says once more. Then he does touch his face, even grinds his hands into his eyes and groans. In the old days, Clemmons thinks, he would have plucked out his eyes, disfigured that Apollonian visage and turned down the long road alone. But that was the old days.

"Just a minute." Milly stands up. Her eyes are slits. "Just a minute. How long have you known about this?"

"Known about what?"

"How this nerd's name is spelled."

"Well, I guess I've always known how it was spelled," Clemmons replies evenly.

"So you've known about this all the time," she continues in the level voice of a prosecutor. "You've lain there all this time, all this time we've been home you've known about this all . . ."

"Yes, yes, yes. For Christ's sake, so what?" He yells back at her. There were signs about him now that she should recognize and be wary of. "So what?"

"Well, you could have said something," she says. Paul is sitting with his head almost between his legs. His hands slack. He really does look sick now. "But no, you just strut around, laughing."

"I wasn't laughing," he says. "Nor strutting, for that matter." He even thumps the bed with his hands to demonstrate how any movement makes him wince with pain. It doesn't hurt him as much as it should, and this surprises him.

"Don't tell me you weren't laughing. . . ."

"Don't point your finger at me. . . ."

"I know that arrogant, know-it-all, Mr. . . ." Apparently she couldn't think of a name vile enough and switched the attack. "Okay." Her hands on her hips, as if ready to go into a menacing buck-and-wing. "Okay. If you knew about it and weren't laughing, why didn't you say something about it. . ."

"Because I thought that it was meant to be that way!" he almost shouts. "I accepted the way you spelled it. I thought it was some sort of a pun or something. . . ."

"Oh, something cute, is that it? You think it's cute. . . ."

"I don't think that. . . ."

"Something cute! You know how much he made last year?" She points, without looking, back at Paul on the sofa. His head is now thrown back, against the sofa. He seems to have gone into shock. There's sweat on his face. "Do you know?"

"No, I don't know and it doesn't matter. . . ."

"That's right," she suddenly says, her eyes bright. "It doesn't matter. Who gives a fuck how it's spelled. Who cares?"

"I have an idea," Clemmons says, and he is touched by the way Paul sits up, looks eagerly toward him. He is, after all, to be the father of his first grandchild. Perhaps, sometime a few years down the road, they would be able to talk about something else. "How about this? Just add an 'e' to the name now. You could reprint some of the stuff, and the next album could have it printed on." As he talks, Clemmons feels the old press agent within him beginning to set up spilled chairs. "That's it!" He even tries to snap his fingers but only manages to rub them together. "Get some publicity out of the mistake. You could even pretend it was a joke. Flaunt it. Print the final 'e' in parentheses or in a different color so it stands out. Maybe in yellow or pink. Some weird color like that." He uses the adjective deliberately but Paul shows no recognition.

"That's some more of that patronizing chicken shit. We're not going to do anything about it. Hear that!" She turns around and Paul nods. His color is getting back. "Who cares how it's spelled?"

"A lot of people care," Clemmons says. "*I* care."

"You know what that amounts to?" She snaps her fingers before her face. She snaps them again. "It doesn't matter. Nobody cares how it's spelled. Nobody cares."

"I care," Clemmons says again. Wisdom had called for silence, but he ignores the message. "I care."

"Stop saying that," Milly yells. Her outburst soaks up all noise; Clemmons can hear them listening in the kitchen. He can visualize a plate being put down carefully, a pot lid suspended in the vapors above the pot. "You care for nothing. What do you know about it . . . you're full of pieces . . . pieces of . . . nothing all at once, nothing together. . . ." Paul has risen to comfort her. She starts to sob. "Gee whiz," Milly says brokenly. The innocence of her expression upsets Clemmons more than anything that has gone before. He looks at Paul who looks concerned, and frightened. He has probably never seen her like this.

"Oh, leave me alone." Milly pushes the young man away and rushes from the room. If Paul had looked toward him, Clemmons would have said something to him, told him that her anger would pass quickly, that her flamboyant nature would return, and that, in any event, this anger was not meant for him. However, the young man only stares after her, like an attendant figure in a melodrama addressing the vacant aperture of the leading lady's exit, and then goes behind her and down the steps, a heavy, uncomprehending tread behind her turbulent clatter.

Like an invalid trapped on a floor above a conflagration, Clemmons hears Milly carry the coals of her rage into the kitchen where the women's attempts to soothe her only ignite more fury. She was like one of those grass fires that sometimes start in the fall that can blacken acres of meadowland in the flick of an eye. Her anger generated its own energy, a fire storm. *"Don't talk to me like that,"* he hears her shout and then a murmur, a laying on of vocal hands it seemed, ineffectual if not like pouring gasoline on the flames. "Bastard!" A door is slammed. There are several sets of feet running through the house. "Oh my," he hears his mother say from the foot of the stairs, where she stands like some sort of school-crossing guard. The two girls stomp by her and across the hall into the library. He listens to Daisy argue for him, argue for her sister—the self-appointed peacemaker. He knows what will happen and eases himself up. His legs move pretty well, and only when he has to bend over the sink do the chest muscles really hurt. If not a change of season, then a change of place might be required.

The water is cool to his face and the more he splashes, the easier it is to use his arms. He notes how neat Paul had been; the sink counter was spotlessly dry. Clemmons always made a soppy mess around the sink; now the bruised shoulder muscles cause him to jerk as much water on the floor as on his face.

"How can you say that . . . listen . . . listen." That was Daisy's urgent plea. "Bitch," came her sister's reply. "What do you know. . ."

There's a new toothbrush, still in its box, and he puts it along with the tube of toothpaste into a small kit bag. The razor is next. Then some toothpicks. Does he have enough collar stays? "Miss Imperial . . . high-and-mighty ass . . ." He hears Daisy heating up, grappling with the sparse vocabulary that always put her at a disadvantage in these arguments with her sister. He would only take a couple of shirts, anyway. He could get more later, somehow. That could be worked out. He puts the kit into a small satchel. Slowly he selects a few ties to match the shirts; several changes of underwear. Socks. "You asskisser, always sucking around him": Milly. Maybe a sweater. He finds his checkbook. He had very little cash, some change. He might head north. "Whore. Slut": Daisy. She has her own burner started now. From the back of the closet, he takes out a gaudy sport shirt, cut overlarge and flambéed with numerous orange suns swimming in a sauce of coconut palm leaves. His brother-in-law had given it to him; not so much a gift as it had been an evaluation maybe, but Clemmons had never worn it. It somehow seems appropriate now—a new image, as Olive might say, but it is also easy to slip over his taped-up torso. His arms flex more easily but it still hurts to move them ever so slowly. "Who are you to talk to me . . . fucking your way around every truck stop." No pictures. Automatically, he pockets keys. "Groupie. Dyke!" Their voices had become interchangeable. The footsteps march back through the house, a righteous parade of anger. He imagines the furniture in the library shattered, the books smoldering. "Oh dear," his mother says to herself, then leaves her post to follow her granddaughters into the kitchen.

It's hard to zip the bag, the strength in his fingers comes and goes, but he finally manages. "Now just a goddamn minute." There's the heavy voice of Olive, a blanket over the blaze. But sparks are chased up from both sides; unintelligible accusations; all the same. Clemmons takes a last look around the room. He wonders where Paul is standing, in what corner of what room. Where is Claire? Would she be outside, away from the heat? "That's it . . . that cuts it." Daisy? Milly? One of them. A resignation. He listens. The conflagration seems to be contained in the far end of the house, near the kitchen. Olive is strongly, surely, taking control. "But Mama," one of them. "But Mama," the other one.

But Claire is nowhere outside, and he knows he cannot take the time to look for her. He continues to walk down the darkened terrace, slowly and mindful of each step. It would be right for her to stay, he thinks. That Claire was part of that scene inside, had been caught up and woven into the pattern, was one of those lucky, unforeseen accidents. A pan is slammed against a counter. He imagines Claire in one corner, studying this social phenomenon, recording this peculiar rite. She would be wearing her glasses. By the time he reaches his car, Olive's steady voice dominates the other two. A spurt from Milly, "Fuck him!," a sudden outburst to be tamped out. "Now, sister—now, sister": Olive. That pot is slammed down again.

The faces of the wedding guests are softly limned by the light of their fire. They have been cooking something. The burned hay aroma of marijuana mixes with the evening air. They do seem not to acknowledge the commotion in the house, not to hear it. Perhaps they are all too stoned to notice it, or maybe they accept the angry noises as part of the "straight life style," along with the chirp of tree frogs and the sigh of pines. Patronizing, Milly would call that thought. Just now he hears her shout, "I don't care," one last fillip to be smothered by Olive's honeyed eloquence. Perhaps he *is* patronizing, but also, just now, Clemmons decided, he really doesn't care.

The several vans parked in the field across the road screen him, so no one sees his careful traverse down the yard to the graveled bay where his car is parked. No one except Boxer, who leaps into the car as Clemmons opens its door. The dog seems to have been waiting for him, maybe with the same idea of leaving Boston Corners for an arcadia twitching with woodchucks and squirrels. "No. You can't come. Get out." Boxer crouches low on the front seat. "You can't come with me. C'mon boy. C'mon Boxer." The dog's muzzle presses between his paws, his eyes beg. "Listen, you little bastard, who's your friend been all these years? I gave you steak bones with real meat on them when others had you eating turnips." The dog doesn't move. "Please." Clemmons knows he can't drag the dog from the car because of the weakness in his arms. "Woodchuck!" he says quickly, hoping to excite the animal whose ears, in fact, do perk up but he remains like a large dusky figurine on the car seat.

He decides to give the dog time, let it stay there with the door open, while he puts his valise in the back seat of the station wagon. Why not take Boxer with him? The two of them could tootle down the road together. It was his fate, perhaps, to end up with a dog for a traveling companion; probably some wry comment by the gods. On the other hand, Boxer would be another being to talk to, one who would listen or at least would not turn on him if he said something foolish—or even correct. It was because he cared about such things as the correct spelling of a name that caused all the trouble. If he hadn't cared, none of the pandemonium inside would have happened. He listens; it was quiet within the house. The lights in the library have been turned off just now.

But Milly might be right, too. It didn't matter these days how the name was spelled or misspelled. It didn't matter if that sign over there made an error of twenty years on the date of the Sullivan–Morrisey fight. Who was it that decided these things didn't matter? It couldn't be a casual thing. "That's enough now, Boxer," he coaxes once more. "C'mon baby." He suddenly remembers how often the dog would sit in the car for a whole day, only to enjoy the idea, enjoy the remote possibility of a ride as much as an actual trip. What sort of a canine deer-park did Boxer hope to find? Where would he, A. W. Clemmons, go? Right now, his one thought was to escape this sorority he had somehow founded. If only he could share the same dog dream as Boxer, a place where rabbits were all deaf and sat with their backs turned. Probably he would lead them both there, but not be denied the promise. "Moses you are not," Claire once said. "Look at you—still with a foreskin."

"There you are." Olive's voice comes from the darkness behind him. "We were wondering where you got to."

Chapter Seven

The field looks prepared for a sporting event. A wooden platform has been erected at one end of the meadow. Insects feed on the white suns of arc lights. Clemmons thinks of the old fighters. Poor old pugs. Nothing like this for their bloody ceremony. No photographers and film crews laying down sectors of action, checking incidences and perspectives. No one put that contest into a groove of history. Not even the date is remembered correctly.

Perhaps the lack of documentation fattened the myth. Around him, camera crews prepared to record the wedding rehearsal as they are filmed by another set of cameras; continuous narcissistic reflections on magnetic tape. Thirty-seven rounds would prove repetitious—require editing. Have to be "newsed up" to give it punch. He winces at the pun and puts forth a hand to steady himself.

"Careful, sir," a technician warns him. "That panel is hot."

Clemmons nods and backs off from the light board, tripping over heavy cables that have suddenly appeared on the ground like the roots of swamp willows. Studious-looking young men and women perch before control panels around the field's perimeter. Their faces are softly lit by dial lights and they speak calmly to each other through bug-sized microphones clamped to their heads. They speak intimately of degrees, amplitudes. They are going to fly the meadow somewhere, Clemmons thinks. They're going to take it off and pilot it to another location more suitable for the extravaganza. What fun Sam Broome would have had with all these toys—and they would have been toys to him. That had been the trouble. More generators cough, turn into whines; more lights are turned on.

When he had turned from the car door, the women's faces had been luminous in the twilight. They stood together on the lawn's slope, posed for a school album of some sort. "There you are," Olive had said as if they had all spent hours looking for him. He thought they should be linked together by a chain of blossoms, a strand that was stronger than it looked and long enough to wind around him. Boxer had slunk out of the car, his traitorous mission accomplished. Clemmons tried to kick him but the pain in his side was too severe.

"Should you be up, Andrew?" his mother had asked. She stood beside Daisy who held her grandmother's arm. Claire was close behind Olive, put there in the second row by the nonexistent photographer. She looked at him expectantly over his wife's shoulder, while the latter presented Milly to him.

The girl's pale expression had been hesitant, anxious and full of an affection that took him off guard. All the previous anger had been washed away. Her arms rose, buoyant on the night air.

"Papa, will you give me away?"

Her question turned on generators, it seemed, for powerful lights illuminated the old field. Clemmons allowed himself to be moved by the women's hands, the appeal in those hands moved him across the road like a character in one of those old Greek plays he used to do publicity for in the old days; plays done not for any artistic purpose but because no royalties were claimed. For the moment, this role within this chorus of women amused him and he let them believe that he had assumed it for whatever reason they wished. Then, once in the field, he was left alone, not a garland to restrain him. They seemed satisfied that he had crossed some kind of border that would keep him, which he could not recross.

Clemmons feels an arm go around his waist, a friendly arm that makes him wince. "Ooh, sorry, darling," Olive says. "I forgot about the old ribs. . . ."

"It's all right."

"My, my. You really are down in the dumps. You mustn't let Milly get to you. That girl wrings me out too, but we got it all fixed up. She's just anxious about everything." They stroll around the field, her arm loosely fitted about his waist.

"We look like one of those old farm couples at the county fair," Clemmons says. "Walking about, checking on the jellies and preserves and the new fertilizer mix."

"That girl could have got married anywhere. She didn't have to come back here just to get married."

"Yes, but where would she get such a backdrop against which to film it?" Members of the band are setting up equipment on the raised platform.

"Oh, fiddle-de-dee. That old fight. These kids could have gone anywhere. They carry all this equipment around with them like jelly beans. If Milly had chosen to get married down at the town garage, they could have set it up just as easily. That old fight means nothing to them. They don't even know about it. This field, this place isn't important to her. You have that all wrong. You always have had it wrong. *You're* the place."

"I'm not convinced," he says.

"Only because you don't want to be." Olive sucks in her lower lip, seems to wait for him to reply, but he lets her words lead him away from argument in the same way her hands had guided him into the field and away from escape, though he had given up neither the argument nor the escape.

Milly and others have been signaling Olive from the center of the field and with a shrug of her shoulders, she finally acknowledges them, leaves Clemmons to join the conference, which he watches. They move their hands, talk, listen and touch each other as they talk. It's all very intimate out there in the middle of five acres. Wine has been opened. A young man who resembles Paul brings a deck of paper cups and fills one from a gallon jug. "Yessir." The young man continues his rounds. The bass player is meditatively stroking the amplified instrument that hangs from his shoulders. Speakers as tall as Clemmons respond with a heavy throb that is difficult to relate to the casual, minute fingering done on stage. It is only one of many incongruities Clemmons notices, his presence not the least of these. To one side of the stage platform, he sees Paul with other members of the band. Except for their lank hair and mustaches, they remind him of the Jaycees over in Green River, young men in action, who would sometimes invite him to a meeting to speak about real estate. J.C.s. He laughs.

Their deliberation over, Olive and Milly are pacing out the center of the field. They hold hands as they walk, amorous surveyors, turn around at a predetermined point, and retrace the route, taking long, ungainly steps, finally to burst into laughter like children catching sight of themselves in grownup clothes. The slim jug bearer reaches them, but only Olive takes a cup of wine though Milly asks for a sip. As Clemmons watches, the mother holds the cup to the daughter's lips and the girl drinks thirstily, her hands held to her sides. He looks away.

"Hello there." Daisy is flanked by two young men who smile happily with a lopsided glee. "How're you doing, Pop?"

"Fine. Where's your grandmother?"

Daisy's eyes are luminous but unseeing. "Last I saw her she was with Paul, helping set up the lasers."

"Is that safe? She doesn't know about such things."

"She's okay. Paul's taking care of her. He's neat, don't you think? Boy, this is going to be a blast." Daisy's young men nod. They agree.

"Daisy? . . ."

"Yeah, Pop?" She swings the long fall of hair expectantly.

"I was just wondering what I'm supposed to do here."

"They're getting it set up so you won't have to walk too much. The drill is that you'll bring Milly down from the far end to the platform. The band will be up there. And you'll walk—we're all going to walk under these really big arches that she's made out of styrofoam and covered with the most beautiful material. Really. Milly made them."

Clemmons would not be surprised if the decorations were spectacular. Milly had always been creative and she had gone to the best art schools. He also wonders if this were the new way; that instead of trousseaux, painstakingly sewn together, young brides today cut out and glued together huge architectural structures to dress the stage of their weddings—all cut from extruded plastic foam. He likes the idea.

Even as he thinks about it, a couple of technicians lift one of these arches from a large truck on the far side of the field. The piece seems to be about the size of Trajan's Column in Rome, but it is so light that the two men can carry it between them, almost float it between them, to a spot in the center of the field. There, the arch is swung up and guyed to the accompaniment of cheers and applause. "Far out," Daisy cries and claps her hands. The bass player shakes the earth with a flourish. Someone hits cymbals and snare drums. Cowbells clang.

Daisy's eyes are the shape of Christmas mornings but tonight they mirror this arch and not one of the young spruces he would have cut the night before and mounted in a bucket of sand in the library. He and Olive messing up and stepping on the decorations and each other's feelings; getting tangled up with drink and their own body heat so that sometimes—while the children slept—they would put together a frantic, sometimes bungled set of love-making there on the floor of the library under the fragrant boughs of the newly cut spruce, their quick passion quickly assembled not so much for themselves but to preserve Christmas morning for the girls; like one of those elaborate doll houses his mother used to send Milly and Daisy that would have to be fitted together (A into B) for the gift to be realized.

However, the reflection in Daisy's eyes is that of a tall arch covered or wrapped like a huge neat package in some sort of slick material, probably vinyl, and of a purple that is not quite purple. That is, this color might be called purple on some other planet but it had yet to be invented here on earth. "Wait'll you see it under black light," Daisy says and claps again and whistles. Meanwhile, another pair of technicians are bringing a second arch and Clemmons can see yet another one being lifted from the truck. The arches are being erected along the route his wife and daughter had marked off before.

Clemmons is impressed by the preparations and curiously flattered by them as well. "A lot of work," he hears himself say.

"What's that, Pop?"

"I said this took a lot of work and planning." A fourth arch is being set up. The field is beginning to resemble an old forum, one that may have been built in another time frame.

"The great thing about them," Daisy says excitedly, "is that they work for the wedding, too. Paul's putting an album together during the tour in Australia. He's going to call it *Stanley Livingston in Ruins*. He's shown me sketches. The band will work in these arches. Every member has his own arch. Wild, huh? Hey, Milly!" Daisy runs off to grab at Milly. The sisters embrace, overcome it seems by the mere sight of each other. Daisy is followed by the two smiling men. Clemmons notices that Milly seems to have a bodyguard also, a plain-looking girl who stands off to one side, detached but protective all at once. Paul is nowhere in sight.

So it is jelly beans after all. His daughters are trying to whirl themselves into the meadow. It would explain the dizzy, bilious color of the arches—the color of jelly beans. It is typical, he thinks, to take a classic form, one that has been proved functionally and aesthetically perfect, and cover it with silly, irrelevant material.

"Well, so what?" Claire Wolferman says. She has brought wine for both of them. "I think it's ingenious. Shows they're adaptable. That's survival, to adapt." Her large gray eyes inspect him as she sips from her own cup.

"But this isn't a wedding," he replies. "It's a promotion for a record album. Two men tried to kill each other in this field—with their bare hands—and here it's used for a bizarre circus."

"I always thought you made too much about that. Face it, Andy, isn't this nicer, tacky as it is—but better than two thugs beating each other up. What's so wonderful about that?"

He can see she is having a good time, and his own spirits rise to meet hers. Her cheeks were flushed and in the sly, happy slant of her eyes was the same expression he recognizes from other times; say, sitting at a corner table in a saloon near Gramercy Park when her glance would suddenly take on a joyous complicity, as if the thought of pleasures to come had just occurred to her. Even now, standing by one of the large portable transformers, Clemmons can feel himself respond to this look, though he knows his body is deceived, for it was not the thought of sexual pleasures that gave Claire this glow.

"I've discovered something," she says teasingly. "I think I suspected it all along, but now I know. The best thing about you is your family. Quality goods. They give you a resonance, a depth." She is playing with him but he can see she is serious also.

"What were the two of you talking about just now?" he asks.

"Who—Olive and I?"

"Yes, Olive and you." He had watched them speak animatedly, their fingers seemingly ticking off points of agreement. A two-woman consensus. They even walked about arm in arm, with an odd stiff-legged grace.

"Do you suppose we were comparing notes?" Claire smiles. "Those little twitches, the things you say in bed? Is that what you think? Ah, it *is!* It is what you think!" She pounces on his discomfort, chases his eyes when they look away. "What vanity. You are incredibly vain." She berates him softly, smiling, but he only half hears her tone. Clemmons is thinking of this new relationship between these two women. Why *didn't* they talk about him? What else, after all, did they have to talk about? What had sparked such a lively parley out there under the lights, the two of them like officials reviewing the rules of some game about to start? Wasn't he the game?

"I have to sit down," he says.

"Of course, poor Andy." Claire skips over to a control booth and begs a stool from a technician. As Clemmons eases himself up on the seat, he sees Paul lead several of his disciples around behind the stage and out of sight. His mother had been in the group, stepping nimbly and with a large, red paper flower pinned in her hair.

"I guess women always manage these affairs," he says.

"Where were you going back there?" She nods across the road where his car is parked in the darkness outside this field of light.

"Down the road," he says. There is more challenge than curiosity in her eyes, and he senses that she will no longer be his accomplice on desert isles, no more share his fantasies of cool, dark *pensione* rooms smelling of *rosamarino.* Somehow, and maybe as a part of this witless appropriation taking place before him, Claire Wolferman has been taken over by his family. By Olive. By the wily Olive, he thinks.

"It would be no different down the road," Claire is saying. Her hand has come to his neck, to stroke and massage him.

"I thought you guys might want some more wine." Milly has appeared. The same slim young woman walks behind her, even carries the wine jug for Milly and serves. Up close, he sees the waiflike innocence is really a hardness around the mouth and eyes, the same primness pressed into her expression as the creases in her jeans and plain smock. A tightly rolled bandanna is knotted about her throat. More than an indifferent Hebe, Clemmons imagines her a new breed of maiden-warrior, and extends his cup though he wants no more wine.

"How ya feeling, Pop?"

"Better."

"Listen. I thought we'd give the old man here a rest"—Milly turns to Claire—"so would you play the father of the bride for now? That way, he can watch how we do it and save his energy for tomorrow."

"Great idea," Claire says as her eyes dance. "I'd be delighted to play him." Everyone laughs. He's amazed by the way Claire's gone over. The facility of her loyalty. Perhaps all the time he had known her, Claire Wolferman had been waiting for someone to invite her to join this kind of ceremony.

"How's it look to you?" Milly asks him eagerly.

"It has all the elements of a new Augustan Age."

Claire, behind Milly, looks at him sharply, but it is too late. His daughter has looked down quickly, as if something has dropped at her feet. Her face has flushed and the black eyebrows have become hyphens, lie almost as one across the bridge of her nose. "No, what I mean is . . ."

"You could just have said *great* or *all right*. Or maybe those words are not in your vocabulary. It's no big deal, you know."

"You're right. I'm sorry."

"Why don't you show me where I'm supposed to stand?"

Claire asks the companion, even takes her arm. The young woman looks quickly at Milly, then submits to Claire and lets herself be led away.

"You always do this," Milly says flatly. "You're always diminishing me. You put us all down. Nothing we do satisfies you. Nothing we do meets your high fucking standards."

"You're too close to the truth sometimes, Milly."

She laughs now, thinly, almost against her wishes. "Why do you do it?" Her small, bony wrist pummels his breast over the heart. "Don't you know how bad this shit hurts?"

"Credit me with ignorance, at least," he replies. "I don't want to hurt you, Milly. I don't."

Her face is close to his. "Everything seems okay, and then you come out with some smart-ass remark that says you were somewhere else all the time."

Slowly he raises his arms and enfolds her. "I know." He strokes her hair, feeling her lie upon him. The pressure is familiar. Many times, Claire had lain against him so, to talk of her father and their competition that, even when she won, it always hurt her. Had she bought that collection of wedding pictures, Clemmons suddenly wondered? Milly takes a long, wavery breath and nestles against him. She seems about to say something. He can almost feel her thoughts lining up for expression.

"Here-comes-the-bride . . . where-is-the-bride . . . we-need-a-bride . . ." Voices chorus from across the field.

"You better go," he says to her. They kiss. He watches her stroll toward her companions, her steps gaining momentum as she nears them.

Now is the moment. A. W. Clemmons stands away from the stool and moves his arms, slowly at first then faster, like a man trying to warm himself, keep the circulation moving. But more than heat is hoped for. His arms move like the counterweights of a curious engine, gathering up impetus for a flight that has only encountered a slight delay.

Claire had said that he would only set up another place

somewhere down the road: A. W. CLEMMONS, COUNTRY REAL ESTATE. He could see that. He'd be one of those vagabonds forever heading out for the territory to start a version of something left behind. A few years from now, he might drive down Route 22, like any stranger, and he'd be tempted by the pretty little side road that led to Boston Corners. He'd be curious to see who was living in the house and then, like a tourist, read the historical marker by the road. Still the wrong date.

Laser beams cut through the paintbox-colored lights. The field looks like an old aerodrome or a movie set of an old aerodrome. The procession has begun its march through the arches, and these laser beams catch the members of the wedding, jerk them along their way with a strobic effect and silently—for the band has not yet caught up with the production chart. Clemmons feels he's watching a silent film. An unintelligible voice, Paul's amplified a hundred times, turns everything back to the beginning and the rehearsal starts once more, accompanied by the crash-croon music of Stanley Livingston—without the *e*. It wasn't Mendelssohn, Clemmons thinks, but then it wasn't Elgar either.

Julia Clemmons leads the way through the purple arches. She has taken the red flower from her hair and holds it before her together with a bouquet of meadow grasses, flowerlets of Bouncing Bet. The series of arches have been set aglow by the lights, and they look like a Stonehenge turned atomic. His mother walks through them with the demeanor of an ancient divine. Clemmons turns to share this outrageous idea with someone, but the young faces near him are fixed with seriousness. He dares not intrude.

The rest follow his mother. Several young women, bridesmaids he would guess, appear in the first archway, a squad of graces separated from their company of dryads. They drink beer from cans, performing strange jigs and steps. Then comes Daisy and Milly's friend. Their mouths are rounded and opened in song, though he cannot hear their voices above the band's din. Then another small vanguard of bridesmaids, one of whom even squats, takes aim, and slices an orange frisbee into the night. The disc glows unnaturally in the lights and Clemmons wonders if all the articles and possessions of this generation have been treated to respond to black light. Was there any part of them that would not glow in the dark?

Olive now stands alone within the first arch. She is probably humming to herself in that fruity, watered contralto, probably humming some conventional tune, to counter the elastic barrage laid down by the rock band. More bridesmaids, this group curiously sedate, followed by Milly and Claire. His daughter, on Claire's arm, looks down and away as if overcome for the first time in her life, or maybe only looking for a contact lens—while the older woman presents a forceful profile. Claire's deep bosom is thrust before her like a shield and the features of her face—the high, arched brow, the strong nose, and plump lines of her lips—are etched by the lights, drawn together into a point of focus.

No, not graces, Clemmons thinks, but sybils. They resemble a band of ancient sybils, and not very well done at that, but like one of those drab panels fostered by an imitator of Martini and that now takes up more space in a provincial museum than it should.

He sees Paul and the local minister standing at the far end, by the stage, and there were other men about, but this spectral procession of women, their motions stung by darts of lights, again reminds him of old movie film, of the thousands of feet of 8mm movies stored on the shelf in the library closet. His mother always asked to see them on her visits—perhaps she visited just to see the film features of herself and Olive, Olive and the girls, the girls alone and together. Always the same women characters, though the backgrounds would vary as the girls magically grew longer on the pull-down screen while the character of Julia Clemmons got older and the role of Olive plumper, more wry-eyed. It took several hours to see all of them. There was no way to argue with Julia Clemmons; every mile had to run through the projector and she knew it by heart too, could recognize any attempt at extemporaneous editing.

At first, Clemmons reasoned that, as the taker of these movies as well as the projectionist, it was somehow pretentious to be in them as well. Moreover, to operate the camera while simultaneously getting in the picture was clumsy—not practical. But not to appear in a single frame? Why hadn't it occurred to any of them to turn the camera on him now and then? The movies all resemble this procession out in the field. When the little green men came out of the blue and began sorting through the artifacts of this lost planet, would they be curious, Clemmons wonders, about this society of women and children as recorded on the millions of miles of home movies? Would they be curious as to what happened to the boy children who mysteriously disappeared from the pictures at a certain age?

Well, make up your mind, Claire would say. He looks to her at the far end of the field. She is beside Milly, about to present her as his stand-in. Do you want to be in the picture or out of it? Do you know what you want? Johnny Appleseed or Charlie Buttondown? Don't call me Charlie, he would say but she had made him laugh. Even now, he laughs out loud. Could he be left out of the picture? Not entirely. What used to turn him on his heel in the old days now turns him toward the middle of the field.

So, not just yet. He'd get into the picture for now, but he could leave tomorrow, or the next day. He could put up his sign elsewhere and listen to Daisy describe Boston Corners on one of her tapes. He wouldn't even have to drive by but just turn on the tape deck wherever he ended up. He imagines her voice telling of the old prize fight. He'd be one of those armchair vagabonds nodding over his daughter's cheerful description of the Sullivan–Morrisey fight, but he'd better remind her—a note would do—about the correct date. The members of the wedding do not notice him. Clemmons has the field to himself. Vanity has skittered him onto the field like a poker chip. Surely, with all the cameras memorializing the event, one might be turned his way? At this moment, a video tape may be assembling magnetic particles into a pattern to give a fair representation of A. W. Clemmons. How he looks, if not a picture of the engine that makes him turn.

Lights. Cameras. The palm trees on his shirt seem to glow with that finely focused luminosity that outlines everything just before a hurricane. But the sky is clear. Clemmons looks up. A moon's hair is caught on the dark velvet of night. His head cocks to one side as if to hear something over the sound of the electronic music. It is a plane flying toward Albany, looking for a place to land.